The Horus Heresy series

Book 1 – HORUS RISING
Dan Abnett

Book 2 – FALSE GODS
Graham McNeill

Book 3 – GALAXY IN FLAMES
Ben Counter

Book 4 – THE FLIGHT OF THE EISENSTEIN
James Swallow

Book 5 – FULGRIM
Graham McNeill

Book 6 – DESCENT OF ANGELS
Mitchel Scanlon

Book 7 – LEGION
Dan Abnett

Book 8 – BATTLE FOR THE ABYSS
Ben Counter

Book 9 – MECHANICUM
Graham McNeill

Book 10 – TALES OF HERESY
edited by Nick Kyme and Lindsey Priestley

Book 11 – FALLEN ANGELS
Mike Lee

Book 12 – A THOUSAND SONS
Graham McNeill

Book 13 – NEMESIS
James Swallow

Book 14 – THE FIRST HERETIC
Aaron Dembski-Bowden

Book 15 – PROSPERO BURNS
Dan Abnett

Book 16 – AGE OF DARKNESS
edited by Christian Dunn

Book 17 – THE OUTCAST DEAD
Graham McNeill

Book 18 – DELIVERANCE LOST
Gav Thorpe

Gav Thorpe

DELIVERANCE LOST

Ghosts of Terra

BLACK LIBRARY

This book is dedicated to the fanatics at Nineteenth Legion.

A BLACK LIBRARY PUBLICATION

First published in Great Britain in 2012 by
The Black Library,
Games Workshop Ltd.,
Willow Road, Nottingham,
NG7 2WS, UK.

10 9 8 7 6 5 4 3 2 1

Cover and page 1 illustration by Neil Roberts.

Poem on pages 186-187 by Horace Smith, first published under the title
"Sonnet. Ozymandias" in *The Examiner* on February 1st, 1818.

A CIP record for this book is available from the British Library.

UK ISBN13: 978 1 84970 061 0
US ISBN13: 978 1 84970 062 7

See the Black Library on the internet at

www.blacklibrary.com

Find out more about Games Workshop
and the world of Warhammer 40,000 at

www.games-workshop.com

Printed and bound in the UK.

THE HORUS HERESY

It is a time of legend.

THE GALAXY IS in flames. The Emperor's glorious vision for humanity is in ruins. His favoured son, Horus, has turned from his father's light and embraced Chaos.

His armies, the mighty and redoubtable Space Marines, are locked in a brutal civil war. Once, these ultimate warriors fought side by side as brothers, protecting the galaxy and bringing mankind back into the Emperor's light.
Now they are divided.

Some remain loyal to the Emperor, whilst others have sided with the Warmaster. Pre-eminent amongst them, the leaders of their thousands-strong Legions are the primarchs. Magnificent, superhuman beings, they are the crowning achievement of the Emperor's genetic science. Thrust into battle against one another, victory is uncertain for either side.

Worlds are burning. At Isstvan V, Horus dealt a vicious blow and three loyal Legions were all but destroyed. War was begun, a conflict that will engulf all mankind in fire. Treachery and betrayal have usurped honour and nobility. Assassins lurk in every shadow. Armies are gathering.
All must choose a side or die.

Horus musters his armada, Terra itself the object of his wrath. Seated upon the Golden Throne, the Emperor waits for his wayward son to return. But his true enemy is Chaos, a primordial force that seeks to enslave mankind to its capricious whims.

The screams of the innocent, the pleas of the righteous resound to the cruel laughter of Dark Gods. Suffering and damnation await all should the Emperor fail
and the war be lost.

The age of knowledge and enlightenment has ended.
The Age of Darkness has begun.

~ DRAMATIS PERSONAE ~

THE EMPEROR — Master of Mankind

Primarchs

CORVUS CORAX — Primarch of the Raven Guard Legion

ROGAL DORN — Primarch of the Imperial Fists Legion

ALPHARIUS/
OMEGON — Twin primarchs of the Alpha Legion

HORUS — Warmaster, Primarch of the Sons of Horus

The Raven Guard Legion

BRANNE NEV — Commander of the Raptors

AGAPITO NEV — Commander of the Talons

SOLARO AN — Commander of the Hawks

ALONI TEV — Commander of the Falcons

LANCRATO NESTIL — Sergeant of the Talons

HADRAIG DOR — Sergeant of the Talons

KEREMI ORT — Battle-brother of the Talons

BALSAR KURTHURI — Battle-brother of the Talons

LUKAR FERENI — Battle-brother of the Talons

MARKO DIZ — Battle-brother of the Talons

STRADON BINALT — Techmarine

VINCENTE SIXX — Chief Apothecary

NAVAR HEF — Novitiate

The Traitor Legions

'ALPHARIUS' — The Alpha Legionnaires

EZEKYLE ABADDON	First Captain of the Sons of Horus
EREBUS	First Chaplain of the Word Bearers
FABIUS	Apothecary of the Emperor's Children
HASTEN LUTHRIS ARMANITAN	Captain of the Emperor's Children

Imperial Personae

MALCADOR THE SIGILLITE	First Lord of Terra.
MARCUS VALERIUS	Praefector of the Imperial Army, commander of the Therion Cohort
NEXIN ORLANDRIAZ	Mechanicum genetor
PELON	Manservant to Marcus Valerius
ARCATUS VINDIX CENTURIO	Warrior of the Legio Custodes

Non-Imperial Personae

ATHITHIRTIR	An antedil, Envoy of the Cabal

'Did the Emperor ever have to contemplate such a thing? Was there a moment when he looked upon his work and wondered who or what had given him the right to pursue it? Did he ever doubt the righteousness of his cause or the methods circumstance forced him to employ? Are such doubts just weakness, possessed only by lesser creatures than the Master of Mankind?

'I look upon my works and I know despair and hope in equal measure. I realise now that I have done a terrible thing, yet I cannot bring myself to ask forgiveness. Even with all that has happened I do not believe that I acted other than with the best of intentions and the noblest of goals. They were the darkest times that we have ever known, and if it seems in hindsight that I acted through selfishness I can only say that we were beset by a foe the likes of which we had not only never faced, but had never contemplated facing.

'All we had created, all that we had striven for long years to bring about, teetered on the precipice of annihilation. It was not just that the glories of the past stood to be destroyed, but that the whole future of the galaxy was hanging in the balance. None who did not live through those times can stand in judgement of those of us who did.

'Even now I cannot understand the motives of those who were to become my enemies by misfortune or intent, and I have even less sympathy. Yet for all that, I know that it was not mere foible or whim that caused this strife. Men of power, men of ambition and means, have goals loftier than others, and justify themselves by morals above those of normal, mortal folk.

'Though I remained true to the greater purpose of my existence, I do not pretend that I did not suffer the same vanity of righteousness that undoubtedly fuelled the actions of others who will also be assessed by future generations. Even when we were at our peak we performed acts that would be considered at best questionable in times of more civilised contemplation. The lesson is not in what happened, but why it happened. In darkness, in desperation, we did something that could only be justified by cruel necessity.

'Do not judge me.

'I am above your judgement, even as I am unworthy of your forgiveness.'

– Recovered record fragment,
author unknown, c.M31

PART ONE

ECHOES OF ISSTVAN

ONE

Memories of Greatness
Brothers Reunited
Branne's New Command

THE LAST TIME he had been in the Isstvan system, his departure had been very different. Eight hundred company banners had snapped and flapped in the strong wind, displaying the company insignias of the Legion in gold, silver and white upon black backgrounds. Wings and claws of various designs fluttered amongst icons of swords and shields. The purple and dark green heather had been trampled flat beneath armoured boots, large patches of blue lichen scuffed away by countless footsteps to reveal dark earth and pale rock beneath.

Drawn up in unmoving rank and file, the legionaries of the Raven Guard filled the floor of the Redarth Valley, their Stormbirds, Thunderhawks and other drop-craft commanding the heights around them, silhouetted against an early evening sky of dark blues and purples. Trails of ragged, violet cloud stretched from horizon to horizon as if dragged across the skies by the fingers of some godly hand. The air above the army was crisscrossed with vapour trails from patrolling aircraft, and pinpricks of light moving across the heavens showed the presence of the ships in low orbit, like slow-moving shooting stars carefully observing the proceedings below.

13

At the head of the valley, to the north, waited the Raven Guard's allies. In red and gold, the Therion Cohort stood beside their tanks and transports, arrayed in swathes of twilight and shadow cast by the immense Titan war machines of the Legio Victorum and the Legio Adamantus.

In front of the massed Legion waited a body of five hundred men. Most were garbed in plated carapace armour of shining black, their hoods drawn back to reveal heads of close-cropped hair, faces tattooed with swirling patterns. The soldiers' targeter lenses gleamed red in the dusk light, gun-halberds drawn up to the salute. At their front stood the elite guard, armoured in enamelled silver, surrounding a handful of civilian dignitaries in ornate robes and coats trimmed with gold braid and heavy epaulettes.

At a signal from one of the elderly men, the soldiers and leaders as one dropped to a knee and bowed their heads to the giant figure pacing slowly out of the ranks of the Raven Guard. The man approaching the Isstvanian delegation was more than a man: he was a primarch. Lord Corax, commander of the Raven Guard, towered above his superhuman warriors, his armour as dark as the night, chased with filigreed designs of towers and ravens and intricate scrollwork. His head was bare, showing pale flesh and straight black hair that hung to the exposed collar of his ornate breastplate. A flight pack fashioned with black wings stretched from the primarch's back, metallic feathers whistling shrilly in the breeze as he advanced. Dark eyes regarded the delegation with solemn pride.

With hands sheathed in clawed gauntlets, Corax gestured for the Isstvanians to rise.

'You kneel as a defeated foe. Now stand as men of the Imperium,' the primarch declared. His voice carried easily over the wind that tousled his hair across his thin face.

'We have waged war against each other, but the Imperial Truth has prevailed and you have sworn to accept its teachings. In complying with the Emperor's wishes you have proven yourselves men of wisdom and civilisation, fitting partners to the many other worlds you now join as part of the Imperium of Man. Not conquered, not subjugated, but free men, who have shown courage and pride in defending their values but who have seen the light of the Imperial Truth and now welcome the benefits it will bring.'

Corax turned to his Legion and his voice increased in volume, echoing to the furthest ends of the valley with little effort.

'We have fought hard and we have fought bravely, and another world is brought from the darkness of superstition and division into the light of the Emperor's clarity and unity,' he told his warriors. 'It is with honour to the fallen and respect to all who stand here that I can declare the Isstvan system brought to compliance!'

A deafening roar of approval sounded from the vocalisers of eighty thousand armoured warriors, joined by cheers drifting down from hundreds of thousands of Therion throats; a clamour which was drowned out by the celebratory blare of the Titans' war sirens.

ALMOST FIFTEEN YEARS later, Corax had returned with his brother primarchs to bring the rebel Horus to account, but at the dropsite his former allies had shown their true colours. Turning on the Iron Hands, Salamanders and Corax's Raven Guard, the traitors had all but destroyed those loyal to the Emperor as they had dropped on the world.

Corax had survived the treacherous ambush, though only just. With the remnants of his Legion, the primarch had attacked and retreated, pursued across the wild hills and mountains of the world by half a dozen Legions.

Now the Raven Guard had been forced to stand at the last, driven into the open to face the wrath of their pursuers.

The Raven Guard's first war at Isstvan had been a great victory. Their latest was a humbling defeat. It was a very different noise that provided the background symphony concluding Corax's latest campaign in the Isstvan system.

The first missiles from the World Eaters' Whirlwinds were streaking through the sky towards the Raven Guard. Corax's legionaries refused to take shelter, proud to stand their ground against this enemy after many days of hit-and-run attacks and desperate retreat. The explosions tore through the squads, slaying dozens. Corax stood amidst it all as if in the eye of a hurricane. His officers looked to him and drew strength from his bold defiance of the World Eaters.

Caught upon the windswept mountainside his Legion remained resolute. Behind the peak stretched great salt plains that had forced them into this last, defiant stand. Ahead of them massed the might of the World Eaters, the rage-driven Legion of Angron, who strode at their head roaring for the blood of his brother primarch. A sea of blue spattered with the red of gore swept up from the valley intent on the destruction of the Raven Guard. Maddened by neural implants and driven into a battle-frenzy by inhuman cocktails of stimulants, the berserk warriors of the World Eaters pounded up the sloping mountainside while their tanks and guns provided covering fire; every warrior bellowed his eagerness to fulfil the blood oaths he had sworn to his primarch.

As explosions rocked the slopes, missiles from the Whirlwinds hammering into legionaries and rock in fountains of fire, Corax glanced up to see more vapour trails crossing the open skies, but something was wrong with their direction.

They came from behind the Raven Guard.

Corax saw broad-winged aircraft plunging down from the scattering of cloud, missile pods rippling with fire. A swathe of detonations cut through the World Eaters, ripping through their advance companies. Incendiary bombs blossomed in the heart of the approaching army, scattering white-hot promethium over the steep slopes. Corax looked on with incredulity as blistering pulses of plasma descended from orbit, cutting great gouges into Angron's Legion.

The roar of jets became deafening as drop-ships descended on pillars of fire: black drop-ships emblazoned with the sigil of the Raven Guard. The legionaries scattered to give the landing craft space to make planetfall. As soon as their thick hydraulic legs touched the ground, ramps whined down and boarding gateways opened.

At first the Raven Guard were in stunned disbelief. A few shouted warnings, believing the drop-ships to be enemy craft painted to deceive. The comm crackled in Corax's ear. He did not recognise the voice.

'Lord Corax!'

'Receiving your transmission,' he replied cautiously, gaze fixed on the World Eaters as they recovered from the shock of the surprise attack and made ready to advance again.

'This is Praefector Valerius of the Imperial Army, serving under Commander Branne, my lord.' The man's voice was stretched, thin with tension, the words snapped out like a drowning man snatching breaths. 'We have a short window of evacuation, board as soon as you are able.'

Corax struggled to comprehend what the man was saying. He fixed on a detail – Commander Branne. The Raven Guard captain had been left in charge of the Legion's homeworld of Deliverance, and Corax had no answer to why Branne was now here at Isstvan. Adjusting quickly to the development, Corax realised that the Raven Guard who had been left as garrison were here, ready to evacuate the survivors of the massacre.

Corax signalled to Agapito, one of his commanders. 'Marshal the embarkation. Get everybody onboard and break for orbit.'

The commander nodded and turned, growling orders over the vox-net to organise the Raven Guard's retreat. With practised speed, the Raven Guard dispersed, the drop-ships launching in clouds of smoke and dust as soon as they were full, heading for the ship or ships that had despatched them. Corax watched them streaking back into the skies as shells and missiles fell once again on the Raven Guard's position. An explosion just to his left rocked him with its shockwave.

Ignoring the blast, Corax glared down the slope at the approaching World Eaters and their leader. The Raven Guard primarch had resigned himself to death here at the hands of his insane brother. It would be a fitting end to fall to Angron's blades, and there was always a slim – very slim – chance that Corax might instead cut down the World Eater and rid the galaxy of his perfidious existence.

A moment later, Commander Aloni was at his side. Like the rest of the Raven Guard, his armour was battered and cracked, a mishmash of plates and parts scavenged from fallen enemies. He had lost his helmet at some point and not found a replacement. The commander's tanned, wrinkled face betrayed a mix of astonishment and concern.

'Last transport, lord!'

Tearing his gaze away from Angron, Corax saw a Stormbird with its assault bay open, just a few metres away. Taking a deep breath, the Raven Guard primarch reminded himself of the teachings he had drilled into his warriors; teachings he had lived by for the whole of his life.

Attack, fall back, attack again.

This was more than a tactical withdrawal. This was surrender. It ate at Corax's gut to depart Isstvan in such shame. Corax glanced again at the drop-ship and back at the World Eaters. They were only a couple of hundred metres away. More than seventy five thousand of his Legion had been killed by the traitors, many of them by the berserk legionaries rushing towards him. It was a dishonour to the fallen to abandon them, but it was pointless pride to believe that he could right the wrongs done here by himself.

Attack, fall back, attack again.

Biting back his anger, Corax followed Aloni up the ramp, his boots ringing on the metal. As the ramp began to close, he looked out across the World Eaters army, baying like frustrated hounds as their prey slipped from their grasp.

'We survived, lord.' Aloni's tone conveyed his utter disbelief at the truth of this. 'Ninety-eight days!'

Corax felt no urge to celebrate. He looked at Aloni and the other legionaries sitting down on the long benches inside the transport compartment.

'I came to Isstvan with eighty thousand warriors,' the primarch reminded them. 'I leave with less than three thousand.'

His words hushed the jubilant mood and a sombre silence replaced it, the only sound that of the drop-ship's roar. Corax stood beside a viewing port, the deck rumbling beneath his feet, and looked at the hills of Urgall dropping away, picturing the thousands of fallen followers that he was leaving behind.

'What do we do now?' asked Agapito.

'We do what we have always done.' Corax's voice grew in strength as he spoke, his words as much a reassurance to himself as his warriors. 'We fall back, rebuild our strength and attack again. This is not the last the traitors will know of the Raven Guard. This is defeat but it is not the end. We will return.'

The cloud obscured his view, blanking it with whiteness, and he thought no more about the dead.

CORAX COULD NOT bear the bleak expressions of his warriors and left to find himself a brief moment of sanctuary in the linking corridor that sloped gently up towards the cockpit. He was alone and had time to consider what had happened.

Twice in the last one hundred days he had stared death in the face and twice he had survived. He had not just been in battle; such hazard was the life of any legionary or primarch. He had been poised moments from death in a way he had never experienced before.

Stooping to prevent his head from banging the passageway ceiling, Corax turned his back to the wall and leaned back, legs braced against the opposite side of the corridor. He took off his helmet and gazed numbly at the battered grille of its faceplate before dropping the helm to the floor from weary fingers. He saw the dents and cracks in his armour, its ornate engravings pitted with bolter-round impacts, the delicate designs smeared into ruin by las-blasts and missile explosions. Beneath the plasteel and ceramite, his wounds ached. He could smell his own blood, clotted across a dozen grievous injuries.

The primarch's keen ears could pick up the background chatter of the communications net receiver in his discarded helmet, his subconscious mind absorbing the flow of information even as his conscious thoughts drifted elsewhere. The danger was not yet over. He knew he should contact Branne and establish the facts of the situation, but could not bring himself to do so just yet. From the vox traffic, he surmised that there was a World Eaters battle-barge nearby. Listening for a few more seconds, as the vox-unit continued to relay the Traitors' position and course, Corax discovered that the World Eaters ship had earlier been on an attack heading but was now slowly withdrawing from the Raven Guard flotilla. The primarch dismissed the threat as minimal as recent events crowded his thoughts.

Danger had been his companion since his first memories, and war had been his calling. Not once had he ever felt afraid to die, and even against the toughest enemies of the Emperor he had approached every confrontation with a certainty of survival and victory. Ninety-eight days had washed away his confidence. Nearly a hundred days of staying one step ahead of his pursuers. Nearly a hundred days of being hunted by his fellow primarchs. Ninety-eight days of constant movement, of attack and retreat, of counter-assault and withdrawal.

He shuddered as he remembered the start of that testing time, when the traitors had revealed their intent and Corax had come so close to death at the hands of Konrad Curze, his brother who took such delight from being called the Night Haunter. Corax knew himself to be numbered amongst the best fighters in the service of the Emperor, and he had never considered Curze his equal. Curze was ill-disciplined, capable of sporadic genius but equally prone to moments of emotional blindness, moments a warrior like Corax could exploit with deadly effect. Yet there had been something about the Night Haunter that had unnerved the Raven Guard's primarch, an aura that had reached into Corax's spirit and found weakness. The hatred of Curze had shocked him, adding to the devastation he had felt at the treachery of Horus and many of his fellow primarchs; yet it was no excuse for fleeing from Curze.

Fear. He had felt a moment of fear when confronted by his demented brother, and in the peace of the passageway he understood what it was that had caused him

a moment of dread, looking into the dead eyes of the
Night Haunter.

They were moulded of the same stuff, Corax and
Curze, creatures born and raised in shadow and fear.

Curze had lived in the night-shrouded streets and
alleys of Nostramo Quintus; Corax's infancy had been
amongst the tunnels and dungeons of the prison-moon
of Lycaeus. Curze and Corax alike had seen worlds
enslaved to the will of evil men, where the weak and
destitute had toiled until death for the power and pleasure of others.

In that moment, subjected to the full brunt of the
Night Haunter's scorn, Corax had realised how close he
might have been to becoming the creature that was trying to kill him. Their lives were the toss of a coin apart.
Corax had been taken in by men learned in politics and
the human heart, and they had shown him compassion
and support; Curze had received no such upbringing
and had become a figure of vengeance and terror.

To look at Curze had forced Corax to see himself as he
might have been, shorn of the civilising influence of others and the code and principles his mentors had instilled
in him. In that moment it had not been fear of Curze
that had unmanned Corax but a dread of himself and,
to his shame, he had fled rather than destroy the object
of his dread.

Alone in that vestibule on the roaring, shaking
drop-ship, Corax despised himself for his moment of
cowardice. He should have stayed and fought, should
have slain the Night Haunter and killed pathetic Lorgar
of the Word Bearers straight after, denying the rebels
two of their commanders, even though it might have
cost him his life. Perhaps that was why he had been so
resigned to die at the hands of Angron, to sacrifice himself to the World Eater to absolve the shame of his earlier
weakness.

The door from the cockpit hissed open and Corax instantly straightened as best he could, resuming the poise of the Raven Guard primarch, Master of Deliverance and Lord of the Legiones Astartes. The co-pilot was startled by Corax's presence just outside the door, his young face a mask of surprise.

Corax smiled to ease the youth's shock.

'What is it?' asked the primarch.

'Sorry, lord, you were not answering your vox. We have Commander Branne on the main link.'

'Very well,' said Corax, nodding encouragement. 'I will speak with him shortly.'

As the co-pilot slipped back into the cockpit, Corax looked past him, through the main canopy. Ahead, the battle-barge of Commander Branne grew larger, a dark shape blotting out a swathe of stars. The *Avenger*, which Corax had last seen in orbit of Deliverance, was now here at Isstvan, against all expectation, a sight that lifted his spirits. Bombardment cannon turrets jutted from dorsal ridge of the ship, pointed at the world below. The weapons batteries were showing, deck upon deck of massed missile launchers and cannons bared like the fangs of a hound. The drop-ship yawed gradually, bringing the painted symbol of the Raven Guard on the battle-barge's beaked prow into view as the pilot steered towards the gleaming light of the landing bays.

Beyond were sparks of light brighter than the stars: the plasma engines of more vessels. The pinpricks of drop-ship and shuttle jets converged on the black-liveried ships as the evacuation came to its conclusion. Already the flotilla was turning away from the planet, ready to speed out into the void with the rescued legionaries.

Corax smiled again, this time with relief. He did not understand how it was that Branne came to be here, but he was grateful for the fact. Deadly absolution at the hands of Angron would have been a righteous end, but

with everything considered, Corax was glad he had survived to fight again.

BRANNE STOOD IN the docking bay watching the drop-
ships landing. The first ones to touch down were already
disembarking their passengers. With weary steps, the
survivors of the Raven Guard filed down the ramps onto
the deck.

They were a terrible sight. Most showed signs of injury.
Their armour was a patchwork of colours: here the silver
of an Iron Warriors shoulder pad, there the red breastplate of a Word Bearer, cracked and broken, bloodied
and stained. Every face Branne looked upon was etched
with fatigue. Glassy-eyed, the last survivors of the dropsite massacre trudged across the loading bay, welcomed
by smiles and cheers from Branne's warriors.

Serfs came forwards with food and drink on plain
metal trays, which the dull-eyed legionaries gulped and
wolfed down without ceremony, replenishing superhuman bodies tested to the limit by their long guerrilla
war. Shoulder pads were stripped off, weapons taken
away for repair, while Apothecaries, Techmarines and
their assistants tended to the most immediate issues of
injury and maintenance.

Though the events that had led up to the return of
the survivors were unique, the doctrine of the Legion
remained the same. A battle, whether won, lost or simply survived, was history and the next battle would come
soon enough. A warrior unprepared to fight again was
no warrior at all. Though exhausted, their guns spent,
their armour battered, their spirits stretched to breaking,
the Raven Guard were in a warzone and so they took
up fresh bolters and magazines of ammunition, and
allowed the Techmarines and Apothecaries to render
such help as was needed to allow them to fight again if
the need arose.

Half-machine, half-human servitors clunked and hissed through the growing throng, bearing crates of ammunition, boxes of grenades and spare parts for Legiones Astartes power armour. Other servitors, hulking things with cranes for arms and tracks for legs, rumbled to the drop-ships, replenishing bombs and missiles from racks on trailers hitched to their metal spines.

The last of the shuttles touched down. Branne approached it as the docking ramp lowered. The first legionary out was a bizarre sight, his armour a mess of colours and bare ceramite. Only his shoulder pad, bearing the Legion's badge, remained from his original suit. He took off his helmet and tossed it to the floor.

'Agapito!' Branne laughed. He slapped a hand to his true brother's chest. 'I knew you would be alive. Too stubborn to let something like this kill you.'

Branne looked closely at his brother, amazed by his outlandish appearance. A new scar ran from his right cheek to his throat, but beyond that it was the same face Branne had known for his whole life. Agapito returned the smile wearily. His deep brown eyes regarded Branne warmly. He reached a hand behind Branne's head and pulled him closer. The two touched foreheads in a sign of respect and comradeship.

'I see you have not managed to stay out of trouble, Branne.'

The commander stepped back from Agapito to see Corax descending the ramp. The primarch towered over his legionaries, his black armour showing as much wear and tear as that of those under his command.

'I was monitoring your transmissions,' said Corax. 'Why did the enemy abort their attack?'

'I have no idea, Lord Corax,' said Branne. 'Perhaps they thought better of taking on three vessels at once.'

'Where are they now?' asked the primarch.

'They've withdrawn to a hundred thousand kilometres,'

Branne replied. 'They don't look as if they'll try to attack again.'

'Odd,' said Corax. 'Signal your other ships to make course for Deliverance.'

'Yes, Lord Corax,' Branne said, holding his fist to his chest. 'And where are we to head?'

'Terra,' replied the primarch. 'I must have an audience with the Emperor.'

Branne and Agapito shared a glance with each other but said nothing as Corax strode out of the docking bay. Branne looked again at his brother and saw a strange look in Agapito's eyes. They roved around the deck, taking in every detail, settling nowhere.

'Relax, brother,' said Branne, slapping his hand to Agapito's arm. 'No enemies here. You're safe.'

Agapito turned a distant look on Branne and nodded uncertainly. His confusion and discomfort passed and Agapito smiled, gripping Branne's arm in return.

'Yes, that's true,' said Agapito. 'I thought I would never see the inside of a Raven Guard ship again.'

A warning siren sounded three times, its piercing blare cutting through Branne's thoughts.

'Strategium to Commander Branne,' a voice announced over the general address system. 'Proximity warning. Enemy ships have altered course towards our position. Intercept estimated at five hours.'

'Stand by to engage reflex shields,' he replied over his vox-bead. He darted a look at Agapito, forcing an encouraging smile. 'Well, maybe not safe just yet.'

THE AVENGER BROKE with the other two ships of the flotilla, all three vessels leaving orbit on different headings to confuse and disperse their energy trails. The other two ships, Triumph and Raven's Valour, would head out-system before translating to the warp and their journey back to the Legion homeworld of Deliverance. Corax

commanded the Avenger to make for Isstvan IV, both
to confuse pursuit and with a hope of linking up with
a small fleet of Therion ships Branne had despatched to
that world several days earlier to misdirect the Traitor
blockade of Isstvan.

The hope that the Imperial Army ships had survived
was faint; the Therions had last been the target of a
World Eaters armada and several other vessels. With the
Raven Guard Legion and fleet on the brink of extinction,
every ship and soldier was a vital asset, and after weighing up the rewards and risks, Corax judged it worth a
few days to see if he could bolster his forces a little more
with the Therions.

Branne had also argued persuasively that the Raven
Guard had an obligation to their allies to at least attempt
to link up. As much as the Therions might be a military asset, the message that those loyal to the Emperor
would not be abandoned was equally important given
the calamitous events that Isstvan had witnessed. Corax
had made it clear to his commanders that the *Avenger*
was now too valuable to risk without good cause, and
that the search would be short. If there was any risk of
discovery, the battle-barge would immediately cease the
hunt and head out-system for warp transit.

As soon as the Raven Guard's ships were far enough
from the planet below to be safe from ground-based fire,
they engaged their reflex shields. An innovation from
the planet of Kiavahr, orbited by the home-moon of the
Raven Guard, the reflex shield was a modified version of
the void shields that protected most Imperial warships
and installations.

A void shield worked by using the power of the warp
itself to displace incoming projectiles and high-energy
attacks. The reflex shield changed the modulation of
the warpcores that powered the void shields, calibrat-
ing them to a much higher tolerance and turning them

inwards, so that matter and energy generated by the ship was redirected instead; all forms of radiation emitted by the Raven Guard's ships could be displaced, rendering them undetectable to scanning equipment.

The advantages of the reflex shield technology fitted well with Corax's ethos of war, allowing Raven Guard ships to approach their targets unseen, striking swiftly and decisively before withdrawing. The low energy requirement meant that such stealth could be maintained almost indefinitely. There was, however, a serious downside to their use. By employing its void shield generators for the reflex shields, a Raven Guard vessel had no defence against physical attack and it took time to power the generators from one state to the other, leaving a ship vulnerable for several minutes with neither its cloaking field nor its energy defence fully operational, hence the swift exit from orbit.

To the augurs and scanning arrays of the Traitor bases and ships throughout the Isstvan system, the three Raven Guard ships seemed to melt away into the stars. To the naked eye they would have appeared to shimmer for a while, as the reflex shields engaged and shifted away the light reflecting from the ships' surfaces, until eventually all such energy was being dampened and the vessels were rendered invisible.

One other problem with the reflex shield, one that Corax had unsuccessfully laboured to overcome for many years, was the low energy threshold for which it could compensate. Reactors could only be run at half power without generating too much energy to be displaced, in turn reducing top speed and blinkering the ship's sensor capabilities. So it was that slowly, half-blind, the *Avenger* slipped away from Isstvan V, tracing an arc around the world until it came to its chosen heading.

The ship did not make directly for Isstvan IV, it being

a doctrine of the Legion to always approach a target by
an indirect route, but instead took a circuitous, zigzag-
ging path, using a timing and distance formula devised
by Corax to maximise the damping effect of the reflex
shields, enough to throw off any pursuer or sensor that
might somehow detect them. Corax did not believe
in taking chances when it came to moving freely and
unseen.

It would be several days before the *Avenger* would bring
Isstvan IV within range of its reduced sensor screen, and
Corax took the time to review the organisation of the
remnants of his Legion.

Including Branne's companies, he had a little fewer
than four thousand legionaries of varying ranks and
specialisations. The majority he had formed into the
'Talons' – tactical companies under Agapito's command.
The survivors of the various assault platoons, along with
several Dreadnought-incarcerated veterans, had been
banded together into the 'Falcons', led by Aloni Tev.
Lastly, the handful of bike squads, land speeders and
aircraft crews still remaining were put together under the
command of Captain Solaro An, and were given the des-
ignation 'Hawks'.

Two days out from Isstvan V, Corax called a council of
his four commanders and explained the reorganisation
and reassignments that would be made once the Legion
was gathered again at Deliverance.

The five of them met in Branne's chambers, given over
to the use of the primarch since his arrival on the ship.
The main room was plainly decorated, the plasteel walls
painted a muted blue, broken only by an armour and
weapons rack on which the commander's artisan-crafted
wargear would normally hang; it was empty at the
moment as every legionary in the force was permanently
geared for battle, so that they even slept in their armour
with a bolter in their hands.

The floor was carved with a relief of the Raven's Guard's device – a heraldic bird with wings and claws outstretched, surrounded by a coiled chain. Upon the symbol was a table of burnished bronze-like metal, inscribed also with the insignia of the Legion, circular in shape and with vox-thieves and display stations for a dozen attendees. The screens were dull slabs of lifeless grey at the moment, their keypads and emitters dormant while silent running protocols were in effect; every watt of energy saved might prove the difference between escape and detection.

Corax stood facing the double doors that led back to the strategium, leaning forwards with his fists resting on the table. Agapito and Aloni sat to his right, Branne and Solaro to his left. As brothers, Branne and Agapito were alike, with square jaws, heavy brows and flat cheeks. Both were from the slave-prison of Deliverance and even the augmentations and manipulations that had turned them into legionaries had not completely eradicated the somewhat sallow and pitted cast to their skin. Agapito was marked out by his fresh scar, but it was the anxious flicker that occasionally crept into his gaze that bore greater testament to the harsh experience he had suffered during the dropsite massacre.

Solaro was the youngest and had been only a child when Corax had freed Deliverance from the tyrannical grip of the Kiavahran overlords. He was pale, like the primarch, with a sharp nose and thin lips, and had an air of constant movement about him. Even as he listened to his primarch, his gauntleted fingers fidgeted on the edge of the table, tapping and scratching.

Aloni was the eldest of the four, and of entirely different complexion. Born amongst the Asiatica dustfields on Terra, his skin was darker than the others, and there was a narrowness and slant to his eyes not found in children of Lycaeus. His head was shaved bald, with many gilded service studs riveted into his scalp.

'And what is to be my purpose, Lord Corax?' asked Branne when he realised that he had not been assigned a command.

'You will be my Commander of Recruits,' Corax informed him.

'Recruits?' Branne did not hide his disappointment. 'But for a quirk of chance, I would have been with you on Isstvan and Aloni or Agapito would have drawn the lot to stay with the garrison at Deliverance. I would prefer a combat command, my lord.'

'And you have it,' replied the primarch, leaning closer to place a hand on Branne's shoulder guard. 'Horus and his traitorous allies will not allow us the luxury of keeping our recruits long from the fighting.'

'With respect, lord, I am not of a disposition to be leading Scout squads,' said Branne.

It pained him to argue with his primarch, and he feared that perhaps pride fuelled his words, but even in the couple of days since the rescue, Branne had noticed a difference growing between those who had been on Isstvan V and those who had not. The Legion once had been bound by common experience, now it seemed that the massacre and escape was a stronger bond than the Legion, one not shared by Branne and his warriors. He wanted to prove himself worthy amongst his peers, and the thought of being left on Deliverance again to marshal recruits soured his mood.

'Perhaps I could be the captain of your guard,' Branne continued. 'Since Arendi was killed at the dropsite you have yet to name a successor.'

There were chuckles from the other commanders, sharing some joke that Branne did not understand. It irked him to feel so detached from his comrades.

'I dispensed with the pretence of an honour guard,' said Corax, not unkindly. The primarch straightened and fixed Branne with his dark, penetrating stare and the commander expected a rebuke for his stubbornness. Instead, Corax smiled slightly.

'It is to you that I am bestowing the greatest honour, Branne,' said the primarch. 'As a reward for coming to our rescue, I am placing you in charge of rebuilding the Legion. There is no more important task I could give to you. In your hands will be the future of the Raven Guard.'

Branne thought about this for a moment, his confidence restored a little by Corax's words. He looked at the others and saw them nodding in agreement with the primarch, sincerity in their expressions.

'I accept the honour, lord, of course,' said Branne, bowing his head. 'But, still…' he muttered to himself. 'Running around with the Scouts?'

'There will not be any more Scouts,' said Corax, his acute hearing catching Branne's slight whisper. 'The existing Scout squads will become part of Solaro's recon forces. Any of them that are close to full initiation will be given their black carapaces and taken into the Talons. Your recruits will have to learn to fight as full warriors from the outset; we do not have years to train them cautiously.'

This brightened Branne's mood further and he felt some contentment at his allotted role. The discussion moved on to other topics, including the need to replenish the Legion's stock of weapons and ammunition as well as its warriors. A full audit of all armour, armaments, vehicles and ships would need to be undertaken to evaluate the extent to which the Raven Guard's claws had been dulled.

'What of the rest of the fleet?' asked Solaro. He looked at Branne. 'Any sign that any of our ships escaped?'

'Unlikely,' said Branne. 'A few might have been able to get away, but I would not hold out any hope. We detected no transmissions, though any Raven Guard vessel would have been running silent by the time we arrived.'

'The *Shadow of the Emperor* was certainly destroyed,' said Corax, referring to his flagship, 'along with the escort flotilla. I received their stand-to and distress broadcasts when the Traitors opened fire. It was cut off within minutes, too soon for the reflex shields to have been raised, and against such numbers that would have been the only defence.'

Silence followed, a tension brought about by mention of the treacherous act committed by Horus and the Legions that had sided with him. Branne saw Agapito unconsciously hunch his shoulders, a distant look in his eyes. Solaro's gauntlets formed fists on the table while Aloni bowed his head in contemplation, eyes closed.

'The fallen will be avenged.'

Corax's words were a whisper, but spoken with such vehemence that Branne did not doubt his primarch for a moment.

The chime of the door broke the pregnant atmosphere within the chamber. Corax operated the control and the double doors slid open to reveal a human member of the crew dressed in a white tunic and black leggings, a digital slate in his hand. Even the *Avenger's* internal vox frequencies had been suspended to conserve energy usage, so that a number of the fittest serfs and crew were employed as runners to convey orders and messages around the battle-barge.

'Forgive the intrusion, lord, masters, but Controller Ephrenia sends word that we are within nominal scanning range of Isstvan IV,' the messenger reported.

'Very good,' said Corax. 'Tell Ephrenia to divert twenty per cent reactor capacity from engines to the surveyor arrays. I will join her shortly.'

The serf bowed and left the commanders with their primarch.

'Someone should inform Marcus,' said Branne.

'Marcus?' asked Corax.

'Praefector Valerius,' explained Branne, 'the ranking officer of the Therions. It was his ships and men I sent to Isstvan IV.'

Branne did not mention that it was also Valerius's strange dreams that had eventually prompted him to come to Isstvan in the first place, overruling his primarch's orders to garrison Deliverance. The whole matter had been unsettling for Branne, and it was something he wished to discuss with his lord in private. An occasion had not yet arisen to do so.

'As you say,' said Corax, gesturing for the commanders to precede him to the door. 'Inform the praefector that we can spare seven hours to perform a sweep for his ships, no more. He is welcome to join me on the strategium during the operation.'

Branne nodded and went, leaving the chamber before the others. Three youths, two boys and a girl, stood to one side in the corridor beyond, dressed in simple tunics and hose. Branne gestured for one of them to step forwards.

'Take a message to Praefector Valerius, ask him...' Branne stopped himself. 'Never mind, I will see him myself. Stand down.'

The commander turned aft and strode away quickly as the others came out of the chamber. He would have to tell Lord Corax about the dreams soon, but it would be better if Valerius did not say anything just yet. When they were away from Isstvan and the situation was calmer, the two of them could broach the thorny subject.

TWO

A Primarch's Summons
Ghosting By Reflex
The Cabal Steers a Path

'WHAT IS IT?' Marcus asked as he heard his manservant, Pelon, calling his name.

The praefector was lying on his bunk, a thin treatise on naval tactics held in his hands, though he had read the last page more than a dozen times since Corax had come on board and not taken in a word of it. He had yet to see the primarch, a matter that gave him a small measure of regret, but equal relief.

'Commander Branne to see you, master,' Pelon informed him. The youth stepped through the doorway from the main room into the bunk chamber, swathed in the shadow of the legionary behind him.

Marcus swiftly hauled himself from the bed and tucked the tail of his shirt into his breeches. He smoothed his hair with a quick hand as Pelon stepped aside and ushered Branne into the small bunk room.

'Commander, I am honoured,' said Marcus, bowing briefly. 'I thought you would be busy with other duties.'

'I am,' said Branne, his expression hard. He glanced at Pelon.

'Leave us please, Pelon,' said Marcus. 'Perhaps you could head to the officers' galley and inquire after my luncheon?'

35

Pelon nodded and left them. Branne said nothing until the outer door had hissed open and closed with a dull thud.

'Lord Corax has permitted us seven hours to search for your fleet,' said the commander. 'No more than that.'

'A vain search, I fear,' sighed Marcus. He sat down on a low, plain couch and gestured an invitation to Branne to do the same. The commander declined with a shake of the head and a scowl.

'You are also invited to attend the primarch on the stategium.'

'Invited?' Marcus smiled. 'That is most welcome. I have been eager to pass on my regards to Lord Corax since his arrival.'

'The dreams, Marcus, have they stopped?' Branne loomed over the army officer, arms folded across his massive chest.

'Yes, thankfully, yes they have,' said Marcus. 'The ravens call no more, the fires have burned out in my nightmares.'

'That is good,' said Branne, his expression lightening slightly. He bent one knee so that his face was level with Marcus's. 'It would not be wise to distract Lord Corax with unnecessary concerns.'

'Unnecessary concerns? I am not sure what you mean, commander.'

'Don't mention the dreams when you see the primarch.'

'Well, I wasn't going to blurt it out in front of everyone on the strategium, if that's what you were thinking,' said Marcus, offended by the suggestion. 'It is a delicate matter, I understand that.'

'More than delicate, Marcus.' Branne's eyes were intent, his expression ferocious. 'There may be something unnatural about those dreams. It is not normal for a man to know what happens to another light years distant.'

'Of course there is something abnormal,' said Marcus. 'It is not natural for a man to have such dreams, but I think Lord Corax is far from natural.'

'You still think the primarch sent the dreams to you? That he somehow called to you across the void to warn of the danger he was in?'

Marcus was unsettled by the note of accusation in Branne's tone.

'Undoubtedly,' the praefector said, standing up. 'Perhaps there is something in your Legion conditioning that hardened your minds to his message, I don't know. I am sure Lord Corax will confide in us when he feels the time is right.'

'Don't embarrass me, Marcus, not in front of the primarch,' said Branne, betraying the cause of his anger. 'He has not inquired deeply as to why we left Deliverance, it may be better that the matter is left to lie in silence.'

'Whatever you think best, commander,' said Marcus, holding up a placating hand, worried by the tension in Branne's voice. 'I will not raise the matter if you or Lord Corax do not.'

'And what of the serf?'

'Who?'

'Your boy, the one that was just here. Can he be trusted not flap his tongue?'

'Oh, Pelon. He is utterly trustworthy. His family have served the Therion nobility for generations. Loyalty is bred into him like that blond hair and flat nose. He attends a praefector of the Therion Cohort and understands his place, and the necessity of discretion.'

'Be sure that he does,' said Branne. 'For your sake, it is better that there is no rumour flying around at this time. Horus's treachery, and the turning of the other Legions, has made everyone very suspicious. Your dream hints at something strange, something that should not be spoken of.'

'I understand,' said Marcus, though he did not. The edgy look in Branne's eyes was something the praefector had never seen in the expression of a legionary before. If he didn't know better, Marcus would have taken it as a sign of fear.

'We had best not keep Lord Corax waiting,' said Marcus, stepping past Branne to unhook the dress coat hanging on the wall. He pulled on the heavy coat, adjusted the braiding and epaulettes to fall smartly, and nodded towards the door. 'After you, commander.'

THE STRATEGIUM WAS silent save for the background hum of the surveyor stations and the mechanical chatter of data-strip printers. Corax stood behind the command throne – the chair was too small for his massive frame – while his commanders waited behind him on the upper tier overlooking the strategium. Marcus Valerius stood, with head bowed, beside Branne, dwarfed by his legionary companions.

It was a risk to stay in the Isstvan system any longer than was absolutely required, and even more of a risk to come so close to Isstvan IV, where a large part of Horus's armada was mustering. Yet for all the risk, Corax knew that he owed it to the brave men and women of Therion to look for any survivors. He held little hope – no hope if he was being truthful with himself – but in times such as these it was important that the debt he owed to the Therions was recognised.

The *Avenger* ghosted towards Isstvan IV on minimal engine power, nothing more than a smear of background radiation on the screens of the enemy fleet. It was not solely to honour the Therions that Corax dared approach so close. Any intelligence he could gather regarding the capabilities and dispositions of the Traitors might prove vital, for the war that was to come as well as his chances of leaving Isstvan alive.

There were dozens of ships, perhaps even hundreds. They belonged to the Sons of Horus, the Word Bearers, the World Eaters, the Iron Warriors, and others who had, for reasons Corax would never understand, turned on the Emperor.

He had not seen the like since first coming to the system, when the Raven Guard and the Therions, along with vessels representing the Mechanicum of Mars and others involved with the Great Crusade, had brought compliance to Isstvan. He had been sent here by Horus, before he had been elevated to Warmaster. Back then it had been a request, an invitation even, rather than an order, but to Corax, a word from Horus had been like a command from the Emperor.

The primarch of the Raven Guard had never been on cordial terms with Horus. He had always found him too extravagant, too ready to make displays of power during his conquests. Corax preferred to be understated, to obtain compliance with the minimum of fuss and posturing.

Yet for all he had disliked Horus, Corax had admired him. He had admired his easy camaraderie with those under his command, and had known that Horus was the more accomplished commander over many campaigns, gifted with a rare ability for both the overview and the fine management of details, something that Corax had never quite equalled.

Physically, Horus and Corax had proved an even match for each other in their mock-duels and wrestling bouts. Such sparring had not created any greater bond between them, as it had done with the other primarchs, but Corax had never considered the possibility that one day he might have to test his worth against Horus for real.

He had been happy to provide the services of the Raven Guard, to lead the attack secretly against those that held out against compliance, fighting behind enemy lines, attacking shipping like a common pirate to weaken supply lines, while Horus and his Legion – they had been the Luna Wolves back then – had reaped the glory with their eye-catching drop assaults and massed battles.

Corax had allowed Horus the plaudits; he had no need for them. The Emperor had told Corax as much on several occasions. The Master of Mankind knew Corax's worth, even if it was not loudly praised, and that was enough for the Saviour of Deliverance.

Now Horus's brashness looked like vanity, and his extravagance seemed to be warmongering, when viewed through the lens of his treachery. He had teetered on the precipice of self-aggrandisement, and he had dragged many of Corax's gene-brothers with him when he had finally fallen.

'Quadrant six report is in, lord,' announced Controller Nasturi Ephrenia, breaking into Corax's thoughts. She was a short, ageing woman, a native of Deliverance. Ephrenia's skin was deeply wrinkled, her white hair thinning, but her eyes were sharp and intelligent as she bowed over the cluster of screens at the primary surveyor station. Artificial tubing snaked just beneath her skin, pulsing gently from the life-sustaining fluids passing within. Augmetic braces glinted on either side of her neck and along the fingers of her hands as she tapped protocols into a keypad.

The strategium controller was dressed in simple grey trousers tucked into short boots, the lapels of her black, wide-collared jacket pierced with a single ruby-headed brooch in the shape of the Legion's icon to signify her position as controller of the strategium. Her expression betrayed nothing as she looked at the most recent scanner returns and communications sweeps.

She always had been cool-headed, even as an infant.

There was almost no light at all. Something glittered through a crack in the rocks, providing just enough of a glow for him to make out the outline of the objects around him. There was something half-buried in the rubble behind the boy, cracked and distorted by an immense impact, shattered glass spread across the uneven floor.

The light glinted from one thousand and eighty-six shards.

He wondered if that was important, and decided it wasn't. What was important was that the air was breathable, well within tolerable limits, and the gravity a little less than... less than what? What did 'Terran-normal' mean? His thoughts were still scattered. He understood gravity, and if asked could have written out many long equations regarding the calculation of its strength and effect, but it was just one fragment of information tossed haphazardly across his mind, like the shining glass pieces strewn over the floor.

There was quite a lot of nitrogen in the air.

How did he know that? He took another deep breath, and came to the same conclusion. He just knew it to be true, just as he also detected a higher concentration of carbon dioxide. Both of these facts hovered in his thoughts before a connection was made and a conclusion surfaced.

An artificial atmosphere.

It was by no means a definitive conclusion, but seemed a safe assumption given the other environmental factors his body had been steadily assessing since in the few moments since he had awoken in this dark place.

There was definitely a generator close by; he could sense the electromagnetic disturbance emitted from its coils.

The source of the light strobed at a particular frequency that resonated with the generator coils. That was how he knew the light was electrically generated, which was confirmed by his analysis of the spectrum of light falling onto his enhanced retinas.

It was very disturbing.

He had no memory of this place at all. In fact, all he could recollect was soft warmth, some muffled background whirrs and clicks, and a dull light permeating a layer of liquid. Not at all like this cold, dry, black place.

And some voices, disturbing, demented voices that hovered on the edge of memory. He could not recall what they had said, but was left with an uneasy feeling of defiance and distrust.

Air moisture was also quite high. Combined with the low temperature, he was forced to conclude that he was close to ice of some kind. He noticed his breath formed vaporous tendrils against the flickering gleam.

He remembered his ears, surprised that he had not paid attention to them sooner.

There were sounds nearby, sounds that did not seem artificial in origin; sounds that reminded him of occasional visitations while he had been growing and learning. Human sounds.

Voices.

He could understand the concept of language. He knew seven thousand, six hundred and forty-one languages, dialects, argots and cants from across the Old Empire. He was not sure how he knew them, and was trying work out into which of them the words he heard could be categorised. There was something of a Pan-Sannamic lilt to the words, but their expression was harshly pronounced. He could not identify the particular sub-strand of the idiom, but it was not so great that he could not form a cognitive appreciation. In short, he decided what they were speaking and listened in.

'Near four hundred dead, at least.'

'Four hundred less mouths to feed,' said another voice. 'Least, that's the way they'll see it.'

'These arc-drills are not meant for icework,' said another. 'This was bound to happen.'

'Quit gossiping and start digging!' This was spat, filled with false authority. He could hear the trembling beneath the vehemence, the edge of fear that lurked in the speaker's subconscious.

There came a high-pitched whining, and a flickering red

*light shone through the tiny gap while the rock started to
vibrate fractionally more.*

He waited, apprehensive but intrigued.

The laser drill crept closer and closer. Rock splintered and
light flooded in as the chamber was breached. He took in the
scene in an instant. A crowd of humans dressed in shabby
blue overalls, seven male and three female, were directing
the laser, five of them steering its head, another five on the
tracked cart behind. Their age was indeterminate, obliter-
ated by obvious signs of malnourishment and hard labour.
Creased, leathery skin, cracked lips and sunken eyes gave
them all an aged appearance that was probably beyond their
chronological existence.

There was also a child with them. A female infant, clinging
to the leg of one of the women riding on the traction cart that
propelled the drillhead. She had long blonde hair and a narrow face with large lips and bright blue eyes. She seemed very
thin, as fragile as an icicle. She was covered in rock dust like
all of the others, but had smeared it away from her forehead
with a wipe of her hand, revealing skin that was unhealthily
pale.

Every one of them had ceased working and was now staring at him. He swiftly concluded that they had not intended
to find him, and he wondered why his presence here was a
surprise. It was another vexing question.

'What's stopping you?' Another male, bigger built and better fed than the others, stepped from behind the mining cart.
He wore trousers and a jacket of dark blue, covered with a
film of dust. His feet were booted, the thick footwear capped
with metal at toe and heel. His face was concealed behind the
tinted visor of a helmet, and in his hand he carried a whip
whose handle was heavy enough to serve as a cudgel. The man
stopped in his tracks as he also saw what was in the pocket
chamber that had been breached. 'How the...?'

The adults, the ones in the coveralls with the tools, started
jabbering amongst themselves, almost too fast for him to

understand. The one with the whip, the one with the false
authority in his voice, pushed to the front. The small girl had
dropped down from the cart and was walking through the
breach into the chamber.

'Get back,' said the uniformed man, snatching hold of the
girl's hair to drag her from the gap.

He decided he did not like the man with the whip. The
girl's shriek was full of pain and fear, cutting through his
thoughts like a hot knife touching a nerve.

He stood up and walked towards the group. They backed
away from him, still whispering and muttering in fear. The
man who had hurt the girl stood his ground, pushing the
infant aside. The man lunged forwards to grab him, but he
moved so slowly it was easy to avoid the outstretching hand.
The boy nimbly stepped around the flailing grasp of the guard
and grabbed the wrist in both hands. It snapped easily, bringing a howl of pain from the man.

The bullying man reared up as his shattered hand flopped
loosely at the end of his arm, bringing back the whip in the
other. The barbed tip of the lash cracked forwards, but it was
a simple enough matter to elude it and snatch up the end of
the whip in his fist. The man laughed, partly in hysteria, and
yanked, trying to unbalance him. The boy spread his legs and
held firm, jarring the guard's arm, before pulling back. Rather
than release his grip, the guard was hauled from his feet,
landing face first in the dust and rocks in front of the others.

Pacing forwards, the boy saw the look of surprise, terror and
hope in the eyes of the workers. The little girl smiled at him,
even as tears streaked the grime on her face. He wanted to
make her happy, to give her something as a sign that everything would be all right.

'What's your name?' she asked. 'Mine is Nasturi. Nasturi
Ephrenia.'

He grabbed the helmeted head of the guard, twisted and
gave a pull, ripping it free. He offered it up to the girl, who
laughed even as the adults started to cry out in panic. He saw

*himself reflected in the visor and realised the reason for the
alarm he had caused.*

*He was nude, and clothed in the body of a child no older
than Ephrenia. Blood was spattered across his snow-white
skin, his crimson-splashed face framed with a shock of coal-
black hair. His eyes were utterly black, darker than night.*

*He searched for an answer to the girl's question as blood
dribbled down his naked arms. Only one reply seemed appropriate, drawn up from the depths of embryonic memory.*

'Nineteen,' he said. 'I am number Nineteen.'

'NOTHING DETECTED, LORD,' Ephrenia reported. 'A little
background echo on the Therion frequencies, but nothing less than five days old.'

'Enemy?' asked Corax, one hand gripping the back of
the command throne.

'Six more frigate-sized vessels detected, lord,' reported
Ephrenia. 'Two strike cruisers and one battle cruiser. All
using Word Bearers protocols as far as we can determine.
They are moving out-system.'

'It's too dangerous to remain here,' Agapito said from
the gallery. 'That makes it thirty-eight vessels detected in
proximity to Isstvan IV.'

'The Therions are gone,' said Solaro.

'I have to concur.' Valerius's voice was quiet, his face
pinched with emotion. He darted a sideways glance at
Branne and then returned his gaze to the primarch. 'I
hope their sacrifice will be remembered. I will provide a
list of ranks and names when we have returned to Deliverance.'

'They will be lauded, have no worry in that regard,'
Corax assured him. The primarch's dark eyes glittered in
the glow of the screens that covered the walls and station
panels of the strategium. 'Their loss will not go unre-
membered. Nor will it go unavenged.'

'My thanks, Lord Corax,' Valerius said with a deep bow.

A dull tone sounded from one of the main speakers.

'Reactor energy spike, lord,' said Ephrenia.

'Reduce scanning array output to navigational,' the primarch replied quickly. 'There is nothing more we will find here. Adjust course to shortest route to translation distance, evasion pattern three.'

The black- and white-clad serfs moved to their control stations without word and within a minute the warning tone fell quiet.

'Augur sweeps being targeted to our vicinity, lord,' said Ephrenia, her words quick but calm. 'Three frigates have changed bearing, moving ahead of our position. Monitoring increase in closed communications traffic.'

'The traitors smell something amiss,' said Corax. He strode across the strategium to join the controller and looked at the display screens. 'Keep to plotted course. Reflex shield status?'

Ephrenia consulted a sub-screen before replying.

'Masking is at ninety-nine point three per cent, lord,' she told the primarch. 'Should we slow down?'

Corax performed some quick calculations in his head, factoring the scanner ranges of the enemy vessels and the time required to get away.

'No change,' he commanded. 'A little more speed will serve us better than complete masking. When we are two hundred thousand kilometres from the enemy, increase speed by twenty per cent. We should be at the translation point in seven days.'

The primarch looked again at the displays, seeing in his mind's eye the dispositions of the enemy fleet. They had quickly thrown up a blockade position around the inner planets, correctly expecting him to have headed in-system rather than directly out of the star's gravity well. Corax reminded himself that his enemies were commanded by Horus, one of the greatest strategists of the Imperium.

His traitorous brother knew well the capabilities of the
Raven Guard, having benefited greatly from their expertise during his campaigns. They would have to be careful
and take nothing for granted. The Raven Guard might
have been pulled from the trap on Isstvan V, but they
were still far from safe.

IN A DARKENED chamber close to the strategium of the
Vengeful Spirit, a meeting was being held. The room
was large, big enough for several dozen occupants to be
seated, the light of the single great lantern hanging from
the centre of the ceiling barely reaching the banner-
hung walls. A few data stations blinked with ruddy
lights on the far wall, beneath an embroidered standard
depicting the Eye of Horus in gold on burgundy. The
floor was plain plasteel mesh, scuffed to a dull grey by
the countless footfalls of booted feet.

As the door closed behind Alpharius, the primarch's
eyes instantly adjusted to the gloom. The space seemed
cavernous, occupied by only three others. Alpharius was
surprised; he had been expecting several of his brother
primarchs to be attending the council. As he stepped forwards he realised that this was not a war council, it was
an impromptu interrogation. Perhaps even a trial.

The thought did not sit comfortably with him as he
regarded the chambers' other occupants with what he
hoped was an impassive expression. Alpharius knew that
he tested the patience of the Warmaster, and here at the
heart of his lair there was no telling what he might do.

Horus, Warmaster, Primarch of the Luna Wolves – the
Sons of Horus, Alpharius corrected himself – sat on a
broad, high-backed throne, robed in heavy black and
purple, hands on his knees. His face was heavily shadowed, eyes hooded with darkness with just a glint at
their core. Even seated, the Warmaster's presence dominated the room. Alpharius had spent time with Horus

before – when loyal to the Emperor and since – and never before had he felt threatened. This time was different. Horus seemed bigger than ever.

Alpharius was the smallest of the primarchs, but had not allowed this to undermine his confidence. Now that he looked at Horus, tree-trunk-thick arms stretching the fabric of his robes, Alpharius realised that his fellow primarch could crush him, tear him limb from limb, without warning.

Their relationship had changed, that much was clear. The primarchs had once been brothers, equals. When Horus had been made Warmaster he had been treated as the first amongst equals. Looking at Horus now, Alpharius was left with no doubt that Horus considered himself master, a lord to whom fealty was owed. The obedience of his co-conspirators was no longer demanded, it was expected.

There was also no mistaking the Warmaster's perception of his role in the coming meeting. He was the judge at a trial. His eyes remained fixed on Alpharius as the primarch walked to the centre of the room. The gloomy surrounds, the half-lit shapes at the edge of vision, were a crude trick, Alpharius told himself, only capable of intimidating lesser individuals. For all that, the primarch of the Alpha Legion felt a cold trickle of uncertainty creeping through his gut.

At the Warmaster's right shoulder stood First Captain Abaddon, fully armoured and with a power sword at his hip. He had a look that matched his reputation: his hard eyes were those of a stone-hearted killer. At the Warmaster's left was the Word Bearer Erebus, his armour painted a lavish crimson, adorned with golden sigils and hung with fluttering pieces of parchment covered with tiny scrawls of Lorgar's meandering litanies. The Word Bearer leaned closer and whispered something in Horus's ear, so quiet even Alpharius's superhuman hearing could not detect it. The Warmaster looked sharply at the primarch of the Alpha Legion, eyes narrowing.

'It would be unwise to take my name in vain, Alpharius,' said Horus, fingers tightening with anger. 'You claimed my authority and misled Angron and his World Eaters, allowing Corax and his Legion to escape.'

'Perhaps your conversion to our cause is less than complete,' added Erebus, before Alpharius could reply.

The Alpha Legion's primarch held his tongue for the moment, quickly adjusting his demeanour in the face of Horus's hostility. He stood in front of the Warmaster, helm under one arm, head bowed in obeisance, the picture of the diffident servant.

Abaddon put his hand to the hilt of his sword and growled.

'Your duplicitous nature is well known,' said the captain, teeth bared in anger. 'The Warmaster saw fit to bring you into the light of his plans, I hope you have not made a mockery of his fair judgement.'

'I seek to place Horus on the throne of Terra, the same as you,' replied Alpharius, lowering to one knee in deference. It was an instinctive reaction, though such submission grated at the primarch's pride. 'If I acted out of turn it is only because circumstance forced me to make a decision quickly.'

'I have not yet heard an explanation for your actions,' said Horus.

The Warmaster's gaze was piercing, as if trying to bore into the primarch's mind to see his thoughts. Alpharius matched the stare without fear. Horus knew nothing of the Alpha Legion's true aims. If he had any inkling of the part made out for him by the Cabal, Alpharius would already be dead. 'I consider it a grave crime to usurp my authority, a crime compounded by the severity of the consequences.'

'The Raven Guard have not yet been apprehended,'

said Erebus, a sneer twisting his lips. 'Though but a shadow of their former strength, it was foolish to allow them to escape.'

'You must trust me,' said Alpharius, ignoring the two legionaries, his attention focused on his brother primarch. It was the Warmaster's will, or whim, that needed to be swayed to Alpharius's cause. 'The military potential of the Raven Guard has been expended, they are no physical threat. Their survival, Corax's escape, will play a greater role in this war we have unleashed.'

'Will it?' Abaddon spat the words, his scorn etched into the creases in his brow. 'What greater role?'

Alpharius kept his gaze on the Warmaster, noting that his displeasure did not seem so deep. It was clear that he did not have Horus's full trust, but Alpharius did not care for that. His brothers had always been wary of the Alpha Legion, always suspicious of their methods, if not their motives. Horus was no different. He had consistently underestimated the power of subterfuge, eschewing the subtler weapons of espionage and misdirection in favour of overt action. Alpharius had not answered the Warmaster's summons to excuse his actions, he had come to persuade Horus of their merit. That he could do so without the interference of the other Legion commanders was an advantage.

'The Alpha Legion have infiltrated the Raven Guard,' Alpharius said bluntly.

He saw Horus's eyes widen slightly with surprise, and suppressed an expression of pleasure at the Warmaster's nonplussed moment. Far from an admission of guilt, it was a declaration of strength; the unveiling of a weapon that the Alpha Legion kept hidden.

Alpharius could see the calculation behind the Warmaster's eyes. If the Alpha Legion could infiltrate the Raven Guard, they could have done the same to any Legion. The Warmaster cocked his head to one side, momentarily perturbed, his eyes flicking away from Alpharius for the first time since he had entered, glancing at Abaddon.

'To what purpose?' asked Horus, recovering his composure, his stare returning to its previous intensity. 'Had they been destroyed, what would be the point of spying on corpses?'

'You allowed Corax to get away from the World Eaters to protect your operatives.' Erebus levelled the accusation with a pointed finger, pushing Alpharius's patience beyond its limit.

'I am a primarch, genetor of the Alpha Legion, and you will show me due respect!' snapped Alpharius, standing up.

He took two steps towards Erebus, eyes glittering. Abaddon moved to intercept him, half-drawing his blade

'Don't make the mistake of letting that sword leave its scabbard,' said Alpharius, fixing Abaddon with a venomous glare. 'I may prefer to work in subtle ways, but if you continue to insult me, I will slay you here and now.'

Horus held out a hand, waving Abaddon back, a thin smile on the Warmaster's face. He seemed pleased at Alpharius's anger. 'You are somewhat defensive, my brother,' he said, gesturing for Alpharius to seat himself on one of the chairs arranged around the throne. 'Please explain to me the benefits of allowing Corax to escape.'

Alpharius sat down, reluctantly accepting the Warmaster's invitation, darting a warning look at Erebus just as the Word Bearer opened his mouth to speak.

'Save your posturing for those that are swayed by it,' said Alpharius. 'Your change of loyalty proves the vacuity of your proselytising. You are privileged to stand in the presence of your betters, and should know not to speak until spoken to.'

The primarch enjoyed the contortions of anger that

wracked the First Chaplain's face, but Erebus heeded the
warning and said nothing.

'I have good information that Corax will attempt to
return to Terra,' Alpharius said, turning his attention
back to Horus. 'He will entreat the aid of the Emperor,
and be given access to some secret of Old Night that we
can use to our advantage.'

'From where does this "good information" come?'
asked Horus, affecting disinterest though Alpharius
could see that the Warmaster was intrigued.

'We each have our own means and sources,' replied
Alpharius, flicking a meaningful gaze towards Erebus.
The Alpha Legion had made it their business to know
as much as possible about their fellow conspirators, and
Alpharius was well aware of the strange rituals that Lorgar and his Word Bearers now indulged in. The Alpha
Legion's allies in the Cabal had furnished them with
much information concerning the Primordial Annihilator, the Power of Chaos. It would not hurt to pretend
that the Word Bearers were not the only Legion who had
influence with the powers of the warp. 'I am not of a
mind to share mine with you at the moment.'

'Are you not?' said Horus, irritated. 'Why would you
keep secrets from me?'

'Perhaps it is just my nature to do so. Secrecy is my
best weapon.' Alpharius smiled apologetically and gave
a slight shrug. 'Also, I do not believe myself or my Legion
indispensable in your endeavours, so it would be unwise
to surrender the few small advantages I possess. I know
that my behaviour in the past and in recent times does
not engender trust, but I assure you that this information is not only legitimate, but accurate.'

'I will accept your assurances,' said Horus, 'for the
moment.' He leaned back in his throne, visibly relaxing as if to back up his words. Alpharius knew not to be
lured into a sense of security. The Warmaster's temper

might change at a wrong answer from him or a sly word from Erebus. 'What is your intent?'

'We will allow Corax to obtain whatever it is he seeks, and then take it from him, turning it to our purpose.'

'How do you think your operatives will remain undetected?' Abaddon asked. 'Our reports show that less than four thousand Raven Guard fled from Angron. New faces will be easily spotted, your legionaries exposed.'

'That is why they wear old faces,' Alpharius told him. He smiled and explained further when the others' frowns deepened. 'The Raven Guard were scattered as they fled the massacre at the dropsite. It was several days before they convened their strength again, during which time many were cut down in pursuit and anarchy reigned through their organisation. It was no simple matter for my Apothecaries to transplant the facial features of several fallen Raven Guard onto volunteers from my Legion, but they have had a lot of practice. As you may have heard, such facial surgery is not uncommon in the ranks of the Alpha Legion. My warriors are skilled and experienced, able to blend in without attracting attention. Even now they are with the Raven Guard, waiting for the opportunity to report.'

'You stole their faces?' Abaddon's expression was a mixture of incredulity and disgust.

Alpharius nodded and looked for Horus's reaction. For a moment the Warmaster had the same guarded look as earlier, but his aggression swept it aside as he leaned forwards, brow furrowing.

'You are sure of their success?' asked Horus, the words laden with accusation. 'You have heard from them since they began their infiltration?'

Alpharius hesitated at this question, not sure of his reply. There was no point lying at this stage, even though the truth might upset the Warmaster further.

'They have not yet been in contact,' Alpharius admitted.

'It is possible that they have been discovered, or perhaps slain in the fighting, but it is unlikely. They will send word when there is something of note to report.'

'That will be a feat in itself, considering how far away they might be,' said Abaddon.

'As I said before, I have my means.'

Saying nothing, Horus regarded Alpharius for some time, his shadow-hidden eyes never leaving the face of the Alpha Legion primarch. Erebus bent down to say something but the Warmaster held up a hand to stop him.

'You should have come to me with this intelligence before you interfered with the World Eaters,' Horus said, his voice quiet. Alpharius chose not to repeat his point that he had had no such time to seek the Warmaster's authority, and certainly didn't voice his view that permission would not have been given. The judge was about to pronounce his judgement and Alpharius could not tell which humours held sway over the Warmaster. He held his breath, trying not to tense lest his anxiety was seen as guilt. 'Angron has been given further cause to doubt my commands, and he is not shy in voicing his displeasure. I do not appreciate your scheming, brother, and I will be watching you closely.'

Which meant that no action more imminent would be taken against the Alpha Legion. Alpharius breathed out slowly, still on his guard.

'We have a possible contact with a Raven Guard vessel heading out-system from Isstvan IV, Warmaster,' said Abaddon. 'Should we call off the pursuit, if it is your desire to let them escape?'

Horus looked to Alpharius, one eyebrow raised, seeking his opinion, though Alpharius sensed he was still being tested.

'I would humbly suggest that the pursuit continues as normal for the moment,' said the primarch. 'Corax may already be suspicious of the events that allowed him to elude the World Eaters, any further deficiency in our attempts to bring him to battle might cause him to act with greater caution and ultimately thwart the reasons for allowing the Raven Guard their freedom.'

'I concur,' said Horus. 'I have every confidence in Corax's ability to escape my clutches without further help, and it will cause further consternation and questions amongst our allies if I am seen to interfere again.'

'A wise decision,' said Alpharius, bowing his head. 'If there is nothing more to discuss, I must return to my Legion and continue the operation.'

Horus signalled for Alpharius to depart and the primarch felt the Warmaster's heavy gaze on his back as he walked towards the door. The hydraulically-locked doorway remained closed to him, but Alpharius did not turn around.

The murmur of Erebus hovered on the edge of Alpharius's hearing as the primarch waited for the portal to open.

'If I thought for a moment, brother, that you were working against me, I would destroy you and your Legion,' Horus declared.

Alpharius looked over his shoulder at the Warmaster and his two advisors.

'I have never doubted that, brother.'

The door hissed open in front of Alpharius and he stepped out of the star chamber, trembling at the experience.

WHEN ALPHARIUS HAD left, Abaddon asked leave of his Warmaster.

'Wait a moment, Ezekyle,' said Horus. His gaze moved between Abaddon and Erebus. 'If the Alpha Legion have managed to infiltrate the Raven Guard, I believe they will have no compunction about doing the same to their allies. We have already suffered from disloyalty, I will allow no further disruption. Erebus, send word to Lorgar before he leaves for Calth. I want more of his Apostles spread through our forces. Ezekyle, conduct a thorough security review of our protocols, and report anything directly to me. Conduct any further purges as required.'

'What of Alpharius?' asked Erebus. 'He plays a game with us, of that I am sure.'

'He follows his own agenda, that much is certain,' replied the Warmaster. He stood up, dwarfing the two legionaries. 'I am equally certain that we will never have definitive proof of treachery. What is the current position of his battle-barge?'

'The *Alpha* is in orbit over Isstvan III,' said Abaddon. 'Should I assign a ship or two to watch them?'

'Yes,' said Horus. 'And pass on my command that the *Alpha* is to join my fleet when we leave the system. Let us keep Alpharius on a tight leash for the moment, until we see how his scheme plays out.'

WHEN HE HAD returned to the *Alpha*, Alpharius headed straight for his personal chambers. The meeting with Horus had unsettled him, more than he had expected. He wondered if it would be simpler to reveal the existence of the Cabal to the Warmaster. If Horus knew of the ancient pan-alien conglomeration that had persuaded Alpharius to side against the Emperor, the loyalty of the Alpha Legion would not be in doubt and they would have more freedom to pursue their goals.

In the longer term, that knowledge raised other questions, questions whose answers would be counterproductive, and Alpharius always took the long view. The Cabal had shown him Horus's self-destruction after the Warmaster's victory over the Emperor, ultimately sparing the galaxy from the eternal threat of the Primordial Annihilator. This outcome had to remain a secret.

If that knowledge were to be revealed, Horus would be forewarned and it would not come to pass, meaning the Alpha Legion's treason against the Emperor would be for nothing.

As they had done so many times before, Alpharius and his Legion had stepped upon a narrow path, playing a part to two opposing sides to achieve a third, more desirable outcome. One distraction, one wrong step, would see them utterly isolated and most likely destroyed.

These thoughts occupied Alpharius as he made his way along the dimly-lit corridors of his battle-barge. The massive vessel seemed empty and he passed only a few of the Legion's human serfs and half-mechanical servitors. They bowed their heads in deference to their master, as befitted one of the Alpha Legion, but were unaware that he was the primarch. His appearance was nondescript and his movements, like those of all of his warriors, were ever masked in distraction and diversion, so that his whereabouts were never certain even to those under his command.

Most of the Alpha Legion was still on Isstvan V, where they had taken part in the massacre at the dropsite, destroying the Iron Hands, Salamanders and Raven Guard, fighting alongside the other Legions who had thrown in their lot with Horus.

It had been a subterfuge worthy of Alpharius's twisted schemes, but there had been survivors, and news of Horus's great betrayal was surely spreading. The Alpha Legion would act as the Warmaster's eyes and ears across the galaxy, keeping watch not only on those remnants that still backed the Emperor, but also on those Legions that had sworn loyalty to Horus. According to the Cabal, there was a balance to be achieved. Horus must be victorious, but his hold on power precarious enough to precipitate the implosion of the traitor forces after the victory. This would result in the destruction of the traitors that Alpharius had already begun to engineer.

In keeping with Alpharius's usual appearance as a normal legionary, his chambers were just one of the many assigned to the Legion captains normally aboard the *Alpha*. A nondescript metal door in a side passage marked the entrance to his personal chambers. According to the small nameplate beside the door they were the rooms assigned to Captain Niming; a conceit of an ancient, dead Terran language that Alpharius found as amusing as it was useful. When more of his Legion was on board, several different individuals would use the quarters, according to secret rota, and there were other such 'blind' chambers on the other ships of the fleet. With such methods, Alpharius could move amongst his Legion without drawing attention to his presence.

Alpharius punched in the lock code and the door slid open, revealing a small, wood-panelled antechamber just a few strides across, leading to another sealed portal. He locked the outer door behind him and checked the security log terminal hidden behind one of the timbers, assuring himself that none of the chamber's other pseudo-captains had returned to the battle-barge yet.

Entering the cipher for the second door, Alpharius entered the quarters proper: three linked rooms furnished sparingly with old Terran cabinets, chairs and tables of nondescript origin. The floor was carpeted with a dark red, the plascrete bulkheads obscured behind more wooden panelling. In the main chamber were three high-backed couches, reinforced to support the weight of several legionaries. The archway to the right led to the sleeping chambers, but it was to the left that Alpharius turned first, to the arming room.

The primarch did not divest himself fully of his armour; such a thing required the attendance of several serfs and he was not prepared to let anyone else into the chambers while he still had his secret visitor on board.

The room was plain save for the weapons racks on the walls and the steel stand for his armour. An alcove in one wall contained two automated, mechanical arms. He backed into this space and activated the backpack removal system. With a hiss of disengaging cables and crackle of detaching power conduits, his backpack was lifted from his armour, turned one hundred and eighty degrees and plugged into a recharging port at the back of the alcove, linked to the *Alpha*'s energy grid.

With this completed, Alpharius took off his helm and shoulder guards and placed them on the armour stand. He removed his gauntlets, vambraces and elbow guards and locked them in place too, before removing the outer greaves protecting his lower legs.

He had eschewed his more formal ceremonial garb for the audience with Horus. This particular suit of armour was the same as that issued to many of his legionaries, bearing no symbols that would mark out Alpharius as anything other than an ordinary warrior of the Alpha Legion. Painted with several coats of blue over the bare ceramite, it was the third such suit Alpharius had possessed on board the *Alpha*, though he had others on several different vessels, each identical to this. The first had been abandoned on Thiatchin after anti-compliance forces had compromised Alpharius's desert bunker complex and the primarch had been forced to retreat without it. The second had been half-destroyed during fighting against orks on Actur Three-Eighteen and the battle damage had rendered it easily identifiable. This suit had lasted for twelve years so far, but Alpharius's meticulous maintenance and attention to the replenishment of the livery and insignia meant that it was as flawless as the day the artificers had created it. There was not a scratch, burr, mark, dent or even brushstroke that marked it out as exceptional, not a detail that might be used to identify Alpharius amongst the other warriors of the Legion.

+I sense a presence.+

The clipped, false tones of his guest's translating device sounded from the sleeping chamber. Alpharius, now divested of much of his armour, crossed the main room quickly and entered the bunkroom.

The Cabal's emissary hovered at the foot of the low bunk. At first glance it appearance to be a glass sphere no larger than his palm, filled with swirling yellow and green gases, several digital devices attached to the globe without any obvious pattern. Looking more closely, one could see the creature itself inside its artificial habitat. It looked like a tiny skeletal hand, with seven fingers and no thumb, its sensory organs dark, shimmering lines against the brittle, pale flesh of its body.

Its true name was unpronounceable, its gender uncertain, but Alpharius thought of the alien as a 'him' due to the thin, reedy voice emitted by the translator, and referred to the creature by the approximate name of Athithirtir.

Bubbles formed in the gas, though from what orifice Alpharius was not sure, and the translator emitter set at the bottom of the globe rattled into life.

+I sense you have met the Warmaster.+

'Horus has allowed us to continue with the infiltration of the Raven Guard,' said the primarch. 'Everything will proceed as we have discussed.'

+I sense that you are not being forthright.+

Alpharius suppressed a growl of annoyance. Athithirtir had some kind of empathic ability which even his primarch mind could not block. The envoy had introduced itself as an antedil, and mentioned a gas giant homeworld somewhere on the rim in the galactic north. Its psychic sense had developed under the crushing pressure and intense gravity of such a planet, where normal senses and limbs would have been inadequate.

'Horus is suspicious, that is all,' said Alpharius. 'He will need to be handled carefully.'

+I sense reticence. Your role is clear. Horus must win this war outright. The Primordial Annihilator gathers strength. It is linked to the Warmaster now. Rituals are being performed and creatures summoned from the–+

The translator let out a stream of incomprehensible high-pitched sounds.

'From the warp, you mean?' said Alpharius.

+Such a short word for such a complex phenom-enon.+

'Creatures are being summoned from the warp? You mean daemons, yes?' Alpharius sat on the end of the bunk and the environment globe lowered, floating level with the primarch's face, just out of reach. Different coloured bubbles flashed in the depths.

+Wheels are turning. Traps are being laid. Your brothers loyal to the Emperor will face their darkest foes. They must fall.+

'So you have said before. For the moment we must wait to find out what Corax will do and if your prophecies are true.'

+Not prophecies. Accurate. True. The Raven will meet the Emperor and he will be given a gift that can change the course of the coming war. This must be destroyed.+

'It seems such a waste, to destroy this gift,' said Alpharius. He stood up and paced to the door before turning to look at Athithirtir. 'I think it would be better in the hands of the Alpha Legion than turned to scrap.'

+That is not what we agreed. I insist that you remem-ber our agreement. The device and the Raven Guard will be destroyed. The plan must continue.+

'I think not,' said Alpharius. 'Already my twin brother Omegon is on Kiavahr, the world around which Deliv-erance orbits. We have allies amongst the people there, old foes of Corax who do not like their new Mechani-cum masters and who strive for independence from the Imperium. Rest assured, the Raven Guard will be destroyed, but not before Omegon claims this prize for the Alpha Legion.'

The alien's words came out as a flutter of untranslatable mechanical shrieks, and its globe bobbed up and down in agitation, the gas roiling within.

'Settle yourself,' said Alpharius with a laugh. 'We wouldn't want you to break on something, would we?'

+Your dishonesty will be communicated to the Cabal.+

'When I have the prize in my hands, and Horus is one step closer to overthrowing the Emperor, we shall see if the Cabal disapproves of my actions,' said Alpharius as he stepped out of the bunk chamber. 'Until then, you can keep your opinions to yourself.'

He hit the lock switch on the bedroom door, cutting off Athithirtir's enraged metallic screech.

Everything had been set in motion, and now came the hardest part: waiting. Waiting for his counterpart on Kiavahr, his twin Omegon, to make contact with the anti-Imperial forces on the forge-world; waiting for his operatives within the Raven Guard to make themselves known to Omegon.

Alpharius sat on one of the couches, elbows on knees, fingers steepled at his chin, as his mind went over the plan as it stood. With Horus now set up to play his part, there was nothing to interfere with the smooth enactment of the Alpha Legion's scheme. Everything would pan out as Alpharius had envisaged.

THREE

A Traitor in the Midst
Blacklight
Corax Makes a Speech

'PICKET SHIPS DETECTED.' Ephrenia's announcement stilled the activity on the strategium.

'Three destroyers, overlapping sensor sweeps, detecting plasma trails of three more vessels, probably light cruiser class,' she continued.

The *Avenger* was only two days from reaching translation point, far enough away from the gravitic pull of Isstvan's star to make a safe warp jump. For the last three days the net thrown up by the traitor ships had been closing in, but this was the closest they had come, only a few hundred thousand kilometres away.

Corax glanced at a screen in the arm of the command throne, showing the relative positions of the vessels. In a moment he had assessed their trajectories and the coverage of the scanner sweeps.

'Too close to alter course,' he declared. 'We will have to make a dash for the translation point. Shut down all auxiliary systems, impose blacklight protocols, divert power savings to the engines.'

A series of affirmatives chorused from the assembled staff and legionaries. The primarch turned his attention to Commander Branne.

'I want you and Agapito to make a stern-to-prow inspection. Ensure all support systems are at minimal output. Pass the word to Solaro and Aloni to enforce the blacklight protocols.' The primarch raised his voice. 'I want full energy balance in ten minutes, no later.'

'Aye, lord, I'll see to it,' replied Branne.

'Detecting launch, Lord Corax,' said Ephrenia. 'Picket ships are firing torpedoes, wide dispersal.'

'Direction?' snapped Corax, returning to his place behind the command throne, eyes fixed to the small data screen.

'Crossing pattern,' Ephrenia replied. 'Even at our increased speed they will pass ahead of us.'

'Clever bastards,' muttered Branne from behind the primarch. 'Hoping to get lucky with blind firing.'

'Save three per cent of energy output for manoeuvring, just in case,' said Corax. 'All personnel to attend to battle stations.'

'Weapons, Lord Corax?' asked Ephrenia. Her expression was as calm as ever, but the primarch detected the slightest hint of tension in her voice. 'Shall we reserve any output for the weapons batteries?'

'No,' replied the primarch after a moment's thought. 'We won't be able to fight our way out of this one if we are discovered.'

'And the void shield transformers, Lord Corax? Shall I have them running on standby?'

'No,' Corax said. 'All power to reflex shields and engines, nothing else. If they hit us, it will be too late anyway.'

Taking the shield transformers offline would add almost four minutes to the time required for the reflex shields to revert to defensive void shields; extra minutes during which untold damage might be incurred by the *Avenger*. For the first time since he had come aboard, Corax noticed hesitation in the controller. It lasted only a heartbeat before Ephrenia nodded and turned to the task at hand. He heard the doors opening and glanced over his shoulder to see Branne departing on his inspection.

He checked the display again. They were two hundred and fifty thousand kilometres from the Traitor picket. Seven more vessels had been picked up by the low-band sensor screen, creating three layers of defence between the battle-barge and the safe translation point. If there was even a momentary blip in the reflex shields, or one of the torpedoes caught the *Avenger* in its blast, the primarch's ship would quickly find itself surrounded by enemies.

He could not outpace his foes and he could not outfight them. Corax's only option was to hold his nerve and stay focused on evading detection. It was something he had been good at since he was a boy, and he was not going to start making rash decisions now.

BLACKLIGHT PROTOCOLS MEANT the complete shutdown of all non-essential systems. One by one, life support, lighting, heating and other environmental systems powered down to their minimum levels; just enough for the human crew to survive. Even the artificial gravity was lessened to one-half Terran normal, freeing up valuable power for the plasma drives.

In the busy transport compartments in the depths of the hold, nearly fifteen hundred legionaries were packed together as darkness descended. The battle-barge had been designed to carry a fraction of that number.

Space had been made in storage holds, weapon bays, and amongst the gantries and decks of the engine rooms. Squads had found room in maintenance crawlways and in stairwells, and several dozen elevator and conveyor shafts had been decommissioned to provide even more space. Even with such measures, the warriors

of the Raven Guard had little freedom of movement.
Only the main access corridors had been kept clear, to
allow runners easy access between the strategium and
other essential stations.

Amongst the throng, Alpharius watched the lights
dimming and then going out. Of course, he was not *the*
Alpharius, but by some clever mind-programming and
a little psychic intervention by the Legion's Librarius, he
had chosen to forget his real name. To all intents and
purposes, he now *was* Alpharius.

And he was a little concerned. He sat with his adopted
squad on a gangway above the plasma reactors, clad in
his armour. Environment warning sigils lit up in his
display as the air thinned and gravity lessened. Without
thought he gave a sub-vocal command to power up the
auto-senses of his helmet.

'What do you think you're doing?'

Alpharius turned his head as Command Aloni's voice
rang along the gantry. He realised the captain was talking to him.

'You know what blacklight means,' continued Aloni.
'Power to minimal. Do you realise what kind of energy
signature one and a half thousand power armoured
legionaries are going to give off? Everybody pay attention! Everything is to be set to minimum output, lowest
cycle. Rebreathing, moisture recycling, locomotion. Everything. No communications, no external address, no
movement.'

Nodding his compliance, Alpharius powered down
his suit, becoming an immobile statue of ceramite, plasteel and adamantium. His secondary heart began to
beat, compensating for the lower temperature outside,
and his multi-lung inflated, enabling him to cope with
air that had not been properly recycled.

Around him the others were doing the same. Here,
out by the reactors, all life support was being withdrawn,

leaving each legionary cocooned within his own personal environment. Artificial night descended, broken only by the wink of illuminated gauges and monitor lights on the twin reactors fifty metres below the walkway. Moisture began to ice over the armour of the legionaries, thin trails of vapour dribbling from face masks and backpack exhaust vents.

Locked inside his suit, Alpharius realised how precarious his position was. Discovery was not an immediate problem. What with the reorganisation of the Legion, and the general unwillingness of the others to discuss what had happened on Isstvan, it had been simple enough to take up his new role.

His face was still sore from the grafting surgery, particularly where the implanted flesh of his new face met his original skin at the base of his neck and around his throat. The bone beneath had been remoulded and ached, while tendons and muscles that had been shortened or lengthened felt raw beneath his stolen skin.

Alpharius swallowed, remembering where the body had been found, no more than five minutes dead, leg blasted off by a Whirlwind rocket, spine snapped across a ridge of rock. The Apothecaries had acted as quickly as possible. For decades the Alpha Legion had striven to look alike, modelling themselves on their primarch, glorying in their anonymity. To have black hair, to have distinctive features and eyes that were a pale green, was a new sensation for him.

And the memories lurked inside his mind too. He knew a little about the legionary whose persona he had taken. He had taken in the meat of the fallen Raven Guard, allowing his omophagea to dissect and absorb the information about his prey. Bolstered by the abilities of the Librarians – abilities forbidden by the Decree at Nikaea but still widely practised by the Alpha Legion – he had gathered what fragments he could of the dead legionary's life.

He could feel them, flashes of images, snippets of conversation. More than that, Alpharius could feel how his new persona had felt. He had been proud, a veteran of the Lycaeus uprising, and had earned distinction with the Raven Guard since they had been united with their primarch.

The memories itched as well, jarring inside his thoughts, confusing him occasionally. Over the time he had spent fleeing across Isstvan V with his new comrades, he had learned their names and faces and the way they fought. The most fraught time had been the first few days, when commands had been issued in code-phrases, and formations called out in battle-lingua that he did not know, a language evolved on Deliverance that he had not grown up with. Yet he had been picked for this mission because of his gift with languages, his quick mind and his instinct for adaptation. His deficiencies had been covered by the efficiency and cohesion of the Raven Guard themselves and soon he had managed to blend in during the hit-and-run attacks, avoiding the suspicion of his squad comrades as well as the deadly attention of those pursuing the Raven Guard.

All of that seemed to be poised on the verge of pointlessness now, as he sat immobile over a reactor that would turn into a small star the moment it was breached, aboard a warship ghosting through an enemy fleet protected by nothing more than a few metres of bonded plasteel and adamantium. One lucky hit and he would be incinerated, along with the rest of those aboard the *Avenger*.

He did not know how many others of the Alpha Legion had been successful in taking their place; he did not know if he was the only one or if there were dozens of them. It did not matter. For the moment he was alone, and had to act accordingly. He had to do all he could to stay alive, remain undetected, observe Corax and get in touch with Omegon once they returned to Deliverance.

As fervently as he had ever hoped for success, he now hoped for his allies to fail. Whoever it was out there chasing the ship – Word Bearers, Alpha Legion, World Eaters, Sons of Horus, Iron Warriors, Imperial Army – Alpharius wished them every disaster that he could imagine: engine failure, outbreaks of disease, weapons malfunction, anything that would stop that one lucky hit from eradicating his existence. He was prepared to give his life for his primarch and his Legion, but not this way, not without a foe to fight and a mission to protect.

It would be such a pointless way to die, he thought, as the sound of a detonation echoed dully through the hull.

'NOVA CANNON SHELL,' reported Ephrenia. 'Six thousand kilometres, starboard bow.'

Corax did not react immediately. Two cruisers had joined the destroyers, the growing enemy flotilla saturating the intervening gulf of space with torpedoes, missiles and plasma blasts in an attempt to catch the *Avenger* in a blanket of fire. It was not a particularly effective tactic. The volume of void they were trying to cover was vast and they were trying to get very lucky, or frighten Corax into an act that would betray his location.

That the Traitors knew the battle-barge was in their vicinity was beyond doubt, but the question that now concerned Corax was whether they knew any more than that. The nova cannon detonation had not been so close as to convince him it had been deliberately aimed at the *Avenger*, but neither had the margin of the miss been enough that it was outside the normal margin of error for such a long-ranged shot. Could he afford to wait for a second plasma explosion to prove things one way or the other?

'Decline by fifty thousand metres, three degrees

starboard,' he snapped to the men at the helm controls.

'Navigational shields absorbing plasma residuals and debris,' announced another crewman. 'Nearing reflex shield tolerance levels.'

Corax gritted his teeth. The low-power navigational shields were usually in place to ward away micro-asteroids and other space-borne debris, but now the nova cannon blast was swamping them with more than they were intended to handle. If he increased power to prevent any of the shockwave reaching the *Avenger*, the energy spike would reveal their position.

'Ride it,' he said, as the ship started shuddering around him. 'Implement previous order.'

The battle-barge made best use of the space available, using all three dimensions to change course away from the point at which the nova cannon had been targeted. It was not an eventuality Corax had expected – the nova cannon was still considered highly experimental by most Imperial forces, and few commanders would allow one to be mounted on their vessel.

'Can you calculate the launching vessel?' he asked Ephrenia.

'Just detecting a third line-class ship, Lord Corax,' the strategium controller replied. 'Probably a grand cruiser. Approaching from almost directly astern, broadcasting Iron Warriors identifiers.'

'Typical,' Corax whispered. Give one of Perturabo's captains the chance to mount a bigger gun and he would snatch your hand off to take it.

'Detecting another nova cannon launch,' warned Ephrenia.

In her worry, she had forgotten his title, something the primarch had thought impossible. Corax noticed her face paling and the knuckles of her thin hands whitening, supporting callipers flexing, as she grabbed the edge of the display console, expecting an impact. There

was no way a warning could be given to the crew without giving away the battle-barge's position, and if the
nova cannon scored an unlikely direct hit, no amount
of bracing and preparation would save lives.

'Passing to port, fifteen thousand kilometres and
increasing, Lord Corax,' Ephrenia said, smiling slightly
and relaxing her grip. 'Detonation detected. Seventy
thousand kilometres away.'

'It is safe to assume the fire is random. Set in a course
for closest translation point.'

Corax had noted the two separate detonation points
and filed them away in his memory. It seemed likely
the Iron Warriors were using a firing formula to calculate their target points. Three or four more detonations
would allow Corax to calculate the formula in retrospect and take appropriate action to decrease the odds
of another close call. Other than that, there was nothing
else to do except continue to hope for the best.

THE AVENGER CONTINUED on, dipping and rising, zigzag-
ging its way towards the translation point, cutting an
elusive path through the net of Traitor ships. At times
Corax headed directly towards the enemy, passing
within ten thousand kilometres of battle cruisers and
frigates, trusting the reflex shields to mask any emission
that would betray their presence.

The cordon tightened, the glimmers on the traitors'
scanner displays drawing in more and more vessels,
chasing ghost returns that were little more than fuzzy
mirages against the backdrop energy haze of the universe.

Sitting in the darkness of his requisitioned command
chamber, Corax felt the change in vibrations that signalled another course alteration. They were less than
half a day from the translation point. It was tempting to make the warp jump now and take the risk of

gravimetric interference, but he stayed patient.

There had been some close calls: torpedoes unleashing their warheads a few thousand kilometres from
the *Avenger*, last moment changes in direction to avoid
enemy scans, nova cannon detonations that had pushed
the navigational shields to the limit, random reactor
spikes that had brought the battle-barge to a virtual halt
to compensate for the energy flare-ups.

The primarch had taken all of this without a moment's
fear. There was no room for error, but there was also no
room for uncertainty. His situation was very stark: escape
and survive or be detected and destroyed. Such extremes
made clarity simple, and drove away other thoughts that
might have clouded his judgement.

For the moment they were exploiting a small break
in the traitor cordon and had had several hours of
unopposed travel. Blacklight protocol was still in full
operation, and so Corax sat at the large command console staring at the blank screens and dead displays, his
eyes picking out the details of the room in the smallest glow from blinking red standby lights and the gleam
from the doorway leading to the strategium.

He was used to waiting.

Over long years, he had learned the lessons of patience,
of precise timing. During hundreds of battles he had
known the moment to act and the moment to pause,
and had known victory every time because of those decisions.

The massacre at the dropsite had caught him off-guard.
It troubled the primarch that he had perceived nothing
of the traitorous intent of his fellow Legion commanders. Sitting in the dark, alone with his thoughts, he
wondered if he had been blinded to their treachery by
some weakness in himself. Had he been too trusting?
Ignored subtle signs of his brothers' intent? Been over-
confident?

What had happened had been unthinkable, and that was part of the problem for Corax. Should it have been so outlandish that he had never considered having to fight his brothers? He had been sent with the others to Isstvan to bring Horus to account – surely he should have wondered whether Horus had acted entirely alone. Had the shock of the Warmaster's turn against the Emperor befuddled him, caused him to blunder into an obvious trap?

The questions were all the harder because they were unanswerable.

Another vibration, another course change. The hours ticked past. The primarch needed no data-screen to tell him what was happening. He had a picture in his mind of the *Avenger* and the ships arrayed against it, their courses plotted in his thoughts as accurately as any schematic. Any notable divergence from the picture he had drawn would be reported, and he had received no such communication from Ephrenia. The complex web being woven to catch the *Avenger* was not tight enough, there were always gaps.

Patience.

Hours, days, weeks of waiting. Years, in fact, when he had been making his preparations, hidden amongst the prisoners of Lycaeus. There was something of a purity in the stillness; something energising about the solitude.

His wounds still pained him, occasional stabs of sensation that broke through the walls of his semi-mesmeric state. He would shift his weight to relieve the stress on ravaged ribs, to move pressure away from damaged organs. Corax's engineered body could withstand incredible amounts of damage, and yet there was something deeper than the physical wounds that afflicted the primarch. The pain was something he forced himself to endure, as a reminder of his failure. He suffered a hurt that no superhuman body could rectify: a grievous injury that the attention of the Apothecaries would not cure. Until he could bring an end to that internal agony, he would not allow his body to heal.

Roused from his contemplation by one such brief burst of pain, Corax activated a data-screen. Analysing the intersecting courses displayed on the monitor, Corax spotted something he had not seen before: a convergence of possibilities brought about by some minor alterations in the enemy's disposition a few hours ago.

There was a gap. Or rather, there was not a gap, but a coming together of four Traitor ships. The wash from their own plasma drives, the emissions of their reactors, would obscure the *Avenger* and provide a pathway to the transition point earlier than he had planned, if he dared take it.

Seeing the possibilities unfolding, Corax stood up, re-examining the chart. He was sure he was correct. Passing from inaction to motion in moments, the primarch leaned over towards the communicator activation stud.

He stopped with his finger millimetres from the switch.

Corax weighed up the situation once more, cooling his excitement, ignoring the lure of sudden activity. The manoeuvre would bring the *Avenger* within range of the guns of at least three enemy vessels. If he changed to the new course, they would be committed. Any significant alteration by the enemy would change the dynamic, revealing the Raven Guard's position dangerously close to the foe.

He discarded the idea.

Though Corax was eager to reach the relative safety of the warp – eager to do anything proactive – there was more to be said for caution than daring at the moment. He had gone after Lorgar at the dropsite, driven by a thirst for revenge, briefly abdicating his responsibility as a Legion commander. Had that emotive response cost his Legion, more of them falling to the ambush than would have done had he been commanding the retreat? He would not act rashly again.

The most important thing was that he had lived, and that was as true now as then. Half a day was not important; survival was important. That need to survive, that animal instinct to keep drawing breath had driven him on, filled him with purpose. He would not lie down and accept death willingly. Even now, his Legion almost wiped out, his enemies outnumbering his allies, Corax knew that he could not give up. His duty now was to keep the Raven Guard alive, no matter the temptations and instincts to act with resolve and daring.

On Deliverance, when it had been called Lycaeus, there had been true desperation. Weaker men had fallen and lesser men had balked at the task ahead. Not Corax. He had dragged Lycaeus, bloodied and screaming, into freedom, and not once doubted the righteousness of his effort. Why now did he wonder if he had the resolve to triumph?

He sat immobile in the darkness once more. He liked the dark; the shadows had always been an ally. He might spend the last hours of his life like this, waiting, anticipating the next shudder of a course correction, expecting a knock at the door to bring a fresh report of the enemy's movements, trying not to relive the mistakes and horrors of Isstvan.

Trying, but failing.

THE ROOM WAS dank with the smell of sweat, the air thick with the stench of his own fear. Marcus was more than happy to face any foe in an open fight, or even to stand firm while battleships destroyed each other with blasting broadsides. This war, the Raven Guard way of war, vexed his nerves and tightened his chest around his heart.

The praefector lay on his bunk, his eyes closed, wishing the ventilators could be activated to siphon away the filth of his perspiration. His hands trembled on his chest, his hair was lank across his brow and the pillow and sheets were soaked beneath him.

All it would take was one warhead to find the *Avenger* and they would all be killed. Valerius was certain of it; the reflex shields provided no defence against a dozen megatonnes of atomic destruction. The walls vibrated with the shockwaves of distant detonations – thousands of kilometres away, yet all too close for the praefector's liking.

Pelon was in the antechamber. Marcus could hear his short, panicked breaths and imagined his servant sitting in the corner of the room hugging his knees to his chest. The praefector understood well the dread that gripped his man, because he shared it.

The bombardment had started less than half an hour ago. He had been sent from the strategium by Corax as the first nova cannon shells had erupted, far from the battle-barge yet too close for comfort. As he had hurried down the corridors and descended seemingly endless stairwells, he had felt the ship vibrating beneath his tread, the metal of the handrails quivering under his fingers.

He had tried not to run. The Raven Guard he had passed were unperturbed by their predicament, trusting their existence to power of the reflex shields in a way that Marcus simply could not. He was Imperial Army, a Therion, and he was used to fighting an enemy he could see, his life entrusted to power fields or tank armour or the metres-thick walls of a bunker. He had endured artillery duels and orbital attacks, but nothing compared to the helplessness he felt right now.

The darkness was absolute. No lights could be lit. In a way, he was grateful. It was better that he was confined to quarters, where Lord Corax and the others could not see his cowardly reactions, could not hear his suppressed whimpers with each rattle of a passing shockwave.

Yet it was also a nightmare to be alone. Pride might have helped him master the fear, had he been within sight of others. With just himself to impress, his resolve was revealed to be woefully weak. The darkness was as cloying as the sweaty air. It weighed heavily on his chest, pushing the wind from his lungs, throttling him.

He choked and gasped and swung to the edge of the bed, booted feet touching upon the bare decking, arms hugged tight around his chest as he winced at another vibration that rattled from starboard to port, accompanied by creaks and cracks from the bulkheads around him.

'This is insanity,' he muttered.

His words were a whisper, but echoed inside his head. Sanity had been a scarce resource of late for the praefector. At first he had been relieved that the nightmares had ended. The blissful oblivion of sleep had been returned to him and he had embraced it.

The sensation of relief had not lasted long. Barely a few days after the evacuation of Lord Corax and the Legion, Marcus's empty dreams had started to nag at him. He woke in the middle of the night watches, a void in his thoughts, feeling dragged down into an abyss. Soon he had come to fear the nights as much as when the fires and the cries of dying ravens had haunted him. It was not the searing hot terror, the paranoia that had gripped him before, it was a cold dread that trickled down his spine and sank to the bottom of his stomach.

Alone in the dark of his cabin, that dread had returned, seeping out of the darkness while missiles and shells lit up the firmament beyond the steel and rockcrete walls. The nothing that awaited him was too much like the vacuum of space. In his dread, Marcus was convinced that he was going to die. Just as he had dreamt of the Raven Guard's predicament, now his sleeping thoughts were bringing him a vision of his doom. He would die alone, freezing in the void, swallowed by the emptiness of the universe.

Marcus let out a whimpering moan and threw himself face-first into the pillows and covers, trying to bury his head, striving to block out the emptiness that was leeching away his existence.

'THAT WAS A little too close,' remarked Branne as a nova cannon shell blossomed into nuclear life a few thousand kilometres off the starboard bow.

'Too close is a hit,' replied Agapito. 'Anything we survive is far enough away for me.'

'Hush,' said Lord Corax. His voice was calm, his features expressionless, as he watched the dull glow of sensor readings on the primary display. 'I am thinking.'

The primarch had taken over the helm controls as soon as the latest raitor fusillade had started, guiding the *Avenger* along a safe course that only he himself could see, his mind constantly calculating and adapting with each launched torpedo salvo and nova cannon detonation.

'Lord, we are heading to danger-close proximity with an enemy cruiser,' warned one of the attendants at the scanner array.

'I know,' replied the primarch, eyes locked on the display.

'Lord, they will detect our plasma wash if we pass that close,' Controller Ephrenia added, her tone quiet and respectful, yet tinged with concern.

'That is not all they will detect,' Corax replied, turning to smile at the woman. He paused for a moment and then held up a finger. 'I judge that we have reached safe distance for translation.'

'Lord?' Ephrenia's confusion was matched by Branne's. A sideways glance at Agapito and Aloni showed that his fellow commanders were tense, eyes narrowed.

'We will not be fleeing without a last remark to our enemies,' said Corax.

'Should we power up the void shields and weapons batteries, lord?' asked Ephrenia, hand hovering over the command terminal.

'No,' said the primarch. 'I have something more dramatic in mind.'

ON THE STRATEGIUM of the *Valediction*, Apostle Danask of the Word Bearers was finding his latest duty a stretch on his patience. The joyful anarchy and slaughter of the dropsite attack seemed a distant memory after days of fruitless searching for the fleeing Raven Guard. His latest orders were no more exhilarating. For more than a day his ship had been sporadically firing torpedo spreads into the area the Warmaster had ordered, with no result at all. It was a waste of time, and made all the more insulting because his brother legionaries were already en route to Calth for their surprise visit to the Ultramarines. It was hard not to feel that this was in some way a punishment for some breach of Legion rules of which he had not been made aware.

Danask wondered if perhaps he had not been dedicated enough in his devotion to this new cause. He had noticed Kor Phaeron looking at him strangely on occasion, and was sure that the Master of Faith was testing him in some fashion. He had offered no complaint when he had received his nonsensical orders, and had offered effusive praise to the primarch for considering him for such an onerous but essential duty.

'Energy signature detected!'

The words of Kal Namir came as a triumphant shout

from the scanner panels, snatching the Apostle from his thoughts.

'Where?' demanded Danask, rising up from the command throne. Sirens blared into life, shattering the quiet that had marked most of the patrol's duration.

'Almost on top of us, two thousand kilometres to port,' announced Kal Namir. 'Weapons batteries are powering up. Void shields at full potential.'

'Mask energy signature and get me a firm location. Brace for impact,' snapped the Apostle, realising that the enemy would only reveal himself to open fire.

He heard Kal Namir mutter to himself, swearing under his breath.

'Speak up or stay silent, brother,' rasped Danask. He was in no mood for his subordinate's grumbling. He punched in a command on the arm panel of the throne and brought up a real-time view of the enemy's rough location. A shimmer against the stars betrayed the presence of the Raven Guard ship.

'The scanners must have malfunctioned. This makes no sense,' Kal Namir said. He checked his displays again and then turned to look at Danask with eyes wide from shock. 'Signature is a warp core spike, commander...'

On the screen, the enemy battle-barge came into view, dangerously close, black against the distant pale glimmer of Isstvan's star. Moments later the space around the vessel swirled with power, a writhing rainbow of energy engulfing the ship from stem to stern.

'Take evasive action! yelled Danask, but even as he barked the words he knew it was too late.

The Raven Guard ship disappeared, swallowed by the warp translation point it had opened. The warp hole roiled wider and wider, washing over the *Valediction*. Danask felt the flow of warp energy moving through him, a pressure inside his head accompanied by a violent lurching of the cruiser.

'We're caught in her wake,' announced Kal Namir, somewhat unnecessarily, thought Danask.

The *Valediction* shuddered violently as the spume of warp energy flowed past, earthing itself through the void shields. Tendrils of immaterial power lashed through the vessel, coils of kaleidoscopic energy erupting from the walls, ceiling and floor, accompanied by the distant noise of screaming and unnatural howls.

More warning horns sounded a moment before an explosion tore apart the stern of the ship, the void shield generators overloaded by the surge. Secondary fires erupted along the flanks of the *Valediction*, detonating ammunition stores for the weapons batteries, opening up ragged wounds in the sides of the vessel.

The shriek of tearing metal accompanied fiery blasts of igniting atmosphere gouting from the massive holes to port and starboard. The *Valediction* heaved and bucked, artificial gravity fluctuating madly, tossing Danask and the others on the strategium to the ceiling and back to the floor. To the right of the Apostle, a communications attendant fell badly, snapping his neck on the mesh decking.

Then there was stillness and silence.

The shielding of the reactors had held firm and no further explosions occurred. Several minutes of disorientation ensued, during which the strategium staff busied themselves getting damage reports. The scanners were all offline due to the warp wash, the dozens of screens surrounding Danask all grey and lifeless.

'Get me helm control,' he rasped.

Anti-damage procedures continued for some time. Danask's head throbbed, an ache in the base of his skull growing in intensity until it threatened to be a significant distraction.

'That could have been worse,' said Kal Namir. 'At least we survived.'

Blood started to drip from the Word Bearer's eyes and nose, thick rivulets of crimson streaking Namir's face. The blood vessels in his eyes were thickening and his skin was becoming stretched and thin. Danask held a gauntleted hand to his nose as he tasted blood, and saw a drop of red on his fingertip.

One of the weapons console attendants gave a scream and lurched away from his panel, his robes afire with blue flames. The man flailed madly as others tried to help him, pushing him to the floor and swatting at the flames with cloaks and gloved hands.

'Get them off me! My face! Get them off my face!' shrieked another serf, tearing at his eyes and cheeks with his fingers, stumbling from his stool.

A subscreen flickered into life at one end of the scanning panel. Danask knew what he would see but looked anyway. Outside the ship the stars had disappeared, replaced by a whirling vortex of impossible energies that hurt his eyes to look at, even through the digitisation of the display.

They were in the warp.

Without their Geller fields.

Unprotected.

As realisation settled in the Apostle's numbed mind, he felt something clawed scratching inside his gut. He dared not look down.

A detached part of his brain marvelled at what had happened. To engage warp engines close enough to drag the *Valediction* into the immaterium yet far enough away not to destroy the cruiser was an incredibly difficult thing to do. He wondered what manner of man could do such a thing.

Around him, madness reigned. He felt apart from it all as his serfs and legionaries howled and roared, limbs cracking, warp energy swirling through their bodies, distorting and tearing. He realised he had asked the wrong question. Exposure to the warp was the most horrific death that could be visited upon any living creature. It was not what manner of man *could* do such a thing, it was what manner of man *would* do such a thing.

He never got to answer his own question. Moments later, a horned, red-skinned beast erupted from his innards, splaying out his fused ribs and chest, his twin hearts held between fanged teeth.

Danask's agonised scream, so inhuman, so unlike a legionary, joined with cries of the rest of his crew.

THEY WERE SAFE in the warp. As safe as the warp could ever be, though the *Avenger's* Navigators had complained about a roiling tempest as soon as they had translated. The Astronomican, the light that guided them through the immaterial aether, was all but obscured by storms of immense proportions.

Corax had told them to do the best they could. Their goal was simple: head to the source of the Emperor's light and they would reach Terra.

The primarch stood on the strategium with his commanders, the pick-up for the internal vox system small in the palm of his hand. Blacklight protocols were over, the reactors running at full capacity. The strategium was awash with light, bright after the days of gloom. The primarch's disposition did not match the brightening of the environment.

Hesitating, Corax wondered what he would say to his warriors. What words of encouragement could he speak when he felt so devoid of hope himself? The Traitors had struck so well, their concealed blow aimed with deadly effect; it seemed unlikely that they could be stopped. He had given many speeches in his life, to rouse the weary to fight on, to inspire his warriors to acts of great bravery; all of the words that sprang to mind now seemed to the primarch to be hollow platitudes.

It did not matter. He drove out the doubt with a surge of will. Now was the time when he needed most to display the leadership for which he had been created. It was at times like this, not in the heat of battle where his physical abilities could sway the day, that his true worth was judged. He was the primarch of the Raven Guard and his legionaries would look to him for guidance and strength. Many had seen rough times before, though nothing compared to the cataclysm that Horus had now unleashed upon them. Some were survivors of the Unification Wars, others the veterans of Lycaeus's rebellion. All of them were warriors, with the pride of the Legion in their hearts.

'We leave Isstvan in defeat,' he said, his words broadcast the length and breadth of the ship. 'It is not a pleasant feeling, but I want you to remember it. Take it into your hearts and nurture this sensation. Let it flow through your veins and fuel your muscles. Never forget what it feels like to fail.'

He stopped for a moment, taking a breath, letting another emotion replace the hurt and the despair.

'Do not give in to feelings of desperation. We are the Legiones Astartes. We are the Raven Guard. We have been bloodied but we have survived. Take that sorrow and pound upon it with your anger, until you have forged a new purpose. Those who we once called brothers...'

Corax stopped again, the words catching in his throat as he said them. He glanced at Agapito, then Branne, then Solaro and finally at Aloni. His commanders' eyes were bright with emotion, jaws clenched with suppressed fury. The primarch let out a growl, giving vent to feelings he had put aside since fleeing Isstvan.

'Those who we once called brothers are now our enemies. They have betrayed us, and worse still, they have betrayed the Emperor. They are dead to us, and we will not give them the dignity of our sorrow. Anger is all we shall have for them. Anger the likes of which we have never unleashed before. Only months ago ago we still unleashed our fury in the name of Enlightenment. We brought war to the galaxy in the name of the Imperial Truth. Those days have finished. The Great Crusade has been brought to an end by the treachery of those we now call foes.

'Hate them! Hate them as you have never hated an enemy before. Loathe the air they breathe and the ground upon which they tread. There is nothing so cowardly as a traitor, nor anything so worthy of our abhorrence. Hate them!'

Pain flared through Corax's chest. In his agitation he had opened up the wounds he had suffered, causing blood to trickle down his body. A normal man would have been slain by any one of these injuries, but the primarch bore the pain without visible sign, stoically moving the agony to the back of his mind.

Corax's hands were trembling and he took a moment, trying to bring some peace to his thoughts.

'They tried to kill us, tried to annihilate the Raven Guard and erase us from the pages of history. But they made one mistake: they failed. We are bowed but not broken, wounded but not slain. I swear by my oaths to the Emperor and by my dedication to you that we will have revenge on those that have so wronged us! They will pay for their mistake with blood and death, and not until the last of them lies dead by our hand shall we know any measure of contentment or satisfaction. We will destroy them wherever we find them, as only the Raven Guard know how.

'Swear with me now, my children, to follow me wherever this road leads. Swear to show no mercy to the traitors. Swear to slay them with hatred in your heart. Swear to excise this cancer that Horus has nourished

in the heart of the Imperium. Swear to bring again the
Imperial Truth to the galaxy. Swear that we will never
fail again!'

DEEP IN THE bowels of the Avenger, Alpharius listened to
the primarch's words and could not help but feel stirred
by them. Such defiance was noble. Pointless, but noble.

FOUR

Journey to Sol
Meagre Repast
The Way is Barred

THERE WAS MUCH work to be done. With blacklight protocols lifted, the warriors and crew of the *Avenger* could direct their efforts towards the consolidation of their strength. The hasty rearmament and reorganisations after Isstvan were superseded by more deliberate measures. Ad-hoc squads were broken up and reformed; legionaries were promoted to sergeants, and sergeants raised to higher ranks still.

Amongst those who were busiest were the remaining handful of legionaries from the armourium. The Raven Guard had lost most of their equipment during the long hit-and-run battles of Isstvan V, and to the Techmarines now fell the task of ordering and repairing and restocking the wargear of the reconstituted squads. The *Avenger's* holds gave up a great store of ammunition, but new power armour and weapons were insufficient for the two and a half thousand legionaries on board. Armour replacements and spare parts were also at a premium, and so, along with his fellow Techmarines, Stradon Binalt spent much of his time working on the guns and armour the Raven Guard had salvaged from their defeated foes.

His existence became a blur of work, every waking hour filled with the crackle of arc-welders, the smell of livery paint, the squeal of pneumatic ratchets and the heat of the ceramite kilns.

Binalt was intrigued by the wargear that he came across, some of it very familiar, some of it of radically different design, issued to other Legions from dozens of forge-worlds across the Imperium. As best he could, he cobbled together repairs for the Mark IV suits of armour worn by the majority of his comrades, bastardising pieces from the older Mark II and III suits taken from the bodies of Word Bearers, Iron Warriors and World Eaters. Nothing was perfect and every patch and jury-rig came only with the assurance that it would last a battle or two, should the *Avenger* encounter the enemy again before reaching Terra.

There was little enough aboard the *Avenger* to work with, so compromises had to be made. Most of the Legion's armoured vehicles had been destroyed or abandoned at the Urgall plateau, so spare parts for tanks and transports were not in short supply. Binalt and his fellow Techmarines devised a way to reinforce the armour they had created, using the molecular bonding studs usually employed for affixing armour and ablative plates to Rhinos and Predators. This gave the suits a particular appearance, the shoulder guards sealed with rows of large rivets that looked like nodules or blisters. Other vehicle parts – transmission cabling, servos, even spare track links – were pressed into service as makeshift components for the new armour design.

Slowly the legionaries started to look like Raven Guard again. Greaves, plastrons, shoulder guards and vambraces that had sported the colours of all the Legions that had fought on Isstvan were painted in the black of the Raven Guard, insignia lovingly applied, each stroke of brush or sweep of spray obliterating the colours of former friend

and foe alike, as if the Legion were cleansing itself of the
memories by covering their marks with their own livery.

Spare time was in short supply, and in the few breaks
he had, Binalt contemplated another, more personal
project. He had secured himself a small space between
two of the starboard gun towers, a noisy little chamber
that reverberated with the *clank* of the auto-loaders and
drummed with the feet of the crew as they performed
their gun drills, ever ready for battle.

There was room only for a small worktop and a set of
shelves – no chair for Binalt, so he stood instead. The
Techmarine looked at the large pile of broken parts gathered on the table and wondered where he would begin.
Pieces of shattered ceramite and twisted metal sat under
nuts and bolts and a nest of wires and cables. Here and
there he could identify a servo or actuator or muscle-like
fibre bundle, all systems he was used to dealing with in
a suit of power armour, but fashioned in a way he had
never encountered elsewhere.

He admired the beauty of the craftsmanship even as
he marvelled at the engineering and design that had
been laboured upon the haphazard scattering of pinions
and power relays.

Binalt started by sorting through all of the parts,
splitting them into piles by form and function, leaving some aside whose purpose he had not yet divined.
Day by day, sometimes snatching only a few minutes at
a time when others were gratefully taking their allotted
few hours of rest, he began to make sense of the mess.
Alone with his thoughts, bringing rational observation
to emotions thrown into disorder by recent events, he
contemplated the nature of the daunting project he had
chosen to undertake and broke it down into achievable
goals. It was relaxing in an odd way, removing the Techmarine from the clutter of the Legion and the memories
of Isstvan; a perfectly self-contained sphere in which he

could operate, with definable outcomes all within his
control.

It would be a long time until he was finished – perhaps longer than he would survive – but Binalt was
determined, filled with a need to do this particular work
of artifice. If he could complete this, the world would
be right again, and his existence would make sense once
more.

THERE WAS LITTLE to do except drill, eat and rest. The
Avenger had translated from Isstvan seventy days ago
and the warp storms were making progress slow.
Alpharius worked with his squad, each day learning
more about them and more about the person he was
supposed to be.

He had heard rumours that they were not going to
Deliverance, but were en route to Terra. The thought
intrigued, excited and worried him in equal measure. He
had never been to Old Earth, and for many years had
aspired to do so. Before the twin primarchs had commanded that the Legion back Horus, Alpharius had often
quizzed the older Alpha Legionnaires about the world of
mankind's birth. None of them had been back since they
had embarked upon the Great Crusade, and certainly
none of them had truly believed that they would ever
again witness the glory of the Imperial Palace.

Alpharius knew that his loyalties were now to a different cause, but the thought of being close to the Emperor
still sent a thrill through him, matched only by the
pleasure he had experienced on being singled out by the
true Alpharius for this mission. The primarch had taken
him into his confidence and explained the nature of the
Legion's change of allegiance. The Emperor had, perhaps
unwittingly, betrayed his sons and their Legions. He had
abandoned them, and in turn had allowed the Great
Crusade to falter. The primarch could not explain why

this had happened, but had been adamant that Horus would set mankind back on the path of the Imperial Truth.

Alpharius wondered if he would get a glimpse of the Emperor, and then fretted that if he were brought into the Imperial presence, his duplicitous nature might be revealed. Surely a man as gifted as the Master of Mankind would not be fooled by an altered face and name change?

More than that, Alpharius's guise was Terran-born. What if the others born of Terra – only a handful left after the massacre but still alive the nonetheless – saw some flaw in his disguise; what if he betrayed his lack of knowledge to the other Terrans?

There was little time to worry about the future, Alpharius had to stay constantly alert to maintain the facade he had adopted. He was fortunate in one sense: his new self had a reputation for being taciturn, and this meant he was not expected to speak much. With the help of the Apothecaries and the material absorbed by his omophagea, his vocal chords and mouth had been reshaped to better resemble that of the legionary whose identity he had assumed, but to the keen ears of a Space Marine, any small difference might give rise to suspicion.

His greatest defence, shared by the others he hoped had also succeeded in their infiltration, was in the unlikelihood of what the Alpha Legion had done. Why would any Raven Guard suspect that their foes had taken on the faces of the fallen? It was a wonderful machination by the primarch and so characteristic of his genius. For another legionary to have doubts about Alpharius's true nature was to invite thoughts of paranoia. It was so improbable that any suspicion without good evidence was likely to be dismissed out of hand.

Alpharius bent his mind to ensuring there would be no evidence, training and eating and sleeping alongside his adopted Legion. He showed pride as his ragtag armour was replaced, speaking words of vengeance and swearing oaths of loyalty to the Emperor and Lord Corax alongside his new brothers-in-arms while they repainted their icons.

There had been a few occasions when Alpharius had come close to revealing himself. Each day he learned a little more – small mannerisms, turns of phrase, and Legion protocols – that enabled him to blend in better with his fellow legionaries, but it was not a perfect process.

His latest close call had come during a hand-to-hand combat drill. The company had gathered in one of the hangar bays, amongst the dormant shapes of Thunderhawks and Stormbirds – the *Avenger's* dedicated training chambers being insufficient for the large number of warriors on board.

Sergeant Dor had called the squad to order and given a disturbing speech.

'We must learn to fight a new enemy,' he had told them. 'For decades we have honed our skills against savages and inferior foes, and faced strange adversaries such as the Isstvan Warsingers and the Ninturnian Devil-Blades. Now we face something entirely different. Now we must fight other Space Marines.'

It was an obvious thing to say but having the situation mentioned so baldly brought home to the legionaries just how much the galaxy had changed. There were mutters of discontent, but Alpharius held his tongue, not wishing to betray his own thoughts on the matter.

'We train against each other every day,' Lukar had said. 'What difference should we expect?'

'We have never tried to kill each other,' had been the sergeant's reply.

The squad had paired off, armed only with their monomolecular-edged combat blades. Alpharius had found himself facing Lukar, and the two of them had started at the sergeant's command, thrusting and parrying, trying to find the weak points in each other's armour, probing for the flexible joint seals, reinforced eye lenses and the gaps between armour plates.

Blades flickering, other pairs duelling around them, Lukar and Alpharius were a match for each other; equal in speed and strength. Their blades clanged against each other, were caught on shoulder guards or deflected by angled movements of their forearms, neither able to find an opening.

It was then that Alpharius had made his mistake.

Feinting high, he had dropped to one knee as Lukar's blade had shot up to meet the blow. Under his opponent's guard, Alpharius had reversed his grip on the knife and swung back-handed, driving its point towards the vulnerable sliver of material between Lukar's upper thigh armour and his groin guard.

Lukar had frozen, Alpharius's blade just millimetres from contact.

'You have me,' declared Lukar, stepping back, shaking his head. There was surprise in his voice. 'Where did you learn such a move?'

Alpharius had hesitated, realising that the manoeuvre had been part of his Alpha Legion training, not replicated in the doctrine of the Raven Guard.

'I saw a Traitor using it at the dropsite,' Alpharius had said quickly. 'I watched a Word Bearer take out one of our brothers from the Salamanders with that move.'

The rest of the squad had stopped their drills and were looking at Alpharius and Lukar. Alpharius did not like being the centre of attention. He had stood up and sheathed his blade as Sergeant Dor approached, helmeted head cocked to one side.

'What was that?' the sergeant had asked. 'Using the tactics of the traitors?'

'It seemed effective at the time,' Alpharius had replied, remaining calm.

'Pay attention,' Dor had said, waving the rest of the squad closer. 'Why don't you show us that again?'

Alpharius did as he was asked, demonstrating the undercutting blow to the others. There were murmurs of appreciation and Dor had slapped him on the chest with a word of thanks.

'This is what we must do,' the sergeant had said. The red of his eyeplates had seemed to fix on Alpharius for some time before he continued, moving his gaze to the rest of the squad. 'We need to learn from our enemies, adapt to the way they will fight. Any other innovations, any edge you can give us, share with the rest, all right?'

'Yes, sergeant,' Alpharius had replied.

Though his cover had remained intact, it was later that same day that Alpharius had realised what he had done. One day, a Raven Guard might use that move on an Alpha Legionnaire, or defend himself against it and so be victorious. Alpharius's purpose was to learn about the Raven Guard, not enhance their skills. The situation was getting more complicated than he had imagined, the considerations more numerous.

Alpharius focused on what was important. He was an actor playing a part, learning more about his role with every day. In his heart he knew he was sworn to the Alpha Legion and felt no guilt at lying to those who he had once called his allies. It was not their fault that they had chosen the wrong side in the coming war. Alpharius did not feel contempt or pity for the Raven Guard, but had only a mild sense of regret that he could never genuinely call the legionaries around him brothers again. Their names slipped from his tongue as easily as the false declarations of allegiance and revenge, but he was not one of them. Like the rest of the Alpha Legion, he had been chosen for a greater purpose, one that the twin primarchs had assured him went beyond loyalty to the Emperor or Horus, and concerned the fate of the galaxy itself.

And like all of those who were blind to the greater truth, the Raven Guard were expendable. They would serve their part and then be destroyed, and he would be returned to his Legion to fight amongst his true battle-brothers again. It was this thought, this goal, that focused Alpharius as he lay awake pondering the unknown task ahead. He was Alpha Legion and so did not expect to be lauded or singled out – such glory-mongering was not in the Legion's traditions. He would fulfil his purpose, take contentment from the knowledge of a mission accomplished and the praise of his twin primarchs, and become one of the many again.

FROM A GALLERY overlooking one of the impromptu mess decks that had once been a live firing range, Corax looked down at several companies of his Raven Guard filling themselves with ship's rations. They stood at long trestle tables – chairs were another scarce commodity on board – and diligently ate from platters laden with synthetic meat and dry soybread. The fare was tasteless, but rich in the proteins and carbohydrates the legionaries needed to sustain themselves. Nutrient supplements were imbibed in the form of fortified water drunk straight from crude jugs turned out by the serfs in the lower deck workshops.

'How are our stores?' the primarch asked. He knew the answer but wanted to make sure that his commanders were abreast of every detail of the ship's running.

'Of no immediate concern, lord,' replied Agapito. Branne and Solaro made up the quartet, with Aloni on watch command at the strategium. 'The *Avenger* was stocked for a full three-year tour, more than enough for our current needs.'

'The Navigators are reporting the same difficulties as before,' added Branne. 'It'll be at least another forty days until we reach the Sol system. They have requested that we make another realspace drop to confirm our location.'

'They are guessing,' said Corax, sighing. 'The rising warp storms almost blot out the Astronomican. We've translated three times already, and every time we have been at least five light years off course.'

'Do you think that the rebels have something to do with the warp storms?' asked Agapito. 'Is that possible?'

'I would not rule out anything at the moment,' said Corax. He knew more about the strange ways of the warp than the commanders with him, and it was not unreasonable to assume that Horus might have acquired some form of technology or other power that had allowed him to conjure the roiling tempest befouling the Immaterium. The nature of what that other power might be, the hints he had learned from the Emperor and gleaned from his fellow primarchs, was best not shared. 'There is the possibility that this turmoil hampers our enemies as much as it does us, but only a possibility.'

'If it is not impertinent to ask, lord, why are we heading for Terra?' asked Branne. 'Although I can't begin to guess at the motives of the Warmaster, the treachery at Isstvan suggests he wants to remove all opposition as swiftly as possible. Would it not be safer to secure Deliverance against attack?'

'Horus might expect as much,' said Corax, turning his back to the balustrade to face his commanders. There was noise from below as the assembled legionaries finished their meals and began to pile up the empty platters. 'That is good enough reason not to go there. I have even stronger reasons for going to Terra.'

The statement floated in the air for a while until Agapito realised it was up to him to ask the next question.

'Are you willing to share those reasons with us, lord?'

'I must speak with the Emperor,' replied Corax. 'We do not know yet whether news of Horus's perfidy has reached the Imperial Palace.'

'Surely the Emperor is gifted enough to know when such a tragedy has befallen his realm?' said Branne.

'The warp storms may serve another purpose beyond stifling travel,' said Corax. He looked at his commanders, seeing confusion in their expressions. 'The warp, the Navigators, the astropaths and even the Emperor are linked together. They derive their powers from its energy, and so the storm cover might shield the Emperor's far-seeing gaze as much as it blinds the Navigators to the route to Terra.'

'Do you think Horus will attack the Emperor directly?' asked Solaro. 'Does he plan to invade Terra?'

'Certainly,' said Corax. 'He has turned from the Imperial Truth and must either destroy the Emperor or be destroyed. The Warmaster's actions have set us on a course to this confrontation; there can be no other outcome.'

This was greeted with intakes of breath and thoughtful silence for a few moments. Corax sympathised with his subordinates. The magnitude of what Horus had done was difficult to comprehend.

'It seems Isstvan will become Horus's folly,' said Branne. 'Even with the backing of so many Legions and the blow he dealt at the dropsite, he cannot hope to stand against the rest of the Imperium.'

'We must assume the worst,' said Solaro, before Corax could speak. 'If those of the other Legions, who we once trusted with our lives, can be turned, we can place no faith in the loyalty of the Mechanicum or the Imperial Army.'

'You are right,' said Corax. 'We have no idea of the true strength of the rebels.' He stopped. The word 'rebels' did not convey nearly enough the gravitas of what Horus and his conspirators had perpetrated. 'The *traitors* will have planned their moves for some time. Horus is prone to grand gestures, to displays of power, but he does not move without due preparation. Be sure of it, he did not act until he was ready, and that must mean he sees now as his best chance of a swift victory.'

'It'll be up to us to deny him, of course,' said Branne, lip curling with anger.

'Of course,' said Corax, smiling thinly. 'It is not in our foes' interests to see the Imperium destroyed. They look to usurp the Emperor and become the rulers of the galaxy. So they must act quickly, destroying the Emperor and those who will fight with him, before the rest of the Imperium is dragged into the war. No matter what powers Horus has at his disposal, I agree with Branne. The traitors cannot win a long war.'

The legionaries were filing out below, while more were entering from the open doors in the far wall. Dozens of serfs were clearing the tables and bringing out heaps of fresh rations for the new arrivals. Corax looked down, meeting the eyes of the Raven Guard looking up at their leader. There was a dreary defiance etched into the features of those passing below, a moroseness that the primarch did not like.

'Sergeant Nestil,' Corax called out, halting the squad leader. The sergeant stood transfixed for a moment, like a target seeing the glint of a weapon pointed in his direction.

'Lord Corax?' Nestil replied. 'How may I serve?'

'Why so glum, sergeant?' Corax kept his tone light-hearted. 'Is the food not to your liking?'

'I have eaten better, I must admit, lord,' said the sergeant.

'I suspect Horus is sitting on a big pile of grox steaks, sergeant. When we have permission from the Emperor, we'll go and relieve him of them.'

There was laughter from the gathered legionaries, a little thin but better than the depression that Corax had sensed before.

'Aye, lord, and no doubt Fulgrim has a few fancies too that we could help him with,' replied Sergeant Nestil, earning more laughs.

'You can be sure of that, Lancrato, you can be sure,' said Corax, laughing along with the poor joke.

The primarch waved the legionaries on and turned his attention back to his commanders. His smile faded quickly.

'We cannot allow the wounds of Isstvan to fester,' he told them. 'The Legion is depleted in strength, but it is the injuries to our spirit that are more grievous. We live or die by our successes, and they have been short of late.'

'We will fight to the last man,' said Solaro. 'Yes,' said Corax. His next words were to encourage himself as much as his companions. 'Yet it would be better if we could get Horus's forces to do that instead. We need a victory, something to restore honour and prestige. If we hole up in Deliverance, we surrender the initiative to our foes. That is not how we fight. With whatever force we can muster, we must take the fight to the traitors. We must prove to ourselves and others that they are not impervious, that an assault on Terra is not inevitable. At the moment we have been dealt a harsh blow, but we cannot run forever. The sooner we turn and fight back, the sooner we will sow doubt amongst the traitors and cracks will appear in their alliance.'

'Are you so sure they will be so easy to break apart, lord?' asked Agapito. Corax started to walk along the gallery. The great arched windows to his right were shuttered with ribbed steel blocking the view of the warp outside, but he could still feel its presence, like an oppressive atmosphere, a tension that permeated everything. To think that it might be under the control of Horus in some way was disconcerting.

'Easy? No,' said Corax in reply to Agapito's question. 'Yet there will be disunity. Even under the banner of the Emperor my brothers and I could find cause for argument. Horus may have the ears of some for now, but each seeks to profit in his own way from this rebellion. When it becomes clearer that those goals will not be achieved without great effort, their resolve will wane and their common cause will fracture.'

'Let us hope we can bring that about,' said Agapito.

Corax directed a stern stare at the commander, stopping just before the narrow doorway at the end of the gallery. Agapito wilted slightly under the primarch's unforgiving gaze.

'We have no room for hope,' said Corax. 'We plan and we act. Hope is for dreamers and poets. We have our will and our weapons and we shall dictate our own fate.'

WHEN CORAX HAD departed, Branne, Agapito and Solaro made their way back to the quarters they now shared.

'Why did you mention hope, brother?' Branne asked harshly. 'Do you not remember those same words he spoke at Gate Forty-Two?'

'It was just a turn of phrase, brother,' said Agapito, clearly taken aback. 'Of course I remember Gate Forty-Two. Who could forget that slaughter?'

'Be more careful with your words in the future,' snapped Branne. 'Lord Corax does not need any extra distractions at the moment.'

Agapito looked as if he would argue, but then bowed his head, accepting the admonishment.

'As you say, brother,' he said. 'I will watch my words carefully in future.'

LOOKING AT THE nearly-empty jars in his small case, Pelon wondered how much longer he could make the spices and herbs last. The praefector had said nothing

of the crude fare Pelon had been forced to serve him
of late – his breeding was far too good and his military
experience too long for such complaints – but it nagged
at Pelon's conscience that a noble of Therion should
endure the same bland meals as a common serf.

He had done his best to make Valerius's sparse quarters
accommodating, setting out such belongings as the praefector had brought aboard on the narrow shelves and
bedside table. Valerius's full dress uniform and parade
regalia were hung on one wall, along with his gold-
hilted power sword, but their bright appearance only
highlighted the drab, unpainted bulkheads, rather than
drawing the eye away from them.

Pelon had managed to procure a few paints and
brushes from the ship's stores, not enough to liven up
the whole chamber but sufficient to add some colour to
the plain furnishings and the bare tin plates and cups he
had taken from the mess. The Raven Guard seemed to
revel in their austerity, he had decided, embracing the
harsh conditions of their home on Deliverance instead
of celebrating the luxuries and frivolities that should
have come with compliance. The manservant had never
thought he would miss those endless corridors of the
old mines, or the empty vistas through the windows, but
since coming on board the *Avenger* he had come to see
the time he had spent on the dusty moon as comparative
opulence.

He heard the outer door hissing open and finished his
fussing around the small table he had set out for the praefector's supper. Valerius came into the main chamber and
sat down without comment, his eyes passing quickly over
the carefully sliced protein slabs dusted with chemyrrh
and orthal. The praefector lifted the dented metal cup, its
edge painted with a fine line of red by Pelon, to his lips,
but stopped before he took a sip. He lowered the cup to
the table and finally looked at his manservant.

'I miss wine,' said Valerius. 'A nice carafe of Mastillian red, a glass of bubbly Narinythe. For shame, I'd even settle for a sip of that stuff Prime Tribune Nathor rustled up on Hedda-Signis.'

Pelon said nothing. It was not his place to speak, but to listen. He had overstepped the mark before, back on Deliverance, and no end of trouble had come from it. With everything that had been going on – and he had overheard a lot from the Raven Guard and the crew about events that had taken place on Isstvan – he was happy to be safe and able to concentrate on his sole duty of providing for the praefector.

'Mustn't grumble, though, Pelon,' said Valerius, as if his servant was the one who had voiced the lament. 'Latest estimate says we're just twelve days from translating into the Sol system. Though judging by their recent success rate, I'd not be surprised if the Navigators took twice that time. It's exciting though, isn't it? Terra, Pelon! Won't that be something of remark?'

Pelon was not sure if he should reply or not. It was difficult sometimes to judge whether he was simply an ear for the praefector to speak into or if his master wanted to engage in conversation. Valerius did not continue, and had a look of expectation that suggested to Pelon that he was waiting for a reply of some kind.

'I would have never have thought I would see such a thing, master,' Pelon said dutifully. In truth, he had been exceptionally anxious about the upcoming stop at the centre of the Imperium. No doubt there would be all manner of dignitaries there to greet their arrival. It would be a shocking failure on Pelon's part if Valerius turned up looking like some ragamuffin officer from one of the professional regiments, but he only had limited resources to launder and repair his master's uniform. 'It is an honour that I can scarce believe.'

'You're not wrong about that,' said Valerius, plunging

his fork into a piece of synth-squash that Pelon had art-
fully carved into a slim-petalled flower. An hour's work
was demolished in seconds by the praefector's chewing.
'There are lord-commanders of Therion who have not
had the privilege.'

'You seem to be of good mood today, master,' said
Pelon, sitting at the end of the bed as he dared to venture
his opinion.

'I have had a conclave with Corax and the Raven Guard
commanders, Pelon,' said Valerius, between mouthfuls
of food. 'I fear our stay on Terra will be short-lived. As
soon as I can secure passage, I am to travel back to Therion to entreat further forces. With the losses the Legion
has suffered, and the regrettable sacrifice of my own
command, it is desired that I raise a new cohort to fight
alongside Lord Corax against the traitors.'

'It is good that he would entrust such a duty to you,
master,' said Pelon. He regretted his words as Valerius
purposefully placed his knife and fork on the half-empty
plate and turned a frown on the manservant.

'Why ever would they not trust me?'

'I was not speaking of you in particular, master,' Pelon
said hurriedly. 'Trust has been in short supply of late,
is all. Even I get wary glances from the crew as they see
me about my business. Times such as these, it's good
the primarch has every faith in Therion to fight for the
Emperor.'

'Yes, you are right,' said Valerius, resuming his meal.
He smiled through the laborious mastication of a faux-
grox fillet, his words coming as a mumble. 'It is quite an
important duty. We'll need every able man and woman
who can carry a lasgun. It'll be like the founding after
compliance. Bigger even!'

The praefector finished his supper, washed it down
with his recycled water and stood up.

'Dark times, Pelon, but aren't all great moments in

history seeded in the dark?' he said, kicking off his short boots and flopping onto the bed. 'Nobody remembers those who lived in times of joy and plenty.'

'Indeed not, master,' said Pelon, collecting up the dishes and cup. He stopped just before the door. 'Will you need me for the next hour, master? I've got some time in the laundries, is all.'

'No, I think I can be without you for an hour,' said Valerius, sounding tired. Pelon glanced over his shoulder and saw the praefector's eyes were closed, his chest already rising and falling gently. 'Perhaps a little more salt next time,' the praefector murmured, his voice trailing away into sleep.

'As you say, master,' Pelon said to himself with a smile of satisfaction, closing the door behind him.

ONE HUNDRED AND thirty-three days after departing from Isstvan, the *Avenger* finally reached the Sol system, heart of the Imperium, birthplace of mankind.

On Corax's orders, the ship came in and deployed its void shields immediately; it would be incautious to arrive without some form of protection but using the reflex shield had the potential to invite immediate suspicion.

The sensor reports were also flooding in, bringing with them a picture of a star system in considerable turmoil. Dozens of warships, haulers and transports were moving back and forth from the Lunar bases and Terra, navigating their way through layer after layer of minefields, orbital defence platforms and out-system heavy monitors. More still were arriving; there was not an hour that passed without at least two or three ships breaking from warp.

Word was spreading across the Imperium. The warp storms that had so hampered the Raven Guard on their journey also disrupted astrotelepathic communication. Even in the best of conditions it took many weeks, sometimes several months, for messages to be relayed from the heart of the Imperium to its outer reaches. Add to this the violence of the warp tempest and it could still be many months before some systems were even aware of the Warmaster's treachery.

This was just the beginning, Corax sensed. Dozens of ships would become hundreds, thousands perhaps. For the moment Horus had the element of surprise, but the behemoth that was the Imperium was being roused to confront this new threat. The resources of the Emperor were vast, but ponderous; but once they had achieved a critical momentum they would be unstoppable. Of this, the primarch was certain. Horus's only chance of triumph was a swift victory, and Corax would do all he could to ensure that such a thing would not happen.

After the standard delays in bringing the scanners and communications arrays online after the warp transit, the Raven Guard found themselves being insistently hailed by the *Wrathful Vanguard*, a strike cruiser of the Imperial Fists Legion. Captain Noriz was threatening all manner of violence if they did not identify themselves.

It was clear from Noriz's hails that unexpected visitors were not welcome.

'This is the *Avenger*, battle-barge of the Raven Guard,' replied Branne, with Corax standing beside him. 'We are carrying Lord Corax to Terra. Please ensure we have a clear path.'

There was a delay before the Imperial Fists communication returned. Even with audio-only exchanges, there was a noticeable time lag between message and response, indicating that the *Wrathful Vanguard* was several hundred thousand kilometres away.

'You are not authorised to proceed. Power down your shields and prepare to receive a boarding party. Failure to comply will be treated as an act of aggression and you will be destroyed.'

Corax laughed at this, but Branne was in no mood to

bandy words with the Imperial Fists captain.

'Watch your tone, captain! Lord Corax will be meeting the Emperor in person. If you have a problem with that, perhaps Rogal Dorn himself would like to come aboard and discuss it. If you have finished insulting my primarch, provide us with escort to get us to Terra without further interference.'

'I am not at liberty to indulge you, primarch aboard or not,' came Noriz's terse reply. 'All non-sanctioned vessels are to be inspected. If you have not noticed, one legionary's word to another doesn't count for much anymore. We will board and if you refuse, your vessel will be destroyed.'

His jaw clenching with anger, Branne reached for the transmit button, but he was stopped by Corax. The primarch gently pushed the commander aside and bent down to the communications array.

'Captain Noriz, your attention to duty and protocol is admirable,' said the primarch, his deep voice edged with humour. 'I am more than happy to welcome a delegation from my brother's Legion aboard, but please dispense with the threats. This is a battle-barge carrying several thousand legionaries; you have a strike cruiser with a complement of fifty legionaries.'

More silence followed, longer than the previous pause.

'Please identify yourself.'

Sighing, Corax shared a glance with the others around him before he activated the transmit switch.

'I am Lord Corvus Corax, Primarch of the Raven Guard, Saviour of Deliverance, Commander of the 27th and 376th Expeditions, acting Marshal of the Therion Cohort and lauded conqueror of a thousand worlds. Please come aboard and I will show you my other credentials.'

Static buzzed across the network for a while, until Noriz had conceived a suitable reply.

'I will lead the boarding party, Lord Corax. Please lower your shields in preparation.'

Corax gave a nod to the technicians at the defence control station and stepped back from the communications panel.

'Be nice, he is only doing his duty,' the primarch told Branne. 'The quicker we sort out this inspection, the sooner we can be on our way.'

'Aye, but he doesn't have to be so stiff about it, does he?' said the commander.

'He's an Imperial Fist,' replied Corax. 'He can't help it.'

Though he kept his tone light, the primarch was wary. He was sure there was nothing on board the *Avenger* that would cause problems, but he had an instinctual aversion to close scrutiny. He suppressed his apprehensions and motioned for Branne to welcome Captain Noriz.

The scraping of a rock chisel smuggled from the mineworkings rang tinnily from the walls of the small cell. Reqaui sat in the corner of the room whittling away at a lump of slag, the form of his latest creation not yet discernable. Corvus lay on the small mattress, listening intently to the old man with his eyes closed, his hands behind his head. It had been only two years since his discovery; two years of moving from prison block to prison block while his body had grown to that of a twelve-year old. Reqaui was only the latest in a line of imprisoned dissidents and anti-establishment intellectuals who had learned of Corvus's existence and volunteered to teach the strange boy what they knew of people, politics and history.

It was the one area Corvus really hadn't known anything about. His technical knowledge was vast, encapsulating the greatest scientific learning of mankind. Corvus could identify the molecular composition of the walls, the door and the bed. He knew the biological processes that had formed the cataracts in Reqaui's eyes. The old man had turned down Corvus's well-meant offer to surgically remove them, saying it would arouse suspicion in the guards.

For all of that immense knowledge, Corvus knew little enough about people. It was if his education had been cut short before that lesson had been learnt, leaving him bereft of the subtleties of human nature, a blank slate waiting for more information to be written upon it. He was aware enough to know he was very naive in this regard, and his first tutor, Manrus Colsais, had swiftly exhausted his own store of wisdom concerning the human condition. So had begun the process of Corvus's education, hidden amongst the masses of the prison-mine that he now knew was called Lycaeus.

'That was the end of the third Facian dynasty,' Reqaui was saying. Motes of detritus floated in the air and created a grey patch on the flagstoned floor around the elderly agitator. His chisel continued its work, seemingly independent of his whitening eyes, which were fixed on a point somewhere near the dim light globe set into the ceiling. 'With the usurpation by Neorthan Chandrapax, the First Settlements began. Lotteries were held for the colonists, so great was the urge to leave Kiavahr's smoke-ridden cities and polluted seas. In a way, it was the first time in seven hundred years that anything like a democracy was in effect. Regardless of station, every family was given equal chance to be crew on the ark-boats being built. Of course, the higher-ups weren't being stupid. While everyone had an equal chance to participate, only the elite would be in charge as officers. The new colonies would have mayors from the old families, the College networks would still be in place and the workers would still be the downtrodden in their new lives.'

'Someone's coming,' said Corvus, hearing beyond the walls the distinctive tramp of boots and the specific noise of the door at the far end of the corridor opening. 'Flash inspection!'

'Quick, lad, you know what to do,' said Reqaui, bounding to his feet with sprightly energy.

Corvus rolled off the bed as Reqaui scattered the evidence of his hobby with a sweep of his foot. The old man stuffed the chisel and lump of slag into a pocket sewn into the bottom of the mattress, while Corvus moved aside the old tin bucket that served as a latrine. He could hear the clank of the locks being unwound from the main lever further down the corridor, and a moment later the latch on the cell door sprang open with a rusty screech. The door swung outwards on its spring, opening onto the brightly lit corridor, letting the thudding of the boots into the cell.

'I don't have to hide,' said Corvus, hesitating as he lifted up the slab that concealed the crawlspace he had dug through the core rock beneath the prison block. 'I can only hear six of them. It wouldn't be any trouble to kill them.'

'Oh, not trouble for you, for sure,' said Reqaui, scowling. 'But where there's six, there's six thousand. Think you can take on all of them, do you?'

'I could try,' said Corvus.

'Not yet, lad,' said Reqaui. 'Not 'til you know what's worth fighting for. Told you before, what you have is a gift, but it could be a curse too. Gotta be right, when you kill a man. Gotta mean something.'

Corvus sighed and slipped into the dark space under the floor. He dragged the slab back into place and fumbled in the dark for the matches and candle stub. The youth did not really need them – there was enough light trickling through from the crack around the loosened slab for him to see perfectly – but Reqaui had provided them for Corvus's comfort and he felt honour-bound to make use of them.

As the candle flickered into life, its light gleamed from Reqaui's carvings that Corvus had placed on a narrow shelf that ran the length of the crawlspace. There were all kinds of animals and birds, some complete, others just heads or faces. Each seemed a grotesque parody of the creatures locked inside Corvus's head, but Reqaui assured him that they were real, true-to-life representations of mutant creatures that dwelled in the slime pools, acid grottos and sprawling enzyme marshes of Kiavahr.

Corvus wondered much about this world. He had seen it

several times through the armorplex windows on the transit galleries, like a red and blue eye glaring up at Lycaeus.
Manrus had explained that Lycaeus was a prison, on a moon
orbiting Kiavahr. The first prisoners had been sent here centuries ago, for speaking out against the coronation of the Fourth
Dynasty. Then the mineral deposits had been discovered, and
more and more were found guilty of dissent and sentenced to
work to death in the burgeoning mines.

That much Corvus had understood, even if Manrus had
spelled it out in no uncertain terms that such political imprisonment was immoral. To remove one's enemies made sense
to Corvus, especially if they could be turned to a more profit-
able endeavour. It was the condemnation of the families that
Corvus had not fully understood. Again, he could perhaps
justify the imprisonment of those related to the first agitators
and demagogues, because there would be grounds to suspect a
criminal's beliefs might be shared by those around him. What
stretched Corvus's comprehension was the continued internment of those born and raised in the mines.

The people of Lycaeus were no longer just prisoners, they
were a colony, of families and children, whose entire lives
would be spent in the stuffy false atmosphere contained by the
energy domes and mineworks. No child could be accused of
insurrection, surely?

Manrus had explained carefully that Lycaeus was a prison
only in name now. It was a slave factory, its purpose to provide resources for the great manufactories of the world below.
That had made Corvus angry, especially when Manrus had
revealed that only a few hundred members of the tech-guilds,
the descendants of the old Colleges, benefited from the mass
industrialisation. Manrus considered this deeply unfair, and
therefore so too did Corvus.

Corvus listened to the guards above shouting for the prisoners to stand in the corridor for inspection as he crawled
along the narrow tunnel, admiring the skill with which each
sculpture had been fashioned. Every feather, scale and hair

was rendered in fine detail, etched from the hard slag by that tip of chisel.

The candle flame flickered slightly as someone moved across the false flag above. There was a strange hollow thump and Corvus froze, realising he had not replaced it properly. There was a confused exchange between the guards and two further stamps on the offending slab.

Corvus blew out the light and retreated to the far end of the hideaway, some three metres from the entrance. There was a scraping noise as a knife was inserted into the narrow gap between the flag and its neighbours.

Bunching his muscles, Corvus formed his hands into fists and bared his teeth, ready to slay those who could discover him. He must not be found. Over and over, from everyone through whose wardship he had passed, he had been told this: do not be found. He was an anomaly, something beyond the understanding of the Kiavahrans. If they discovered him, he would be taken away.

Corvus did not want to be taken away. He had friends here. Friends like Ephrenia and Manrus and Reqaui.

The slab lifted up and the beam of a flashlight flickered around the tunnel mouth.

'What have we here?' said one of the guards, ducking his head into the opening.

Corvus shrank back as far as he could, pressing himself against the jagged rock wall, eyes narrowed. The beam of the torch moved towards him and stopped when it reached the shelf of sculptures.

'Seems Raqaui's been up to his scrimshawing again,' said the guard. Corvus did not detect much malice in the man's tone.

'Leave it be,' said another voice from above. 'It does no harm. More paperwork for us if we report it.'

'I don't know,' said the guard squatting above the hole. 'It is contraband, and if someone else finds it, we'll be up for penal shifts, or worse.'

'Let me see.'

The guard moved away and his helmeted head was replaced by another, this time with the silver strip across the nose guard that signified a wing corporal. He flashed the torch around some more, the beam of light coming to rest directly on Corvus.

The youth tensed every muscle, ready to leap forwards and tear off the corporal's head the moment he tried to raise the alarm.

To Corvus's amazement, the corporal said nothing. He played the flashlight around the tunnel for a few more seconds, its beam twice more moving slowly over Corvus, and then stood up.

'You're right,' said the wing corporal. 'Not worth reporting that. We'll get him to hand over whatever he's using as a tool, might use it as a weapon otherwise.'

The slab slammed down with a ring that shook Corvus. He squatted panting in the dark, unable to work out why he had not been discovered.

Eventually the boots thudded away and the door creaked shut again. There was a gentle rap on the concealing slab.

'You still down there, lad?'

With a laugh of relief, Corvus crawled to the slab and pushed it up, glad to see Reqaui's perplexed, bearded face.

'Still here,' said Corvus.

'I thought they'd find you for sure,' said Reqaui, helping Corvus up through the hole, though the youth needed no such aid. 'I swear they was looking right down there.'

'They did,' said Corvus. 'They didn't see me. How's that possible?'

Reqaui shook his head and slumped onto the mattress while Corvus replaced the slab, this time ensuring it fit as snugly as possible.

'How's anything possible where you're concerned?' said the old inmate. 'How's it possible a baby boy's found a kilometre deep inside a glacier? How's it possible he pulls off the head of

*a grown man? How's it possible he ages five times faster than
any other folk? There's all sorts that's possible when we're
talking about you.'*

'They looked right at me, and didn't see me...' The possibilities were flashing through Corvus's mind. He thought how
wonderful it would be to travel the wings without concern,
moving from one block to the next without the guards ever
noticing him. Deep inside himself, from some place of instinct
rather than intellect, he knew this was something he could
do. Like all of the other gifts he had been given, this was an
ability that was meant to be used, though to what purpose he
still was not sure.

'It was nice of the guards not to take your sculptures,' said
Corvus, bringing himself back to the present.

'Nice, my arse,' said Reqaui. *'That corporal gave me a truncheon in the gut before he left. They're all bastards, lad, never
forget that.'*

'I won't,' said Corvus. *'They're all bastards. Don't worry,
Reqaui, one day we'll be settling the score.'*

Reqaui smiled and leaned forwards, gesturing for Corvus to
sit beside him. He placed a wiry arm across the boy's shoulders and gave him a hug.

'Sure enough, lad,' said the inmate. *'A few more years,
you'll have to be patient. A few more years and you'll be
ready. You'll make the bastards pay, no doubt about it.'*

Corvus smiled at the thought.

TRUE TO HIS word, Corax met with the arriving Imperial
Fists, accompanied by his senior officers and company
captains. Noriz arrived with a full complement of
legionaries, who disembarked from the Stormbirds in
the docking bay and formed a guard of honour for their
captain.

Noriz appeared last, crested helmet under one arm,
a long cloak of scarlet trailing from his armour. He
seemed very young for a captain to Corax's eye, his head

covered in a short-cropped nest of blond curls, bright blue eyes fixing immediately upon the primarch. The captain swallowed hard and continued to stare at Corax.

'Is there something amiss, captain?' asked the primarch.

'No, not at all,' said Noriz. 'We thought... We did not expect to encounter Raven Guard, much less yourself, primarch.'

'And why would that be?'

Noriz's discomfort increased.

'We have received word that you were all dead,' he said quietly. 'The Raven Guard, Salamanders and Iron Hands... We, that is Legion command, were told that there had been no survivors from Isstvan.'

'I am pleased to contradict such rumours in person,' said Corax. 'As you can see, the Raven Guard continue to serve the Emperor.'

The captain said nothing in reply. Corax realised that Noriz had to consider an alternative explanation for the Raven Guard's survival: that they were loyal to Horus.

'I understand your suspicions, captain,' said the primarch. 'When so few have survived such treachery, it is hard to believe we did so without collusion. I would assuage your doubts in any way that I can. Whatever assurances you require, we will provide them.'

'My apologies for this necessary inspection, primarch,' said Noriz, eyes averted. 'I am under standing orders to conduct a search of every vessel entering this quadrant without authorisation.'

'The Raven Guard will cooperate in any way we can,' replied Corax. 'We understand well the need for security at this time. What do you require of us?'

Noriz looked along the line of Raven Guard officers: a row of scarred faces regarding him with distaste bordering on hostility. He sought sanctuary in the more welcoming expression of Corax.

'We are ordered to conduct a thorough search of the ship and all personnel aboard, primarch.' He glanced back at his legionaries. 'We shall conduct our investigation in ten teams, if that is possible. If you would appoint a liaison officer, I can brief him on the details of the process.'

'I do not wish to be delayed, captain,' said Corax. 'I am on my way to an audience with the Emperor.'

'I am sure that, with your cooperation, we can be thorough and efficient, primarch,' said Noriz. 'It should take no longer than a couple of days.'

'Very well,' said Corax, though the thought of being kept here for any longer irked the primarch. He pointed to Branne. 'Commander Branne is captain of this vessel, you may conduct all communication through him. He will make other officers available to assist your inspection. All holds, bays, storage areas, weapons lockers and barracks will be opened to your men. I shall have my Legion prepared for the inspection.'

'Thank you, primarch,' said Noriz. He looked as though he was about to say something else, but stopped himself. Corax was not sure, but he had the sense that Noriz had wanted to offer more than just gratitude: sympathy perhaps. 'We will begin our inspection immediately.'

FIVE

Inspection and Appraisal
Arrival at Terra
Malcador

ALONG WITH THE rest of his company, Alpharius stood to attention in one of the primary cargo bays. The order had gone out across the *Avenger* for all squads and crews to make ready for an inspection. In full armour, bearing their weapons, the Raven Guard had turned out en masse, filling the flight bays, storage areas, gun decks and mess chambers with rank upon rank of warriors.

The Alpha Legionnaire waited patiently while an officer in the livery of the Imperial Fists, introduced as Captain Noriz, prowled between the ranks, checking every legionary in turn. Every now and then he would ask a question, probing for some hint that the Raven Guard were traitors.

'Do they think the rebels are just going to turn up and ask to see the Emperor?' muttered Doril to his left.

'Maybe they think we're on some kind of scouting mission for Horus,' replied Ordin, standing on Alpharius's right. 'They probably have no idea who is friend and foe.'

'It'd be a pretty brazen Traitor to turn up with just one battle-barge,' said Doril. 'If that's Horus's strategy this'll be over in a year. I don't know why the primarch is allowing this.'

'Because he has nothing to hide,' said Alpharius. 'Every Legion is under suspicion at the moment, and nobody, least of all Dorn, is going to take anyone's loyalty for granted.'

'Well, I've got a scar on my left arm from a World Eater chainaxe if this jumped-up policeman wants any proof of my loyalty,' said Ordin.

'Quiet!' snapped Sergeant Dor.

They fell silent as Captain Noriz continued his tour through the lines. Alpharius stayed calm as the captain approached from the left and stopped in front of him. His helmet was on his belt, leaving him fully exposed to the scrutiny of the others, but there was nothing outward that would betray his true identity. He met the Imperial Fist's gaze with an emotionless stare as the captain eyed him closely.

There were no questions. Noriz moved on further down the line. Alpharius quashed the urge to sigh with relief, realising how tense he had become, even though he had kept his exterior utterly placid.

Soon enough, the order to disperse was given and the company broke into squads.

'What next, sergeant?' Ordin asked as they filed out of the chamber.

'The Imperial Palace,' replied Dor with a grin.

DESPITE FINDING NO hint of suspicious activity on his inspection, Captain Noriz insisted that his orders required the Imperial Fists contingent to remain aboard the *Avenger* until it reached Terra. Not wishing to create more problems, Corax agreed, placing him under the stewardship of Branne. As ship's captain, it was his responsibility to accommodate the visitor and Branne did his best to be helpful and cordial, if not outright friendly. Noriz did not make the task any easier; he was a tight-lipped warrior, monosyllabic for much of the time, unwilling to shake a certain distrust of his hosts.

The journey from the translation point to Terra would take eleven days, during which time Noriz was invited by the primarch to brief him and his command council on the current intelligence regarding Horus and the situation at Isstvan.

They convened in the command chamber beside the strategium, Corax choosing to stand while the others were sat around the table. As a courtesy, Noriz had brought over some personal stores from his strike cruiser before despatching it to continue on patrol, and so there were several bottles of wine, plates of fresh meat and bowls of ripe fruit for the council to enjoy. Branne would have been grateful for the gesture, had it not been performed in a manner that indicated Noriz believed it his honour-bound duty to offer this gift rather than acting out of genuine comradeship for his fellow legionaries. For all that, the commander showed no hesitation in consuming the fresh provisions with gusto, as did the other commanders.

'You must be aware that I am not privy to high levels of intelligence,' Noriz began, casting a worried glance at Corax, who stood a little apart from the rest of them, looming over the group like a shadowy statue.

'Just tell us what you already know,' said the primarch.

'Details are scarce, as you might expect,' said the Imperial Fist. His uncertainty continued, either from genuine lack of knowledge or reluctance to share what he knew with the Raven Guard. 'Some of our Legion were sent to Isstvan and are still unaccounted for. The rest are garrisoning Terra and dealing with the Martian situation.'

'What situation?' said Solaro. 'What is happening on Mars?'

'Insurrection, bordering on civil war,' replied the captain with a sour expression. 'It seems Horus has allies within the Mechanicum as well as the Legiones Astartes and Imperial Army.'

'There is fighting on Mars?' Agapito's incredulity was betrayed by his tone. 'That puts the traitors within striking distance of Terra already!'

'I expected as much,' said Corax, leaning forwards to pick up a wine bottle in his giant hand. He delicately poured himself a glass of red, the crystal goblet seeming tiny in his fingers as he raised it to his lips. 'Horus would not be able to launch a war against the Imperium without support from the tech-priests. That it reaches as far as Mars is worrying, but not a revelation.'

Corax sipped his drink and nodded to Noriz to continue. The captain cleared his throat and looked at the assembled commanders.

'If you do not trust us now, Horus has struck an even keener blow than I had feared,' said Corax, sensing the captain's continuing reluctance. 'Your reticence is starting to become tiresome, captain. Are we wasting our time here?'

'Our primary focus is the fortification of Terra and the defence of the Sol system,' Noriz told them, pouring himself a drink. He looked long at Corax and the commanders and then gave a single, unconscious nod, indicating that he was willing to trust them. 'The turncoats on Mars are contained, their defection destabilising our efforts rather than directly threatening them. With the loyal Mechanicum occupied with the enemy within their ranks, they can provide little support for our growing war effort.'

'Which is all very interesting, but we want to know what happened to other Legions on Isstvan. Who is left to fight Horus?' This was from Agapito.

'I was hoping that you might know more than me on that account,' confessed Noriz. 'There has been scattered traffic returning from the system, a ship or two bearing survivors, but little else. We're not really sure what happened out there. As I said before, we had heard that the Raven Guard had been eliminated.'

'Though the news has proven false in that case, we must still assume for the moment that the Salamanders and Iron Hands have been wiped out,' said Corax. 'Ferrus Manus was slain, I saw as much myself, and nothing has been seen of Vulkan. It is likely that their Legions were also destroyed. What of other loyal forces? How far has the taint spread to the Imperial Army? Any news from Guilliman, or Jonson, or the Khan?'

'I do not know,' Noriz said with a shrug. 'Nothing has been passed down to me from Legion command, you will have to speak to Lord Dorn about that.'

'The Emperor, what is the Emperor doing?' asked Aloni. 'Surely he will lead the fight against Horus.'

A pained look crossed the face of Noriz.

'We have heard nothing directly,' said the captain, placing his cup on the table in front of him. 'Lord Dorn has been placed in charge of the Sol defence and the fortification of the Imperial Palace. Malcador appears to be acting as regent on Terra, with the authority of the Emperor alongside the primarch. We have been told that the Emperor is engaged fully in his own endeavours to defeat the traitors, though what that means I have no clue.'

The Raven Guard commanders muttered shock and disapproval at this revelation, until Corax stepped up to the table.

'Quiet,' said the primarch. He cast a stern look at the legionaries. 'If the Emperor is embroiled in some unseen effort, we must trust that it is the surest road to victory. Did you think he would come out of the Imperial Palace, sword in hand, and cast down these traitors with a single blow? The Emperor created us to be his warriors, and we will bring him victory.'

With further questioning it became clear that Noriz could furnish them with little more information other than the ongoing defensive measures being undertaken. Jaghatai Khan and his White Scars were presumably en route to Terra, having been recalled from Chondax by Dorn himself, but no other communication had been received from them for some time. The First Legion, the Dark Angels under Lion El'Jonson, had not been heard from and were likely unaware of the recent treachery of Horus. Leman Russ and his Space Wolves were equally incommunicado, having been despatched by the Emperor to deal with the problem of the Thousand Sons and their continuing sorceries many months before. The Ultramarines, largest of the Legions, had been sent to the opposite side of the galaxy by Horus prior to the massacre, and were unlikely to be able to intervene any time soon. For the moment, the only Legions that could be accounted for and depended upon were the Raven Guard and the Imperial Fists.

The council ended with little learnt, but what small amount of intelligence Noriz had passed on was far from comforting. The warp storms were, as Corax had suspected, widespread; perhaps the whole galaxy was engulfed. Certainly the region around Isstvan was cloaked in a massive tempest that blocked navigation and communication.

It seemed increasingly likely that the warp disruption was part of Horus's strategy. The last time warp storms had raged like this, the worlds of mankind had been divided and isolated, leading to the onset of Old Night and the dissolving of the original human empire. Unable to unite properly, prevented from coordinating their strategy or enforcing loyalty to the Emperor, the disparate planets of the Imperium would be much easier pickings for the traitors. With a swift strike to secure power on Terra, Horus could emerge as a new uniter of humanity, sweeping away the rule of the Emperor at a stroke.

* * *

THE PREPARATIONS FOR Terra's defence became more evident as the *Avenger* moved in-system towards Terra. The Sol battlefleet, the largest single armada in the Imperium, was gathering in strength. Dozens of warships blockaded Mars, while hundreds of other vessels took station in orbital positions over the other planets, their sensors turned outwards in readiness for the arrival of Horus's fleet.

The communications networks were overloaded with activity, the strat-net frequencies used by the Legiones Astartes and Imperial Army sometimes so clogged with data that it took many hours for messages to be relayed. There was a tangible aura of desperation amidst the turmoil, as though any day would see the warp tearing apart with the arrival of hundreds of traitor ships.

As they neared their destination, the Raven Guard encountered increasing numbers of security screens. Warship patrols hailed them frequently, while massive star forts locked their guns upon the arriving vessel, keeping watch until it had passed out of range. Passing further and further into the heart of the Sol system, the *Avenger* was subjected to constant scrutiny, though its passage was never barred outright.

Gaining orbit over Terra was an expedition in itself, despite the assurances and assistance of Captain Noriz. After three days entangled in the security protocols of half a dozen different military jurisdictions and organisations, Corax finally lost patience. Dismissing the communications attendants from their posts, he keyed in a failsafe code for the most secure channel: an ultra-secret frequency used by only the primarchs and, before his self-seclusion on Terra, the Emperor himself.

There was no reply for half an hour, as Corax paced back and forth across the strategium. Finally the vox crackled into life, with a voice that was deep and thoughtful, every word carefully enunciated, every syllable spoken with crisp authority.

'Is that you, Corax? It is about time you contacted me, brother. I was wondering if the news that you were still alive had been yet another breakdown in communication.'

'Brother Rogal, yes it is Corax,' replied the primarch. 'If you do not find me an orbital station in the next five minutes, I'm going to use my weapons batteries to make a space for myself.'

There was a short but hearty laugh over the vox.

'That would not be a good idea!' said Rogal Dorn. 'I heard that you had arrived, but then I must admit that your whereabouts were washed away in all of the other clutter. Do you want to berth at a platform or take up an independent orbit?'

'We need to resupply,' said Corax. 'I'll shuttle down with an advance guard.'

'I will send you the coordinates of Beta-Styx platform. It has a fully-stocked victualling yard. You can come down to Lion's Gate port and I will despatch a delegation to meet you.'

'A delegation? Too busy to greet your brother in person?'

'Yes. I will be back at the Imperial Palace within the day.'

'Understood, brother. I wish our reunion was in much lighter times.'

'It is not for our kind to meet in peace, brother, you should know that. We will talk more tomorrow; I have something I must attend to urgently.'

With that, the frequency devolved into static once more. A data screen flickered into life, a list of spatial coordinates scrolling across it in yellow lettering and signed with the insignia of the Imperial Fists.

'Prepare for docking manoeuvres,' Corax announced. 'And ready me a Stormbird. Agapito, choose a company to act as honour guard. Branne, you have command.'

A series of affirmatives chorused across the strategium as the primarch walked towards the doors. Corax stopped as they slid open and turned his head.

'Branne?'

The commander froze, halfway into the control throne. He stood and looked back at the primarch and saw a lopsided smile on Corax's face.

'Yes, lord?'

'As much as I appreciate your arrival at Isstvan, please stay where I put you this time.'

'Aye, lord, I will.'

AS THE AVENGER powered towards the orbital dock, preparations were made for Corax and a small entourage to descend to the surface of Terra. Branne found Agapito on the launch deck, with a company of his legionaries. The clatter of a heavy servitor's tracks echoed from the metal walls, blotting out the dormant whine of a Stormbird's engines. Branne thought he sensed some anxiety in his brother's demeanour.

'Relax, brother, this is not a combat mission,' said Branne.

'And all the more dangerous for it,' replied Agapito. 'Suspicion surrounds us like a cloud. You saw how Captain Noriz treated us. I expect no warm welcome on the surface.'

'So it will be up to you to assure our allies that we can be trusted,' said Branne.

Agapito hesitated, and glanced over Branne's shoulder. Corax entered the flight bay, nodded to the two commanders and strode up the Stormbird's boarding ramp without a word.

'I'm not the only one that feels it,' said Agapito, his

gaze on the drop-ship, his thoughts clearly on the primarch now aboard. 'Now is not the time for rash displays of loyalty. I'm worried Lord Corax will promise more than we can currently deliver.'

'We can't afford to let the traitors make their preparations without pause,' said Branne. 'Would you want us simply to let them proceed as they wish?'

Leaning closer, Agapito's voice dropped to a whisper.

'We were nearly wiped out, brother,' he said. 'If we do not tread carefully, the execution Horus planned for us at Isstvan will be carried out at another place. You know that we lack the strength to fight at the moment.'

Concerned by his brother's words, Branne slapped a hand to Agapito's shoulder guard.

'What happened on Isstvan is over,' said Branne, guessing the source of Agapito's hesitance. 'We lost most of the Legion, but we survived.'

'"We" survived, brother? I don't remember you at the dropsite.'

'Through no fault of my own!' snapped Branne, snatching back his hand. He was infuriated that of all his comrades, it was Agapito who had given voice to the accusation Branne had suspected lingered in the minds of his battle-brothers. 'How can I be held responsible for the drawing of lots that left me as garrison commander?'

'You misunderstand me, brother,' said Agapito, with a sorrowful shake of the head. 'It is not personal, but you can never understand what it was like to be there. I don't begrudge your absence, I envy it.'

'You haven't talked about the dropsite at all, to me or the primarch,' said Branne, his anger punctured by Agapito's confession. 'Some of the others, they have found it helpful to discuss what they saw, to share their stories. Tell me, what happened to you at the dropsite?'

'No,' said Agapito, stepping away. He signalled to his warriors to begin boarding as the launch bay lights

dimmed in readiness for the main doors to open. Overhead, klaxons sounded the five-minute warning. 'Some
stories are best left untold. You do not want to know what
I did at the dropsite.'

Branne said nothing as his brother turned away, confused by the change he had seen in Agapito. His fellow
commander had once been the first to swap war stories
on the ship back to Deliverance, taking great delight in
recounting his kills and close calls with death. Even
as young boys, when they had fought for the liberty of
Deliverance, before the Emperor had come and brought
the Legion, Agapito would rouse the flagging spirits of the
freedom fighters with tales of his daring and their victories over the Kiavahran enslavers.

He watched as Agapito stood at the bottom of the ramp,
counting off the squads as they ran into the Stormbird
amid the thunderous falls of boots on metal. As the last of
the legionaries passed him, Branne noticed something on
their shoulder guards, a small device painted under the
Legion symbol. It was a grey skull, almost as dark as the
black of their armour. Now that he noticed it, Branne saw
it in the insignia of all the company's warriors. He waved
aside one of the squad leaders as he jogged past.

'Sergeant Nestil, a word,' said the commander.

'Yes, captain,' said Nestil, coming to attention in front
of Branne.

'What does this mean?' asked Branne, prodding a finger
towards the small sigil.

'Isstvan veteran, captain,' replied the sergeant with no
hint of reluctance. 'There was no official campaign badge
or honours issued, captain. We thought it would be good
to remember the fallen.'

'You have all taken this on?' said Branne.

'All of us that fought there, yes, captain, at least in the
Talons,' said Nestil. He glanced towards Agapito, and
Branne took his meaning.

'Whose idea was this?' asked Branne.

'I'm not sure, captain,' admitted Nestil. He looked away, glancing again at Agapito. 'It was just one of those ideas that seemed to catch on.'

'Sorry to delay you, sergeant,' said Branne, waving Nestil to carry on.

Not good, thought Branne as he watched Agapito follow Nestil up the ramp onto the Stormbird. A commander being close-lipped about what he had done and legionaries giving themselves honours. The drop-site massacre had caused serious damage to the Raven Guard, even more than the seventy-five thousand dead legionaries.

STRAPPED INTO HIS berth beside one of the viewing ports, Alpharius had a good view of Terra as the Stormbird dipped away from the *Avenger*. It had been a fortunate turn to be included in Corax's honour guard and would provide, he hoped, a good opportunity to see the defences being prepared to welcome Horus. Aside from whatever else he might be asked to do, his role in the Raven Guard was to gather intelligence for the final, inevitable assault on the Emperor's stronghold. Everything he could learn now would give the Warmaster and his allies a valuable warning of what to expect.

'What is that?' one of the legionaries asked from further down the compartment. Alpharius turned to see the other Raven Guard straining at their harnesses to look out of the starboard windows. 'It's bigger than a star fort!'

Alpharius could not see clearly from his position but glimpsed a massive vessel in low orbit. It seemed to stretch on and on, a gilded construction shaped like an eagle with outstretched wings, bedecked with fortified gun towers, lance batteries, missile tubes and bombardment cannons. So vast was the orbiting station, its faint shadow could be seen on the cloud layer wreathing Terra. The flicker of void shields surrounded the immense floating edifice, dappling the gold of its heavily-buttressed superstructure with purple and red. Smaller ships – some of them mighty battleships in their own right – were dwarfed by its presence, its turret-encrusted docks large enough for cruisers several kilometres long.

'That's *Phalanx*,' said Sergeant Nestil. 'Base ship of the Imperial Fists. Impressive, isn't it? Never mind a battle-barge, that's what we should've taken to Isstvan.'

It certainly was impressive, but no surprise. Everyone had heard of *Phalanx* and its presence in the Sol system was to be expected. Horus was well aware of the star fortress's capabilities and defences already, and no doubt had devised a way to counter them. This was not the object of Alpharius's mission. Of more interest to the Alpha Legionnaire was a golden-hulled cruiser rising out of the dock neighbouring the *Avenger*. Though he was not sure, it looked like a vessel belonging to the Legio Custodes, the Emperor's elite protectors. He wondered where they were going, when all other effort was being directed towards the defence of the Master of Mankind.

And then everything outside turned white as the Stormbird dropped into the thickening Terran atmosphere, enveloping the craft in bright flames. As they descended, the visibility momentarily cleared, revealing a vista that sent a thrill through Alpharius.

Large platforms could be half-seen amongst the dense cloud, drifting serenely through the air surrounded by swarms of shuttles and cargo-lifters. The closest floating city, its name unknown to Alpharius, was glimpsed between breaks in the whiteness, a mass of towering buildings, winding roadways and landing aprons. Sunlight glittered from coiling spires made of multicoloured glass and dazzled across the mirrored plates of photo-receptors and vapour condensers.

The splendour of graceful lines and arcing bridges was marred by blocky aberrations: gun towers and bunkers surrounded by scaffolding that was thick with workers. As the Stormbird banked onto its final course, Alpharius's augmented eyes could see flashes of yellow armour amongst the robes and overalls of the work teams: Imperial Fists supervising the construction of the defences.

The nose of the Stormbird dipped and cloud again swathed Alpharius's view, blotting out the vision of the hovering city. The engines whined as the craft slowed for its landing, and banked once more, circling over the Lion's Gate starport that spread darkly across the bare rock of Terra's surface in a vast maze of ferrocrete and plasteel. Alpharius had a glimpse of landing platforms that stretched for kilometres, shadowed beneath control towers and defence laser turrets.

The Alpha Legionnaire was glad that his arrival was in the guise of a friend and wondered if, at some point of the future, he would be returning here as a foe. He had made dozens of combat drops during his long years of service, but seeing the immense barrels of the orbital defence cannons and the flicker of power fields, he knew that whichever Legion ultimately had the task of securing Lion's Gate would suffer heavy casualties.

Even as he thought of the assault that was sure to come, Alpharius's mind was analysing the growing defences. Any insights he could glean from this opportunity to examine Dorn's fortifications first-hand might prove invaluable to Horus, and so in turn were of significant worth to the Alpha Legion. His eye caught the telltale capacitors and conduits of power field generators, while he calculated the zones of fire of the smaller rings of protective pillboxes and automated lascannon mounts.

With a thud and a hiss of hydraulics, the Stormbird extended its landing gear, breaking Alpharius's thoughts. So engrossed had he been in his intelligence-gathering,

he had quite forgotten where he was. Alpharius took a
deep breath as the Stormbird touched down, rocking
slightly on its gear, clouds of smoke and plasma-wash
billowing around the craft.

He was on Terra, the capital of the Imperium, home
to the Emperor.

AS PROMISED, THERE was a contingent waiting for the
arrival of Corax. As the primarch descended the Stormbird's ramp, he saw a group of thirty gold-armoured
Custodians. In height and size, they were the match
of the Legiones Astartes, if not bigger, though Corax
was taller still. Every warrior of the Custodian Guard
was armoured uniquely, their heavy gorgets decorated
with eagle devices, winged skulls and other icons, their
high, conical helms topped with flowing scarlet crests.
Clusters of studded red leather pteruges hung from their
belts and high shoulder guards, tipped with pointed
gold weights, and their wide greaves and heavy vambraces were chased with intricate designs that matched
the rest of their armour. They held guardian spears with
red power field-clad blades held across their chests, carried behind tall shields emblazoned with designs of the
Imperial aquila and laurel-crowned skulls.

With them stood an ageing man Corax recognised
immediately: Malcador the Sigillite. The Regent of Terra
wore a voluminous robe, unadorned in stark contrast to
the ornamentation of his guard of honour. His weathered, ancient face was half-hidden behind the fold of his
hood. The gusts of wind blowing across the open landing
apron tugged at the rim of the hood, showing glimpses
of reinforced pipes connected to a collar around the
Sigillite's throat that disappeared into the swathe of his
garments. In his hands he held a black marble staff taller
than himself, its head a soaring eagle shaped in gold,
wreathed in flames that sprang from the rod itself. The

Emperor's regent leaned heavily on his staff of office but nonetheless managed to maintain an air of statesman-like authority.

Malcador bowed his head in greeting and Corax returned the gesture as his guard of honour filed into ranks behind him.

'I hope they are for ornamentation and nothing else,' said Corax, directing a purposeful gaze at the armed Custodians.

'Purely ceremonial, I assure you,' replied Malcador. 'I apologise for the formalities you have been forced to endure, but you understand that we cannot afford any laxity in our security in these times.'

'It seems a primarch's word is no longer his bond,' said Corax as he stepped forwards, the Custodians moving to form two lines of escort around him and Malcador, encircling the primarch's entourage of Raven Guard.

'Only for some, Corax,' said the Sigillite. 'A number of your brothers remain true to their oaths of allegiance. Your loyalty is greatly appreciated.'

The primarch laughed, but there was no sign of humour in the Sigillite's expression. Malcador continued to talk as they walked from the landing apron.

'Rogal asked me to assure you that he will be joining us tomorrow as he promised. We are very keen to hear everything you can tell us about Horus's forces and perhaps what you think he intends to do.'

'I can add little to the discussion,' said Corax. They passed under an arching silver gateway a hundred metres high and headed down a ramp leading to a line of silver-hulled shuttle craft. They looked like giant scarabs, with steel wings that fluttered under the vibration of idling engines. 'It sounds like there are other survivors.'

'Of course,' said Malcador, waving for Corax to precede him onto the ramp of the closest atmospheric shuttle. Inside, the main compartment was furnished like an

austere lounge, with low couches and tables on a carpeted deck, the walls covered with hangings depicting
scenes from the Unification Wars. Corax assumed it was
Malcador's personal transport. The Sigillite sat down on
one of the long couches and instinctively waved a hand
for Corax to do the same. The primarch declined with a
shake of his head, knowing that the furniture was totally
unsuited to someone of his height and weight. He leaned
against the bulkhead instead, head dipped beneath the
shuttle roof.

'There are not only those like yourself who escaped the
ambush,' the Sigillite continued, 'but also brave warriors
who have recently arrived from within the traitors' ranks.'

'And you can be sure of their loyalty? Misdirection and
falsehood seem to be Horus's primary weapons at the
moment.'

'We are convinced of their continuing support for the
Emperor,' said Malcador. 'They will have a very important role to play in the waging of the war to come.'

'The war has started already, if you haven't noticed,'
growled Corax. He had noticed Captain Noriz using a
similar turn of phrase, implying that somehow the massacre at Isstvan had been an end point rather than a
beginning.

The two of them were alone in the shuttle, the Custodians and legionaries being directed to the other transports.
With a growl, the engines of the craft throttled to full,
the hull trembling as the ornithopter's wings sprang into
blurred life. The shuttle lifted quickly away from the starport and turned northwards, rising to clear a range of
mountains that thrust up from the ground. The mountains were as much artifice as natural phenomena. Corax
could see vast galleries and windows several storeys high
cut into the crags and ridges, betraying the labyrinthine
structure hidden beneath the snow-capped peaks.

Corax sensed Malcador studying him at length, but the

two of them sat in silence for some time as the ornithopter sped over the mountains, shuddering slightly in the
buffeting winds. Occasionally the primarch glimpsed
one of the other shuttles through the oval windows,
their shining fuselages glimmering against the white and
grey of the sheer-sided peaks.

'And what is the opinion of the Emperor?' Corax
asked, realising that Malcador had yet to mention him
specifically. 'Dorn said that he had been placed in charge
of the defence.'

'The Emperor is very aware of the situation and Dorn
has his full support,' replied the regent.

'That's it?' said Corax. 'His Warmaster turns half the
Legions against him and all he has to say is that Dorn
has his full support?'

'He is entirely absorbed in another matter, one which
overshadows his thoughts even more than this distraction with Horus. If his current endeavour is successful,
this rebellion will be short-lived.'

'I have come to Terra to seek audience with the
Emperor,' said Corax. He glanced out of the window
and saw cranes and earth-movers remodelling a massive shoulder of the mountain below, crafting immense
revetments and fortifications from the naked rock.
Swarms of thousands of labourers were at work.

'It is with regret that I must warn you that is highly
unlikely,' said Malcador, his gaze unwavering as Corax
turned his stare back on the Sigillite. 'His current project
requires all of his attention. I have seen him only a handful of times since we learned of the events at Isstvan.
Dorn has not spoken to him at all, receiving the Emper-
or's instruction only through me. I cannot give you any
guarantee that our master will grant you an audience.'

The firm expression on Malcador's face forestalled
any further comment Corax might make on the matter.
Though he did not say as much, the primarch believed

that he would be seen by the Emperor. No matter what Malcador said, there could be no endeavour so pressing that the Emperor could not find time to speak with one of his primarchs at this dark hour.

Then a thought occurred to him, which would explain why Malcador was being slightly evasive and seemed so convinced that Corax would not get an audience.

'The Emperor *is* aware of my arrival?' asked the primarch.

'No,' said Malcador. 'I have been unable to contact him since you first entered the Sol system.'

'Unable or unwilling?'

If Malcador took any offence at the question, he did not show it. His reply was calm, his face earnest.

'The Emperor wages a different sort of war to the ones you and I have ever seen,' explained the Sigillite. 'To attempt to contact him whilst on one of his... expeditions, would be to endanger his cause. When he has returned, he will be immediately informed of your presence, rest assured.'

'You make it sound as if the Emperor is not on Terra.'

As before, Malcador hesitated, though Corax did not sense any duplicity in him, merely reluctance. The regent's thin fingers slowly tapped the haft of his staff as he contemplated his answer.

'That is not a thing I can easily quantify,' said Malcador. 'Forgive my vagueness, but I am not at liberty to discuss the Emperor's plans, nor am I in a position to fully comprehend them. It would be indiscreet, a betrayal of my position as regent, if I were to furnish you with information that the Emperor has not chosen fit to share with you himself.'

What Malcador was saying unsettled Corax greatly. Ever since his return to Terra after the victory at Ullanor, the Emperor had shrouded himself in secrets, when once he had walked freely amongst his sons and shared his

plans and visions. Malcador spoke with such a reverent
tone that Corax was left in no doubt that the Emperor's
current campaign was indeed very important, but the
Sigillite's assurances that it was more worthy of attention than Horus's treachery rang hollow. The Imperium,
the spreading of Enlightenment, had been the Emperor's
great scheme, and now it was all for nothing. Surely he
would have to emerge from his cloistered endeavours to
lead those still loyal to him?

As the squadron of ornithopters swept along a high-
sided valley, Corax wondered what he would do if he
could not speak with the Emperor. After the debacle at
Isstvan, the primarch was not sure of anything, including his ability to effectively command. He needed the
Emperor's guidance now more than ever, and the
thought of returning to Deliverance without seeing his
gene-father filled him with a subtle dread. With primarch turning on primarch, Corax wanted to bend his knee
to the Emperor once more and assure him of the loyalty
of the Raven Guard.

THE FLIGHT UP into the mountains took the Raven Guard
past the burgeoning fortifications being erected under
the leadership of Dorn. The scale of the endeavour was
vast, larger than anything Corax had witnessed before,
and he had seen the rebuilding of worlds shattered by
his Legion.

The mountains themselves were being shaped into
great bastions, carved by explosive charges and mono-
lithic machines into buttresses and keeps, curtain walls
and towers. The shadows of the ornithopters flitted over
many-tracked cargo haulers in convoys kilometres long,
bringing loads of ferrocrete and adamantium, ceramite
and thermaglas, plasteel and diamatite. With them came
cranes with booms half a kilometre long, and shovel-
fronted earth movers the size of tenement blocks.

Snaking multi-compartment crawlers edged along
newly laid roadways, their cargo more workers to join
the hundreds of thousands already labouring on the
upper slopes. These caravans were in turn supplied by
forage trucks and water tankers numbering in the hundreds. Everywhere was seen the blazon of the Imperial
Fists and the splash of their golden livery.

'My brother does not take half measures,' said Corax,
looking across the cabin to Malcador.

The regent roused himself from a half-slumber and
glanced out of the window, barely interested by the gar-
gantuan effort laid out below.

'A wall unmanned is no defence against attack,' said
the Sigillite. 'If Horus's forces were to strike now, who
would hold the ramparts and gates?'

'I thought the White Scars were headed for Terra.'

'Jaghatai Khan was ordered to return with his Legion,
but we have had no contact with the White Scars since
the warp storms began anew.'

Corax absorbed this news in silence, still looking at the
edifice taking shape around him. Peaks were being toppled, the material thus created used to erect walls closing
off the passes and valleys between. Huge lifters powered
by dozens of rotors and thrusters hovered over the vales,
carrying generators and building-sized capacitors to new
defence laser silos. The barrels of these weapons were
transported on flat-beds a hundred metres long, over
bridges and through tunnels carved from naked rock.

Within this growing outer cordon, the activity was
less frenetic. Here and there a slope was broken by high
gallery windows or the curving front of an embrasure.
Roadways disappeared into dimly-lit passages and for-
ests grew around flattened landing pads. These were the
outer reaches of the old palace, first raised up by the
Emperor as the Great Crusade began. Buildings fashioned in layout to appear as Imperial aquilas from above

clustered atop a peak to the east. To the west, down a winding valley, hundreds of square kilometres were covered with huge wind farms powering the city hidden beneath, each fan three hundred metres high.

Ahead were the tallest mountains, still silhouettes against the sky. One of the floating sky platforms had been brought down to dock, a thirty kilometre-wide city jutting from the side of the mountain like a balcony, resting on a maze of piles and girders stretched between two summits. The shuttles banked away, turning more to the west where the sun was setting behind jagged peaks. The last rays of sunlight glinted on golden arches and pearlescent towers, stark against the blues and purples of the dusk.

After several hours, the shuttles reached a cavernous dock set into the side of a mountain whose peak had been flattened and replaced by a sprawl of jutting antennae and communications dishes. An immense pillar stood to each side of the kilometre-wide opening, carved with lightning bolt designs that forked between rising, turning columns of eagles.

Swallowed up by the dark interior of the shuttle port, the ornithopter's lights flickered on inside and out, strobing navigation lights illuminating row after row of craft on the wide landing apron beneath. Corax saw Thunderhawks and Stormbirds, plus dozens more of the ornithopters. There were larger craft too: slab-sided Harbinger drop-ships in the varied colours of many Imperial Army regiments.

Into this vast dockyard descended the craft carrying Corax's warriors, spiralling down after each other before scattering to their allotted landing spaces. The primarch glanced towards Malcador with a frown.

'Accommodation has been made for your legionaries,' said Malcador. 'They will be well catered for.'

The Sigillite's shuttle did not land amongst them,

however, the pilot steering it up towards a much smaller opening a little below the vaulted roof of the port. Rising towards this tunnel, the shuttle's lights passed over gallery after gallery overlooking the port. The area was strangely deserted, a city delved for millions of inhabitants who were now absent. The thrum of the ornithopter's wings echoed in the immense hollow, interrupted by no other sound.

Passing into an opening between the legs of another carved eagle, the ornithopter followed a narrow channel for several hundred metres until it came to land in a circular chamber situated at the heart of the mountain. Its walls were of plain dressed stone, showing the striations of the mountain rock. A single door led from the docking site, fashioned from bronze, embossed with two crossed lightning bolts beneath an armoured fist. With a whine of decreasing power, the shuttle's wings settled and Malcador's craft lurched to a halt on the stone floor. The doorway opened with a rush of escaping air and immediately Corax detected an atmosphere far thinner than at ground level. Malcador led the primarch out of the shuttle, seemingly unaffected by the low oxygen content in the air.

'If you will follow me, I will show you to the quarters that have been set aside for you, while your warriors will be garrisoned close at hand.'

The door opened at the Sigillite's approach, Corax hearing the faintest buzz of a communications connection emitted from Malcador's staff. Beyond, steps led steeply downwards into the bowels of the Imperial Palace.

WATCHING THE GOLD-ARMOURED figures of the Legio Custodes advancing ahead of him, Alpharius could not help but measure himself against them. Physically they did not seem to be any more impressive than a legionary,

though certainly their armour and weapons seemed to
be individually fashioned, something only a captain
might expect in the Legions. He had heard before that
each warrior was also a product of unique effort, as
hand-crafted by the genhancers and tech-serfs as his
wargear was by artisans of the Mechanicum. Since he
had gunned down several Salamanders at the dropsite,
he had been confident that the Alpha Legion were the
match of any in the Legiones Astartes, but it was not
until he had been confronted by the ranks of the Custodian Guard that he had contemplated fighting against
the Emperor's other servants.

There was some idle chatter from the other Raven
Guard as they followed the Custodians deeper into
the Imperial Palace. Corax and Malcador had left them
not far from what Alpharius assumed was the Sigillite's
private shuttle chamber – another little nugget of intelligence to pass on – and they had descended through
forty-six floors in a gigantic elevator to the barracks level.

The upper parts of the palace had been ornate, fashioned from marbled stone and obsidian, hung with
banners and paintings of scenes from before the Unification Wars. Alpharius had seen depictions of old cities
with onion-domed towers and ruined pyramids jutting
from desert, rivers flowing in swift torrents over wide
falls and landscapes of green pastures. Nothing of those
times remained except for these pictures; the beauty of
ancient Terra had long ago succumbed to millennia of
pollution and war.

After leaving the elevator, the Raven Guard had been
brought into an area far more functional and austere in
appearance. The walls were of rough ferrocrete, covered
by plain whitewash. The long dorms that opened out
through arches on either side of the corridor were empty,
and the smell of fresh paint and residual particles of rock
dust still in the air indicated that they had been newly

built, no doubt to house more defenders in the future.

There was little enough to report at the moment, but Alpharius kept his eyes and ears open for anything that might be of value. It was impossible to tell how deep within the mountain they were. There were no windows, the light provided by endless glowing stripes set into the ceiling and walls, the air coming through ventilator housings too small to allow entry or exit except perhaps by a child. The only way in or out was through the doors at each end of the main corridor, a defensive measure in all likelihood, but it also made for an effective prison. There was some discontented muttering amongst those Raven Guard who had been raised in the cells of Lycaeus, but this was stilled by a few words from the sergeants.

The leader of the Custodian Guard stopped and pointed with his spear to an archway on the left, beyond which was a dormitory housing several hundred beds in long lines. There were lockers and shelves, as well as weapons racks and armour stands. Everything was proportioned for legionaries, larger and more robust than the furniture required by normal men.

'Remain here,' the Custodian leader said sharply, his voice coming through the grille of his helm tainted by an external emitter. 'Food and drink will be brought to you. There are drill rooms suitable for close-quarters weapons practice at the southern end of the hall,' his spear tip pointed further down the corridor, 'and should you wish to conduct live firing exercises you will be taken to an appropriate part of the facility.'

'And how will we contact you?' asked Commander Agapito, his voice conveying his displeasure at this abrupt treatment. 'We are here to escort our primarch, not lounge around down here with you for company.'

'Lord Corax is under constant watch, be sure of that,' replied the Custodian, his metal-edged voice betraying no hint of whether that was for the primarch's safety or other reasons. 'You will be assigned a secure communications frequency. You may make full use of the barracks and its attached facilities, but you are not authorised to move beyond the southern and northern extents of this hall. Failure to abide by these restrictions will result in summary execution.'

'Nice to be trusted,' said Agapito.

The Custodian turned his head towards the Raven Guard commander, bringing the black lenses of his helm to focus on the legionary.

'Trust is a depleted resource, commander. There will be no exceptions. I have been given personal authority over your stay here. I am Arcatus Vindix Centurio. All communications will be directed through me. My companions are not authorised to communicate with you, so save both your time and theirs by sparing them any questions or complaints. I will return in one hour to conduct a full security briefing.'

The Custodian Guard filed out through the gigantic lock-door at the end of the corridor, leaving the Raven Guard to their own devices. Squad by squad, the quarters were allocated. Alpharius found his squad assigned bunks close to the corridor, but he did not entertain any thoughts of sneaking out for further investigation. His primarch had made it clear that he was to remain undiscovered at all costs, until the full nature of his mission had been revealed. He was not going to risk exposing himself to go on a sightseeing jaunt under the noses of the Custodians.

When the legionaries had ordered the dormitory to their liking, stowing weapons and other gear on the racks bolted to the walls, Agapito called the company to attend him.

'I know this is all quite strange, and those Custodian Guard are stiffer than a dead man's fingers, but this is the situation and we must deal with it,' said the commander.

'When we have communications access, I will signal *Avenger* that we have arrived and I will parley with Arcatus to arrange a suitable routine. I don't know how long we will have to stay here, so let's just keep alert and wait for the primarch's orders.'

There being little point in staying at combat readiness, the Raven Guard aided one another with the removal of their armour, each legionary stripping down to bodysuits and robes. Normally such assistance would be provided by the Legion's army of non-augmented attendants, but there was no such personnel available here. Despite the apparent security of their barracks, a watch rota was drawn up and the squads allocated shifts on duty. A lifetime of routine and discipline could be quickly eroded by periods of inactivity and Agapito was not going to allow any laxity to grow in the minds of his warriors.

As Arcatus had promised, attendants arrived with food, which was brought to the dining area in the chamber on the opposite side of the main passage. The serfs came and left in silence, obviously under orders not to fraternise with the legionaries in any way. They were all middle-aged men and women, wearing identical white jackets embroidered with the aquila of the Emperor, baggy black trousers and slippers of the same thick material, their faces etched with polite indifference from years of experience.

Alpharius was able to loiter in the passageway for a little while, and had a look past the sealed door at the end of the corridor when the attendants were leaving. As he suspected, beyond lay another chamber and another lock-door. There certainly would not be any way to slip out through there.

He rejoined his squad and sat down at the long table, taking a welcome lungful of steam that was rising from the roast meats laid on platters before each legionary.

Fresh fruit and vegetables were heaped in bowls along the length of each table, along with an assortment of other foodstuffs. After many days of ship's rations, it certainly was a feast. There were harsher conditions in which he might have found himself trapped, and as Alpharius ripped a leg from some giant poultry bird in front of him, he considered this one of the less arduous duties he been asked to perform for the Legion.

SIX

A Guest of the Emperor
Hall of Victories
Omegon Prepares

IN CONTRAST TO the confinement of his honour guard, Corax was quartered in some comfort and opulence, given a villa-like suite of chambers that overlooked a vast underground lake. Lit from below the water's surface by powerful lights, the stalactite-clustered ceiling glittered with crystal deposits that glinted in the dappling glow from the waters beneath. The rooms were lavishly furnished with dark wood and gilded furniture, hanging tapestries and deep carpets. From the ceilings hung chandeliers with real candles, something of a novelty to the primarch who had been raised under the dim glow of lumen strips.

The fact that the chambers were scaled to the height and bulk of a primarch was something of a pleasant surprise. It occurred to Corax that primarch-appointed quarters should not have been a shock, given that he was on Terra. He wondered briefly if they had been intended as guest quarters, or something more permanent once the Great Crusade had been finished. His brothers had sometimes quarrelled about what would happen when the last planet was conquered and the Emperor's dream

made a reality, but Corax had been more than content
to allow others to take over the burden of administer-
ing the Imperium in the wake of the Legiones Astartes.
He was a commander, not a governor, and if he had no
more battles to fight, he could have happily spent his
remaining years, however many hundreds or perhaps
thousands that might be, in comfortable retirement; perhaps compiling a treatise on the political lessons he had
learned from his mentors on Lycaeus.

It was quite literally a world away from his quarters
on Deliverance, which were by necessity rather cramped
and functional. Not that luxury had ever been a consideration of the primarch. His home had always been a
battlefield, a ship's deck or the rooms of a command
centre.

Once Malcador had taken his leave, Corax had been
left alone, with a handful of Custodians on hand to act
as guides and guards; and the small company of servants
who had seemed to spring into existence as Corax had
moved from room to room, each more than happy to
see to the wants and needs of their primarch guest. For
the first time since he had awoken in the dark cellar of
Lycaeus, Corax felt as if he was in a place intended for
him. The humans that attended him were dwarfed by
their surroundings, diminutive figures let free to roam
in the house of a giant, but seemed accustomed to the
strangeness of the household in which they served.

For a short time, the primarch tried to relax, though his
ribs were sore and the lacerations on his back plagued
him with spasms of pain. Even on the long voyage to
Terra he had not allowed himself time to rest, to allow his
body to recover. The constant activity and Corax's unsettled mood had prevented any meaningful recuperation.
In a way, the injuries Corax felt were a reminder to him
of what had happened, making real an event that sometimes seemed to have been a nightmare. Every twinge of

torn muscle and stab of ripped flesh was a physical companion to the torments of his thoughts, a memorial of the tens of thousands that would never return to Deliverance.

The novelty of the environment wore off as lights were dimmed in an approximation of night. Agitated by what he had heard from Dorn and Malcador, Corax was full of energy and had no desire to sleep. At his request, a writing tablet was brought to the primarch and he started to make notes of everything he had seen since he and the other Legions had arrived to bring Horus to justice for his actions at Isstvan III.

At first his words were functional, listing the dispositions of the different Legions, their agreed strategy and the intelligence reports concerning the Sons of Horus. He remembered in exact detail the initial fleet manoeuvres performed to encircle the ships of the Warmaster, even as drop-pods, Hawkwings, Thunderhawks and Stormbirds were readied for the assault on the planet below. At the time nothing had seemed amiss, but on reflection Corax could see the plots of his treacherous brethren already being set in motion.

The integration of the Legions had seemed a wise move given the circumstances, a united front against the perfidy of Horus and his legionaries. In retrospect, it had allowed the traitors close, their battle-barges and cruisers alongside those of the Salamanders, Iron Hands and Raven Guard.

Ferrus Manus had led the attack against the reasoning of Corax and the strategy devised by Dorn, determined that the traitors would be brought down. Perhaps he had been goaded into it by some quiet word from Fulgrim or Lorgar. They would never know, as the Gorgon had been slain on Isstvan V. That the second wave was composed entirely of those who had sworn allegiance to Horus was the greatest machination, an attack against which the loyalists could muster no defence.

As he wrote, Corax's account gradually grew more personal. It was impossible to separate himself from the bald facts of what had happened. His fingers flew over the screen of the writing pad, charting his feelings of horror and disgust as the Iron Warriors and Word Bearers had opened fire from the hills overlooking the Urgall Depression. He could not help but recall his own burning rage as his claws had scythed through the traitors, every sweep of his weapons accompanied by a surge of anger.

He stopped as his memories brought him to Lorgar.

How could he find the words to describe the loathing he had felt for his brother? And if he found the words for that, how would he then explain his feelings when the Night Haunter, Konrad Curze, had stopped Corax's lightning claw milliseconds from Lorgar's throat?

The servants were bustling again, and hearing their scattered conversation, the primarch realised that the night had already passed and they were preparing a breakfast for him. He scanned the last few paragraphs he had written, amazed by the vitriol let free from his thoughts. He considered deleting the whole document, expunging his memories at a stroke, but resisted. As painful as it was, he had to carry on.

He described his encounter with Lorgar and Curze in a few brief lines, reverting to the perfunctory style with which he had started, swiftly moving on to his withdrawal to a nearby Thunderhawk; a withdrawal that had been cut short by enemy fire, bringing the craft down only a few kilometres from the massacre.

The account came easily again, the turmoil in his thoughts subsiding as he recounted the gathering of the Raven Guard and the retreat into the mountains, striking back at the traitors when they could, fading into the shadows of the caves and valleys when the enemy came with too much strength.

He finished with a terse telling of Branne's arrival as it had been relayed to him by the commander, and the extraction from Isstvan. Corax was sure he had not heard the whole of the story. For Branne to have disobeyed his orders and left Deliverance had been a bold move. Also the Therion, Praefector Valerius, was involved somehow. That part of the story did not yet make sense, and Corax resolved to find out the truth behind it when he returned to the *Avenger*.

He took the tablet with him as he moved to the feasting chamber, compiling and annotating tables of warships and other forces he had documented during the entire campaign. As he wolfed down the food, barely registering its taste or texture, Corax added an appendix detailing the enemy forces and tactics he had seen on Isstvan, and a few more notes regarding the fleet movements observed as they had fled the star system.

His account complete, he sealed the file and passed it to one of the attendants, commanding that it be taken to Malcador. The Sigillite would ensure that the information was passed on to Dorn and any others that would find it of benefit.

Writing down his experiences on Isstvan had not brought any sense of satisfaction or release. There were still so many unanswered questions, Corax could not begin to articulate them. Again and again he was left with a sense of loss and emptiness, not knowing what had turned his brothers against the Emperor.

Seeking peace and distraction, the primarch left the chambers and walked out onto the balcony overlooking the inner sea. He put aside all of the thoughts crowding into his head and tried to focus only on the ever-shifting play of light and the constant gurgle and ripple of water.

After spending some time marvelling at the beauty of the lake cavern and taking a few minutes to explore his immediate surroundings, the primarch chose to rove further afield. There were several other self-contained habitats in the vicinity, facing onto a circular plaza decorated with an abstract mosaic. All of the other residences looked empty at the moment. Corax counted twenty of them, a number that was surely not coincidence. That answered the question of how long ago they had been built, for surely a more recent construction would have numbered only eighteen.

From outside there was no way of telling one apartment suite from the other, and Corax quickly grew bored of trying to guess who might have been housed behind which doors. He was about to summon the elevator situated in a grand column at the central plaza when one of the residence servants came hurrying out.

'Lord Corax, there is a message for you!' The primarch turned back to see a woman of middle years running across the plaza. 'Lord Dorn has returned and wishes to meet with you and Malcador.'

At that moment a chime sounded from the elevator and a panel in the marble-like pillar slid open to reveal a captain in the livery of the Imperial Fists.

'That would be your guide, Lord Corax,' said the servant. 'Sorry for the delay in finding you.'

'No matter,' said Corax.

The Imperial Fist slapped a hand to his chest in salute and bowed his head as Corax stepped into the elevator. The door closed, enveloping the primarch and legionary in a soft blue glow of artificial light.

'Where am I going to meet my brother?' asked Corax.

'Malcador will host you in the Hall of Victories, lord,' replied the captain. 'It will only take a few minutes to get there.'

They said nothing further to each other as the elevator continued to descend, dropping several kilometres into the heart of Terra. Eventually the conveyance slowed and Corax estimated that they were some distance below sea level. A short distance from the shaft the Imperial Fist brought him in front of a massive set of double doors, each gilded and engraved, showing a picture of a man and a woman facing each other. On the left door, the woman held a babe in the crook of one arm and a sword in her hand, her hair flowing like a waterfall, mingling with a billowing dress that in turn merged with the long grass at her feet. On the right, the man, dressed in a worker's overalls, a chain with the crossed lightning bolt of Unification hanging around his neck, had a wrench in one hand and a pistol in the other, looking to the skies. Between them burned a stylised star, surrounded by other pinpricks in the sky.

Ornate scrollwork held a caption across the heavens, in one of the Terran languages of old. Corax had not been much of a scholar and had studied little of pre-Imperial Terran culture, unlike many of his brothers. He had felt little interest in the past, preferring to concentrate his thoughts and actions on the proper shaping of the future. Despite that, he could instinctively decipher the emblazoned message, crudely translating it as *'People of Earth, Together.'*

The doors opened easily at Corax's push, swinging silently inwards to reveal a hall several hundred metres long. Corax was surprised to see arched windows along the wall to his right, with sunlight streaming through them.

Given the name of the place, Corax had expected to see lines of battle honours and banners, displays of armour and weapons lining the walls. Instead there were many glass cabinets varying from those small enough to fit in Corax's palm to some the size of battle tanks, arranged in rows across the hall, each containing an object from across the galaxy and dating back centuries, millennia, tens of millennia.

Stepping up the nearest cabinet, Corax stooped to

examine the contents. He felt a tingle of static and heard the faint buzz of a stasis field generator. Enclosed within was a small circuit board, its function unknown. On the stand below, a small steel plate etched with plain text revealed its importance:

Navigational Circuit from the first warp-capable starship

Corax stepped back in surprise. Intrigued, he turned around and found himself looking at the skeletal form of a wheeled vehicle, barely large enough for a normal man to sit inside. Its balloon tyres made up the greater part of its bulk. Corax stepped up to examine the title plate.

Titan Rover

The primarch was not sure what to make of it. It certainly looked like no Titan ever produced by the Mechanicum, which were towering war machines tens of metres high. He looked more closely at the vehicle, but could not see anything that might be a weapon mount.

With a grunt of confusion, he moved on, eyes passing over various technological artefacts and coming to rest on a glass tube filled with a pulsating liquid coloured a deep blue, located about a dozen metres further down the hall. The words beneath, though written in Imperial Gothic, might well have been an alien or lost language, for all the sense Corax could make of them.

Mendelian Eukaryotic Genesis Formula

Raking his fingers through his hair, which had slipped across his face, Corax straightened, bringing something else into his eyeline. It was a small cabinet, less than half a metre to each face, but its positioning on the central aisle seemed to mark it out as of particular importance.

Within was a broken piece of pottery. It was utterly unremarkable, shattered into eight curved shards of crude unpainted clay, marked with fingerprints and dents. Piercing the parts together in his mind, Corax worked out that it was a bowl of some kind.

He heard the whisper of the doors opening and turned back to see Malcador entering the hall, striding with purpose. His face was flushed with blood, his eyes bright and alert.

'What is this place?' Corax asked. 'What manner of victories are celebrated?'

'The most important kind,' said the Sigillite, joining Corax beside the shattered bowl. He pointed with a skeletal finger at the contents of the cabinet. 'One of the first pieces of pottery ever made by human hand. Hundreds of thousands of years old.'

'It doesn't seem like much of an achievement, compared to some of the things in here,' said Corax. 'It's so simple, a child could make it.'

'And yet perhaps one of the most important advances in our entire history, Corax,' said Malcador. 'Without this bowl, without the mind that devised it and the hands that shaped it, the rest of the hall would be empty. We have come a long, long way since one of our ancestors noticed a certain type of mud hardening in the sun and decided to make something, but without a first step, no journey is ever begun.'

'All of these are technological achievements? First steps into new epochs of human history?'

'Most are technological or scientific, a few are cultural,' said Malcador. He waved his hand towards the far end of the hall where a number of paintings, statues, carvings, tapestries and other works of art were stored.

Before the primarch could investigate, the doors opened again, revealing a figure almost as tall as Corax and broader at the shoulders. Rogal Dorn's white-blond hair was cropped short and spiked, framing his weathered features like a corona. He was dressed in demi-armour: chest, shins and forearms protected by plates and sheaths of golden metal etched with swirling designs similar to those on Corax's own suit. A cloak of deep red reached down to Dorn's ankles, held with a clasp shaped into a clenched fist on his left shoulder, pinned with a brooch in the form of the Imperial aquila on the right. He wore a skirt of golden mail that hung to his knees, and at the primarch's waist was a belt that held a chainsword with fang-like teeth and a holstered bolter. Dorn's hands were covered by segmented gauntlets of gold, each knuckle embedded with a sizeable ruby. His skin was leathery and heavily tanned, covered by traceries of thin scars and brand marks.

'Brother!' Dorn called out with a hand raised in greeting, his voice booming down the hall, disturbing the air of quiet reverence.

The two primarchs met and clasped wrist-to-wrist in welcome. Dorn slapped a hand to Corax's shoulder and smiled briefly.

'I promised I would be here today,' said Dorn.

'As ever, your word is as secure as the fortresses you raise,' replied Corax, stepping back and releasing his grip on his gene-brother. Dorn's expression darkened.

'I hope that my latest work proves equal to the task.'

'Your work is as exceptional as ever, Rogal,' said Malcador. He waved for them to accompany him to the line of benches beneath the high windows. 'There is not another in the galaxy the Emperor would want to raise up his walls for him.'

Corax stopped before sitting and looked out of the windows. Beyond was a wide valley, which appeared to be made entirely of metal. Glancing up, he saw the dull sky several hundred metres above. The entire edifice was delved into a deep fissure and continued to stretch below out of sight, storey after storey of windows and walkways, the divide criss-crossed by covered bridges, curving railway tracks and black roads.

'The clerical tenements,' explained Malcador, peering

past Corax. 'Three million men and women devoted to the administration of Terra and the Sol system.'

'Three million? For one system?' Corax could not believe what he heard. 'Why so many?'

'Oh, that's just a fraction of the civil population, Corvus,' said the Sigillite. 'It's barely enough to keep track of all the comings and goings here. Most of the others live in the service towers over at the Chivolan Heights, about seven hundred million of them.'

'It is barracks space that concerns me more,' said Dorn, lowering himself to the dark blue couch. 'Your army of scribes and auditors are not going to keep Horus at bay.'

'Give them guns and I am sure they will do their best,' countered the Sigillite, sitting on the next bench.

'I've already sent your honour guard to the new garrison quarters not far from here,' Dorn told Corax as the Raven Guard primarch continued to look out of the window. 'There is room for several thousand more, once the rest of your Legion arrives.'

Corax turned, eyebrows raised in surprise.

'You think I'm bringing the Raven Guard here?'

'Where else would they go? By the sounds of it, there are barely enough of you to make Deliverance look inhabited. We need every warrior we can to defend Terra. Captain Noriz tells me that you had one thousand, seven hundred and fourteen legionaries and other ranks on board *Avenger*. How many more can I factor into my plans to arrive from Deliverance?'

'You are getting ahead of yourself, brother,' Corax said, crossing his arms. 'I came here to see the Emperor and will seek his permission to launch attacks against the traitors.'

'Unwise,' muttered Malcador, obviously to himself yet not quiet enough to avoid Corax's keen hearing. The primarch rounded on Malcador.

'I am not staying here to get trapped like a rat in a

hole,' snapped Corax. He calmed down and looked at Dorn again. 'You know how we fight, brother. We were never expert at manning a tower or trench line. If the Raven Guard are to play their part, we need freedom to operate without our backs to a wall.'

'Impossible,' said Dorn. 'Like it or not, I must insist that your Legion be stationed here to bolster the defence of the Emperor. Horus will be coming here, make no mistake about that. Our first duty – our *only* duty – is the protection of Terra. What damage do you think you can do on your own? You have, what, three thousand warriors? Horus now has many hundred times that number, and who can say how his ranks might swell? Your place is here, on Terra, like it or not.'

'I like it not, and I do not care what you insist,' said Corax, infuriated by Dorn's assumption that the primarch of the Raven Guard would demurely acquiesce to his demand. 'I swore my oath to the Emperor, not to you, and nor to you Malcador, before you start claiming any authority as regent.'

Dorn and the Sigillite said nothing as Corax stepped away from the windows, one hand rubbing at his brow in agitation. The Raven Guard primarch stopped his pacing and turned back to the others, hand held out in conciliation.

'Why do you assume that Horus must attack Terra?' Corax asked.

'If he wishes to depose the Emperor and claim the galaxy for himself, there is no other way,' said Malcador.

'We will not allow that to happen,' added Dorn.

'You misunderstand me,' said Corax. 'You assume that Horus will reach Terra. You have already surrendered the initiative to our enemy and now run around making the best you can of the time he will allow you. We need to strike back fast, dull any momentum he has gained from the massacre at Isstvan, and stop this rebellion in its infancy.'

'That was why you were sent to Isstvan,' said Malcador, sighing heavily. 'It is you who does not understand the situation fully. Horus has the allegiance of his own Legion, the Word Bearers, the Alpha Legion, the Iron War–'

'I know the faces of the traitors, I saw them first hand at Isstvan,' snarled Corax. 'We are not without allies. The Khan and his White Scars, the Lion with the First. What of the Ultramarines and the Thousand Sons?'

There followed an uncomfortable silence, while Dorn and Malcador exchanged a worried glance. The primarch gave Malcador a slight nod.

'The Thousand Sons cannot be numbered amongst those loyal to Terra,' said the Sigillite. 'I won't go into details, but Magnus proved his untrustworthiness and has been dealt with. Leman Russ and his Legion were despatched to bring Magnus to account for breaking the Nikaea Decree.'

'What does that mean?' said Corax.

'What happened is uncertain so far,' said Dorn, his tone blunt. 'The Wolves of Fenris were over-zealous. They have destroyed Prospero and wiped out the Thousand Sons.'

'What would you expect, unleashing the Wolf King like that?' said Corax.

'If that were true, our woes would be lessened,' said Malcador, his gaze moving between Corax and Dorn. 'Only this morning I have reports from Prospero that Magnus and some of his Legion escaped the attack. I fear the numbers of our enemies will be swelled by Russ's headstrong actions rather than reduced. Though there is no great kinship between Magnus and Horus, it seems we have given them a common foe '

Dorn let out a growl of irritation, his fist thumping

down onto the fabric of the bench. The primarch stood up and stared at Corax.

'Every warrior will count,' said Dorn. 'We need you on Terra. We cannot stop Horus coming here. Accept that as fact and bring your Legion to the defence.'

'Not unless the Emperor himself commands it,' said Corax, once more pacing back and forth in front of the other two, driven by agitation. 'I will not sit idle while Horus and our other traitorous brothers bide their time and ready themselves for the battle. They must be harangued and harried, made to pay swiftly for what they have done. They will be brimming with supreme confidence at the moment. I will puncture their pride and show them that they have not won yet.'

Corax stopped and fixed his glare upon Dorn.

'I trust no one more than you, brother, to see the Emperor safe, but I do not have your confidence or patience. I must fight back and hurt the traitors, for what they have done to my Legion.'

'A personal vendetta?' said Malcador.

'An act of defiance,' replied Corax. 'There are those that Horus will try to recruit. He can virtually guarantee them victory at the moment, with no evidence to counter his claims. I will send a message across the Imperium that the Emperor and his Legions have not abandoned them.'

The Raven Guard primarch spun away and strode towards the doors.

'Where are you going?' Dorn called out, standing up.

'To see the Emperor!' Corax snarled in reply.

'He won't see you, Corax, do not disturb him,' Malcador cried out, hurrying after the departing primarch.

Corax hauled open the doors and found himself confronted by a contingent of Malcador's Custodian bodyguard.

'You,' he snapped, pointing to their leader. 'Take me to the Emperor.'

The Custodian said nothing, but turned his head to look at Malcador as he came up beside Corax.

'This is unwise, Corax,' the Sigillite said.

'Be sensible, brother,' said Dorn, laying a hand on Corax's arm. The Raven Guard pulled away from his brother's grip.

'I am primarch of the Raven Guard, son of the Emperor,' said Corax. 'It is my right! Take me to the Emperor now, or I will find him myself.'

Dorn met his glare with a doubtful expression, his hand straying to the hilt of the chainsword at his hip in warning.

'Enough! I will brook no dispute in my palace.'

Corax and Dorn looked at Malcador, who had spoken, though the voice was deep and resonant, unlike the whisper of the Sigillite. Malcador's eyes shone with golden light, his face a mask of beatific happiness. His lips moved again, as though divorced from the rest of his body, and he held out a gnarled hand surrounded by a shimmering aura.

'My Emperor?' Dorn lowered to one knee and bowed his head. 'I am sorry for causing conflict.'

'Do you not share your brother's shame?' said the voice through Malcador's flesh as the Sigillite's golden eyes turned on the primarch of the Raven Guard.

'My apologies, father,' said Corax, dropping to one knee beside Dorn.

Malcador's form leaned forwards and rested his palm atop Corax's head.

'Heed my wisdom.'

Light and warmth pierced Corax's thoughts, blinding him to all else.

FOR A MOMENT, Corax glimpsed a vast chamber. The hall was filled with machinery: coiling pipes and cables snaked across the floor and walls from banks of equipment set with thousands of dials and gauges. The air was thick with ozone, the rattle and hum of generators making the floor throb underfoot. Transformers crackled with energy and pistons thudded in the distant shadows.

In the glimmer of light and dark, Corax could see hundreds of robed figures attending to the machinery. Beneath red cowls he spied half-machine faces and from scarlet sleeves protruded limbs of metal and wire.

Corax took all of this in at a glance, his eye being drawn to the strange but magnificent edifice at the centre of the hall. It was a gigantic, towering dais, stretching away to the far wall, sheathed in gold that reflected the thousands of surrounding lights and inlaid with silvery circuitry. Dozens of cables and pipelines connected the dais to the accompanying machines and electricity thrummed across its surface. A huge pair of doors was set into the base of the plinth, large enough to allow a tank or even one of the Mechanicum's scout Titans to pass through.

Yet it was not this that fixed the primarch's gaze.

The upper part of the building was fashioned in the form of an immense chair, ringed about by sparking conduits and pulsing energy fields. Seated in the chair was the Emperor, garbed in golden armour, his head bowed with eyes tightly shut in fierce concentration. Waves of purple and blue energy flowed across his skin, a miniature lightning storm playing about his furrowed brow.

As Corax watched, a single bead of glittering sweat broke from the Emperor's brow and fell like a golden droplet from his cheek. The Emperor's jaw was clenched, either from effort or pain. The primarch had never seen his father look as he did now, and he felt a moment of worry.

The scene faded, replaced by a landscape suffused with light. It seemed to exist nowhere, formed of the light and nothing more. At the heart of the glare the Emperor was sitting as he was before, though now he was upon a golden throne that blazed with energy. A giant eagle sat atop its back, two-headed, glaring at Corax with ruby eyes. The Emperor's face was calm here, showing no evidence of the strain the primarch had glimpsed before. The Master of Mankind seemed to be in deep meditation, unmoving on his seat of gold.

'Father, my Emperor, it is Corvus,' he said, lowering himself to one knee. 'If you can hear me, please heed my words. My Legion is all but dead and our enemies grow stronger with each passing day. I would know what you would wish me to do. It is in my heart to strike back at these traitors, to shed their blood as they have shed mine. All I ask is your blessing on this endeavour and I shall take the battle to the foe with righteousness in my heart and your glory in my mind.'

There was no change in the Emperor's demeanour.

'Father! Hear me!' In his straining, Corax felt his wounds reopening under his armour, thick blood trickling down his side. He ignored the surge of pain. 'The Raven Guard will fight to the last to protect the Imperial Truth. We are not so strong as once we were, but we will lay down each life left to us in your defence. But I need your help. Please, give me your wisdom, grant me your guidance.'

He broke down, collapsing as a wave of fatigue washed through him. For more than three hundred days he had fought back the injuries of Isstvan, pushing himself on. At first his Legion had needed him. Later, he had held on for this moment, enduring his agony in silence so that he might come before the Emperor and seek his lord's command.

He had failed.

He had failed on Isstvan and he had failed here. Blood was leaking from his many wounds, as if in response to the hurt he felt in his psyche. With it, his vigour died and his will faded.

'Son.'

That one word resounded across the glowing firmament, echoing and rebounding, filling Corax's thoughts even as the sound came to his ear.

The Emperor's eyes were open, glittering orbs of gold that bored into Corax's soul. Motes of golden energy danced in those orbs, but their look was not without kindness. The Emperor stood, his armour melting away into wisps of golden threads to be replaced by robes of flowing silver that cascaded from his body like an argent waterfall.

The Emperor stood, seeming diminished in size, but not presence, by the removal of his armour. Particles churned as smoke, forming insubstantial steps that allowed the Emperor to descend as effortlessly as a normal man walks down a flight of stairs.

The Emperor reached out a hand and Corax felt hot fingers upon his brow. Energy flowed through the primarch, knitting his shattered bones, stemming his pouring blood, healing wounded muscles and organs. The primarch gasped, filled with love and adoration.

'Stand.' Corax did as the Emperor commanded, his strength restored.

'I am sorry, father,' said Corax, dropping to his knees once more. 'I know that your labours are important, but I have to speak with you.'

'Of course you do, Corvus,' said the Emperor. The majesty and power had gone from his voice, leaving only a tone of respect and admiration. 'You have endured much to come here.'

Corax felt a hand on his arm and he straightened under the Emperor's guidance. His father appeared less majestic, the light dimming beneath his skin, his face taking on the features of a normal man with brown eyes while long, dark hair flowed from his scalp.

'Is this your true face?' asked Corax.

'I have no such thing,' replied the Emperor. 'I have worn a million faces over the millennia, according to need or whim.'

'I remember this one,' said Corax, dimly recalling a dream he had glimpsed when overcome by his wounds in the crashing Thunderhawk. 'This was how you appeared to me when I was born within my pod.'

'Yes, it is strange that you should remember that,' said the Emperor. His expression became sterner. 'What do you wish to ask of me, my son?'

'The Raven Guard verge on being a spent force, but I would rebuild them if I had the chance,' said Corax. 'Yet I cannot spare a warrior from the fighting to come, nor the time to raise up a new generation of the Legion. I seek your permission to launch attacks against the traitors, to mark our final passing in the glory of battle.'

'You wish to sacrifice your Legion?' The Emperor seemed genuinely surprised. 'In what cause?'

'I do not do it out of woe but necessity,' explained Corax. 'I must atone for the failure at Isstvan, for it will tear me apart as surely as my wounds did, if allowed to fester in my heart. Forgive me, but I cannot defend Terra, idly awaiting my fate to come to me.'

The Emperor did not reply for some time, his brow creased slightly with deep thought. Corax waited patiently, eyes fixed to the Emperor's face.

'I concur,' the Master of Mankind said eventually. 'It is in your nature to cry havoc and wreak the same upon your foes. Yet there is no need for sacrifice. I am reluctant, but you have my trust, Corvus. I will grant you a gift, a very precious gift.'

Once more the Emperor reached out his hand and laid it upon Corax's head.

For an eternity Corax was overwhelmed by the mind of the Emperor. An existence that had spanned more than thirty millennia tried to crowd into the primarch's thoughts, sending pain searing through him.

In a moment the pain had ceased, the imprint upon his memories a shard of what had come before, the tiniest fraction of the Emperor's being. Still reeling from the psychic onslaught, Corax wondered if this was how the astrotelepaths felt during the Soul Binding, their minds conjoined with the psychic might of the Emperor.

Flashes of new memories coursed through his thoughts, blocking out all other sensation, a succession of images burnt into his psyche. The primarch's body quaked with the sensation, rebelling against the patterns and images thrust into his brain.

He could smell the tang of cleansing fluids, and hear the buzz of machines and the hiss of respiration devices. Corax glimpsed metal cylinders with glass viewplates, arranged in a circle at the heart of a clinically sterile chamber, a maze of wires and pumps and tubes splaying from each steel sarcophagus.

The primarch did not just see the scene, he was part of it, speaking to a white-coated technician in a language he did not understand. There were other orderlies, with cloth face masks and tight hoods drawn over their heads, their hands gloved in white.

Corax walked amongst the incubators, noting at a glance the digital displays plugged into each, satisfied with the life signs beeping and chiming from each device. He felt enormous satisfaction.

There was still much to do. The physical bodies were being nourished, their superhuman forms each developing over the genetic matrix inlaid inside each chamber. They were only empty shells though, and the greatest part of the project was yet to come. Their nascent brains were ripe for the template integration.

Even as he had these thoughts, Corax did not understand them. More arcane and technical phrases came to him, their meaning lost in the translation to his mind. Yet for all their complexity, the primarch felt on the verge of recognition.

Like his brothers, Corax's intellect was as enhanced as his body and his brain was a vast repository of knowledge, both military and technical. There was something new in there as well, placed at the same time as the memories. In his mind's eye he saw genetic splicing and hybridisation calculations, and understood now that the Mendelian eukaryotic genesis formula was the first ever successfully cloned human gene-code.

He understood the mechanics behind his own creation and marvelled at the ingenuity of the mind that had conceived of them. There were areas that were left blank though, intentionally he assumed. Details of the parts of the Emperor's own genetic strand that were employed in the creation of the primarchs. Obviously the Emperor did not trust Corax that much.

There were other memories too: the dismantling of the laboratory after the strange warp phenomena that had swept away the incubators and scattered them across the galaxy. Corax saw it being reassembled in another place, far from prying eyes.

He knew where that place was.

CORAX REALISED HIS eyes were closed and opened them. The Emperor was watching him, waiting patiently for his son to explore the gift he had given him.

'You have given me the secrets of the primarch project?' said Corax, his voice a whisper of amazement.

'The parts that were relevant to the creation of the Legions, yes,' said the Emperor. He did not smile. 'I must return to the webway, my absence will be sorely missed. That is all the help I can offer you.'

'The webway?'

'A portal into the warp, of sorts,' said the Emperor. 'This is my great endeavour. Beyond the veil of reality, the forces of the Imperium wage war with a foe just as deadly as the Legions of Horus. Daemons.'

Corax knew the word, but did not understand why the Emperor had used it.

'Daemons?' said Corax. 'Insubstantial creatures of nightmare? I thought they were a fiction.'

'No, in truth they do exist,' said the Emperor. 'The warp, the other-realm we use to travel, is their home, their world. Horus's treachery is greater than you imagine. He has aligned himself to the powers of the warp, the so-called "Gods of Chaos". The daemons are now his allies and they seek to breach the Imperial Palace from within. My warriors fight to hold back the incursion, lest Terra be overrun with a tide of Chaos.'

'I still do not understand,' admitted Corax.

'You do not have to,' said the Emperor. 'Know only that my time is scarce and my power bent towards securing our ultimate victory over these immaterial foes. It is to you, and your brothers who have remained true to their oaths, that the physical defence of the Imperium must fall. I have shown you the way by which the Raven Guard might rise from the ashes of their destruction and again fight for mankind.'

'It is an incredible gift,' said Corax, 'but even with this I am not sure what you intend for me to do.'

'I have already informed Malcador of my intent and he gathers such aides and companions as you will need to recover the gene-tech,' said the Emperor. 'You asked me for help, but now you must help yourself. Rebuild the Raven Guard. Strike down the traitors and let them know that my will shall still be done.'

'Yes, I shall,' said Corax, bowing his head and lowering to one knee. 'The Raven Guard will rise from the grave of defeat and bring you victory.'

'I not only give you the gift of these memories and this technology, I place upon you the burden of its protection. You will have the power to create armies as I once did, and that in itself would be reason enough to jealously guard its existence. More than that, the gene-store contains the means to destroy what it created. That which I bound within the fibre of every Space Marine can be undone, unravelling their strength and purpose at a stroke.'

'I understand,' said Corax. 'I will defend it with my life.'

'No, you must swear more than that, Corvus,' said the Emperor, his voice becoming aggressive, his words sending a surge of energy through Corax. 'Swear to me that should our enemies learn of its existence, you will destroy it, and everything created by it. It is too dangerous to keep if there is even the possibility that Horus might take it. With its power he could unleash devastation even greater than you can imagine, and raise up such a force that no defence Rogal might build could withstand it. Swear that oath to me.'

'I swear, as your son and servant,' said Corax, trembling with the ferocity of the Emperor's demanding voice.

'Even if it means the destruction of the Raven Guard and all that you have striven to build?' The Emperor's words were like an implacable storm, pushing into Corax's mind, demanding obedience.

'Even so.'

The Emperor turned away and walked back towards the Golden Throne. The light consumed him once more, burning through his flesh, his robes forming the hard edges of armour. He stopped just before the throne and looked back at Corax.

'One other thing, my son,' he said, calmly and slowly. 'The gene-tech is protected. Only I can deactivate the defences in person, but I cannot spare the time away from this place to do so. I am sure with the knowledge I have given to you that you will find a way through.'

Corax said nothing as an aura of golden light surrounded the Emperor, lifting him up to the seat of the Golden Throne. The Master of Mankind grew in stature once more, as armoured plates slid into place and his form was again encased in the golden aegis that Corax had seen on many battlefields.

The Emperor closed his eyes and with a pulse of energy that rocked the whole chamber, sparks flew and psychic energy danced, embroiling the seated figure in a storm of power.

CORAX CAME TO his senses, lying on a marbled floor with Dorn and Malcador bent over him, still not sure he believed what had passed. The memories were there, embedded in his brain, like a vault of treasures to be unlocked, and he clung to them as proof of the Emperor's will.

'Thank you, father,' Corax said. He looked up at Malcador, who nodded in understanding.

'You have been set a difficult task, Corax,' said the Sigillite. 'We should begin your preparations.'

STEAM AND OTHER vapours filled the sub-level chamber with distorting clouds and whorls of gas. The thump of heavy machinery made the whole basement shudder every few seconds, setting the cable bundles on the wall rattling and sending the glow-globes circling in eccentric orbits about their hanging wires.

It was certainly not the most pleasant location for a lair, and by far one of the noisiest Omegon had ever inhabited, but it served its purpose well. Situated below the forges of the Wellmetal district of Kiavahr's largest city, Nabrik, the four adjoining rooms occupied by the

primarch of the Alpha Legion were at the heart of the
old industrial complex from which the technocrats had
ruled the world before the coming of the Emperor.

These days the furnace rooms and manufactories bore
the symbols of the Mechanicum of Mars, but for thousands of years before their coming, Kiavahr had been a
powerhouse of weapons manufacture and shipbuilding.
The old tech-guilds had divided their planet's resources
between them and each taken to themselves rulership
of Kiavahr, trading very successfully with the few neighbouring systems that had been within reach during Old
Night.

It had been a blow to the prestige of the tech-guild
when Corax had led the rebellion of the mining colony
of Lycaeus, Kiavahr's largest moon; further insult had
been added to this gratuitous injury when the Emperor
had arrived and the tech-guilds had been sworn in as
members of the Imperium. Had they known then that
the Martians would dismantle their monopoly and re-
order their society, the tech-guilds might have resisted
further.

Omegon was pleased that they had not fought to the
last. Enough of them remained alive, kept from death
over the decades by inhuman augmentations and anti-
ageing narcotics – many of them now illegal under the
regime of the Mechanicum – that he had a ready core of
resentment from which to recruit. He had been here for
less than a hundred days and already he had established
contact with three of the surviving tech-guild overseers.
Progress had been swift, their agreement to cooperate in
the liberation of Kiavahr quickly accomplished.

With the network of the Alpha Legion spreading across
the forge-world, both in terms of Omegon's own operatives and the agents of the tech-guilds, he was confident
that the remaining five houses of the old rulers, those
who had some surviving scion hidden away amongst the

smoke and flames of the irradiated wastelands, would soon add their support.

Omegon had little interest in the freeing of Kiavahr from the Emperor's clutches, except insomuch as it would inconvenience his enemies and prove to be the downfall of Corax. Though the Kiavahrans measured themselves amongst the highest in terms of technical accomplishment, they were in truth of only average ability and output in comparison to many of the Mechanicum's forge-worlds. The primarch was ever quick to further inflate the bloated self-esteem of the tech-guilders though, and with promises and veiled assertions he had led them to believe that once they had thrown off the yoke of Imperial tyranny – he had used that phrase so often of late – the Kiavahrans would be the equal of Mars.

Sitting beneath a scalding hot pipe, nestled between a reactor feed core and a colossal drive shaft, Omegon opened up a tripod on the bare floor in front of him and set upon it a small communications device about the size of his fist.

He keyed in a sequence of frequency ciphers from memory – cracking the security protocols of the Mechanicum's on-world communications network had taken him five whole days of calculations – and began to set up the signal. He routed the transmission through fifteen different sub-stations, bounced the carrier wave from two orbiting stations, established three dead-end backtrace locations, including one on Deliverance for his own amusement, and finally entered his personal command code check.

As Omegon worked, he felt a measure of contentment. While he had no preference regarding the existence or extinction of Corax and his Legion in themselves, their removal, and the securing of the Terran tech which the Cabal had assured they would come in possession of,

would be a step closer towards achieving the aim of the
twin primarchs. If Horus were to be given the greatest
chance of success, the Emperor had to be isolated. In
their death, the Raven Guard would provide further
means for that to be accomplished.

Satisfied that only the most diligent search would
indicate he was hijacking the constant datastream that
criss-crossed the Mechanicum's new estate, Omegon
finally punched in the frequency address of Iyadine
Nethri, his contact within the White Iron guild.

The communicator crackled for a while and then an
affirmative beep told the primarch that the connection had been established. His eyes went to the small
schematic readout on the front of the communicator,
assuring himself that the transmission was free from
monitoring. He pressed the acceptance key.

'Councillor Effrit, I was expecting contact earlier.'
Nethri's voice was muffled from the many layers of
compression and encryption through which the transmission was being squeezed. 'I hope that nothing is
amiss.'

'All is well,' replied Omegon. His voice as it would
emerge at the other end of the line would be nothing
like his own, modulated and warped several times over
to eradicate any trace of his identity. 'I had to confirm
certain orders and agreements.'

Omegon had not had to do any such thing, but
was masquerading as an intermediary rather than the
orchestrator of this particular coup-in-waiting.

'We are ready to make our report to the revolutionary
council,' said Nethri.

'Go ahead,' said Omegon, smiling. He had created
three different cells, one for each of the guilds already
sworn to his cause, and while he waited, intelligence
from the Alpha Legionnaires hidden in the Raven
Guard had sent them on all manner of inconsequential

missions and information-gathering expeditions. It was good to keep them occupied and distracted, and also necessary to test their competence and security procedures. So far his operatives had done well, and the Kiavahran authorities had no reason to suspect anything was wrong with their world.

'The storage bays at Pharsalika have been emptied of their usual promethium consignments. We are investigating to what purpose. Coldron Diaminex has been promoted to Vice-Regent of the Augmetical Society. He was one of the most vocal political opponents of the Imperium before compliance.'

Omegon continued to listen as more pointless trivia was rambled out to him by Nethri, until one particular piece of information piqued his curiosity.

'Please repeat that last section,' he said.

'Output from manufactorum thirty-eight has been re-routed to manufactorum twenty-six, councillor,' Nethri said again.

'Confirmed,' said Omegon. Manufactorum thirty-eight had been employed since the coming of the Raven Guard in the construction of power armour energy conduits. That the factory had ceased production was intriguing, and ran counter to Omegon's expectation. He would have thought that all elements of armour production would have increased since the massacre, but the opposite was proving true. For the last eighteen days, production was being scaled down.

'Any reason given as to why this has happened?' he asked.

'We are not sure, councillor. There has been an increase in astrotelepathic traffic through the Cortex Spire, and I have heard gossip that a new armour design is being awaited.'

'Understood,' said Omegon. He checked the passive interference monitor again. There was still no sign the transmission had been detected. The primarch could not bring himself to listen to the rest of the agent's interminable report and so asked for the only piece of information he considered pertinent. 'What news of the Raven Guard? Is there any sign of Corax?'

'There is no news concerning the usurper, councillor,' replied Nethri. 'Current reports show only those ships and personnel previously communicated to you. We have not heard of anything that would suggest when, or if, he intends or is able to return.'

'Very well. Please submit the rest of your report by standard data packet. Ending transmission.'

He cut the link and set about dismantling the maze of communications loops and checks he had erected. While he did this, he used his Legion transmitter to contact Verson. The operative answered within moments.

'We need an operative inside manufactorum thirty-eight,' he said.

'Understood,' replied Verson. 'I'll have someone in place by moonfall.'

There was no need to say anything further and the communicator buzzed and fell silent.

Having completed his shut-down, Omegon dismantled the communicator and stowed it in a hip-sack that he slung onto his belt as he stood. He wore the red robes of a Mechanicum acolyte, and put on a silver and pearl mask to conceal his face before pulling up the gold-trimmed hood. Amongst a populace that contained vat-grown slaves, half-machine servitors and the augmetically-enchanced, Omegon's size would not be worthy of remark. Even so, when forced to move openly, he travelled only during the 'tween-shift hours and through the areas of least traffic. It was better to be certain than sorry.

It was time to quit his uncomfortable environs and move on to the next safe area. Two days was long enough to be staying in one place. He already had his next location in mind.

SEVEN

Servant of Terra
To the Mountain
Hold Fire

MARCUS VALERIUS BLINKED hard, his thoughts clouded with a vision of a golden panorama and the echoes of a resonant voice whose words he could not quite understand. His temples throbbed painfully and his eyes ached for some reason he could not fathom. The voice in the praefector's head changed, becoming more mundane and insistent, close at hand.

'Are you all right, praefector?'

Blinking again, Valerius focused on the man in front of him. It was Pelon. After-images of golden eyes faded from memory, replaced by the manservant's plain features.

'Yes, I am fine,' said Marcus, rubbing his brow with his knuckles. He turned and looked out of the metres-thick plasglass at the ship tethered alongside the viewing gallery.

His strange daydream becoming more unreal with each passing second, Marcus felt a moment of pride as he looked at the *Servant of Terra III*, lit by the dock lights against the shadowed orb of Terra. His new command, it was nothing more than a messenger cutter, smaller than a destroyer, but still large enough to boast a warp-capable engine. His requisition had been fast-tracked through the station's official channels, countersigned by Corax himself, and the refitted cutter had been found to take him back to Therion.

'The shuttle will be here in five minutes, praefector,' said Pelon.

Valerius turned his head and saw his manservant being followed by a motorised trolley, steered by the half-form of a servitor. Several chests and bags were piled on the bed of the trolley.

'Is all of that mine?' said Valerius, startled by the amount of luggage. 'We have a cutter, not a bulk hauler!'

'Most of it is supplies I have managed to acquire whilst on the station, praefector,' confessed Pelon. The trolley whined to a stop beside Valerius. 'I spoke with one of the crew of the *Namedian Star*, which arrived this morning. The warp storms have been continuing. I thought it better to prepare for a long journey. Even before the storms, it would have taken us forty days or more to reach Therion.'

'Very good,' said Marcus. His sigh made a lie of the words.

'What is wrong, praefector?' Pelon shot an accusing glance at the baggage. 'Have I forgotten something?'

'Not at all, Pelon. Your attention to your duties, as ever, is nothing less than absolute.' Valerius glanced up and down the gallery and saw they were alone. He felt an odd sensation of anti-climax. His visit to Terra had been short and uneventful, his time taken up with administrative work concerning the loss of his regiment. 'I must admit to mixed feelings about our return to Therion. My command has been destroyed and I return in ignominy.'

'Far from it, praefector,' replied Pelon. He rummaged through the bags and produced a small silver flask and cup. The manservant poured a measure of dark red liquid from the flask and handed it to Valerius. 'If not for you, the Raven Guard would have been wiped out.'

'But nobody can know that, or at least my part it in,' said Valerius, keeping his voice hushed. 'Branne was right, the dreams that led to our rescue attempt will be viewed with suspicion.'

'Then it is with admirable humility that you must bear the secret, praefector,' said Pelon. 'It was not to further your own fame that you went to Isstvan.'

'They'll strip me of my praefecture, Pelon,' said Valerius, with another deep sigh. 'I would not blame them. I have proven myself a less than competent commander.'

'Again, I think your modesty does you injustice, praefector. The sacrifice of your command was a terrible but necessary thing to do. Had Commander Branne not insisted on your staying on the *Avenger*, I am sure you would have proudly led the diversionary attack in person. To preserve life when its sacrifice is required is worthy, praefector, but wrong. You showed your merits in making that difficult decision.'

'That is true.' Valerius was heartened a little by his servant's assurance, though doubts lingered still. Past his reflection in the window, he saw a glimmer of light from a shuttle's engines emerging from the hull of his new ship. He turned to Pelon. 'You have the air of a philosopher about you, Pelon. Where did you learn such a thing?'

'A life below and between the decks of a warship, praefector,' Pelon said with a sly smile. 'There's enough personalities and merchantry going on there to give any man a sound understanding of politics and trade. Though I wouldn't be expecting an Imperial governorship any time soon.'

'Where is this shuttle picking us up?'

'Bay fourteen, praefector,' said Pelon. He said

something to the driver-servitor and the trolley wheeled around on its thickly tyred wheels. 'Follow me.'

Valerius took another look at the starship, and wondered if it would be the last thing he ever commanded. He took a deep breath, straightened the blood-red sash across his body and stepped out after his servant, determined to make a good first impression on his new crew. It might be his last command, but that was no excuse to make it a bad one.

IN A SECLUDED valley a few kilometres from the mountain keep where Corax had met with Malcador and Dorn, three ornithopters and two bulk-lifters waited on the main apron of the terminus. Sleeting rain drenched their metal hulls and formed small lakes on the wide circle of black asphalt. Distant thunder rumbled, adding to the noise of idling engines and the tramp and splash of booted feet.

The wind whipped Corax's hair across his face and drove the icy rain hard against his skin, but he did not flinch from the elements. Being raised in the claustrophobic confines of Lycaeus, he relished the outdoors, whether sun or snow, night or day. To breathe air under an open sky – even air as tainted as that of Terra –was a luxury the primarch had only dreamed of during his early years.

His Raven Guard filed quickly onto the transports, accompanied by long lines of servitors carrying weapons and equipment for the expedition. The Emperor had not been more forthcoming about the defences that protected the ancient gene-tech and so Corax had prepared for all eventualities.

Alongside the black armour of his legionaries strode twenty figures of gold: Legio Custodes led by Arcatus. Malcador had said they were assigned by the Emperor, but Corax wondered if they were not present to keep an eye on the legionaries rather than aid them. Corax had detected a degree of animosity between his Raven Guard and the Custodians, brought about by his legionaries' forced internment for the last few days. It mattered little to Corax, he was glad of any extra aid that could be offered, and if the Custodian Guard turned out to be a hindrance he could demand that Malcador recall them from the expedition, though whether that demand would be met was less certain.

A splash of red came into sight: Nexin Orlandriaz. He wore the robes of the Mechanicum, and with him came an entourage of half-machine orderlies and brain-scrubbed servitors. Malcador had assured Corax that the genetor majoris was loyal to Terra, and considered the foremost expert in genetics currently able to assist. The primarch could not process all of the information and memories implanted by the Emperor – it came to him in flashes and starts, nightmarish and fragmented – and was sure the knowledge of Nexin would prove a useful guide in unravelling the secrets of the gene-tech.

A hydraulic hiss followed by the whine of armour caused Corax to turn towards the door leading from the control tower's interior. Dorn stepped up to the parapet, now fully armoured in gold and yellow inlaid with obsidian and malachite, his gauntlets ornamented with rubies and black gemstones. Lines of concern furrowed Dorn's heavy brow.

'You have everything you need?' asked the Imperial Fists primarch.

'If not, it is too late to worry about it,' replied Corax. 'We will adapt.'

Dorn did not meet Corax's gaze, but stared out into the distance to where sheets of rain fell on the steel-girdered gantries and black-tiled roof of a half-built gun tower.

'I know that the Emperor has given his permission for this venture, but I cannot allow you to leave without asking you one more time,' he said. 'Will you not bring the Legion to Terra?'

'My mind is set,' said Corax. 'The Emperor has shown me a way to bring the Raven Guard back into the war, in a way that suits us all.'

'I don't know what it is you are after and, unlike you, I know better than to ask,' said Dorn. 'I trust the Emperor to know best.'

'That implies that you do not necessarily trust that I do.'

'If the Emperor wills it, I am agreed. I do not have doubts about you, brother. We must forever hold the Emperor's judgement as the highest there is, or we must wonder if we are nothing more than creations of vanity. He is the Master of Mankind, and he will steer us to Enlightenment.'

'He made us what we are, but I cannot divine his purpose any more,' said Corax. 'Do you think we have failed?'

'We conquered the galaxy in his name, brother. We brought humanity into the light from the darkness of Old Night. He created us for that purpose and no other.'

'The Emperor also created Horus and made him Warmaster,' countered Corax, unsettled by Dorn's words. 'He brought the likes of the Night Haunter into his plans.'

'What else could he have done?' said Dorn. 'Curze is one of us, though perhaps a victim of circumstances none of us can even imagine. I know better than anyone exactly what he is capable of.'

Corax nodded grimly. 'The likes of Curze and Angron were broken from the start. You know the ultimate sanction open to the Emperor. He could have–'

Dorn raised a hand before he could finish. 'I find your doubts disturbing, brother.' The wrinkles on his forehead deepened further in annoyance as he gazed across the shuttle port, his fists clenched by his sides. 'It is still the Emperor's will that mankind become the masters of the galaxy.'

'And we shall ensure it,' said Corax. He took hold of Dorn's arm and guided the Imperial Fist to look at him. 'I will do nothing to endanger the Imperium, brother. I just have to do this. You have not seen your Legion crushed, not heard the dying cries of thousands of your sons in a few minutes. Understand, brother, that I will do anything to destroy Horus.'

'I can tell that the Emperor showed you something of what I have also glimpsed. This war is greater than Horus. There are eternal powers out in the universe that crave dominion over mankind, that lust to turn humanity into their servants and playthings. Horus is just a figurehead. He must be destroyed, but not at a cost of losing the wider war. There can be no room for pity.'

'I have no pity for the traitors,' snapped Corax.

'No, it is self-pity that I warn you against,' Dorn replied calmly. 'Whether yourself or for others, your pity will be turned against you, and become a weapon of the enemy. You are a primarch, harden yourself to loss and woe. We were born to greatness, but we must endure tragedy.'

Corax stayed silent. He saw nothing but earnest concern in the face of Dorn, and he nodded, accepting his brother's wisdom.

'Whatever it is you are looking for, it is not worth risking your life,' said the Imperial Fist.

'Is that concern I detect?' said Corax with half a smile. 'You are becoming sentimental, Rogal.'

'Not at all,' came the other primarch's gruff reply. 'I have few enough allies as it is. To lose another would be inconvenient. You intend to leave as soon as you have retrieved your prize?'

'Yes, I must return to Deliverance as soon as possible. I will not see you again before I depart.'

'Travel well and fight hard, Corvus,' said Dorn.

'Protect the Emperor, Rogal,' replied Corax.

They clasped wrist-to-wrist, as they had greeted, and parted with a respectful nod to one another.

THE SNOW CAME in flurries, whirled about the rocky ledge by winds gusting over the shoulder of the mountain. It had taken Corax several days to find this place, guided only by snatches of the Emperor's memories. To find one mountain amongst the many had proven a difficult task, made all the harder for the decades that had changed the appearance of the peak since the Emperor had been here. Aerial survey had been all but impossible in the harsh weather, so the Raven Guard had searched on foot, a difficult mission for heavily armoured warriors forced to forge across metres-deep snow drifts that hid sheer-sided ravines and treacherous cliffs.

As the Raven Guard unloaded their equipment, the edges of the ornithopter's blades were already beginning to sparkle with accumulating ice. Agapito coordinated the disembarkation, the air thick with vapour from the mouth grilles and backpack vents of the Raven Guard as they pounded up and down the ramps, helping the servitors to speed the disembarkation and allow the shuttles to depart before their engines froze.

Alpharius did as he was asked, heaving up a crate of bolter ammunition and jogging back down the bulk hauler's gangplank. He felt no slight at performing work normally carried out by serfs and servitors, sharing with his adopted brothers some excitement at finally reaching their goal. The snow had been packed almost to ice by the comings and goings of the legionaries and their half-human servitors, but the grip of his boots was secure underfoot.

He placed the crate in the designated space and stepped aside for a moment. He caught sight of Corax standing beneath the great overhang that protected the shelf from the deluge of snow from above. The primarch appeared to be staring at a bare wall of rock.

There had been little explanation as to the purpose of the mission. Agapito had simply told the Raven Guard that they were venturing into the depths of an old storage facility to retrieve a weapon for the Legion. Alpharius had felt a thrill of achievement from this announcement. It was obvious to assume that this was the reason he had been sent to the Raven Guard. Whatever was being held in that facility – a well-protected facility judging by the amount of materiel being unloaded – was sure to be of some value to the Alpha Legion. Though he would have to confirm his conclusions with Omegon once he had reached Deliverance, Alpharius was sure that his real mission was just starting.

'It can't be that much of a big deal,' Lukar said from behind Alpharius, startling him from his thoughts.

'What?' replied Alpharius, unsure if he had missed the start of the conversation.

'Whatever is hidden here, it can't be that important,' Lukar explained.

'How so?' Sergeant Dor joined the pair of them beside the pile of crates. 'It is important enough to keep us on Terra.'

'No towers, no defence turrets, nothing to protect it at all,' said Lukar. 'If it was a big deal, this place would be more heavily guarded than Ravenspire.'

As Alpharius considered this, slightly deflated by Lukar's theory, he heard the crunch of snow underfoot and turned to see Corax looming over the group. Evidently he had overheard the exchange.

'A simplistic approach to defence,' said the primarch, looking displeased. 'Have you forgotten the doctrines of the Raven Guard?'

Lukar said nothing, glancing at Sergeant Dor in his confusion.

'The most powerful defence is to never present your-self as a target,' the sergeant said, banging a fist against the side of Lukar's helm.

'There is nothing that says "attack me" like ten kilo-metres of curtain wall and a hundred gun towers,' said Corax, glancing back at the bare cliff. 'On the other hand, a nondescript stretch of mountain pass would be the ideal place to conceal a powerful weapon.'

'Forgive my stupidity,' said Lukar, bowing his head to the primarch. 'I was not thinking clearly.'

Alpharius's eyes narrowed in suspicion behind the lenses of his helm. As yet he had not made contact with any other member of the Alpha Legion. He had no means to do so until instructed by Omegon. Lukar's mis-take hinted that he did not think in the same way as a Raven Guard. Alpharius decided to keep an eye on his squad-brother to see if there was any other cause for con-cern. If one of the Alpha Legion betrayed the presence of infiltrators, it would go ill for all of them.

'How do we get in?' asked Alpharius, seeking to change the subject and divert attention away from Lukas.

Corax looked down at the legionary.

'We knock,' the primarch said with a thin smile.

WHEN ALL HAD been unloaded and his warriors assem-bled, Corax called the expedition to order. His troops lined up in their squads, while the Custodian Guard and agents of the Mechanicum gathered in their own groups to one side.

'Though we stand on the rock of Terra, we are about to put our lives in peril,' the primarch announced. 'Ancient defence systems protect the prize we seek beneath this peak. Know that this mission we are about to perform is not only necessary for the future of our Legion, it will allow us to strike back at those who sought to destroy us. This day will live long in the annals of the Raven Guard and you will all be remembered for your role in it. The past is history. It matters not what went before. All that should concern you is how we act from now on. The future lies beyond this wall.'

Corax turned and strode towards the seemingly impenetrable cliff face. His first sight of it had triggered one of the memory-shards implanted by the Emperor. The primarch had not been joking when he had told the legionary that they would knock to enter.

The vault beyond was barred by a harmonic lock, attuned to an extremely narrow frequency of sound wave. There were certain parts of the rock that were linked to amplifiers within the structure, and the location of these had been revealed to Corax by the Emperor's memories. He raised his fist to the first area and ran through the position and timing of each blow required to generate the correct harmonic key.

He banged his gauntlet against the rock face, the blows resounding deep within the hollow beyond the cliff but muffled by the howling wind and snow.

Knock. Knock-knock knock-knock. Knock-knock.

The dull echoes faded away and Corax wondered if he had mis-timed the blows or directed them at the wrong spots. His doubt disappeared as the grinding of gears and wheeze of pneumatics shuddered across the cliff face.

The primarch stepped back as a massive portal swung inwards, two doors of solid rock several metres thick effortlessly parting, revealing a mosaic floor. The wind blew flurries of snow over the small black and red geometric designs and howled madly as it entered the cavernous space beyond.

'Wait for my command,' Corax told his warriors as he took a stride across the threshold. The Emperor's memories contained nothing that suggested the outer gate was lethally defended, but that was no guarantee of safety.

He felt the faintest of tremors and, from the knowledge passed to him by the Emperor, knew that many
kilometres below, ancient power plants had been stirred
into life by the opening of the doors. Plasma was flaring within containment fields, electricity searing along
cables and wires throughout the mountain's depths.

Lights flickered into life, ruddy strips that ran the
length of the arched ceiling, bathing the interior with a
hellish glow. The walls and ceiling ran straight ahead,
covered with slabs several metres across and engraved
with a simple lightning bolt design. At the far end, a
little less than two hundred metres into the mountain,
the hall-like chamber ended abruptly, several of the
wall-slabs replaced with gilded portals. Square pillars
lined the corridor every ten metres, decorated with
sparse geometric carvings.

Looking along the broad corridor, Corax saw that the
floor tile designs were not simply ornamentation. He
could recognise the pattern, discerning its message in a
complex numerical code; whether from the Emperor's
memory or his own knowledge he was not sure. The
tiles contained a message, a quote in an ancient Terran
tongue; probably intended only for the Emperor himself, a small conceit by the Master of Mankind. Though
it was in a long-dead language, Corax understood it.

In Egypt's sandy silence, all alone,
Stands a gigantic Leg, which far off throws
The only shadow that the Desert knows:
'I am great OZYMANDIAS,' saith the stone,
'The King of Kings; this mighty City shows
'The wonders of my hand.' The City's gone,
Nought but the Leg remaining to disclose
The site of this forgotten Babylon.
We wonder, and some Hunter may express
Wonder like ours, when thro' the wilderness

Where London stood, holding the Wolf in chase,
He meets some fragments huge, and stops to guess
What powerful but unrecorded race
Once dwelt in that annihilated place.

The primarch considered the words, but could not divine their meaning. His mentors on Lycaeus had taught him of poetry, of rhyme and metre and cadence, but he had never quite been able to see the appeal. Poems reminded him too much of the work-songs the prisoners had invented to keep up their spirits while they had hewn with pick and laser drill at the unforgiving stone of the penal colony. The last three lines left Corax feeling disquieted, though, as if the Emperor had suspected that his Imperium could not endure any more than the great empires of mankind's long history.

Questions gnawed at Corax as he signalled for his expedition to prepare to enter the vault. If the contents of this trove were so dangerous, why had the Emperor kept them? He had abandoned the primarch project after the strange scattering of his progeny by the warp-bound entities called the Primordial Chaos. This much the Emperor had explained to Corax on their first meeting. Had the Emperor conceived of a time when this technology would be needed again? Had he, in truth, foreseen that one day one of his sons would require its secrets? Was it simply pragmatic not to destroy that which had taken so much labour to build? Or was this simply an extension of the Hall of Victories, in spirit if not location, a secret museum standing testament to the Emperor's greatest achievement?

The noise of armoured boots echoed around Corax as the Raven Guard and Custodians entered, oblivious to the concealed warning beneath their feet. The clank of servitors and the drone of wheeled equipment transports filled the hall with raucous echoes, dispelling the reverent atmosphere of silence.

Searching the fragments of the memories lodged in his mind, Corax knew that the bulk of the facility lay beneath them, deep within the rock of the mountain. The doors ahead were elevators that would take them down to the hidden levels. He could not recall any traps or alarms in this place, but warned the expedition to proceed with caution nonetheless – the Emperor's recollections were hazy in places and a slight delay for caution would do no harm.

'Squads seven, eight and nine, secure rearguard,' said Corax as the last of the Raven Guard passed through the portal. He moved to a slab about twenty metres from the entrance. It angled up at his touch, revealing a bank of controls. Corax punched in a sequence dredged up from his borrowed memories and the outer doors began to swing shut. 'Transports to leave. Monitor secure channel epsilon-six for our transponder signals.'

The doors came together with a surprisingly delicate thud, leaving the Raven Guard in the red glow of the lights. Corax took the lead, quickly striding to the front of the column, where he found Agapito and the Mechanicum agent, Nexin Orlandriaz. The two of them were having an argument.

'But it is imperative that we preserve any technology we find,' the genetor was saying, the words coming as a clipped whisper from a mechanical grille set beneath the left side of the man's jaw. His mouth was sealed with a pipe that looped over his shoulder into some form of rebreathing unit that hissed and whirred with metronomic precision.

The genetor was swathed in a voluminous red robe, the sleeves and hem threaded with gold designs in the shape of a cog's teeth. A heavy chain bearing the gear-rune of Mars hung across his chest, and the device was repeated on several small ceramic studs above Nexin's right eye.

Other than the lung unit, he showed little outward signs of the heavy mechanical augmentation seen on many of the Mechanicum's agents, but there was a strange lustre to his skin, a sheen of silvery quality. His eyes were also bizarre, seeming too large for his face, with no visible iris and dark red pupils. Given Nexin's particular expertise – a genetor of the Magos Biologis – Corax concluded the Mechanicum operative had experimented on himself with other, less obvious, artificial enhancements.

'The lives of my warriors are more important than any piece of equipment,' Agapito replied. 'We have lost enough legionaries already, I will not see any more fall without good cause.'

'You do not seem to understand the weights being brought to the balance,' argued Nexin. 'A single warrior is limited. He can achieve only so much and then his light is extinguished. A weapon, a piece of technology, a fragment of our past glories, can live on for eternity, transforming the lives of billions.'

'Life is just a commodity, right?' Agapito snarled. He towered over the slight form of the magos, causing Nexin to flinch. 'I remember well that attitude. That was the Kia-vahran creed.'

'Commander, what is the problem?' Corax said briskly.

Agapito kept his gaze firmly on the genetor when he replied.

'This half-man says we cannot fire our weapons in this place,' said the commander.

'Live rounds and explosive contain the potential to inflict irreparable damage to the contents of this vault,' the Mechanicum agent added, turning his unnatural eyes to Corax. 'Our quest will be in vain if we destroy that which we seek.'

'And what do you know of our objective?' said Corax. 'What do you think might be endangered by weapons fire?'

'The Sigillite did not furnish me with much data,' said Nexin, stepping away from the brooding presence of Agapito. 'However, given my proclivities and technical disposition, I have compiled my own theory on the issue.'

'And your conclusion?' asked Corax, gesturing for Agapito to stand down.

'I am a genetor, therefore it is logical that we seek an object that is genetic in nature. I do not speculate, but it is reasonable to deduce that this would relate in some way to one of three prior endeavours by the Emperor: the Thunder Warriors, the primarchs and the Legiones Astartes. I do not know which.'

'Is that right?' asked Agapito, turning his helmeted face to the primarch. 'Gene-tech?'

'A means to rebuild the Legion,' replied Corax. His gaze moved between the two of them when he next spoke, his displeasure clearly visible. 'We are the Legiones Astartes and we do not relinquish our weapons. If at all possible, we will act to preserve the contents of this vault. If any life is put in immediate danger, we shall respond without hesitation. With that understood, there is to be no weapons fire in any other situation unless authorised by me.'

'Yes, lord,' said Agapito, with a nod.

'My entourage and I will comply with your policy,' said Nexin.

'Agapito, if you have any cause for dispute, bring it to me,' Corax told the commander, before turning the full force of his glare on the genetor. 'Understand that I and many of my warriors have no fondness for those who pursue industrial strength or mechanical domination at the expense of lives or liberty. Your presence here is by no means essential, magos.'

'I wish merely to participate and elucidate where possible,' said Nexin. 'Please also understand that I know something of your Legion's history. Your oppressors were not part of the Mechanicum and it is inappropriate to conflate the misguided tech-guilds of your home system with the great endeavours of Mars. However, I recognise that we all share the same goal and at this time I will ensure that my acolytes are sensitive to any issues your past misfortunes may bring about.'

Not sure whether this amounted to an apology or not, Corax simply turned from the genetor and looked further down the hall. The end could be dimly seen in the ruddy glare: three immense doorways.

The expedition reached the far end of the corridor to find that the three doors each had a keypad set into the wall next to them, with only two buttons on each.

'Perhaps some kind of binary code is required?' suggested Nexin, examining the central doorway.

'Or a finger,' said Agapito, pushing an armoured digit into the upper button. 'It's an elevator.'

The door rumbled up into the ceiling to reveal an enclosed conveyor large enough for thirty or forty men, or ten legionaries with all of their equipment.

'We will have to descend by squad,' said Corax. 'Agapito, I'll leave it up to you to organise the details. I will, of course, be going down first.'

The order was not as simple to execute as first seemed. Agapito wanted to send down the Raven Guard with the primarch to act as a vanguard in case of danger. Arcatus was adamant that he and several of his warriors were in the first shift. Though the Custodian did not say as much, Agapito believed he did not trust Corax out of his sight. On top of this, Nexin was also insistent that he be included in the first party, but would not be separated from his two hulking gun-servitors.

After some further negotiation, it was agreed that Corax would descend with the Custodians while Nexin and his armoured servitors would accompany one of the

Raven Guard squads. Several of the legionaries had to
suffer the indignity of riding on the backs of the tracked
servitors as there was not enough room for all of them
to fit into the elevator.

Corax paid only vague attention to these arrange-
ments, confident that Agapito would find a solution.
The primarch searched his memories, trying to work out
what awaited the expedition at the bottom of the shafts.
Try as he might, he had no recollection of this place, just
as he had had no memory of the main door until he had
laid eyes upon it. Whatever gifts the Emperor had given
him, they were highly contextual. Corax wondered if
this was intentional or simply a side-effect of the psychic
implantation process.

The sight of Agapito bathed in the ruddy glow, guiding
a squad into the right-hand elevator, triggered an altogether different kind of memory.

*The security alert lighting flickered orange and red, in time to
the slow warning klaxons ringing along the corridor. Twenty
inmates, dressed in their standard coveralls and heavy boots,
gathered in a group beside the tower transit shaft. They carried an assortment of wrenches, picks, hammers and other
tools – improvised weapons that had been carefully stashed
after the work-shifts for the last thirty days.*

*'Are you sure this is the right way?' asked Nepenna, his
grease-covered face screwed up with consternation, blond
hair matted with oil. The ex-engineer knelt beside the open
mechanical access hatch, his kit of handmade tools spread out
on the bare rockcrete floor next to him. 'If we don't shut down
these lifters, the guards will be here in minutes.'*

*'It is the right way,' Corvus assured him. The layout of
the entire facility was etched on his memories. He could not
explain to his companions how he had managed to explore
the maze of corridors and mineworking unseen by the guards,
but they had to trust him. 'The diversionary riot in the hangar
block will take the security forces away from the guard block*

above and along to the transit hub two miles towards the spire. That is why I chose the hangar area to catch their attention.'

'What if you are wrong?' This came from one of the youngest prisoners, a youth barely in his teens called Agapito, a third-generation internee. His skin showed the characteristic sallowness of those who had spent their entire lives in the artificial habitat, his eyes dark and brooding.

'Has he ever been wrong?' Dorsis was the team leader, a middle-aged political poet appointed by Corvus for his steady head and creativity. The others looked up to him and took comfort from Dorsis's calm demeanour. 'We all know the plan. The guards evacuate the block up-tower, we break into the arms lockers and take ammunition. In and out, nothing fancy.'

The patter of feet alerted Corvus to the approach of Ephrenia. She was three years older now than at their first encounter. They had shared a few months as friends when he had been found, but his swiftly maturing mind and body had left her far behind. Even so, she was devoted to Corvus, a nimble-minded and -footed messenger who was adept at using crawlspaces and service ducts to elude the pickets of the sentries.

'The fire has been started on deck four of the north hangar,' she reported breathlessly. 'Danro and the others have holed up in the maintenance bay like what you said.'

'Good,' said Corvus, ruffling the girl's hair. Her smile sent a shiver through him, of joy and despair in equal measure. Joy that he might be the one to free her from this life of bondage; despair that he might get her killed in the attempt.

It was not good to think about such things. Corvus knelt down beside Ephrenia.

'There will be guards on the overhead monitoring gallery,' he told her. 'You know which way to go?'

'Yes, Corvus, of course,' she replied, in a tone children seemed to reserve for patronising adults. 'I'll pass by the kitchen flues, the ovens will have been damped at first alert.'

'Good,' Corvus said again, sending the girl on her way with a paternal smile. 'Get something to eat.'

She nodded and ran off down the corridor.

'Come on, come on,' muttered Standfar, a white-haired old-timer who had been chosen as lockpick on the mission.

'Relax,' said Dorsis. The team leader glanced at Corvus and then at the battered bronze chronometer he had been given. 'At least another two minutes until the next patrol.'

Corvus nodded in agreement. He needed no timepiece, his internal clock as accurate as anything that could be fashioned or stolen by the prisoners. They waited in tense silence as the rumble of the lift grew louder and louder.

With a heavy thud, the elevator arrived. Nepenna was packing his tools into a soft leather cloth, placing each into its pocket in the fabric. Agapito and Laudan grabbed the concertina doors and hauled them open. The others had their tools raised, ready to fight.

The elevator was empty.

'I wish you were coming with us,' said Agapito, as the others hurried into the lift. The youth craned his neck to look into the face of the prisoners' guerrilla commander, who now stood more than a head higher than the tallest amongst them, his unnatural growth showing no signs of abating. No worksuit would fit him any more, and so his followers had tailored him a uniform out of stolen blankets, wire thread and dyed sheets. Black and grey, it seemed an appropriate yet underplayed mockery of the commandants' gaudy outfits. The suit fitted perfectly for the moment, but Corvus knew that in only a few weeks' time his constant increase in mass would have it bursting at the seams.

'Too much chance that I will be seen,' replied Corvus, slapping the young man on the arm. 'If a guard were to see me, our secret would be out. Better that I keep my head down for the moment. I know you will do just fine without me.'

With a nod, Agapito stepped into the conveyor with the others. Corvus slammed the doors closed with a smile and an

encouraging wink. Now alone in the hall, he felt very exposed.
The clatter of the elevator chains sounded dully from the shaft
as the lift ascended towards the upper levels.

It was hard not to get excited. The nascent rebellion was
barely started, but momentum was surely building. Corvus
had spent a year planning this first phase, travelling far and
wide across Lycaeus, invisible to the eyes of the wardens. He
had scouted out the forces opposed to him, learnt every step
of the complex that housed several million internees. He had
established communications cells in each wing and tower,
and devised a dead-drop system to pass messages between the
groups as the work-shifts changed.

Corvus had watched and noted the guards' actions when
a few small-scale incidents had been staged. A fight here, a
sit-in protest there. He had, somewhat foolhardily he realised,
sat unnoticed in security briefings and listened to the vice-
commandants detail the patrols and schedule the inspections,
and with this information he had set up smuggling circuits
and hidden caches that avoided the security sweeps.

This exercise was just the latest in the last few days to test
out his theories. It would not be wise to act too soon, and
every tiny insurrection and discipline breach had been carefully timed not to arouse suspicion. If the enemy had any idea
that their charges were building up to something, the patterns
would change and Corvus would be forced to start over. Even
so, he was committing his followers to a road that would lead
inevitably to outright rebellion. The ammunition that would
be stolen by the party he had just sent would not be missed
for another ten days – he had checked the manifest inspection
dates that morning. By then the guards might connect the
theft to the weapons missing from Tower Four, and a full-
scale security clampdown would ensue.

In fact, Corvus was depending upon it.

When the guards left their blocks, they were vulnerable.
Though they outgunned the prisoners, they were hugely outnumbered. When the revolution proper was started, they

would be swept away in a few bloody days.

The clump of a boot forced Corvus to retire into the nearby shadow of a support girder. Three guards, one of them a corporal, marched directly past him, their eyes passing over Corvus as if he was not there.

As they were about to turn the corner, the corporal stopped. His head turned towards the maintenance access panel. Corvus could see nothing wrong, but the guards were suddenly wary for some reason. It was then that Corvus saw what the corporal had spotted: tiny flecks of oil spattered on the white-washed wall.

Unnoticed, Corvus emerged from his hiding place, stepping silently to come at the guards from behind. He flexed his fingers and decided which two of the three would have their necks snapped first. He chose the one on the right and the one in the centre. The third would be silenced by an elbow smash.

It would mean a step up in the timetable. The death of three security men would not go unpunished. Corvus considered his contingency plans as he loomed over the guards.

'Find out who's on cleaning rota for this sector,' the corporal said, jabbing his truncheon towards the offending oil stain. 'Punishment detail, five days.'

'Yes, corp,' replied one of the guards.

Corvus stopped mid-stride, hands moments from the necks of his chosen victims, who were still oblivious to his presence.

The trio moved on and Corvus breathed out slowly, fading back to the shadows.

All was well. The plan was still on track. In forty days from now, Lycaeus would be free.

'WHAT'S HE DOING NOW?'

Lukar, as usual, felt the need to give voice to the question that the rest of the squad had not dared ask. Sergeant Dor had Alpharius and the others covering three of the dozens of branching corridors that led away from the chamber at the bottom of the elevators.

The rest of the Raven Guard were placed in defensive positions close to the other entrances.

Alpharius glanced quickly to his right to where Corax paced back and forth between the various openings, head bowed in thought. The Custodians stood close to the primarch, helmeted heads turning left and right as they followed his reciprocating course. The Mechanicum contingent were fussing over one of the combat servitors, which had burst several hydraulic lines under the weight of the legionaries that had ridden on it during the half-hour long elevator descent.

'We're stuck,' said Canni, his multi-melta directed down the leftmost of the three passageways. 'What else would it be?'

'No, that can't be right,' said Sergeant Dor. 'He must know the way.'

'Something isn't right,' said Alpharius. 'Everything about this mission has been ad-hoc so far. We've barely had a briefing. I'm with Canni, I think we're trapped here.'

'We can't be trapped,' insisted Dor. 'There's only been one way to come so far: one big entrance tunnel and then the elevators. Marko, watch your sector! That goes for the rest of you.'

Marko turned his head back towards the passage with a grunt of apology.

'But he doesn't know where to go next,' said Lukar. 'Or if he does, he's taking his time deciding what to do.'

'Ancient defences,' said Dor. 'There must be something up ahead that he's trying to figure out.'

'He has a plan.' Marko's interjection silenced the others. The heavy weapons specialist did not say much, but when he spoke it was usually insightful. 'The primarch knows it is going to be dangerous. He is facing a difficult decision.'

'Aye, that's it,' said Dor. 'Weighing up the different

options. Just like that time in Fellhead.'

The Lycaeus veterans laughed. Alpharius, masquerading as Terra-born, knew not to join with their reminiscing from the time of the rebellion.

'A right bad job that was,' chuckled Lukar. 'Do you remember Thaneus getting his finger snapped off by that vent slam-door?'

'Shouldn't have been poking around in dark places,' said Dor. His laugh stopped quickly. 'Wait, it looks like the primarch's ready to go.'

Alpharius risked the sergeant's wrath with another glance towards Corax. He was in conversation with the ranking Custodian and Commander Agapito, finger pointing out one of the arched openings.

'Squad, stand by for orders,' said Sergeant Dor.

EIGHT

Akin to Theseus
Dark Alliances
Hidden Defences

THE EMPEROR REMEMBERED this place as the Labyrinth, a
name from ancient Terran legend that only had vague
meaning for the primarch. Corax knew that it did not
matter which of the corridors they followed initially.
Each led into a randomly shifting network of passages
and bridges that responded to the presence of intruders,
directing them away from the inner vault. There were
also numerous automated defences, both in pre-planned
killzones and wandering the maze. It was a cunning artifice, allowing no strategy because there was no logic to
out-think.

Corax remembered that the shutting and opening of
doors, the shifting of movable gantries and the spinning of
enormous turntables, was directed by the random melting
of a glacier on the other side of the mountain, impossibly
intricate to predict even for his superhuman mind.

He could have the entirety of his old Legion and not
be able to find a route through by trial and error. At first
he had been dismayed by the thought of getting trapped
in the Labyrinth, but the more he had considered the
problem the more Corax had convinced himself that

the Emperor had implanted some clue or stratagem that would outfox the random nature of the situation. If not, he had been sent on a fool's errand, and that seemed equally as impossible as the task at hand.

There had to be a way, and so the primarch wracked every memory he could pull from his thoughts, seeking some tiniest nugget of truth that would provide a solution. The Labyrinth had been activated after the Emperor's final visit, and so the Master of Mankind had never traversed its depths. There was nothing to be learnt from first-hand experience.

A flash of inspiration had come to Corax. The Emperor had overseen the construction of the Labyrinth, and in that there was a pattern. As ingenious as its operation was, the Labyrinth was not infinite; there were only so many possible configurations it could align itself to at any given time.

Slowly an image formed in the primarch's thoughts, of passages being delved and bridges erected. He saw the great engines being sunk into the rock that would power the Labyrinth, the power channels that linked those engines to the sensor beneath the glacier, the pneumatics and gears that drove the whole machine.

Just like the mosaic behind the door, there was a formula to be discovered, a single equation that could sum up the immense operation of the Labyrinth. Corax could not compose such an equation in his head, it was too vast, but from what he could now remember of the construction it was possible to make a start.

As the workings of the Labyrinth unravelled in front of his mind's eye, Corax saw a weakness. It was possible to present the Labyrinth itself with a dilemma it could not solve, requiring it to respond in contradictory ways that could not be physically accomplished.

The Labyrinth could be tricked into jamming itself open.

'I need three exploration teams,' he told Arcatus and Agapito, speaking quickly. 'Take the sixth, eighteenth and thirtieth corridors.'

'Is it wise to split our force, lord?' asked Agapito. 'You warned us of defence systems.'

'We *must* split our force, commander. The squads must be on full alert.' Other memories were becoming fixed in Corax's mind. 'They will encounter mobile sentry devices as well as fixed gunnery emplacements. They employ laser weaponry and solid shot cannons, easily powerful enough to penetrate Legiones Astartes armour. These devices use broad spectral analysis, heat and vibration detectors, and proximity trips. Blind grenades and plasma discharges will render them inoperational for short periods. Tell the legionaries to look for sensor plates, they are likely to be mounted on the weapons themselves as well as at points on the walls. Do not forget to check the ceilings and floors.'

'Destroy the sensors and the guns will be blind?' said Arcatus.

'Best to destroy the guns as well,' said Corax. 'There may be redundancies and cross-weapon networks in the defence grid. Warn your warriors that the battlescape will be changing constantly. The area they are about to enter is highly active, capable of transitioning from one format to another. They will come across meeting points between the elements of the maze, likely doorways and bridges. Crossing the threshold of these points will activate a transformation of the layout. Our warriors must also be prepared for environmental and gravitic changes?'

'Gravitic changes?' said Arcatus. 'What sort of place is this?'

'Some of the tunnels can invert, and there are chambers set with gravity devices counter to the standard field,' continued Corax. 'Also beware of thermal and atmosphere changes. The maze is hazardous, but it contains nothing that our troops cannot surmount.'

'This sounds like a nightmare,' said Agapito. 'How are we supposed to get any kind of force through that? And what about those who get left behind?'

'I know how the maze will react, and every action will be guided by me. All movements and contacts are to be reported directly to me across the command channel. All orders from me must be acted upon without delay. Arcatus, you must be my spearhead.'

'I am under orders not to leave your side,' replied the Custodian.

'I must remain here to coordinate the mission,' Corax told the gold-armoured warrior. 'I need your group, there are not enough Raven Guard to unlock the Labyrinth. I need your warriors, Custodian, and their complete obedience.'

'My orders were specific,' said Arcatus, shaking his head. 'Who can say what will happen to us in that maze?'

'You must trust me, Arcatus,' said Corax.

'The Legio Custodes cannot afford the luxury of trust,' came the reply.

The primarch searched for an alternative, eyes settling on the cyborg creations of the Mechanicum. He dismissed them. The servitors were too slow to respond to orders, and would be more of a liability than an asset during this part of the operation. Corax turned back to Arcatus.

'I am asking for your help, Custodian,' said the primarch. 'Your orders may be to watch me, but your role is to protect the Emperor. With the secrets held beyond the Labyrinth, I can forge a new Raven Guard Legion. That Legion will fight against Horus. If the Custodians wish to have such allies, you must aid me now.'

Arcatus remained silent for a while, the mask of his helm hiding any thoughts and expressions.

'Do you require all of my men?' he asked.

'Preferably,' said Corax, making quick calculations. 'Fifteen may be sufficient.'

It was some time again before Arcatus spoke next.

'Very well,' he said. 'We will all venture into this labyrinth. What do you require of us?'

'Thank you, Arcatus. Adjust your communications to the Raven Guard frequencies, Commander Agapito will furnish you with the details. Please divide your Custodians equally between the three expeditions. Agapito, you will lead team one. Arcatus, I will give you command of team two. Senior sergeant in the force is Nestil, correct?'

'Yes, lord, Nestil has seniority,' replied Agapito.

'He shall be commander of the third team. Teams are to advance in combat squads, five men each, with ten metre dispersal in each squad and a twenty metre gap between squads. Is that understood?'

'Yes, lord,' said Agapito. 'I shall start the briefing.'

'This seems too dangerous work for uncertain reward,' said Arcatus. 'I hope it is worth it.'

Considering Arcatus's words, the primarch took a moment to evaluate his course of action. From the moment the Raven Guard entered the Labyrinth, Corax and his warriors would be committed. The deadly series of traps and defences would be set in motion and there would be no chance of withdrawal. They would either reach the vault or die in the attempt. The leader of the Raven Guard was sure that the gene-tech held the key to resisting Horus, no matter the sacrifice required to acquire it.

'It will be worth it, Custodian,' replied Corax. 'The Emperor would not go to all of this effort to protect something of no value. This gene-tech contains the secrets of our creation, and with those secrets the forces of the Emperor will multiply a hundredfold. When the

Raven Guard strike back at Horus, you will be thankful of the choice you have made.'

'If we survive that long,' said Arcatus.

'That will depend on your discipline and swift reactions,' said Corax, 'and I am in no doubt the Custodians have both in ample supply.'

With a nod, Arcatus returned to his men. The large hall rang with the thunder of boots as the Custodians and Raven Guard moved to their designated positions. Corax blocked out the chatter over the vox. He closed his eyes, creating a picture of the Labyrinth in his mind. No one had set foot within its walls since its completion, and so the primarch knew the starting layout from the schematics gifted to him by the Emperor.

The Emperor had designed the maze to outwit any foe, but had given Corax just enough insight to tip the balance. It was up to the primarch now to make the correct decisions. Corax had learnt to pick locks from Olda Geb back on Lycaeus, but he was about to pick the most complicated lock in all of the Imperium, devised by the Emperor himself.

He took a deep breath, focusing on the first fifty metres of the Labyrinth. He would know within that distance whether he could crack the secret of the maze. If not…

Corax chided himself for the moment of doubt. There would be no failure. He could not allow it. He had not said as much to Agapito, but in his calculations he had allowed for a ten per cent attrition rate. If that proved to be true, those Custodians and Raven Guard who gave their lives to the Labyrinth could not be allowed to die in vain.

He let out the breath.

It was time to start.

THE DRONE OF the air barges powering through Kia-vahr's polluted skies thrummed constantly through the cracked tiles on the roof, the vibrations sending a tiny but constant stream of dust across the glimmer of light that crept through a crack between the ill-fitting metal plates of the wall. The workers' shack was dark except for that single glimmer, which created a dim pool of light in the centre of the hut and touched upon half-seen machines and tools piled along the walls. The air was thick with the smell of rust, moisture seeping through a small culvert beneath a broken sink on the wall opposite the door.

Omegon heard footsteps on the metal gantry outside. He stayed immobile, hidden by the shadows, his bolter held ready.

The plate of the door creaked open, shedding flakes of oxidised iron into the light that trickled through the opening. The doorway was lit from behind by the glow of a strobing searchlight, flickering through a red haze of rust-polluted air. A man with a loose tunic and baggy trousers appeared in silhouette. He darted a glance over his shoulder before stepping inside and closed the door behind him, blocking out the glow of the air barge navigation lights.

'Councillor Effrit?' he asked, stepping into the thin shaft of light. His pupils were wide, ineffectively trying to pierce the gloom. Omegon could see that his clothes were well-tailored, fashioned in the style favoured by the guilds before the coming of the Mechanicum. Layers of ornate cloth obscured the man's figure, but from his pinched face and vein-heavy hands, Omegon could see that he was frail, his skin worn thin from decades of anti-agapics. His voice shared a reedy quality with his body. 'It is Armand Eloqi.'

'I can see who you are,' said Omegon. The voice modulator trembled at his throat, adding two octaves to the pitch of his words. 'Welcome.'

'I cannot see you,' said Eloqi.

'That is for the best, for the moment,' Omegon told him. 'There is a seat to your left. Make yourself comfortable.'

'It is a risk, meeting like this.' Eloqi's eyes continued to dart nervously from side to side, unable to locate Omegon. He did not sit down.

'You were not followed,' said Omegon. 'You will be returned to the guild hall by the same means you arrived, with no suspicions aroused.'

'Still, it seems to be an awful risk for no reason.'

'Please, sit down, guildmaster,' said Omegon. 'We have a little while longer to wait.'

'Wait?' There was an edge of panic in Eloqi's voice. Omegon smiled in the darkness. It was good that the guildmaster, and his allies, were on edge. In truth, there was no cause for them to be suspicious. The Mechanicum were totally unaware of any plot in their midst, but it suited Omegon's need for secrecy for his pawns to be ever vigilant. Their nervousness also made their negotiating position weaker.

'Sit down.' Omegon did not bark or snarl the words, but he added just a little of the authority he could muster; authority that had sent warriors into battle without fear and equally despatched operatives to their necessary deaths.

Eloqi hesitantly sat on the rickety remnants of an old armchair, the fabric worn thin by generations of foremen who had slunk off their shifts to this hidey-hole to enjoy a moment's peace from the docking yard below. It had not been used in years, not since the coming of the Mechanicum.

'Your fortunes have failed of late,' Omegon said quietly, his words delivered in a sympathetic tone. 'Once you and your guild claimed rulership of Kiavahr, now you are reduced to underlings of the Mechanicum. A whole continent used to labour for your benefit, guildmaster, and the populace of an entire moon worked to death to bring ore and aggregate to the guilds' workings. You grew powerful and your lives were filled with luxury. Do you miss that time, guildmaster?'

'Of course,' the old man snapped. 'The dogs of Mars have swept away everything with their stupid hierarchies and cults. Not a die stamps nor a bolt is tightened without their artificial eyes watching, their mechanical brains counting. Scraps from their table, that's what we must survive on now. They have not the courage to do away with us entirely, instead they inflict this wasting disease upon the guilds, bleeding us dry so that we will eventually wither and die, leaving them with the riches of Kiavahr.'

'And you want to take that power back,' Omegon prompted. 'That is understandable. Why should you slave for the distant, uncaring Emperor or the Magi of Mars when your halls stand half-empty, your tables sparse and your treasuries looted.'

'Exactly,' said Eloqi. 'Exactly my point, councillor. We were cowed, broken by the threat of annihilation, but the Mechanicum made a mistake in letting us live. We will take back Kiavahr. It took a hundred generations to build this world, and if it takes a hundred more to reclaim it, we will.'

'Your freedom is so much closer than that,' said Omegon. 'Within the year, I predict, the guilds will control Kiavahr again. You have a powerful ally, whom I represent. The Warmaster himself, Horus Lupercal, saviour of the Imperium, stands ready to support you.'

'Horus?' There was awe in the guildmaster's voice. It turned to suspicion. 'What interest does Horus have in humble Kiavahr?'

'You will hear soon many disturbing tales about the Warmaster,' said Omegon, ignoring the question. 'There will be lies, spread by agents of the Emperor to sow

discord amongst those who doubt the rightful rule of
Terra. You must see through the deceit and stay true to
your ideals. Horus looks to those who have suffered
the tyranny of the Emperor to stand up for the cause of
justice. Across the galaxy there are hundreds of worlds
like yours, denied their freedom, denied the right to rule
themselves because of some misguided notion of compliance. Horus will give you back your freedom, and in
return he expects nothing more than the support of Kiavahr should he ask for it.'

'Wait, this sounds a lot more dangerous than it did a
moment ago,' said Eloqi, standing up. 'I am not sure I
like where this is heading. Why have you only just mentioned Horus's interest? What does he care for the fate
of Kiavahr?'

'Relax, Armand,' Omegon said, in his most concilia-
tory tone. 'We are allies, but we must be cautious. The
Emperor and the Mechanicum will do everything they
can to cling on to their power. You must understand that
I had to assure myself of your dedication to freedom.
Throwing off the shackles of the Mechanicum will not
be easy, but you must understand that you must also
face down the warriors of the Raven Guard.'

'We cannot afford a war against the Legiones Astartes,'
said Eloqi. 'You mentioned nothing of overt action,
councillor. Do you think we are fools? Our aim is to
gradually usurp power, not to openly wrest it from those
who deny us the right to rule ourselves. I do not like the
way in which you have changed the stakes.'

'No trickery is intended,' said Omegon, lying through
his teeth and enjoying the manipulation of this weak-
willed, ambitious man. He had said much the same
thing to the other guildmasters, making each feel indispensable to the cause, massaging their precious egos. 'It
is because I can trust you that I reveal this information.
You alone are privy to this knowledge and I know you

will guard it with your life. The Raven Guard will pose little threat to the true rulers of Kiavahr. I can tell you now that they have suffered a massive reversal. I am sure you will learn the same from other sources soon.'

This much was true. By some means, news of Horus's actions would spread and it would come to Kiavahr that half of the Legiones Astartes had turned on the Emperor. It was better that Horus's version of events was heard first, casting doubt on the rumours and propaganda that would be following. Part of the bargain agreed with the Warmaster was for the Alpha Legion to spread disinformation ahead of this, whilst seeking new forces for Horus's cause. It was a mission Alpharius and Omegon were well prepared to undertake. On many other worlds, Alpha Legion operatives and legionnaires were already sowing discord amongst the Emperor's followers and stoking thoughts of rebellion in those who had been forced into compliance by the Legiones Astartes.

'I have heard whispers that Deliverance is all but empty, guarded by a handful of ships and no more,' said the guildmaster.

'They attempted to defy the Warmaster and now the Legion has been all but destroyed. With your help, we will finish their destruction and restore the rule of Kiavahr to those who deserve it.'

'I do not understand this,' said Eloqi. 'The Raven Guard attacked the Sons of Horus?'

'Indeed, just so. The Emperor, jealous of Horus's power and popularity, sought to withdraw the rights he had granted his Warmaster, and sent several Legions to force Horus to surrender. Horus is not without many friends, though, and the lackeys of the Emperor were destroyed. The Raven Guard escaped by a twist of fate, but they are spent. Now is the time to strike. Unless, of course, you do not support Horus in his fight for liberty.'

Omegon left the consequences of such a view unsaid,

but he could hear Eloqi's heart beat a little faster as he filled in the blanks left by the primarch. A vague reference to punishment was worth a dozen specific threats in the minds of the weak. Whatever the guildmaster imagined would happen to him was far more worrying and personal than anything Omegon could devise.

'The Warmaster will respect the power of the guilds? He will allow us to reinstate the old laws?'

Omegon could hear the calculation in Eloqi's tone; the greed and desire to rule. The primarch knew what the guildmaster wanted to really hear but was too afraid to voice.

'Deliverance will be overthrown and the colony of Lycaeus returned to the guilds,' said Omegon. 'Horus will give you autonomy, from Terra and Mars. He does not even demand your fealty, only your friendship. He asked for you by name, guildmaster.'

'My name? Known to the Warmaster?'

A slight wheezing outside the shack came to Omegon, almost unheard amongst the clatter of a passing freight car.

'My other guest will be arriving in moments,' he told Eloqi. The guildmaster was nervous enough without having another arrive without some kind of warning. 'Do not be alarmed.'

The door opened a few seconds later. A robed figure entered, swathed in folds of black and red. A gold mask glinted beneath a heavy cowl, cables and pipes protruding from the faceplate, linked to an ornate brass machine on the newcomer's chest.

'What is this?' hissed Eloqi, backing away from the new arrival. Omegon silently side-stepped into the other corner, to avoid the guildmaster stumbling into him. 'You have betrayed us.'

'I said not to be alarmed,' said Omegon. 'Do not judge by appearances.'

'I am Magos Unithrax, guildmaster,' said the new-comer, his voice ringing from behind the mask. 'I am here to help you overthrow the tyranny of Mars.'

'You... You are one of them! One of the Mechanicum!'

'Yes, and no,' Unithrax said calmly. 'I come from the Order of the Dragon, and answer to a different power from Terra. With the aid of my associates, I will see the guilds restored to power on Kiavahr.'

Eloqi was speechless, his terror still gripping him.

'Unithrax will ensure the grip of the Mechanicum is broken from within,' Omegon explained, speaking slowly to ensure the guildmaster heard him. 'With the magi in disarray, the guilds will be able to overthrow the usurpers. You need his help, Armand. Believe me, you need his help.'

'What if I choose not to ally myself with this thing?' said Eloqi. 'Maybe we do not want any more of your conspiracy.'

'It is too late,' said Unithrax. 'Already wheels are in motion. You can either be elevated to power or be crushed by the forces we will unleash. The guilds will control Kiavahr and Lycaeus again. Whether you choose to number yourself amongst those guildmasters or not is irrelevant to our plans.'

Seeing that he had no choice, Eloqi nodded firmly, affecting an air of bravado.

'Well, it seems that I was right to trust you, councillor,' he said. 'I knew there was more to you than a simple alliance of the guilds. The Warmaster can expect my full support.'

'Good, I am glad that we are in agreement, Armand,' said Omegon, suppressing a laugh at the hollow arro-gance of the man. He could imagine the guildmaster's ambitions growing, seeing himself in audience with Horus, perhaps a master of a dozen worlds or more. It was pitiful, really. 'It would be wise of you to leave now.

You will be contacted again in due course.'

'Yes, very well,' said Eloqi, circling around Unithrax to reach the door.

'One other thing, guildmaster,' said the magos as Unithrax was about to leave.

'Yes?'

Unithrax held out a hand sheathed in a silvery gauntlet.

'I am pleased to make your acquaintance,' said the magos.

Eloqi grunted and took the proffered hand in his grip. A moment later he squealed and ripped away his hand as if stung.

'A guarantee of your cooperation, guildmaster,' said Unithrax, holding up a fingertip that glinted with a needlepoint in the low light.

'What have you done?' demanded Eloqi, looking at his wrist.

'A neurotoxin, guildmaster. It is inactive at the moment, of no threat. However, should you disclose my presence or betray our cause in any way, you can be assured that the catalysing agent will be introduced into your system: air, food, water, all can be used.'

Aghast, Eloqi stared at the puncture mark on his wrist and then glared at the magos before stumbling from the cabin.

'Was that really necessary?' Omegon asked, cautioning himself not to get too close to the renegade magos. It was possible that the Order of the Dragon had a poison that would work on primarchs too. 'You can be so unsubtle at times.'

'Let us hope it is a needless precaution, but it is not without benefit,' replied Unithrax. 'When the Order of the Dragon takes control, the guilds will be of no further use. Better to lay the groundwork now and ease their disposal later. Before I leave, I have messages for you, from the Fabricator-General, concerning developments on Mars.'

'I am sure you do,' said Omegon. 'I am sure you do.'

THE WALLS OF the passageway were lined with large panels of a dark grey material. Alpharius ran a hand over it, the sensors in his gauntlets conveying its smooth texture to his fingertips. Tiny temperature detectors told him it was cold to the touch. Slamming his fist into one of the panels, Alpharius noted hairline cracks appearing, radiating out from the impact.

'Ceramite,' he said. 'Like our armour.'

'Don't touch anything,' snapped Sergeant Dor. 'Not without the primarch's say-so. If something shoots at you, shoot back, but don't do anything else without orders.'

'Yes, sergeant,' said Alpharius, regretting his action immediately. Curiosity was not a trait that would be rewarded in his current situation. He stepped back into the group of legionaries, realising he had drawn attention to himself.

Dor and his squad were the lead element, split into two five-man groups. Alongside Dor were Alpharius, Lukar, Velps, and Marko with the multi-melta. They had covered perhaps seventy metres of the passageway, which was lit by strips inserted into the angle between ceiling and walls, bathing the legionaries in an unwavering yellow glow.

'Look at that,' said Lukar, pointing to one of the ceramite slabs ahead. 'Switch to thermal.'

Alpharius did so, a film of red falling over his vision as his armour's auto-senses tracked through the frequencies to the infra-red end of the spectrum. Behind the panel Lukar had pointed at he could see a tracery of brighter lines.

'Power cables,' said Alpharius. 'Sergeant?'

'I see it,' replied Dor, holding up his hand to signal the halt. 'Commander, we have some kind of power conduit ahead.'

'Understood.' Agapito's reply was immediate, his voice tense. 'Await orders.'

'Proceed thirty metres, Sergeant Dor.' The primarch's deep voice cut across the vox. 'You will see a sealed door ahead of you. Wait by the door for further instructions.'

'Affirmative, lord,' replied Dor, waving his hand to set the squad moving again. 'Keep an eye out for weapons systems.'

They had advanced only another five metres when a panel in the ceiling hinged open and a multi-barrelled gun dropped into view. Lukar was the first to react, unleashing a salvo from his bolter into the opening, the explosive shells tearing through a nest of cables. Sparks showered down and the weapon wilted on its mechanical arm, twitching fitfully.

'If that's the worst this place has to offer, this shouldn't be too hard,' said Lukar.

As if in response to his bravado, there was a shout of alarm from behind the squad, followed immediately by the crack of a laser bolt.

'Eyes front!' snapped Dor. 'Not our problem. Keep advancing.'

The chatter of bolter fire and the distinctive crackle of a plasma gun echoed along the passageway as the squad continued on. As Corax had told them, they came upon a chamber a few metres wider than the corridor, bare except for a door in the opposite wall. The portal was slightly recessed into the ceramite, made of the same material. Alpharius could see no sign of a handle or lock, though his thermal vision showed several power cables leading into the sill around the door.

'We just wait here?' asked Velps. He pulled a

melta-bomb from his belt and held it up. 'This'll burn through that door in no time.'

'Don't you do anything,' said Dor, warning Velps back with a raised hand as the legionary took a step across the room.

Alpharius looked around the square chamber. Other than its dimensions there was nothing to mark it out from the passage that had led to it. The featurelessness of the corridor, the perfect uniformity of it, unsettled him. He was an Alpha Legionnaire and intimately knew the disorientating power of anonymity. It would be very easy to get lost in such a place, and Alpharius had no intention of ending his life in this bland but deadly warren of passages and rooms.

'Perhaps we should mark our progress somehow, in case we get turned around,' he suggested.

'What do you mean?' asked Dor.

Alpharius drew out his combat blade and etched a cross into the ceramite wall to his left.

'If we see that again, we know we've come in a circle,' he said.

They waited for several minutes. Alpharius looked back down the corridor and saw the other half of the squad a dozen metres behind, still in the corridor. The heat from the power packs of the following legionaries was building up, distorting the air with a haze. To Alpharius's thermal vision the vents on the backpacks of the other legionaries were bright white.

'Commander, we are giving off a high heat signature,' said Alpharius. 'The primarch said that the defence systems had thermal registers.'

'Good point,' replied Agapito. 'All squads, set cooling systems to minimum. Reduce heat signatures.'

'Negative, do not adjust heat signatures.' Corax's tone was quiet but terse. Alpharius realised the primarch had to be monitoring every squad communication, a considerable mental feat. 'I need you to trigger the thermal sensors if necessary. Team two will shortly be in position. Their progress will trigger the first transformation. The door ahead of you will open in two minutes. Stand ready.'

IN THE ENTRY chamber, Corax had his eyes closed, the totality of his mind focused on picturing the mechanism of the Labyrinth and the positions of his squads. He had blocked out all input save for the constant narration that streamed across the command network into the communications bead in his ear.

Like a burglar examining the most complicated lock ever devised, the primarch imagined the interplay of revolving rooms, rising bridges, closing doorways and collapsing arches. The three forces had already begun to divide, combat squads directed through new openings to trigger the next transformation of the maze. With each random change, Corax's plan evolved and solidified, as possible avenues of approach opened or were shut. He could not predict every movement of the Labyrinth, but he could respond swiftly to each development. The timing of each move had to be precise, and he snapped out orders in a clipped voice, redirecting the combat squads to where they were needed.

He blotted out the sound of gunfire and the rumble of mighty engines and immense pistons. He ignored the curses and warnings of his warriors. His sole purpose was the unpicking of the lock.

Twenty-three minutes and one hundred and seventeen metres after first entering the Labyrinth, the Raven Guard suffered a casualty. A legionary under Agapito's command was struck in the chest by a laser bolt from an automated turret that had risen from the floor.

'We have no Apothecary,' the sergeant reported. 'Mathan looks in a bad way.'

'You must leave him behind, Sergeant Cannor,' Corax replied quickly. 'We will return for him later. Move the rest of the squad up to the second archway on your left. The doorway ahead of you will be closing in seven seconds.'

'Mathan is still alive, barely. He needs treatment.'

'You have your orders,' Corax said coldly. The gene-tech – the rebirth of the Raven Guard – was a prize greater than any individual life. There could be no delays. The Labyrinth would already be moving towards its next configuration. To falter would be to fail, and that would make every life lost a vain sacrifice. 'Move your squad now.'

'Confirmed, Lord Corax.'

Distracted by the event, the primarch had almost missed an opportunity to get Agapito's lead squad across a bridge that might ascend into the heights when Arcatus's men entered the chamber ahead of them. Corax made a swift calculation and judged there still to be time enough for the crossing.

THE RAMP AHEAD seemed innocuous enough to Arhuld Dain, special weapons bearer of Squad Seven, though Lord Corax had warned the squad to approach with caution. The ferrocrete causeway rose ten metres above the floor of the chamber, leading to a circular door that looked like a ship's airlock. Dain looked up and saw a similar opening directly above, and what appeared to be the rungs of a ladder leading from one of the walls across the ceiling.

'How would anybody get up there?' he asked, adjusting his grip on his flamer as the five-man combat squad advanced towards the causeway.

'I have no idea,' replied Sergeant Caban. 'Stay focused.'

With a loud hiss, the double doors through which the squad had entered slid shut behind them. Dain detected vibrations pulsing through the floor at the same time as a distinctive crackling came to his ears.

'Wait!' the legionary snapped, stopping in mid-stride. Sergeant Caban took another step onto the causeway before turning back.

'What is...' The sergeant's voice trailed away as the whole chamber lurched, spinning quickly on its axis, spilling the squad into the air.

Dain felt himself go light, drifting away from the floor. The ceramite underfoot provided no purchase for the magnogrips of his boots and he floated away, the rest of the squad lifting up around him. Sergeant Caban slipped past him, propelled through the air by his last step, gently inverting as he slowly glided towards the wall behind Dain.

The Raven Guard found themselves suspended about three metres above the floor, which had become a wall. Dain tried to twist towards the rungs of the ladder, whose purpose became clear. Angling his flamer, he fired a short burst, using it as a crude propellant to send him flying towards the ladder.

'What are you doing?' demanded Caban. The sergeant came to halt against the far wall, one hand outstretched to stop himself.

Dain reached out with his left hand, flailing for the closest rung. His fingers closed around the metal.

The crackling noise increased in pitch, becoming a pulsing whine. Dain looked around, trying to find the source. The ladder was thrumming with energy between his fingers. Realising his error he let go and tried to push himself away with his legs.

Lightning arced from the ladder, coruscating across Dain's armour, earthing through exposed cabling around his midriff. The muscles in his abdomen tightened as electricity surged through the legionary, his spasm causing him to kick out, hurling himself across the room as spark erupted from his armour and flames burst from melting seals and blown circuits. He could feel his flesh charring and cracking, the pain muted by a sudden rush of anaesthetic compounds produced by his body. Dain's jaw felt as if it had been welded shut while agony flared through his head.

Spinning madly, he blacked out, his last vision that of the room turning again, his companions plummeting towards the new floor.

'INCOMING ORDERS,' SAID Dor, motioning with his bolter for Marko and Alpharius to move through the doorway ahead. 'Distributing on squad channel.'

Alpharius and Marko edged through the opening with their weapons ready. They found themselves on the edge of a large, vaulted chamber. Ten metres from them, the floor dropped away into a dark chasm, a natural fault in the strata of the mountain. With the thermal sight of his suit, Alpharius could see the telltale glint of power cables and weapons positions on the ceiling above, not yet activated.

'In thirty-two seconds, a bridge will descend to your position,' came Corax's voice, relayed through Sergeant Dor's vox-unit. 'You will have forty-three seconds to cross that bridge.'

'There are seven weapons turrets,' Marko reported. 'Irregularly spaced. We only have clear lines of sight to three of them from this side. We will have to get onto the bridge before we can see the others.'

'No cover,' added Alpharius. 'We'll be targets on a shooting range.'

'Blind grenades,' replied Corax. 'They will disable the units for twenty seconds.'

'Still not enough time, lord,' said Dor. 'The gorge must be at least two hundred and fifty metres wide.'

'Sprint, sergeant,' came the primarch's clipped response.

Alpharius was about to protest but held his tongue, as if the order had been given by his own primarch. The others seemed willing to trust in Corax's judgement and he could not afford to show any dissent.

'I'll go first,' he said. 'Marko, can you target that second turret on the right?'

'From the edge of the chasm, yes,' said Marko.

'Wait!' snapped Dor, as Alpharius readied a blind grenade from his belt. The Alpha Legionnaire froze in place.

The sergeant took a few steps past the pair, looking around.

'Save it for when we reach the bridge,' said Dor, lifting his bolter towards the darkness that hid the far side of the chamber. 'We can take out these turrets before we cross.'

A deep rumbling reverberated around the cathedral-like hall, sending dust shaking down from jagged stalactites that had grown up around the heavily riveted girders that held back the weight of the ceiling. From a recess far above, a metal structure descended into view, swaying on dozens of chains each as wide as a legionary's shoulders.

'You have forty-three seconds.' Corax's voice was calm, almost emotionless.

Dor spat out a string of orders and the squad burst into action. Alpharius headed towards the metal pillars that marked where the bridge would fall. The *clump* of his boots activated a sensor and a turret directly above his head extruded from the metal of the ceiling. Lukar fired his bolter, shredding the gun's casing in a storm of sparks.

Alpharius carried on, trusting to his squad to protect him as he primed the blind grenade in his fist. The whine of the multi-melta filled his ears for a split second before another turret disintegrated into a mist of molten metal that rained down on the Alpha Legionnaire's armour.

With a thunderous clang, the bridge hit the braking pillars and rocked to a halt. Alpharius was already bounding along its length as it settled, his boots sending up flakes of rusting metal from the mesh of its floor.

'Thirty-five seconds,' Dor warned them, his words almost lost in another blaze of bolter fire, this time from Velps. Another turret burst into flames.

Alpharius ran across the bridge, blind grenade held ready, arms and legs pumping, his armour-assisted run covering three metres with every stride. He heard the clamour of the others following behind, and tensed, waiting for the distinctive snap of a las-bolt.

'On the right, quadrant three!' barked Dor. Alpharius did not look, but heard the sound of Velps behind him sliding to a halt. A red flash blazed from the gloom, melting through the bridge just a metre behind him. Velps's bolter roared and the defence turret was silenced.

'Grenade away!' Alpharius bellowed, hurling the blind field detonator far ahead of him. The orb arced through the darkness, glinting ruddily as another turret opened fire, its blast scorching a line across Alpharius's vision as it bit into the bridge decking just in front of him. The machines controlling the turret had adapted and anticipated his run; only the momentary pause to throw the grenade had saved Alpharius from a direct hit.

He bent forwards into a full sprint as the blind grenade erupted into life at the far end of the bridge, forming a whirling cloud of silvery particles and swirling forks of electromagnetic energy.

Again the system controlling the defences had evolved. The turrets were blinded, but whereas before they had ceased their fusillades, now they opened fire with a storm of bolts, flashing randomly around the chamber with a criss-cross of ruby beams. As a beam

seared past his right shoulder, Alpharius almost cursed
in his native tongue, the words stopped by his gritted
teeth as he plunged into the storm of the blind field.

Clanking gears and hissing pistons sprang into life.
The bridge lurched under Alpharius's feet, almost sending him toppling over the low rail. The blind cloud
raged around him, blotting out all of the data being fed
through his armour's auto-senses. In silence and blackness, Alpharius leapt, powering himself into the air.

It seemed to take an age for the legionary to land,
swallowed up by the blind field, oblivious to the crackling las-bolts that were undoubtedly flaring all around
him.

He landed with a heavy thud and almost lost his
footing, coming down hard on one knee, the impact
sending alarm signals through his suit. He surged to
both feet and pressed on, trusting that the others were
following him, trusting also that Corax was correct and
there was an archway or open door ahead to provide
sanctuary. The blind cloud was already collapsing, the
chaff and distortive energies fluttering into the darkness.

Freed from the effects of the blind grenade, Alpharius's comms and auto-senses sprang into life again.
Las-fire blazed around him, sending up wisps of molten rock from the floor. There was no point trying to
dodge the haphazard fusillade and he pressed on up
the slightly sloping floor while his auto-senses shuddered. Patches of light swam across his eyes and a dull
ringing sounded in his ears as the suit's systems recovered from the blind field.

'–igh and left,' Dor was shouting as he emerged from
the spreading miasma of disruptive energy. 'High and
left!'

Alpharius swung his bolter up to a firing position and
saw through the infrared haze a flicker of the turret's

artificial eye blinking in the darkness. He fired three
rounds, puncturing the casing of the gun position,
sending shards of metal through the air.

'Keep moving,' Lukar said, slapping a hand to Alpharius's shoulder as he ran past. Alpharius looked ahead
and saw a blast door descending over a yellow-lit opening.

The legionaries ducked under the closing portal in
quick succession, armour clattering. Marko was the last
in line, slightly slower due to the weight of his heavy
weapon. A red beam of laser energy spat down from
the ceiling and shattered the armour of his right leg.
Twisting, Marko tried to fall under the closing door but
fell short.

'Leave him,' Dor snapped.

Alpharius ignored the command and acted out of
instinct, dropping his bolter to grab Marko's backpack
with both hands. He hauled with all of his strength,
dragging the stricken legionary under the door
moments before it slammed closed with a resounding
crunch.

They were in a corridor much like those they had first
encountered in the maze, with drab grey walls without
markings. It curved away sharply to the right, the route
ahead hidden after ten metres.

'Sergeant Dor, report status.' Corax's voice was
assured, confident that his warriors had succeeded.

Dor looked at the squad, the lenses of his helm glinting in the bright light that came from a single strip in
the roof.

'We're through, Lord Corax,' he reported. 'Marko is
hurt, though.'

'Can he move?' The question hung in the air while
Marko pulled himself to his feet with Lukar's aid. He
hefted his multi-melta, checking the power cabling that
linked it to his backpack.

'I'm not staying here,' Marko said, voice strained. 'But don't expect me to do any more running.'

'He can move,' Dor passed on the legionary's assessment. 'What are our orders?'

'Continue along the passageway for thirty metres.'

'Understood. We are advancing,' Dor replied.

At that moment, something came around the bend in the passage, clanking and hissing. It was a strange mix of bipedal machine and small tank, with tracked feet of metal links, its main body shaped like a turret with two multi-barrelled cannons protruding menacingly from the front. Sensor discs and artificial eye lenses dotted a small module atop the machine.

Alpharius watched as the barrels spun up to speed, momentarily taken aback by the machine's sudden appearance; Corax had warned of such a thing but until now they had only encountered the fixed defences. Even as he lifted his bolter to fire, he realised he had reacted too slowly.

A weight smashed into the side of Alpharius, sending him reeling to his left just as the guard-machine opened fire. Lukar was firing his bolter as he took the brunt of the cannonade, fist-sized shells hammering into his armour in a welter of ceramite shrapnel and ripped metal.

Lukar was hurled backwards by the impact, his shattered armour slamming to the floor, cratered and cracked. Alpharius fired his bolter, targeting the sensor array, smashing lenses and aerials.

The side of the machine exploded into a shower of molten drops from the blast of Marko's multi-melta, exposing steaming circuitry and wires. Dor's bolts slammed into the rent a second later as the turret spun towards Marko. Velps leapt forwards with a melta-charge in his fist. He ducked beneath the blaze of bullets as the guardian opened fire again, smashing Dor from his feet. With a snarled oath, Velps slapped the charge on the casing beneath the guns and dived away.

The machine detonated, its destruction filling the tunnel with incandescent fury that caused heat warnings to flare across Alpharius's helm display, an explosion far greater than that caused by the melta-bomb alone. Shrapnel carved into Alpharius's chest and shoulder, but his armour held. The ceramite walls were similarly crackled and pitted with debris.

'Self-destruct,' said Velps, the paint of his armour blistered away by the fiery blast. He fired several rounds into the smoking, twitching mechanical remains, snarling curses.

Alpharius turned to where Lukar lay awkwardly on the grey floor. The face of his helm was a mess, the Raven Guard symbol embossed on his breastplate mangled beyond recognition, blood seeping from a dozen gouges in his armour.

'The sergeant looks alive,' reported Marko, kneeling beside Dor's supine form. The sergeant weakly held up his hand to confirm the fact.

'Lukar's dead,' Alpharius said quietly. The Raven Guard had taken the full brunt of the attack, saving Alpharius's life. As he looked down at the blood-spattered, broken armour of Lukar, Alpharius shook his head with disbelief. 'Why did he push me out of the way?'

'Why did you drag me to safety?' Marko replied, pulling Dor to his feet.

Alpharius had no answer. These warriors were Raven Guard, his enemies. His sole purpose was to ensure their destruction, but the mission required that they succeed in retrieving whatever it was that Corax sought in the vaults. That meant they had to stay alive to breach the inner sanctum of the mountain.

Yet there was more to it than that. Their eventual deaths would be a necessity, but as individuals Alpharius had respect, perhaps even friendship, for his fellow

squad members. Whether this was some remnant of
memory from the warrior-material in his omophagea,
or something altogether more vexing and problematic,
he did not like to guess.

'We are brothers-in-battle,' Dor said quietly, crouching to place a hand on the shattered remnants of Lukar's
chest.

'Aye,' said Velps, pressing his fist to his chest in salute.
'Battle-brothers.'

'Battle-brothers,' Alpharius whispered, pulling his
gaze from the dead legionary, unable to deal with his
confused thoughts.

ARCATUS EYED THE channel ahead with suspicion. The passageway was long and narrow, no more than two metres
wide and at least three hundred metres long, turning
abruptly to the right to continue out of sight. About
fifty metres away, a small gutter-like trench emerged
from the wall, cutting diagonally across their line of
advance. He called his Custodians to a halt and waited
for instruction from Corax. In the three and a half hours
since he had entered the Labyrinth, Arcatus had found a
new respect for the primarch, and perhaps even a little
trust. Four times, Corax's last-minute warnings or orders
had saved the him and his group of Custodians and
Raven Guard from deadly traps and mechanical attack.
Only a few minutes earlier, Arcatus had drawn back just
in time to avoid a vaporous acid spray that would have
melted through his armour in seconds.

A rivulet of liquid ran along the channel, a dark green,
viscous fluid that flowed sluggishly, its level growing
higher.

'I think this passage is going to be flooded, Corax,'
Arcatus reported.

'It is just lubricating fluid,' the primarch replied. 'It is
no threat. Proceed to the end of the passageway. There

will be three doors. Take the door on the left. Beyond is some kind of energy grid, a laser trap perhaps. Be wary.'

This last comment seemed unnecessary – Arcatus had been wary from the moment he had first stepped into the deadly maze. He followed Corax's instructions, taking the squad to the bend in the corridor. A shouted warning caused him to turn as a previously invisible hatch opened in the ceiling. Three silver orbs, each no bigger than his fist, dropped into view.

The first exploded into molten shards as Custodian Ganius swept the blade of his guardian spear through it. The other two detonated of their own accord, showering Ganius and the Raven Guard next to him with jagged, smoking shrapnel. Wisps of vapour rose from their armour as the acidic compound melted swiftly through to flesh.

Ganius cried out – the first time Arcatus had ever heard a Custodian react to pain – and struggled to disconnect his breastplate. The Raven Guard legionary toppled to the floor with a crash, a hole melted through his helm, a slush of liquefied skull and brain matter dribbling onto the bare floor.

'It's through my ribs!' snarled Ganius, dropping to one knee, clutching at his chest.

Arcatus acted without thought, to spare Ganius the inevitable agony of having his heart and lungs melted. His power halberd gleamed with energy as he swung the weapon, taking Ganius's head from his neck in one stroke. Ganius's decapitated corpse flopped to the ground, the echo of the impact resounding along the passageway.

'Move up, door on the left,' Arcatus snapped, waving his halberd to get the survivors advancing.

He stood over the remains of Ganius, alert for any more of the silver globes. Arcatus followed after the last of the Raven Guard to pass, remembering the primarch's promise that the vault contained something that would ensure Horus's defeat. With a last glance back to Ganius's body, which was collapsing in on itself as the acid chewed through his spine, Arcatus vowed to himself that he would hold Corax to his word.

NINE

The Depths of Terra
Nikaea's Legacy
Genesis of the Primarchs

THE GENE-TECH VAULT lay within reach. Corax allowed himself a moment to see if he remembered anything about the inner defences, but there was nothing in the Emperor's memories. Once through the Labyrinth, Corax would simply have to unlock the vault doors and they would stand before the prize.

'Ready your servitors,' the primarch told Nexin. 'We enter the Labyrinth in two minutes.'

Twenty-three Raven Guard were dead, another seventeen crippled and left in the Labyrinth to be recovered later, a further thirteen wounded but able to continue. The Custodians had also lost three warriors. Corax had committed all of their names to memory but now was not the time to mourn or mark their passing. The Labyrinth remained to be unlocked.

Corax's commands continued to spill from his lips in a constant stream, moving the pieces of the puzzle to where they were needed. He tried not to think of them as living, breathing warriors. Ever since he had first sent his prison-army to fight against the guards of Lycaeus, he had known his orders would see men die. Though

the adversary he now attempted to outwit was no sen-
tient foe – though, in a sense, he was being pitted against
the guile of the Emperor himself – the sacrifices required
were no different. Millions, probably billions, of the
Emperor's followers would die if the Raven Guard failed
today and could not cause Horus to pause in his advance
on Terra.

So it was that the chatter of bolter fire that now echoed
distantly from the maze and blared harsh over the vox-
net did not divert his attention from the task. He thought
only of report and command. His Legiones Astartes had
sworn oaths to lay down their lives in his service and for
the cause of the Emperor, and it would be vanity to think
this battle was any different.

The lead elements of the force were almost two-thirds
of the way through the maze. Parts of the Labyrinth had
been secured – the positions of the squads and the routes
they had taken forcing the mechanism of the Labyrinth
into impossible choices so that engines broke, pistons
froze and gears seized.

The hardest part was over. The remaining possible configurations had dwindled to the extent that Corax could
clearly see the path ahead. It was just a matter of time
until the Labyrinth was bested. The primarch warned
himself against complacency. The Labyrinth was still a
random device, constantly changing, and could throw
up a challenge he had not yet encountered and could
not foresee. His brave Raven Guard and the warriors of
the Legio Custodes still placed their lives in his hands.

He directed several squads to converge on a massive
turntable that would open up a main accessway towards
the inner reaches of the mountain. This done, he signalled Arcatus on a direct channel.

'Custodian, you must move your men into the chamber flanking your right,' he said. 'You will be breaching a
line of strong defences. Be prepared.'

'The Custodian Guard is always prepared, primarch,' Arcatus replied. 'It seems from the reports I have been hearing that you have directed my squad into the teeth of the hardest opposition. Perhaps you hope we will fall, and thus rid yourself of our scrutiny?'

'I have no desire to do so,' Corax replied without rancour at the accusation. 'Had I wished you disposed of, I have had many opportunities already. Your warriors see the hardest fighting because they are the best under my command. You and your men have abilities even above those of my legionaries and so it is against the toughest challenges you have been pitched. The Raven Guard owes you a debt of honour for your aid, which I have found of the highest value, making this task a little easier for all of us.'

There was no reply for a while, the Custodian perhaps taken aback by Corax's words.

'Very well,' Arcatus said. 'We shall continue as you say.'

The whine of hydraulics caught Corax's attention as Nexin and his servitors joined the primarch.

'The vault is open?' the magos asked.

'It will be soon,' said Corax. He worked out the quickest route through the Labyrinth to the front of the advance and pointed to one of the openings. 'This way. Follow me.'

STANDING CLOSE TO Corax, Alpharius could hear the primarch's conversation with Arcatus, Agapito and the tech-priest. They discussed the immense vault door that now barred further progress. It was circular, five metres across, and of a metal that reflected the light dully, something which Alpharius had not seen before. The hinges were massive, as tall as him, but there was no sign of a locking mechanism: no runepad, no scanner, not even a keyhole. Around the door smoked the remains of four gun turrets that had sprung from the floor as the lead elements of the force had approached.

Alpharius listened patiently as the commanders discussed the options. Agapito favoured melta charges, but the primarch was not convinced they would breach the barrier. The magos claimed his servitors could cut their way through.

More squads were emerging from the beaten Labyrinth; some of them bearing dead warriors. Corax had assured his force that the fighting was over for the moment. Alpharius had been alarmed when the maze had been held in the grip of a titanic shuddering, the screeching of metal echoing along the tunnels and rooms, smoke from burning oil drifting through the air. It had lasted several seconds, and the Alpha Legionnaire had thought the whole complex was collapsing.

When it had finished, Corax had announced calmly that the Labyrinth was stuck, unable to respond to further movement. He had despatched search teams to return to isolated and fallen brethren, but Alpharius and his fellow squad members had been directed towards the vault entrance along with the majority of the expedition. It was there he had come across the senior leaders of the force, baulked by this final obstacle. The conversation had reached an impasse.

'Burrowing through would take many hours, days perhaps, if it is even possible,' Agapito was saying. 'Is there no other way?'

Corax seemed lost in thought for a moment, eyes half-closed, before he replied.

'It is a psychic lock,' said the primarch, his whole demeanour changing, shoulders slumping with disappointment. 'It can only be activated by the mind of the Emperor.'

'Then we must rely upon physical means,' said Orlandriaz. The magos gestured towards the two heavy servitors looming over the group. 'I shall prepare my servants.'

'There is another way,' said Corax, straightening, filled with purpose again. He glanced at Arcatus before his eyes came to rest on Alpharius. The Alpha Legionnaire was disturbed by that dark gaze but did not react. 'Balsar Kurthuri is in your squad, yes?'

'He is, lord,' replied Alpharius, glancing towards the named legionary who stood a few metres away from the group.

'He was once a member of the Librarius,' Corax continued.

Alpharius did not know his squad-brother was a psyker, and was taken aback by the thought, but assumed Corax would not have misremembered. He nodded.

'Yes, lord, he was,' said Alpharius, unsure of the primarch's intent. He called for Balsar to join his superiors.

'This is unwise,' said Arcatus, stepping between the primarch and the approaching legionary, his halberd raised. 'Do you not remember these words: "Woe betide he who ignores my warning or breaks faith with me. He shall be my enemy, and I will visit such destruction upon him and all his followers that, until the end of all things, he shall rue the day he turned from my light." Such were the words of the Emperor.'

'The Edict of Nikaea,' Corax said with a nod. 'I remember the words well, Custodian. I heard them myself from the lips of the Emperor.'

'Then you understand their meaning: sorcery is condemned. I cannot allow this,' said Arcatus.

Corax pursed his lips in thought and then gently laid a hand on the warrior's shoulder, guiding him aside. He looked at the legionary standing before him.

'Balsar, you have powers of the mind, yes?' he asked.

'I was a Librarian, lord, it is true,' replied the battle-brother. 'I have not exercised my powers since the Librarius was disbanded by your command, and have sworn not to employ them.'

'To whom did you swear that oath, Balsar?'

'To you, Lord Corax,' the legionary replied.

'And if I release you from that oath, can you use your powers now?'

'My lord… I also swore in the name of the Emperor to cease using my abilities,' said Balsar, his voice trembling. 'Are you ordering me to break my oath?'

The words struck a chord in Corax, his lips twitching with frustration. It lasted only for a few seconds before the primarch's expression hardened again, dark eyes narrowing.

'This will not happen,' barked Arcatus before Corax could speak. His Custodians assembled around him, summoned by some means Alpharius had not detected. 'The Edict of Nikaea is absolute.'

Corax ignored them all and addressed Balsar again.

'Have you ever felt "dark temptations"?' the primarch asked, his tone harsh and dismissive. 'Do you feel any now?'

'No, my lord, I have never felt any temptation, dark or otherwise,' Balsar replied dryly. 'My life has been woefully bereft of temptation since I left Terra.'

'I will not allow sorcery, not here on Terra itself,' said Arcatus. A glimmering field sprang into life along the length of his halberd blade and was matched by the glow of the other Custodians' weapons. This was greeted by the raising of several dozen bolters by the assembled Raven Guard. Alpharius followed suit a moment later, directing his weapon at the Custodian Guard.

'You use words whose meaning you do not understand,' said Corax, his expression growing grim. 'The Emperor guards Terra from the most unnatural powers. Do you think he will allow such a thing on his world?'

'I do not guess the mind of the Emperor, I merely ensure his decree is enforced,' replied Arcatus. He looked around at the legionaries that surrounded him and then back at Corax. 'Sorcery is forbidden.'

'Do you judge the Emperor to be a sorcerer, Custodian, or perhaps his regent, the Sigillite?'

'The edict does not concern my superiors, only the warriors of the Legiones Astartes,' Arcatus said coolly.

The two sides faced each other in silence, fingers tight on their weapons. Alpharius looked at Corax, trying to judge the primarch's next move. It would go badly if the Custodians were killed. Investigations would follow that would not only hamper the retrieval of the vault contents but might also lead to the discovery of the Alpha Legion infiltrators. There was also the very real possibility that Alpharius would be killed in the fighting, as Corax's summons had brought him close to the Custodians. It was impossible to guess at Arcatus's intent, his face hidden behind his golden-masked helm. Similarly, the Raven Guard were faceless warriors, their weapons showing their intent with no hint of reluctance.

Only Corax's face could be seen. The primarch looked pensive, but his eyes never moved from Arcatus. Corax held no weapon, but Alpharius knew well enough that the primarch was fully capable of killing Arcatus without armament. He wondered what 'dark temptations' played on the primarch's mind at that moment. A single blow would fell Arcatus and the Raven Guard had the other Custodians surrounded, though the gold-armoured warriors would surely slay many legionaries before they fell.

'Father, do not abandon us.' Corax's voice was a whisper, not meant to be heard by the others. There was anguish in those few words, spoken between gritted teeth.

Alpharius sensed something, a motion or sensation on the edge of awareness. It seemed that he heard distant howling and screaming, for a fraction of a moment. It was as if he was in the heart of fiery battle, his body responding as if he was fighting for his life, hearts pounding, blood racing. A looming presence filled the corridor, an oppressive surge of power that seemed to compress Alpharius's skull. From the disconcerted murmurings of others, he knew he was not alone in feeling it.

A dull clang echoed from the door.

All eyes turned towards the portal, where a golden gleam emanated from the metal, glittering with power. The door swung inwards and lights flickered into life beyond as the auric glow faded to reveal a white-walled antechamber. There was a smaller door beyond, of silvery metal. Every surface was covered in a thin icy sheen. Vapour swirled as cold, sterile air washed from the entranceway.

The silence was absolute as the assembled warriors stared in disbelief at the open doorway. Corax briefly bowed his head, eyes closed, his lips moving, though the words he spoke were too quiet to hear.

Alpharius glanced at Balsar and saw a few golden motes of energy dancing from the lenses of his helm. Corax noticed this too and stepped between the former Librarian and Arcatus, quickly blocking the Custodian's view.

'It seems the Emperor has intervened,' said the primarch, directing his gaze towards the Custodians.

Arcatus and his warriors remained poised. Corax motioned for his Raven Guard to lower their weapons, some of them doing so only reluctantly. The primarch turned his attention back to Arcatus, who stood down his own men after a moment.

'Wait!' said Corax. Suddenly weapons were raised again. Behind the primarch, Nexin had taken a step towards the opening. The magos stopped and looked back to see the scowl on the primarch's brow.

'Apologies, Lord Corax,' said the Martian, with a deep bow. 'You will lead. I will follow.'

Alpharius lingered a moment as Corax and the others headed towards the vault. He stopped Balsar with a hand on his arm.

'That was not the will of the Emperor, was it?' Alpharius said.

'I do not know what you mean,' replied the legionary. 'It is forbidden for me to use my powers. I was not relieved of my oath.'

'But still,' said Alpharius. It seemed unlikely that the Emperor had intervened on their behalf, having not made his presence felt throughout the tortuous journey through the death-traps. It had to have been Balsar's doing. 'That wasn't really the Emperor, was it?'

Balsar said nothing and left Alpharius to fall in behind the departing primarch and commanders. Alpharius could not tell whether Balsar was lying or not, though there had been no trace of deception in his voice. He felt tense at the thought of psykers using their powers again, and equally disturbed by the idea that the Emperor had perhaps witnessed what went on and intervened on Corax's behalf. No amount of deception would protect him if one of the former Librarians decided to delve into his mind, despite the precautions taken by the psykers of the Alpha Legion to shield his mind from casual inspection. The threat of psychic discovery had always been present, but the realisation that such a warrior was in Alpharius's squad was a more distinct worry.

If the Librarians returned, his task would become a lot harder. He would have to watch his thoughts as much as his deeds and words.

THE MAIN VAULT was a circular room, with a domed ceiling carved into the naked rock. There were several other doors leading from it, but it was the contents of the central chamber that dominated Corax's thoughts as he stepped across the threshold. He could not recall

any defences in this inner sanctum though he had a
flash memory of a final failsafe – any interference with
the outer door would have seen the contents destroyed
by a fusion charge set underneath the vault. Perhaps it
was the presence of this memory that had stopped the
primarch ordering the cutters and drills brought forth,
though it was only now that the dire consequences of
such an act were clear to him.

His misgivings about the events that had just tran-
spired evaporated, replaced by satisfaction, curiosity
and a sense of awe. Here was the Emperor's laboratory,
where it could be said the Imperium was truly created.
This was the birthplace of the primarchs.

Everything was pristine, environmental regulators and
stasis fields maintaining the facility in the exact condition it had been left. The air was clean, every surface
brightly scrubbed. A large device sat at the heart of the
room, dormant for the moment but riddled with energy
cables and pipes, not dissimilar to the machinery Corax
had thought he had glimpsed around the Emperor's
Golden Throne. It reached to the ceiling, covered with
glass-panelled openings that showed hundreds of dials
and phials, tubes of coloured liquids and touch-screen
interfaces.

Under the direction of Agapito and Arcatus, the Custodians and Raven Guard fanned out, securing the other
doorways. The Emperor's memories were hazy on what
lay behind them, but Corax had a dim recollection of
vast generators, freezing chambers, databanks and room
upon room of cogitating machines.

Thick cables coiled out from the central machine,
snaking across the plainly tiled floor to twenty other
devices, arranged in a circle around the chamber. Corax
recognised them immediately: the incubators of the
primarchs. They were empty of their artificial amniotic
fluids, their glass cases raised open. Where lights had

flickered, gauge needles had wavered and monitoring systems chirped and beeped, now there was lifelessness and silence.

Magos Orlandriaz started gasping and muttering, wandering from one machine to the next with wide eyes. Corax smiled at the almost childlike delight with which the tech-priest was drawn from one sight to the next, occasionally pausing to place a reverent hand on a piece of technology, often stopping to gaze dumbly at something suddenly revealed to him.

Each of the incubators was numbered on its side. Corax quickly sought out number 19, his own chamber. He realised something was wrong as he approached. The incubator was incomplete, its insides missing like a tomb with no coffin within. Only the casing and outer protective canopy remained: a mess of cables and pipes lay loose at the bottom of the shell, disconnected.

He remembered the cracked and broken machine that had been found beside him beneath the glacier. For years, long and lonely years, he had wondered about that machine and its purpose. Only when the Emperor had come to Deliverance had the primarch learned what he was and how it was he had awoken on that strange, desolate moon.

Corax still vividly remembered that meeting. Laying his hands upon the incubator chamber brought it back to his thoughts.

'Scanners have picked up an object moving towards the main dock,' reported Agapito, standing at one of the scanner arrays. The youthful freedom fighter was wearing the black trousers of a guard, the jacket that had completed the disguise discarded once the tower had been opened to the guerrillas. A curving slash was slowly forming a scab across his bare chest and his left arm was wrapped in a fresh bandage. 'Trajectory implies a landing pattern, but it is impossible to say what sort of craft.'

The main tower was still heavily damaged and in disarray from the fighting. Corvus's followers manned the stations as best they could, but the equipment was barely functioning and most of them were working from guesswork rather than training. That anything had been detected by the shattered scanner array was remarkable.

The bodies of those who had worked here before had been removed, but there were still bloodstains on the grille of the floor and brushed metal consoles; cleaning up the detritus of revolution was low on Corvus's list of priorities whilst there remained men alive on Kiavahr who opposed his rebellion. Many of the screens and keypads were shattered from weapons fire and exposed wiring burst messily from larger rents in the equipment banks, but power had been restored and a few crackled with life under the nurturing of Corvus's most technically gifted followers.

The defence turrets that littered the immense spire of the main guard tower were definitely operational. The revolutionaries under Corvus's command had ensured they had been taken intact, as their leader had instructed.

'Bringing the weapons systems to lock-on,' announced Branne, standing at the firing console. Like his brother, he showed the wounds of war, sporting a graze across his cheek, a patch of blood matting the light scattering of downy hair on his chin.

The tower rumbled as immense turrets moved into position, targeting their mass drivers towards the incoming vessel. Branne looked expectantly over his shoulder at the revolutionary leader, tousled hair falling over his youthful face.

'Shall we fire?' asked Branne.

'No,' replied Corvus.

He stood at the armoured window of the control room looking out into the darkness. Kiavahr was waxing towards full, looming large behind the mineworkings and crane gantries on the horizon. From this distance it looked the same as ever, but Corvus knew that below the welter of swirling red clouds *the planet was in turmoil. He fancied he could still see the aftermath of the atomic detonations unleashed by the mining charges his forces had dropped down the gravity well to the import station below, but it was just a fancy.*

The guilds were broken, that much he had already learned. Denied the resources of Lycaeus, their counter-attacks against the moon bloodily repelled, they had taken to fighting amongst themselves, pitting the strength of their city-factories against each other. Some had sent signals asking for truce, fearing further atomic bombardment from orbit. Corvus had ignored their pleas. Let them kill each other, he thought, staring at the world that had enslaved millions for generations.

Corvus's reflection was superimposed over the rising orb of Kiavahr against the thick glass. He was a grown man now, more than a grown man. There was barely room for him to stand straight in the control chamber at the summit of the Black Tower. They were calling him the Saviour now, those he had led to freedom, and he had felt their awe at his continued growth. A decade had passed since his first encounter with the inmates of Lycaeus, but it was only now that he enjoyed his first moment of celebration.

Victory was his, the overlords had fallen.

'Craft still approaching,' said Agapito, his voice betraying nervousness. 'Branne, how is that lock-on holding up?'

'Still have half the weapons systems targeted, brother, no problems,' replied Branne. 'Corvus, we only have a few minutes until the flight path brings the approaching craft too close to fire.'

'We will not fire,' Corvus said, turning to face his companions. 'It may be a diplomatic mission from Kiavahr. I can see it: it is a shuttle, nothing more. It can't hold more than a dozen men at the most, no threat to us. Have a company of the Eighth Wingers meet me at the main dock.'

There was something else about the shuttle that intrigued Corvus. At the moment it was barely a glint of gold in the distance, but the revolutionary leader was filled with a sense that its passengers were important. The sense nagged at him, not as a warning, but something else he was unable to define. Corvus felt assured that those aboard the approaching craft bore him no ill intent, though he could not say why he felt such conviction that this was true.

'Let me know if anything changes,' he told the others, patting the bulky communications handset hanging from his belt.

Corvus ducked under the rim of the mangled security door and into the corridor beyond. A handful of prisoners with scavenged shotguns stood guard outside; an unnecessary precaution, but one that had been insisted upon by his followers. The self-appointed bodyguard fell in behind their commander without command, joining him in the chamber of the Black Tower's main conveyor.

The elevator rattled down several dozen floors until it reached the accessway that led to the main port landing apron. Ignoring his companions, Corvus strode quickly along the passageway, past work teams that were busy labouring with welders and metal panels to reinforce the repairs that had been hastily made after the tower's occupation. Blue sparks danced in the air as Corvus made his way towards the landing port.

Gapphion, one of his senior lieutenants, waited for him on the main deck with a hundred of his men from the company of the Eighth Wing. Above, the energy dome of the landing field crackled yellow against a starless sky.

'That was quick,' Corvus remarked to his lieutenant.

'We were close by,' Gapphion replied, a hint of a smile on his lips. The left side of his face was heavily bruised, his eye closed tight, a cut running across his brow. His grey hair was cropped short but his beard dangled almost to his belt. He still wore his grey prison coveralls, but the collar was marked with half a dozen lapel studs taken from dead security officers. There was blood on most of them.

'A happy coincidence,' said Corvus, directing an inquiring stare at the man. Gapphion shrugged away his leader's *suspicion and turned to shout an order to his men, directing them to set up perimeter around the landing apron.*

They moved like soldiers, Corvus thought as he watched the ex-prisoners spreading out across the ferrocrete. A few years ago they had been gangsters and philosophers, thieves and agitators. Now they were his army, well-drilled and highly motivated. He knew much of the credit was his, but in turn he owed a lot to whoever had given him the gifts he possessed. People listened to him without doubt, and he had an innate understanding of fighting. To direct an attack or devise a strategy came as naturally to Corvus as breathing.

Some of the men were pointing upwards and shouting.

A craft appeared beyond the field barrier, twin trails of plasma bright against the dark sky. As it descended through the barrier high above, Corvus saw that it was shaped like a great mechanical bird of prey, golden in colour, with angled wings that stretched back like those of a diving hawk.

It hovered for a moment, and plasma engines dimmed as the pilot switched to anti-gravitic impellers to land the craft. Falling slowly, the shuttle came to rest at the centre of the apron, within the inner circle marked there in red paint.

Corvus looked through the canopy and was surprised to see that the cockpit was empty. He suddenly felt a hint of suspicion at the seemingly unmanned craft; perhaps it was loaded with explosives, a desperate act of petty revenge from one of the guildmasters.

'Ready weapons!' Gapphion called out.

The men raised an assortment of slug-throwers, shotguns and lasrifles looted from dead guards and captured weapons lockers.

A door opened in the side of the shuttle beneath the right wing, directly opposite Corvus. Light spilled from within as a gangplank extended from the craft with a clang. A shadow appeared in the light, waiting for a moment at the entryway before emerging into view.

Whispers spread through the men, of surprise and

amazement. Guns quivered in shaking hands and there were clatters as some of the soldiers dropped their weapons. Seemingly without prompt, the men lowered themselves to the ground, putting aside their weapons and bowing their heads. Some prostrated themselves, whispering fervently.

Corvus glanced to Gapphion beside him. The lieutenant was on his knees too. There were tears in his eyes and an expression of joy etched on his slack-lipped face.

'So majestic…' Gapphion muttered. 'What glory. What power.'

Confused, Corvus directed his attention to the man descending the landing ramp. He seemed unremarkable. In fact, he seemed so unremarkable that Corvus could not discern a single distinguishing feature about him. He was of average height, with dark hair and moderately tanned skin. In build he was neither bulky nor slight, but of normal proportion, slightly larger than the malnourished men who now abased themselves before him. He was dressed in a robe of white linen, free of ornamentation except for a necklace of gold on which hung a pendant fashioned in the shape of an eagle with outspread wings, a lightning bolt in its claws.

The man's eyes were as indistinct as the rest of him, neither blue nor green nor grey nor brown, but a flecked mixture of all. Yet there was something in those eyes that reached into Corvus and touched upon his inner self. There was wisdom and kindness there, and antiquity that was very humbling but also disconcerting.

And at the same time as Corvus saw this, he also witnessed the arrival of a demigod, wreathed in golden light and dressed in white finery that burned with its own light. He saw a stern face set with two golden orbs for eyes, piercing in their intensity, searing into the core of his being. The stranger seemed to tower over the kneeling men, borne forwards upon a carpet of undulating flames.

It was impossible to reconcile the two images. The supreme, grandiose king of men approached Corvus, but all the while *the slight, unimposing man flickered within. Finally Corvus's mind could fight no longer against the glamour and he saw the new arrival as his followers did, and was filled by an overwhelming urge to pay obeisance to this stranger.*

He fought that instinct. He had waged a war so that his people would not bow before another man. The newcomer's effect on Corvus's men unsettled the rebel leader. He stared with narrowed eyes, unable to discern which image was true and which was illusion as the stranger paced slowly and confidently across the ferrocrete.

'Who are you?' Corvus demanded. 'What have you done to my men?'

The stranger looked around at the guerrilla fighters regarding him with adoration, seeming to Corvus slightly nonplussed at the scene. His blond hair fell in waves across his shoulders as he turned his head, spilling like fiery liquid. Another wave of majesty swept over Corvus and again the guerrilla commander had to make a physical effort not to fall to his knees.

'An occupational hazard,' said the man, returning his attention to Corvus. He fixed the rebel leader with a stare, his eyes now permanently golden like bottomless wells of light. There was a glow of power beneath his skin, as if the stranger's flesh were embers masked behind thin paper. Corvus experienced a momentary fluttering in his breast and a knot of anxiety in his gut, a fraction of the effect the man was having on his warriors. 'I am the Emperor of Mankind. I created you.'

Hearing these words was like a veil lifting from Corvus's eyes. He saw the Emperor as he had seen him before, watching the growing infant through the canopy of an incubator. His face had been distorted by curved plates of glass, but the features were unmistakeable. The guerrilla leader had long pondered the face from his earliest memories, wondering to whom it belonged. Now vague recollections became sharp memory. Corvus recalled the noise and lights and booming voices that had engulfed him, remembered the surge of power and disorientation as unnatural forces had borne him away from the place of his creation.

Now he saw and knew for certain the face of his father, the only individual worthy of Corvus's unwavering obedience. He lowered himself to one knee in deference, understanding that the stranger spoke the truth. Here was the Master of Mankind.

'What do you call this place?' the Emperor asked.

'It used to be called Lycaeus,' Corvus replied. 'Now we know it as Deliverance.'

'A good name,' said the Emperor. 'Please, rise, my son. We have much to talk about.'

And they did. Corvus withdrew from his men and took the Emperor to his quarters, an old guard station in the mid-levels of the Black Tower. Corvus sought out food and drink for his guest, ashamed at the meagre fare he could offer his father. The Emperor waved away his concerns, sitting on the rough bunk that served as a chair for the massive rebel commander.

'Do you recognise me?' the Emperor asked. His expression was hard to read, but Corvus thought he detected a hint of surprise behind the question. Whatever glamour had befallen the guerrillas had a lesser effect on Corvus, and the man before him was definitely the same as from his old memories.

'As if from a dream,' he replied.

'Interesting,' said the Emperor, with a smile and a nod.

They spoke about many things. Though Corvus was bursting with questions, about the Emperor, himself and the wider galaxy, he found that he did most of the talking, answering constant queries from the Emperor concerning what had taken place on Deliverance and Kiavahr. Corvus furnished him with all the information he could concerning the history of the star system and the war for freedom he had waged over recent years.

Corvus paced the room while he spoke, animated and energised. The Emperor sat on the bunk and nodded occasionally, *in understanding rather than approval. In fact he showed no judgement of any kind: no condemnation or endorsement of Corvus's actions. He listened intently to everything Corvus told him, sometimes asking exceptionally pertinent questions about the tiniest of details, wishing to absorb everything about Corvus's life.*

'But there is one piece missing that I cannot answer,' Corvus said, finally voicing what his heart had yearned to know since his first discovery. 'How is it that I came to be here?'

The Emperor's mood darkened and his face grew grim. For the first time, he took a sip from the glass of water Corvus had given to him hours earlier, eyes haunted.

'There is another universe,' he said. 'It lies alongside ours, part of it but also separated. It is called the warp.'

'I know of it,' said Corvus. 'Though I have not seen it, I hear that ships can use it to travel to distant stars. Some of the machines of Kiavahr are said to harness the energy of the warp.'

'It is a universe of boundless power, and can be accessed as you say, by ships and by the minds of special men that we call psykers,' the Emperor continued. 'Like our galaxy, the warp is inhabited, by creatures not of flesh but thought. Sometimes they hunger for our material lives, wishing to feast on our mortality. You and your brothers were taken from me by denizens of the warp before you were ready.'

'Brothers?' Corvus was excited by the prospect, pushing aside the questions that the Emperor's answer had prompted. Though he had made many friends amongst the prisoners of Lycaeus, always Corvus had been aware of his otherness, and when they had started to call him Saviour any hope of normal relationships had ended. That there were others like him filled Corvus with hope again.

'Yes, you have brothers,' said the Emperor, smiling at his son's delight. 'Seventeen of them. You are the primarchs, my finest creations.'

'Seventeen?' Corvus asked, confused. 'I remember that I

was number nineteen. How can that be so?'

The Emperor's expression grew bleak, filled with deep sorrow. He looked away as he replied.

'The other two,' he said. 'That is a conversation for another day.'

'Where are my brothers now? Are they with you?'

'You and the other primarchs were snatched from me by strange powers of the warp, thrown across the galaxy on unnatural tides. That is how you came to rest beneath a glacier on this moon. Yes, I have seen what befell you, learning your life the moment I laid eyes upon you. The rumour of you, of a magnificent being who led a rebellion here, has travelled farther than you realise, and it was word of this that attracted my attention. Your brothers, those I have found, were similarly scattered to far-flung worlds. Like you, they are all great warriors and leaders. That was my gift to you. You are supreme commanders, with intellect and physical ability unmatched by anything in the mass of humanity. I engineered you from my own genetic structure, to be my sons and my lieutenants in the Great Crusade.'

'What is this crusade? How many of my brothers have you found?'

'Most of them,' replied the Emperor. 'I have vast armies: the Legiones Astartes. As you are crafted from me, so they are created from you. The primarchs are the generals of those armies, leading humanity's reconquest of the galaxy. The Long Night, the Age of Strife, has ended. The remnants of the old empires smoulder out in the darkness, the dying coals of humanity almost smothered by the dark. The Great Crusade fans the flames into life, bringing with it reason to drive out superstition, Enlightenment to replace barbarism. With your help, I will unite humanity and lead mankind to rule the stars.'

It was so much to take in, but Corvus knew it to be true. Not only the words of the Emperor seemed certain, the idea of what he described meshed with a much deeper feeling.

Knowing he was a primarch, that he had been created to fight and to command, explained much that Corvus had never understood about himself. On a level that he understood in his spirit and was encoded into every cell of his body, Corvus knew what he was.

'I swear my loyalty to you,' said Corvus, sinking to one knee in front of the Emperor. He met the Emperor's gaze and felt elation like no victory had given him before. 'I am your son, your primarch, and your will shall be my command.'

'That is good,' said the Emperor. 'I have an army waiting for you. They are the Raven Guard, highly decorated and distinguished in my campaigns already. When you are ready, you will assume command of the Legion.'

'Am I not ready now?' Corvus said, having been elevated and then deflated by the Emperor's words.

'Not yet, my son,' said the Emperor. 'But soon you will emerge to join your brothers and take your place at my side and at the head of the Raven Guard. First though, tell me of Kiavahr. What are your intentions?'

'To bring peace to both the world and its moon, and to heal the wounds of the past,' said Corvus. 'With your help, I will succeed.'

'Peace is the hardest goal to achieve,' said the Emperor. 'Victory, the cessation of war, the demilitarisation of our opponents, these we can obtain with might of arms and perseverance. Peace? That is an altogether different beast.'

Corvus frowned, but nodded slowly.

The Emperor sipped from his glass, his gaze unmoving. 'Tell me again, then. Tell me of the wounds you and your followers inflicted upon this world, and of the peace you would bring to it with my help.'

THERE WAS PALPABLE excitement amongst the legionaries within the inner vault. Alpharius had seen many things in the service of his Legion – sights that would stay with him until he died, of strange worlds and even stranger foes – but the very mundanity of his surroundings added to their mystique. This was a place of science, the laboratory where the Emperor had set about bringing to life his vision for the galaxy.

Unnoticed by the others, Alpharius walked around the circle of incubators until he came to the one numbered 20. The last, always overlooked, his primarchs had begun their lives in this metal and glass construction. It looked the same as the others, no larger to account for the twins that had been nurtured within. Perhaps the Emperor had not intended for there to be Omegon and Alpharius. That the two had been nourished as one accounted for their strange bond, and perhaps their slighter build in comparison to their brother primarchs.

Had the Primogenitors of the Alpha Legion known this was where they would send their agent? Surely not, Alpharius thought. Who would have believed that this place still existed?

Everything was pristine, exactly as it had been for decades, centuries perhaps. Alpharius wondered why this place had been kept in this way. What purpose did it serve? He heard Magos Orlandriaz talking excitedly as he accessed a data terminal in the central tower. Wires snaked from the wrist of the tech-priest, plugged into a series of sockets beneath a flickering holographic runepad. A wide screen scrolled with a mass of symbols, the green light reflected in the magos's eyes.

'This… This is amazing,' gushed the tech-priest. 'So much is here. So much!'

'What have you found?' asked Corax, as the primarch looked over the magos's shoulder.

'Everything, I would say. All of the genetic files for you and your brothers. I have studied the splicing of genes and the manipulation of the same for over a hundred years and I cannot comprehend more than a fraction of this.' The magos glanced at Corax, his strange eyes wide.

'The root factors alone will take several years of analysis to deconstruct.'

'We do not have years,' said Corax. 'Horus readies himself for his offensive. I need something that will enable me to rebuild the Raven Guard, not spawn endless theses and theories for your Martian friends.'

'Of course,' muttered Orlandriaz. He busied himself at the console for a while longer while Alpharius absorbed what had been said.

Corax intended to bring the Raven Guard back to full strength, that much was now clear. Alpharius did not know if such a thing was possible, but if it were, a restored Raven Guard Legion would be a serious threat to the Warmaster's plans. The Alpha Legionnaire was confused by the possibility; the Raven Guard had been close to destruction, so what purpose would be served by allowing them to escape and cling to this lifeline?

It struck Alpharius that there was some more complex scheme at work than the simple elimination of his adopted Legion. He considered the possibilities and came to the inevitable conclusion: the Alpha Legion could do what Corax intended. If he was able to secure the secrets of the gene-tech for his primarch, his Legion would become paramount amongst those who had turned against the Emperor. He could see the sense in such a plan, and was pleased that it offered some explanation as to why the Alpha Legion had sided with Horus. The Warmaster had struck the first blow against the Emperor, but it would be the Alpha Legion who would eventually emerge from the shadows to take their rightful place.

His thoughts were interrupted by an exclamation from the magos.

'Look at this!' Corax leaned even closer, brow furrowed as he observed Orlandriaz's work. 'Here we see the derived strands, the foci divergences from the primarch

material that was used by the Emperor for the first of the
Legiones Astartes.'

Everyone in the chamber had heard the magos's
words. Custodians and legionaries all turned towards
the tech-priest as he continued, talking more to himself
than the audience.

'It's a masterpiece of engineering,' Orlandriaz said.
'Such sublime beauty encoded into the structure, yet
imbued with endless potential.'

'Speak clearly,' said Corax. 'What have you found?'

'Evidence of the Emperor's true greatness, proof of
his claim to be the Omnissiah,' exclaimed the magos.
'New life from old life. Millions of years of evolution
extracted, distilled and improved. It is the key.'

'The key to what? You make no sense, magos,' said
Agapito. 'What is so important?'

'We must look for the stasis chamber,' announced
Orlandriaz, turning away from the screen. He flinched,
as if he had forgotten the others around him. He looked
around the chamber for a few moments before addressing himself to Corax. 'It would take many years of
deciphering these files to produce anything of direct use
to you, Lord Corax. However, in the vault somewhere
is a stasis cubicle, which contains the secret we require.'

The magos's words prompted another flash of memory in the mind of Corax. He saw a cylinder, glowing
with silvery light, encased by a mesh of golden wire. A
sequence entered his thoughts, and the primarch tapped
in the code on the holograph.

Dozens of lights lit up on the central console, flashing in sequence as Corax entered the cipher. When he
tapped the last rune, the strobing lights settled into a constant gleam. New messages flickered across the screen,
announcing security protocol deactivation, granting
access to the console's contents. With a puff of escaping
gases, lines appeared in the central spire of the machine,

which resolved into panels that extended outwards and slid down into newly-revealed recesses. Silver glowed from within as an intricate wire cradle emerged from the depths of the device, just as Corax remembered. At the heart of the mesh was a narrow cylinder half a metre high. It was encrusted with suspensor devices that lifted it from the containing web, as if it ascended on the light itself. A bluish green fluid trembled inside, freed from the stasis field that had confined it.

'This is the true secret of the vault,' announced Corax. Around him, the Raven Guard, Mechanicum adepts and Custodians gathered, attention drawn by the spectacle. 'This is the gift of the Emperor.'

'What is it?' asked Agapito, voice hushed.

'The source of our existence, commander. Living genetic material used to create the primarchs.'

THOUGH HE DID not have the expertise of the Magos genetor, Corax knew enough from his own experience and the memories of the Emperor to understand the importance of the discovery. The Emperor had explained to him many years ago how the primarchs' genetic material had been used to create the first warriors of the Legiones Astartes. His Raven Guard were his genetic sons, in a way, as all of the Legions were of their primarchs. Each of the twenty had been created by the Emperor, unique with their own strengths and weaknesses. What the Raven Guard had was the blueprint from which each of the twenty primarchs had been first derived. It was pure, for want of a better word, unchanged by the Emperor's subsequent experiments. The perfect specimen from which to extract gene-seed for future generations of Raven Guard, or to create a whole new generation of primarchs.

'Surely you do not intend to remove this sample from Terra?' said Arcatus. 'I am no magos, but I understand enough history to know that the secret of the primarchs' genetic code cannot be allowed out of this vault. What if it were to fall into the hands of Horus?'

'The Emperor himself led me to this place,' replied the primarch. 'I need no further warning, nor license, from you. It is the wish of the Emperor that I return to Deliverance to rebuild my Legion with this technology.'

'Is it true, lord?' asked Agapito. 'Does this sample hold the key to the future of the Raven Guard?'

'Yes it does,' said Corax, smiling at the thought. 'An untainted source of gene-seed, but more than just that. If the magos and I can unlock its secrets, we can combine its potential with that of the Raven Guard gene-code. The primarchs were created from birth, while a legionary must wait until adolescence before implantation can begin. Imagine a generation of Raven Guard that combines the code of both, the superior growth of a primarch enmeshed with the abilities of a legionary. What would normally take a generation could be accomplished in months.'

'What about training?' said Arcatus. 'What about proper education in the nature of Enlightenment? A legionary is more than just an enhanced body. He is forged in mind as well as flesh. These things cannot be rushed, their implementation is as much an important part of the process as the physical changes.'

'I did not say it would be instant,' said Corax, annoyed by the Custodian's negativity. 'You still fail to understand the full possibility. At present, only the smallest percentage of candidates are suitable for gene-seed implantation. If we can use the primarch material properly, that will no longer be the case. We could take any child, from the earliest age, and accelerate their development, as mine was hastened. *Any* child. Our recruitment pool would expand from a few tens of thousands to millions.'

'But each primarch was crafted by the Emperor himself,' said Agapito. 'A labour of many years by the greatest mind of mankind. We do not have such resources, or the time.'

'Which is why we will not be creating a new generation of primarchs,' snapped Corax, exasperated that his commander showed such doubt. He calmed himself, realising that Agapito and the others, except perhaps for Orlandriaz, could not comprehend the technical issues involved. 'The tech-priest will aid me in isolating those strands of the material we require, and we will then improve the Raven Guard gene-seed with that information. A blend of primarch and Legiones Astartes: a warrior superior to a legionary, yet produced on an unprecedented scale.'

'And I say again that such a weapon cannot be allowed to leave Terra,' said Arcatus. 'If the Emperor had desired such a thing, he would have created it himself. There is a reason why he fashioned the gene-seed of the Legions in the way he did. Unless you think you will achieve something the Emperor could not?'

The retort that sprang to Corax's mind stayed there as he considered the Custodian's words. Was he allowing himself to get carried away by the prospect of rebuilding the Raven Guard? Was it even possible to achieve what he had said? Given pause, he took a deep breath, considering his answer.

'It may be that the Emperor chose to create the gene-seed with its current limitations for good reason, but the galaxy has changed,' said the primarch. 'It is equally ludicrous to suggest the Emperor granted me access to this facility without knowing my full intent. He has allowed us to enter this place so that we might make use of its contents. It is the will of the Emperor that we unravel the secret of this technology and use it in the fight against Horus.'

Arcatus had no reply to this and turned away without

further word. Agapito remained, and he spoke with concern in his voice.

'Whatever the rights and wrongs, I can't say, lord,' said the commander. 'But Arcatus speaks the truth when he says that this is dangerous. We cannot let knowledge of its existence spread too far.'

'What are you suggesting?' said the primarch. 'The only man on this expedition who is not a Raven Guard or Custodian is Orlandriaz, and the Sigillite vouched for his presence.'

'If we return to Deliverance with this technology, it will not go unnoticed by those outside the Legion,' said Agapito. 'The fewer that know of its existence, the better. I think we must learn a lesson from the Emperor here. It will require facilities and technicians to perform the work to unlock the gene-secrets. If such a place is heavily guarded it will attract attention. We know there are still guild sympathisers on Lycaeus, and despite our best efforts they still have the means to know what passes in the Ravenspire. We must avoid rousing their curiosity.'

'You make a good point, commander,' said Corax. 'I have been so focused on the retrieval of the genetic archive I have not considered how we should house it. Your plan has merit, I will consider it.'

'And do you really think it is possible to create a new form of legionary?' asked Agapito, his voice touched by awe. 'One that is as good as any of us, in a fraction of the time?'

'I do not only believe it possible, I guarantee it,' said Corax. 'With Horus poised to strike, we must retaliate in some fashion. Unless we have the means to perpetuate the Legion for the war to come, we cannot risk our current strength in such an attack. The Emperor has placed his faith in me and I will not fall short of the mark. The Raven Guard *will* have a part to play before the matter with Horus is decided.'

'I am sure of that, lord,' Agapito said. 'What of the Custodians? Do you think they will cause further problems?'

'Arcatus overplays his objections,' said Corax. 'He must attend to his duties as he sees them, but I think he understands what we will achieve. I believe I have convinced our companion that we pose no threat to the Emperor.'

THE EXIT FROM the vault was far less fraught with danger than the entry. Having secured the contents of the inner chamber, the precious stasis capsule of primarch material included, the Raven Guard loaded up their supply carriers and heavy servitors to extract their spoils to the surface.

They worked in shifts, escorting lines of cases and crates back through the dormant Labyrinth to the waiting shuttles on the ice shelf at the entrance. Data crystals and storage units were carefully sealed within protective boxes. Larger pieces of equipment, the purpose of which was lost on all except the magos and Corax, were secured to the tracked trolleys that had brought in the expedition's ammunition and food. Only the incubators and a few power generators were left behind.

It took the best part of a day to ferry everything to the surface. During that time, a signal was sent to the Raven Guard ship waiting in orbit. Drop-craft from the *Avenger* arrived as the last of the expedition emerged from the vault, together with the most precious treasures, which were watched over by the primarch himself, Orlandriaz and Arcatus.

Alpharius, along with the rest of Sergeant Dor's squad, again found himself hefting boxes onto the drop-ships while the commanders discussed what was to happen next. Alpharius dawdled as much as he was able, to hear snippets of the discussion, though he learnt nothing that he would not have expected.

'Be very careful with that,' said Agapito, as Alpharius took the handles of a frost-rimed crate, Velps at the other end. A blinking energy monitor on the side of the box indicated the below-zero temperature within. 'Break that stasis generator and we'll have gone through all of this for nothing.'

'Aye, commander,' replied Velps.

They carried their cargo onto the ramp of the closest Stormbird, treading carefully through the drifts of snow. Alpharius was quietly amazed at the contents of the container: the stuff from which the primarchs had been created, from which the Emperor had engineered the Legiones Astartes, and ultimately the gene material that had turned him into an Alpha Legionnaire.

Odd thoughts crept into his mind as he hefted the box over the lip of the entry portal. How long had the Emperor laboured to create the contents of the stasis chest? Decades? Centuries? Perhaps even millennia? For untold generations he had waited, and when the Emperor had shown himself to the galaxy, it was at the head of the Legiones Astartes, his chosen warriors. The Alpha Legion had fought alongside the others for many years during the Great Crusade, seeing time and again their companions reunited with their genetic fathers while they fought on without the guidance of their primarch.

Alpharius remembered the discovery of his namesake, the last of the primarchs to be found. It had been as joyous for the Alpha Legion as the same event had been for the Luna Wolves, or the Iron Hands, or the Raven Guard. Each had been celebrated by all of the Legions as a momentous occasion. Yet the reunification with Alpharius had been a muted affair, almost overlooked by the other primarchs and Legions. That the nature of the twin primarchs was deemed a secret not to be revealed had only deepened the lack of celebration. It had rankled

Alpharius that his Legion had been all but dismissed by those who had found their primarchs. It had been an afterthought, a niggling gap that had been filled, rather than being seen for what it truly was: the apex of the Great Crusade when the last of the primarchs had been brought back into the Emperor's armies. Alpharius's discovery was the culmination of the Emperor's plans, not the mundane arrival of a latecomer.

With the aid of Velps, Alpharius slid the stasis container into a locker beneath the decking. They secured it with tightened straps so that it would not move, and lowered the deck grating over it, stowing it away for the journey to orbit.

'Makes you thankful, doesn't it?' said Velps, pointing down at the container.

'Thankful about what?' replied Alpharius.

'Thankful for the Emperor,' Velps explained. 'I don't know why Horus has turned, or those others, but it confounds me. The Emperor created us. I mean, literally he made us what we are. He gave us weapons and armour and a galaxy to conquer and let us free. He made us the future of humanity, and that is something to be thankful for, deep in the heart. We were right there, it was almost finished. That bastard Horus, he had everything thanks to the Emperor and now he's turned his back on him. There's no forgiving something like that.'

Alpharius did not argue, though he was stung by Velps's words. He could say nothing in defence of the choices the Alpha Legion had made. He did not fully understand why the twin primarchs had sided with Horus, but he trusted them to know what was for the best.

'I'm sure everyone will get what they deserve in the end,' he said, slapping a comradely hand to Velps's shoulder.

It left Alpharius unsettled as they made their way back

down the ramp. The rest of the expedition was already tramping onto the shuttles and drop-ships. Sergeant Dor and the others were waiting to board, not far from Agapito and Corax. Alpharius and Velps joined the squad just as Arcatus approached the primarch.

'I have spoken with Malcador,' the warrior announced, 'and he agrees with me. I and my Custodian Guard will travel with you, in order that this cargo is protected properly.'

'That is not necessary,' said Agapito. 'Your presence will arouse suspicion. Besides, we don't need your help.'

'My commander is correct, if blunt,' said Corax. 'A group of Custodians will attract unwarranted attention, and it is with secrecy that our cargo is best protected.'

'We come with you, or you do not leave,' said Arcatus. 'I leave the choice up to you.'

Corax sighed and nodded.

'Very well, Custodian, have it your way,' said the primarch. 'You will travel with me. Be warned, space is already pushed aboard the *Avenger*. You will have to billet with my warriors.'

'That will not be an issue,' said Arcatus.

'Not a problem,' said Agapito, with some satisfaction. 'The Raven Guard will be happy to extend the same hospitality to the Legio Custodes as they gave to us.'

The group parted, leaving Alpharius and the rest of the squad in the snow. Alpharius looked at the golden-armoured warriors accompanying the primarch and felt on edge. With the vault contents in their possession, the Raven Guard would be more vigilant than ever.

A slap on the shoulder guard snapped Alpharius from his distracted thoughts. Sergeant Dor jabbed a thumb at a nearby drop-ship.

'Get on board,' said Dor. 'We're heading back to Deliverance.'

PART TWO

RECONSTRUCTION

TEN

Return to Deliverance
Unlocking the Gene-tech
Caesari

THE LANDSCAPE OF Deliverance was dominated by a kilo-metre-high needle at the centre of the workshops. Once this had been the infamous Black Tower, the main cita-del of Kiavahr's guards. Now it was called Ravenspire. Spotlights from dozens of gantries pierced the black void, shining down upon transportways and sprawling mineheads. Defence turrets studded its surface, guided by gleaming sensor-lenses in armoured niches, arrayed like the eyes of a fly. Corax's Stormbird descended over the sprawl of the ancient prison towards one of the eight landing aprons that jutted from Ravenspire like grey fungi on a black stalagmite, each surrounded by the pale glow of an energy field.

Looking at the maze of prison wings and guard houses, it would be an observer's first thought that the moon's facilities were in disrepair. Rockcrete housings and metal panels covered the surface of the buildings like patchwork, while some areas were left blasted and burnt, open to the airless vacuum of space. Force domes glittered in the starlight, protecting clusters of high-rise cell blocks, fuel storage tanks and ore transport hubs.

The appearance of Deliverance was deceptive. All damage caused during the rebellion and the subsequent counter-attack by the guilds had been fully repaired. Not a crack leaked air nor a door seal was broken. By order of Corax, the settlement bore its scars as reminders of those who had died to free the moon-colony from the oppressive tyrants on the planet below; as long as such affectations did not compromise safety or security.

As Corax gazed down through the port of the Storm-bird, he could remember every single rupture and ruin, as if they had been wounds on his own flesh. The drop-ship passed over Wing Eight, where he had lived with Antonu, and where the rebellion had truly begun. The once-majestic Twelfth Gate that linked Wing Eight to the Ravenspire bore the marks of the bombs that had been planted by his guerrillas to trap the guards who had come flowing out of the central spire, welts of darker plasfoam that filled the cracks like scar tissue. Naphrem Solt, a thirteen year-old girl, had sacrificed herself to det-onate the last of the charges to bring down the arching gateway on the reinforcements.

Wing Seven was all but a ruin. Burnt-out cells with empty windows stared into the blackness. Four thou-sand inmates had perished there, scourged by a fireball unleashed when the guards detonated the main gas supply. Corax had not anticipated this, and it was with bitter memories that he looked down at the blackened shell of the prison wing. It had taken more than a year to recover all of the bodies from the ash, babes and elders for the most part, Wing Seven having been a low security administrative complex.

Corax had scoured the security logs to find out the man responsible and had tracked down Corporal Theod Norruk four days later. The primarch's revenge had been drawn out, a moment he was not proud of, but which had brought him a small sense of satisfaction at the time.

Only one building stood out as much as Ravenspire, connected by a silvery tunnel to the main edifice. The castle-like structure, with peaked roof and corner turrets, gleamed in the light of the setting star, silver and obsidian, a marvel of Imperial engineering. It was formally called the Primary Administration Core, but to the inhabitants outside its shining walls it was known as the Tax Keep. Corax would be addressing those who worked within later that night, but he had more pressing business to attend to first.

The Stormbird passed through the energy canopy of High Dock, Corax's view becoming one of yellow static for a moment. He turned away from the window as the Stormbird's jets whined into the final descent.

'Do you know what you are going to say?' asked Branne, sitting opposite the primarch. 'I foresee it causing trouble, lord.'

'Not yet,' replied Corax. 'Not every word. They will have to deal with the reality, there is no avoiding what must be done.'

'It's a complication we could do without,' said the Commander of Recruits. Corax agreed but made no further comment.

The drop-ship touched down with a screech of metal landing pads on the ferrocrete.

'A necessary action,' muttered Corax, standing up as the drop-ship settled into place. The door hissed open behind him. 'One that I would have performed without Malcador's insistence.'

The pair departed the Stormbird and made their way the short distance to the Carnivalis, a hall near the bottom of Ravenspire that had been used for large gatherings of the Legion. It was part feasting chamber and part reliquary of the Legion's many victories. Trophies of all kinds – weapons, skulls, armour, banners, even pieces of wall and armoured doors of enemy citadels – were hung upon the walls. There was little organisation to the display, which had once led Iterator Sermis Iconialis to remark that it looked more like the nest of a magpie than a raven.

That same individual now waited with one hundred and fifty-six other men and women in the Carnivalis, having been summoned there by Corax as the *Avenger* had attained orbit. Along with his fellow iterator, Loc Nasturbright, Iconialis was accompanied by Deliverance's remembrancers. Artists, poets, pictographers, sculptors and journalists gazed at Corax with a mixture of apprehension, suspicion and expectation as the primarch entered the vast hall. The small crowd was dwarfed by its surroundings and had gathered about the stage area and lectern at the far end of the hall, forcing Corax to walk the length of the Carnivalis before he could address them. He strode up the stairs to the stage, easily taking the steps four at a time, and turned towards the assembled remembrancers.

'You are all to return to your quarters, pack up your personal belongings and prepare to leave Deliverance,' he said. The announcement was met with shouts of condemnation, groans, pleas and general hubbub. 'Quiet! I have not finished.'

The crowd was stilled as Corax raised his hand for silence.

'Take everything. You will not be returning. All materials you have been compiling for the remembrancing are to be handed over to Commander Branne. You and your luggage will be searched thoroughly, do not attempt to smuggle out even a few rough notes or a doodled cartoon. *Everything* is to be delivered to Branne.'

This caused further outcry, which Corax had been expecting. He caught the gaze of Iconialis, who gave a slight nod of understanding and turned to face the distraught and angry remembrancers. He lifted his hands, stilling the tumult.

'Pray silence for the noble primarch,' said Iconialis, his voice clear and precise, cutting through the few lingering grumbles and whispers. 'I am sure there is good cause for this action. Let us not forget that it is by the grace of Lord Corax that we have remained here.'

'Thank you, iterator,' said Corax. He folded his arms and ran through what he had to say. Malcador's last communication before the *Avenger* had left orbit had been to dissolve the Order of Remembrancers and send them back to Terra for debriefing, in accordance with the Edict of Dissolution. The Sigillite had made it clear that Corax was not to discuss in detail the events that were currently overtaking the Imperium. He had also acknowledged that some explanation was necessary and had furnished the primarch with a few preferred phrases to convey what had happened. Corax dismissed the suggestions, preferring to say things in his own way.

'Horus has rebelled against the Emperor,' he said. There was no point in keeping the situation secret. Better that Corax told the remembrancers the bald facts than they heard half-truths and rumours. He waited, expecting another storm of surprise and protest, but instead his words were met with shocked silence. 'You may have heard before Commander Branne left Ravenspire that a force of the Legiones Astartes had been despatched to confront the Warmaster at Isstvan. That confrontation did not end well. The Emperor gathers his forces and the Raven Guard will be amongst them. We cannot offer you protection here, so you will be removed from Deliverance and returned to Terra.'

'I come from Assyri,' called out a bearded man with a long cowl and paint marks on the sleeves of his loose tunic. Unlike his warriors and Legion attendants, Corax had never bothered to learn the names of most of the remembrancers, seeing them as an inconvenience at the best of times, and an irritation and distraction at the worst. 'I don't want to go to Terra.'

This was followed by several similar protests.

'It is not for you to decide,' said Corax. 'We are not going to shuttle each of you back to your preferred choice of destination. You will all go back to Terra for debriefing by the offices of Malcador the Regent. There will be no exceptions.'

'Why do you want all of our work?' asked a young woman with a pictograph unit hanging on a strap around her neck. 'We've worked for years gathering that material.'

'Intelligence,' Corax replied bluntly. 'Many of you have mingled with remembrancers attached to other Legions, particularly the Luna Wolves. We will examine your accumulated material for insights into Horus's rebellion.'

He did not add that the remembrancers had chronicled most of the Raven Guard's accomplishments and victories, as well as the defences of Deliverance. He could not risk the ship transporting the remembrancers being taken by a traitor vessel with such information on board.

'Just how bad is this?' asked Iconialis, his voice losing its usual timbre, hushed with worry. 'I mean… I do not know what to say. I can scarcely believe it.'

'I won't lie to you, iterator. War is coming, like nothing you've ever seen. A war that will tear the galaxy apart. A war between the Legiones Astartes.'

THE PRISONER WAITED patiently, bemused by his incarceration. He sat on a plain chair that was almost too small for him, dressed in a simple grey robe. He was being kept in an empty storage room not far from Alpha Terminal near the summit of Ravenspire. Corax had ordered the old punishment cells sealed forever after the revolution and it had seemed pointless to open up one of the vacant wings for one legionary. On a world that had once housed nearly ten million prisoners, the massive warrior looked incongruous amongst the metal shelves and cabinets; there was still a mop and bucket in the corner.

Agapito stood to one side of the closed door, Solaro on the other. The commanders stared directly ahead, not looking at their charge. Agapito did so only with immense self-control, and knew that Solaro felt the same. That the prisoner was still alive was a testament to the discipline of the legionaries that had returned directly from Isstvan. He had been taken into custody and treated with a level of dignity that many of them had not known as inmates of Lycaeus. Corax had taught them that there was no honour in heaping the suffering they had endured on others.

A spoken word from the legionary standing outside heralded the arrival of the primarch. Corax had been forced to deal with the remembrancers first, but this matter had been raised between the primarch and his commanders on the return to Deliverance. Agapito opened the door, unsure what his master intended as Corax ducked through, instantly filling the small room with his bulk. The door closed again with a dull clang and Agapito finally allowed himself to look at the prisoner, disgust welling up from the pit of his stomach.

His name was Iarto Khoura and he had come to the Raven Guard shortly after the Edict of Nikaea to ensure the ban on the Librarians was enforced. Like others of his kind throughout the Legions, he had been an unpopular figure, an embodiment of outside interference that aggravated the independently-minded Raven Guard. Despite this, Agapito had never had any personal argument against the man, and had fought alongside him in several wars.

The Word Bearers Chaplain looked up at Corax's entrance, relief on his face.

'Lord Corax,' he said, rising to his feet with a bow of the head. 'I am glad you have returned to right this matter.'

'Be silent,' snapped the primarch, causing the Chaplain to flinch. 'Sit down and do not speak.'

'I have been patient thus far with your men, bu–'

'*Silence!*'

Corax's roar flooded the room, causing Agapito's ears to ring. Khoura fell into the chair, almost breaking it, stunned by the violence of the primarch's outburst.

'You are a traitor,' said Corax, his voice now dipping to an angered whisper, more intimidating than his shout. 'You are an enemy of the Emperor.'

Khoura opened his mouth and then quickly closed it as the primarch's frown grew even deeper.

'Your primarch is a cowardly, treacherous worm,' Corax continued, crouching down so that his face was centimetres from that of the Chaplain. 'Your Legion are worthless scum, whose false praises of the Emperor ring even hollower than ever. Your fellow Chaplains are either dead or fled.'

Fighting against the urge to retort to such accusations, Khoura squirmed in the chair, mouthing wordless defences.

'Why did you not come to Isstvan?' demanded Corax.

'It was not my place,' replied the Chaplain. 'It was better that I remained here to continue my instruction of the Legion's recruits. You agreed with that proposal, lord.'

'Convenient for you. Very convenient that you were not there when your Legion opened fire on my warriors, cutting them down from behind.'

'They did what?' Khoura looked aghast at the thought and shook his head. 'No, that is impossible.'

'There are seventy-five thousand Raven Guard corpses as evidence of its possibility,' snarled Corax. 'How long have you been planning your betrayal, Iarto? Since the Emperor slapped Lorgar back into place? Before then?'

'I am a Chaplain, dedicated to the spread of the Imperial Truth,' replied Khoura. 'I was despatched to Deliverance by the edict of Malcador to ensure the Emperor's will was being done.'

'More lies! You were sent by Lorgar to spy on us, to pervert my warriors to the cause of Horus.'

'That is not true. What evidence do you possess that I am anything but a loyal servant of the Emperor? I have been with your Legion since Nikaea. How can you hold me responsible for the actions of my primarch?'

'Because you are a Word Bearer. You speak with the tongue of Lorgar. That is your dark creed. You masquerade as the bearer of Enlightenment, but you are nothing but an apostle of treachery.'

'You have no right to acc–'

Corax snatched up Khoura by the throat, lifting him into the air, banging the Chaplain's head against the ceiling.

'Liar! Nothing but filthy lies spill from your bastard lips, son of Lorgar.'

Agapito took a step forwards, but was stopped by Solaro's hand on his arm. The other commander silently shook his head. Khoura's gasping face grew redder and redder as the primarch's grip tightened.

'This is my world, my Legion,' rasped Corax. 'You pollute both with your presence.'

There was a loud crack and Khoura's head flopped to one side, neck snapped. Corax growled wordlessly and lowered the limp corpse back onto the chair. He turned back towards the door and stopped suddenly as he saw Agapito and Solaro. The primarch's face was deathly white, his eyes black pits. Agapito felt a moment of trepidation as he looked at his lord's twisted snarl.

'Throw this filth in a furnace,' said Corax. He closed

his eyes and visibly calmed, some of the blood returning to his face. 'I want his quarters searched again. If there is anything to connect him to Horus's plans, I want it found. Check his communications logs to see if he was contacted by Lorgar or any of the other Word Bearers within the last year.'

'Should we not have done that before his execution?' asked Solaro.

Agapito drew in a sharp breath, detecting a hint of annoyance in the tone of the other commander.

'To what end?' said Corax.

'Proof of his guilt, as he demanded,' said Solaro. The commander met the primarch's gaze without fear, hands clasped respectfully in front of him.

'We cannot take the risk of allowing a traitor in our ranks. Besides, I could smell the taint on him, now that I know what it is,' said Corax. He looked at Agapito. 'You saw what had become of the Word Bearers on Isstvan.'

'I saw things that I wish I never had,' replied Agapito. 'The Word Bearers were only one amongst many such.'

'If you are blind to it, I must open your eyes,' said the primarch. 'Too long have we kept this secret. It was the Emperor's will, but that no longer matters. He underestimated its threat.'

'What are you saying, lord?' said Solaro. 'What threat?'

Corax blinked rapidly with surprise and wiped a hand across his face. His expression of torment had gone when he removed his pale hand, replaced by a saner look.

'Nothing. I am not… My judgement is clouded,' said Corax. He opened the door but turned his head as he stepped through. 'Send Branne to me. We must prepare the recruits.'

When the primarch was gone, Solaro gave Agapito a strange look.

'What was that about? What stench?' asked the commander.

'Must be a primarch thing,' replied Agapito. 'I smell nothing here except the sweat of a dead man. You go and fetch Branne, I'll deal with this.'

Agapito spent several minutes looking at Khoura's corpse after Solaro had left, thinking about what the primarch had said. Solaro was indeed blind to it, perhaps had not seen the taint, but Agapito knew what Corax had referred to. The taint had a name, a name he had heard whispered for the first time on Isstvan: *Chaos*.

RAD-FIRES FLICKERED BLUE at the heart of the mangled city, turning the ruddy sky purple with their blaze. The ruins stretched for dozens of kilometres, silhouettes like broken teeth jutting against the glow. For nearly a century the fires had burned, a warning to Kiavahr not to return to its despicable past. The impact site was a cratered bowl of glass, levelled in an instant by the atomic mining charges the rebels had dropped down the gravity well. The stump of the orbital elevator remained as a twisted upthrust of solidified slurry that pointed accusingly at Lycaeus above.

Further out the buildings had survived, though some were little more than molten piles of rubble and slag. Gas pockets and ruptured fuel lines added their own sporadic glare to the scene, brightening the dead landscape with flashes of white-hot promethium plumes and clouds of venting vapour that oxidised into flurries of green and orange before dissipating into the polluted atmosphere.

With no buildings to break it, the wind raged, scouring the ruins with hurricane force, adding its own erosion to the destruction wrought by the improvised nuclear bombs. Bridges over glowing rivers of molten ferrocrete swayed dangerously, their metallic creaks and groans an eerie cry in the desolation. Stairwells ascended into thin air where once stratoscrapers had soared towards the heavens. Foundry cooling pools had become rad-lakes, tumbled aqueducts spilt forth sluggish rivers that oozed rather than flowed along sheer-sided ravines that had once been the streets of Nairhub.

Into this crawled a convoy of armoured vehicles, their broad tracks churning through the dust and ash. Each vehicle was low and broad, carried on four independent sets of tracks. The wind keened from their heavily riveted hulls and whipped communication aerials back and forth. They were marked with the symbols of the Mechanicum, but the armoured legionaries manning the open defence cupolas showed the livery to be a deception.

Five in all, the transports advanced slowly, the lead vehicle picking its way over the piles of rubble, grinding and crushing brick and ferrocrete beneath its bulk. Alpharius manned a turret on the foremost rad-crawler, twin heavy bolters on the pintle in front of him. Despite the ruin, the rad-zone was not without its inhabitants, both humanoid and otherwise. He had been surprised by talk of guilders hiding out in the wastes, protected by flimsy rad-domes and force shelters. Corax had left it to the Mechanicum to clear the last remnants of the old authorities, eager to join the Great Crusade. That the Mechanicum had been lax in their prosecution of the guild survivors would no doubt be of great benefit to the Alpha Legion's task here.

One building stood proud amongst the debris of the old war. Swathed with noxious fog, it stood three storeys high, slab-sided like a hangar, and bore the sigil of the Raven Guard. Armoured towers at each end followed the advance of the vehicles with batteries of lascannons.

'Ravendelve in sight,' Commander Agapito reported over the vox.

It was a training facility, used by the Raven Guard to conduct wargames in the nuclear wasteland. Sometimes the recruits were sent out against the separatist camps that still eked out an existence in the heart of the atomic carnage. It was here that Corax had chosen to set up his new facility, away from the eyes of the Mechanicum.

It was a good choice for seclusion, and with news of Horus's treachery bound to have reached Kiavahr, it struck Alpharius as good cover for the gene-tech laboratory. Those few who might notice would not be surprised at an increase of activity here.

There was an outer wall guarding the compound, ten metres high. Armoured gates slid aside to allow the vehicles to enter, and then ground shut when the last transport had passed. Radiation detectors in Alpharius's suit flashed from green to a warning amber for a moment as they passed along the road to the building: a rad pocket. He had no concerns for his safety. Even without his armour, his modified body was capable of withstanding the levels of nuclear pollution in the area. Further into the wastes would be a different matter, and as the transporter shuddered to a halt in the shadow of Ravendelve, he wondered again how the dissidents could survive at all.

Covered by the defences of the station, the Raven Guard disembarked and formed up beside their vehicles while Corax, Agapito and Branne headed into the facility. The hydraulic ramps on the side of each transport lowered and they began the process of unloading their precious cargo.

Alpharius had noticed something particular about the force sent down to Kiavahr when they had boarded the strike cruiser that had brought them here: they were all from the vault expedition. Clearly Corax trusted only those he was forced to with the knowledge of the gene-tech. There were no serfs, only legionaries, the most trustworthy of the Emperor's servants. The only exceptions were the tech-priest and his servitors, who were

essential to the project. The Alpha Legionnaire wondered what story had been told to the rest of the Raven
Guard to explain the goings-on on the world below.

Secrets made Alpharius happy. In secrecy, Corax hoped
to rebuild his Legion, but secrets were the favoured bat-
tleground of the Alpha Legion. The Raven Guard were
entering alien territory now, and would be made to pay
for their inexperience. Secrecy created its own problems
of communication, and would ultimately hamper Corax.
The primarch had stepped into a twilight world of misdirection, and would be made to pay for the mistake.
The increased security did not bother Alpharius now;
he was already one of the trusted few. The Raven Guard
feared their secret would be discovered and would bend
their efforts to maintaining the falsehood, not knowing
that their security had already been compromised and
the enemy lurked within.

The interior of Ravendelve was far larger than Alpharius had expected. It burrowed into the ground for several
more levels. He followed the rest of the squad down a
ramp towards the sub-levels, a motorised trolley steered
in front of him, into the bowels of the facility. Most of
the space was taken up with the dorm rooms for recruits
and legionaries sent here on exercise – empty for the
moment – with the rest taken up by a huge drill hall and
firing ranges.

'Where are you going?'

Alpharius froze at the sound of Branne's voice. He
looked over his shoulder to see the Commander of
Recruits and his brother standing at a doorway he had
just passed, the twinkling lights of command consoles
winking behind them.

'Pardon, commander?' said Alpharius, not sure what
was expected of him.

'That crate, it's clearly marked for the infirmary,' continued Branne. 'What are you doing down here? We

don't have the luxury of time to dawdle about.'

'Have you lost your way?' asked Agapito, a smile on his lips.

The unease of Alpharius increased dramatically as he realised the two commanders were expecting him to change direction and head towards the infirmary there and then. He had no idea where it was! His eyes scoured the walls for any sign or markings that might indicate its location. There was nothing to aid him. He looked back at Agapito and Branne, something like desperation surfacing in his thoughts.

'You can share the elevator with me,' a voice called down the corridor. Alpharius swung around and saw the white armour of Vincente Sixx, an Apothecary he had met after infiltrating the Legion on Isstvan V. He was standing at the open door of a conveyor in a small vestibule behind Alpharius.

'Good idea,' said Alpharius, breathing a sigh of relief. He thumbed the motor of the trolley into life and guided it towards the waiting Apothecary, who slid the door closed behind him as Alpharius brought his trolley to a stop on the metal floor of the elevator.

'I know how you feel,' said Sixx, pulling a lever to send the elevator ascending to the upper levels. 'It seems like an age since I was last here. Can barely remember where anything is.'

'Too true,' said Alpharius. A thought occurred to him. 'I don't remember you from the expedition on Terra.'

'No, I stayed on the *Avenger*,' said Sixx. 'I'm Chief Apothecary now, though, so the primarch couldn't well start all of this gene-tech business without bringing me in. To be honest, even the little of what I've seen is way beyond anything I know. Nexin, the tech-priest, will be doing most of the work. I'm just here to liaise.'

'A solemn duty,' said Alpharius, 'and a great responsibility.'

'One I am entirely unprepared for,' said Sixx without any hint of humour. 'My brother Apothecaries suffered badly at the dropsite. It would appear that the traitors set out to target us from the outset. Only seven of us got back, and even with only fifteen years in the Apothecarion, it seems I'm the longest-serving. Now I'm supposed to be running the whole project.'

'I'm sure Corax has every confidence in you.' The elevator rattled to a halt and Alpharius dragged open the door. 'We're all depending on you, Sixx. You won't let us down.'

'The infirmary's this way,' said the Apothecary, pointing to the right.

'Yes, it's coming back to me now,' said Alpharius. 'Thanks for the help. Let me know if I can return the favour.'

'I'll find plenty for you to do, have no worry about that,' said Sixx. 'If even half of what Nexin says is true, there'll be no shortage of work for everyone. Rebuilding a Legion is going to be hard work.'

Not as hard as it was to destroy one, thought Alpharius, as he followed the Apothecary along the passageway.

HOLDING THE ELECTROWELDER delicately between his fingertips, Stradon Binalt used his other hand to hold the vent vane in place. Sparks erupted onto his skin, already pockmarked by dozens of similar burns, but the work was so delicate he could not use protective gauntlets. The pain was momentary, barely registered.

The weld complete, he put his tools aside and leaned back on his stool to admire his work. From the other workshops around him came the clatter of pneumatics and the crackle of spark-bonders. The smell of ceramite adhesive was thick, the primitive air filtration systems of Ravenspire's lower levels unable to cope with the vast quantities of the vapour being released by the work of the armourers.

The armourium of Ravenspire was far better equipped
than that of the *Avenger* and progress had been relatively
swift since the return to Deliverance. He hoped it was
swift enough. From what he had heard of the progress
on the new gene-tech, Lord Corax might be leading the
Legion to war again within a few dozen days. He twisted
the nozzle across both axes, satisfied with the freedom of
movement on the joints. Picking up a rag, he wiped away
a small residue on the fuel inlet valves and lifted the vent
into place.

'You said you had something to show me.'

Binalt drew a protective covering over his work as he
stood up and turned to see Commander Agapito at the
door.

'Yes, commander,' said Binalt. 'Follow me.'

He led Agapito between the open-fronted workshops,
where his fellow Techmarines and their non-enhanced
assistants laboured in the glare of fluorescent tubes and
welding sparks. Rows upon rows of shoulder plates and
reinforced greaves hung on the walls. More complete
suits of armour were being assembled in a larger space
attached to the armourium, where a small army of servitors and attendants worked to fit power cabling and
life-support systems into the refurbished suits.

'This way.' Binalt directed the commander to a solid
blast door on the left. The Techmarine punched in a security code on the pad and the door lifted out of view with
a wheeze of hydraulics. Beyond was the test-firing range.

Lights flickered into life as they entered, to reveal a narrow space a hundred metres long, painted white overlaid
with a grid of thin red lines. At the far end stood three
suits of armour in front of a wall heavily cracked and
pock-marked by impacts. Binalt turned to a rack on the
right and lifted up a bolter. He took out a box of rounds
from a shelf underneath and loaded the weapon before
handing it to Agapito.

'Target the left suit,' said the Techmarine. 'Go for one of the shoulder plates.'

Agapito hefted the bolter up and aimed. With the cough of the launching charge, he fired, the bolt-round flaring into life for a second as it raced down the hall. It struck the left shoulder pad of the empty suit. There was another detonation, the crack echoing back down to the two Space Marines. Shards of ceramite scattered across the firing range, but as the dust cleared, the shoulder pad was shown to be mostly intact.

'That is one of our standard rounds, against Mark IV armour,' said Binalt. 'As you can see, the effect is limited.'

'Yes, I can see that,' said Agapito.

'Yet at the Urgall massacre, the traitors cut down thousands of legionaries with their bolters,' continued Binalt. The words sounded cold, but he remembered painfully the sight and sound of his fellow Raven Guard butchered in the ambush. He had felt helpless, the rounds from his bolt pistol barely scratching the armour of the traitors while their weapons cut through the Raven Guard without mercy. 'I recovered pieces, fragments of the ammunition used by the enemy, from the armour of legionaries who withdrew successfully.'

Taking the bolter from Agapito, Binalt swapped the magazine for another and gave the weapon back to the commander.

'I was also able to procure a few experimental rounds our brothers in the Imperial Fists secured from Mars before it was embroiled by division. We haven't got the facilities to replicate them here, but I think I have devised a close approximation.'

Agapito sighted again and fired. This time, the other shoulder pad of the armour erupted into spinning fragments and droplets of molten ceramite.

'*Vengeance...*' muttered the commander. He lowered the bolter and looked at the Techmarine. 'This is impressive, but also profoundly worrying. It means that the traitors had access to Martian developments before Isstvan.'

'The roots of their rebellion have delved deeply, commander,' Binalt agreed with a sombre nod. 'We are not without countermeasures. Please fire at the central suit.'

The middle stand held one of the suits that had been modified by Binalt's multi-plate, reinforced shoulder pads. This time, Agapito's shot caught the armour's shoulder guard flush on the rim. As with the last shot there was a great explosion of debris, but as the ringing died down, both Raven Guard could clearly see that only the outer layer of armour had been shredded; the inner plating was intact.

Agapito was quiet, staring at the armoured mannequins at the far end of the hall. He distractedly handed the bolter back to Binalt, attention still fixed on the damaged suits.

'What is the matter, commander?' asked the Techmarine. 'Is something not satisfactory?'

'I killed at least a hundred Space Marines on Isstvan,' Agapito said quietly. 'They were Legiones Astartes, just like us. Something I had never thought I would have to do.'

The commander shook his head abruptly, breaking his distant stare.

'This war will not end easily. We must all get used to the idea now.'

THUNDER PEALED FROM Therion's dark clouds and lightning split the violet evening sky, glittering from the glass walls of the Great Conservatory. Ten thousand panes of glass reflected the tumult in the heavens, bright even against the lights that glowed within.

The hippocants snorted mist in the cold, their shaggy coats thick with moisture as the coach driver urged them on through the strengthening rain. The road ahead was fast becoming a stream, water flowing down from the tree-lined embankments that flanked it as it speared across the estate towards the sprawling mansion. The driver was swathed in oilskins, only his nose and eyes visible as he turned to speak into the grille on the body of the carriage behind him.

'Almost there, praefector,' said Pelon, voice muffled.

'Very good, Pelon,' came Valerius's tinny reply.

The Therion servant pulled up the lapels of his heavy coat and adjusted the cord under his chin that kept his broad hat from being whisked away by the wind. It was not an ideal arrangement, but Valerius had been adamant that they depart for his father's palace as soon as possible. The rare storm had prevented them taking an airfoil, and a noble of Therion would never be seen travelling in a gascart, leaving the far more traditional means of the coach as the only option.

Broad-tyred wheels hissed through the puddles as Pelon slowed the carriage to negotiate a small bridge that humped over a foaming stream. The hippocants were controlled by a small box set into a pedestal beside the driver. As his deft fingers moved the levers, pressure bladders in the creatures' harnesses reacted to the radio signal, inflating or deflating in sequence to guide the creatures left and right, urge them on or quell their momentum.

The gate ahead was open already and they passed beneath the arch of silver wrought as two coiling serpents: the ruling crest of Therion.

'Take us straight to the west entrance,' Valerius instructed over the tannoy.

Pelon steered the carriage over the gravel of the compound, the clawed feet of the hippocants throwing up stones to clatter against the bottom of the driving board. He brought them to a halt and then guided them forwards step by step until the carriage door was level with the raised brick walkway that led up to the col-umned entrance to the Great Conservatory.

Many of the windows were open despite the tempest. Pelon saw the telltale glimmer of weathershields glow-ing around the open frames. The sound of music and conversation could just be heard over the rain. Pelon engaged the brakes and dropped the anchor lines over the haunches of the hippocants before twisting in his seat to disengage the door lock. With a puff of pneumat-ics, the door swung out. Pelon dragged out a large rain canopy from under his seat and jumped down to the walkway in time for Valerius to step out under the vast umbrella.

'Seems there's a bit of a party going on,' remarked Valerius as he strode up the rain-soaked pathway, Pelon trotting along beside, struggling to keep hold of the red and white canopy acting as a sail in the wind.

'Your niece's birthday, praefector,' said Pelon.

'Which one?'

'Darius's youngest, Nisella,' replied Pelon.

'Oh, her,' said Valerius. 'Such a pretty young thing.'

'Not so young now, praefector,' said Pelon. They reached the short flight of steps that led up to the entranceway. 'She is six years old now. A woman, not a girl.'

'What's that in Terran?' said the praefector as he mounted the steps. 'I don't see why you insist on using the old calendar, Pelon.'

Because it served us well enough for eighty genera-tions before compliance, thought Pelon, but instead he said, 'That would be roughly seventeen Terran years, praefector.'

'Time passes so quickly,' observed Valerius as they passed under the glass awning of the entrance.

Liveried servants took the umbrella from Pelon and

sponged down Valerius's moist uniform without comment. They carried themselves with the easy manner of
men who had served in the Cohort and the skull buttons
on their lapels attested to the fact. They made no inquiry
of the new arrivals and silently stepped aside to allow the
pair entry. That Valerius wore the red sash of the Therion
elite was proof enough of his right to attend the function.
For an imposter to wear the red was the only capital crime
left on Therion.

Pelon led the way across the deep carpets, the rain
rattling on the canopy of glass above their heads. More
attendants waited at the doors to the conservatory with
gold trays holding spiral-stemmed glasses of wine. Pelon
appropriated one for his master, but the praefector
declined the drink with a wave of his hand and stepped
through the door. Pelon downed the glass's contents
in one gulp and placed it back on the tray with a wink,
earning himself a scowl of disapproval from the servants.
Valerius's manservant was not the least worried about
their disapproval. As simple household servants they were
far below an attendant to a praefector in the informal
hierarchy of the serving class.

He followed a respectful distance behind Valerius as
the praefector made his way across the conservatory. The
festivities were in full swing. Gaily dressed women with
jewelled hairpieces twirled and curtsied as they danced
with men decked out in their fine uniforms braided and
brocaded with gold, a whirl of sparkling colour and gems.
Chandeliers hanging from the white-painted iron of the
conservatory lit all with a soft blue glow, adding to the
unreal atmosphere.

On a small side stage a quintet played a tune on hunt-
flutes and rhintars, the slow tempo of their piece dictating
the whole rhythm of the partygoers. Even those not dancing seemed to congregate and separate in time to the beat,
taking measured paces with each skirl and strum.

Valerius was not in time to this rhythm, hurrying towards a set of spiral stairs that led to a gallery overlooking the proceedings. The praefector kept bumping into people or dodging to avoid them at the last moment, so his progress became a series of faltering steps punctuated by bowed apologies. Pelon closed the gap and assisted his master, picking up dislodged hats, dropped scabbards and canes, and smoothing ruffled skirts and jacket sleeves in Valerius's wake.

A broad-chested man with thick sideburns and beetling brows emerged from the throng just in front of Valerius. He wore a red and black sash over his blue uniform, indicating he had served with the Cohort but was no longer a licensed officer. He slapped a hand to Valerius's shoulder, almost knocking the surprised praefector from his feet.

'Marcus!' boomed the man, who Pelon now recognised as Raulius Tabalian, one of the distant family cousins. He was much larger of gut and jowl than when Pelon had last seen him, which had been at least five Terran years before.

'I'm sorry, I have to speak urgently with my father,' said Valerius, pushing past. Tabalian turned to one of his companions with a scowl.

'Apologies, Equerre Tabalian, my master has very pressing concerns to discuss with the Caesari,' Pelon said hurriedly as he came level with the man. 'I am sure the praefector will find time to reacquaint himself with you soon.'

Valerius's progress had caused quite a stir, rippling out from his path like a bow wave of distraction. Tabalian and several others followed him to the spiral stair, the crowd growing to nearly a dozen by the time the praefector was mounting the wrought iron steps. Pelon made his way through the press with as little shoving as possible and ran up the stairs to catch his master.

The ruling dignitaries of Therion sat on low couches overlooking the floor of the conservatory, even more marvellous in their finery than those below. The band finished playing and the half-dozen members of Valerius's family rose to their feet with polite applause.

'Look, father, Marcus is here!' This came from a woman a little older than the praefector, his sister Miania. All eyes turned towards him as he stepped up to the gallery balustrade, tucking his helmet under one arm as he presented himself with a short bow.

'Caesari,' said the praefector, eyes fixed on the plushly carpeted floor.

'praefector,' replied his father with equal formality.

Caesari Valentinus Valerius was one of the youngest to hold the office, just over seventeen years old; in his late fifties as Terrans measured time. He was even shorter and slighter than his eldest son, clean shaven and with thinning blond hair that was pulled back in a short knot at the base of his skull. His uniform was bedecked with frogging and medals; honours he had rightfully earned in the Therion Cohort alongside the Emperor and Raven Guard.

The Caesari extended his hand in greeting, the thumb and two other digits replaced by mechanical augmetics. Likewise his right ear was a prosthetic device, and he stood slightly lop-sided on his bionic leg. Marcus took the hand and briefly pursed his lips to his father's knuckles before straightening.

'Welcome back to Therion, my son,' declared the Caesari, embracing Marcus tightly.

'Do not hoard him to yourself,' said Juliana, the Caesari's wife. She prised her husband's arms from her son and replaced them with her own, planting an audible kiss on the praefector's cheek.

'I have important news,' said Marcus, freeing himself from his mother's grip.

Pelon glanced over the balcony to see that the party-goers were all paying attention to what passed amongst the ruling family: glasses were held halfway to lips, conversations had dried away.

'Get yourself a drink, Marcus,' said Antonius, the younger of the Caesari's two sons. He looked like a fairer-headed version of his older brother, save for the pockmark of a bullet scar on the right side of his chin. 'Why so glum?'

'Yes, son, settle and tell us what you've been up to,' said Juliana, lifting up a wineglass from a shelf set upon the balustrade. 'It's been such a long time.'

'Horus has rebelled against the Emperor.'

The praefector's blurted words carried far across the conservatory, hushing the few discussions that had continued. From below came the clatter of metal and shattering of glass as a servant spilled his tray in shock.

'What did you say?' demanded the Caesari. 'What do you mean?'

'The Sons of Horus are traitors,' said Marcus. He snatched the glass from his mother's hand with trembling fingers and swallowed the contents. When he continued, it was in a whisper. 'The Warmaster seeks to overthrow the Emperor. Many of the Legiones Astartes have sided with Lupercal. There is going to be civil war.'

'This must be a mistake,' said Juliana. 'Perhaps some of his Legion, but Horus himself...'

'What of the Raven Guard?' asked the Caesari.

'This makes no sense,' said Antonius. 'Are you sure?'

'It happened at Isstvan,' said the praefector, the muscles in his jaw clenching at the memory. 'I saw what happened. I and a handful of others are all that remains of the Therion Cohort. The Raven Guard, they are loyal. Lord Corax sent me here. They were all but destroyed, and it looks as if the traitors finished the job on the Salamanders and Iron Hands.'

The Caesari slumped back onto his couch, face as white as snow, mouth open in dumb shock. Pelon heard the chattering on the main floor and saw some of the guests heading towards the doors. He cautiously tugged at the elbow of his master's coat.

'Praefector, might I make a suggestion?'

'Be quiet, Pelon,' said Marcus, pulling away his arm.

'Some of the guests are leaving,' Pelon said, pointing across the conservatory. 'Rumours, master, can be damaging.'

'Your man's right,' said Antonius. He turned to the Caesari. 'Father, if this news spreads in the wrong way, it will cause hysteria and panic.'

The Caesari beckoned with a raised hand and his chief counsellor, Tribune Pellis, rose from his seat at the far end of the gallery.

'Nobody is to leave yet,' said Valentinus. 'Confiscate all personal communication devices. Not until we've drafted an official proclamation. That includes servants. Have the veterans stationed at every exit, I want nobody coming in or out until I say otherwise.'

Pellis nodded wordlessly and withdrew. The Caesari was recovering from the shock and stood up. He gave Marcus a troubled glance and then began to pace, circling around the couch.

'I assume Corax sent you to raise a new Cohort,' he said, receiving a nod of affirmation from his son. 'Manpower shouldn't be a problem, we've been turning away volunteers for the last two years. We'll need ships to replace the losses, though.'

'Natol Prime, there's a fleet there,' said Antonius. 'Old ships, returning with the Natol regiments, but they'll serve well enough if you send word to the council there.'

'Yes, and we can get help from the forge-world at, oh, what's the damned place called?'

'Some of the Mechanicum have allied with Horus,'

Marcus said before the question could be answered. 'You mean Beta Cornix, father. Best to make sure which side they are on before you go to them.'

The Caesari stopped in his tracks and was again struck dumb for a moment with distress at this news, his expression almost imploring his son to retract what he had said. The unease passed in a few seconds and the Caesari continued his striding.

'That will make weapons acquisition a problem,' said Valentinus.

'The forges of Kiavahr can supply any shortfall,' said the praefector.

'Good, good. I'll have Pellis start the muster first thing in the morning. We can sort out the details once the initial orders have been despatched.' The Caesari stopped and gripped the rail. Below, servants were herding the guests towards the main building, corralling them like hippocants. A musician protested loudly as he was man-handled from the stage, waving his lyrepipe above his head like a regimental banner. 'Anything else we need to decide now?'

'The commander,' said Juliana. 'You're not leaving Therion to go running off to war, not at a time like this.'

The Caesari's expression sagged with disappointment as he nodded. His lips twitched for a second or two while he considered the problem. Valentinus smiled and looked at Marcus again.

'Well, no need to look too far, is there, my son?' said the Therion ruler. He slapped a hand to the praefector's shoulder. 'You know more about what is happening than any of us. You can lead the Cohort.'

'I am honoured, father, but I am only a praefector,' said Marcus.

'Nonsense. I'm in charge. You're vice-Caesari now. Full authority. Antonius will take over as praefector.'

Marcus shook his head in disbelief, mouth opening

and closing several times before he remembered his station. He dropped to one knee and took his father's hand, kissing the knuckles.

'I will serve,' he said, speaking the oathwords of the Cohort. 'For the Emperor above all others. For Therion and Enlightenment.'

Pelon suppressed a smile. Being servant to a praefector was one thing, being aide to a vice-Caesari was something far grander. If he was lucky, and he could see no reason why he didn't deserve a piece of luck, he might even be made a sub-tribune to recognise his status.

'Ensure your master's rooms are ready,' Juliana said to Pelon. 'Without warning of his arrival, I have no idea what state they are in.'

With a bow, Pelon accepted the slight admonishment and withdrew. Even as a sub-tribune he would still have to fold down the sheets. It gave him comfort to think that there were some things in life that even the treachery of a Warmaster could not change.

ELEVEN

Rebirth Begins
Unauthorised Transmission
Doubts Arise

THE BEEPS OF the machines and background thrum of energy cables triggered a sense of comfort in Corax as he stepped into the sterile chamber of the new genetech facility. Centrifuges whirred and servitors plodded from work station to work station with samples and tests. Vincente Sixx, divested of his armour, sat at a bank of five screens, data tables and helical displays large on the monitors.

At a long table covered with data tablets and instrumentation, Nexin Orlandriaz pored over a transparent sheet, idly tapping the fingers of his free hand against an empty crucible. Sixx looked over his shoulder as Corax strode across the tiled floor. Orlandriaz was too absorbed in his work to notice the arrival of the primarch.

The thud of the servitor's metal-shod feet disturbed the peace, the clacking of a crude teleprinter burst into life as an analyser spewed out its latest findings. On closer inspection, the room was balanced on the line between order and anarchy. Sixx's area was tidy, disciplined and compact, while the magos's work sprawled

over several desktops and was piled on trolleys left haphazardly around the tech-priest's high stool.

'You reported significant difficulties,' Corax said, stopping to look over Sixx's shoulder at the displays. 'What
is the problem?'

'Compatibility,' said Orlandriaz, emerging from his
contemplation, massively dilated pupils shrinking as
he focused on Corax. 'The Emperor did something to
streamline the primarch material to create the Legiones
Astartes template, but the possible permutations are too
numerous to investigate. My mathematical analysis suggests it would take at least five years of continual study
to narrow down our options to a number more suitable
for physical experimentation.'

Corax looked at Sixx, eyebrow raised.

'It has only been twenty days,' said the primarch. 'A
little early to admit defeat, isn't it?'

'The primarch genetic coding is vastly more complex
than standard Raven Guard gene-seed,' the Apothecary
explained. 'The Emperor extracted only a few elements
of the original data to create the Legiones Astartes strain,
and about a dozen more in the Legio Custodes data we
retrieved from the Terran vault. To isolate the rapid maturation and cell cloning abilities you desire, and graft
them onto our own gene-seed, we have to retroactively
engineer the Raven Guard gene-seed with the appropriate sequence. There are millions of sequences that might
be applied, even from a single primarch strand, and
there are twenty unique primarch codes to choose from.'

'Take this one, sample four, as an indicator,' said
the genetor majoris. 'We have managed to identify at
least six unique sub-complexes and protein strands
geared towards physical durability, above and beyond
that found in the others. In the same sample, there is
a dearth of certain enhanced genes that, in our estima-
tion, boost the cytoarchetectonic structure responsible

for the development of nociceptors and proprioceptory function. The deficiency seems to be deliberate. In subject six there is a whole suite of genetic encoding derived from a non-human source, possibly canine. In subject twenty, a whole suite of growth boosting augmentations is absent. In all, we have catalogued seven hundred and eighty-three variations between the samples. This leaves the common, core material, the primarch essence for want of a better term, exceptionally small compared to what I expected.'

'I see,' said Corax. He knew enough about genetic manipulation to understand the problem they were facing, but even his extensive biological knowledge was insufficient to propose a solution. He stared at the screen for some time, letting the revolving images of different cell helices float into his consciousness. He studied the data tables, absorbing the information without consciously reading it, hoping it would trigger some insight from the Emperor.

All he could remember was sadness.

It was a struggle to keep motivated, to repeat the research that had taken so many centuries to perfect. All had been swept away by... By what, Corax could not quite remember. The Emperor's memories were blank on the matter. The primarch concentrated on what had happened after the period of ignorance.

There was hope in his heart. His ambition had been misplaced. Rather than create twenty superhuman warriors, he could create thousands, hundreds of thousands of next-generation soldiers. Each would have a fraction of the power of the primarchs, it was true, but their numbers would more than make up for the difference. Corax held an image for a moment, a picture of rank after rank of armoured warriors, fists and banners raised in salute. He would create an army. Something more than an army: a Legion.

Intellect fired by his imagination, he set to work with this new goal in mind. There was no need to create this Legion from a single zygotic embryo. Humanity numbered in its billions, just on Terra alone. Through Corax's thoughts, the Emperor discarded swathes of the primarch genetic data, deemed redundant in light of his new plans. He focused on amending all of his findings from the primarch project, filtering out those abilities and traits that could only be gene-bred from inception, concentrating on transferable, implantable genetic strands.

The primarch latched onto those memories, delving deeper. As he did so, Corax edged Sixx aside and pulled a touch-screen interface closer. Hesitantly at first, he began to tap the screen, navigating his way through the mass of coded information. His fingers picked up speed as the memories came faster and faster. Fingertips dancing over the screen, Corax delved into the intricacies of the primarch genes, separating out those sequences and proteins discarded by the Emperor, following in his creator's remembered footsteps. The shifting displays and tables blurred as the primarch continued, isolating gene-fragments and cell duplication segments, tossing some aside, moving others into a separate partition.

For five minutes he worked at furious pace, linking unconscious recall to conscious action. Orlandriaz had moved up beside him at some point and was staring at the flow of information spreading across the screens, nodding ferociously while he muttered to himself.

Corax stopped, taking a deep breath as he straightened.

'Masterful,' whispered Orlandriaz.

'Perhaps if you could spare us five more minutes, lord, we could solve the whole problem,' said Sixx, grinning broadly.

'If only it were that simple,' said Corax. He had not worked out anything, simply remembered it. The

Emperor had never attempted to create what Corax sought, and so there was no base of knowledge for him to recall. 'That still leaves you with seventy-two different gene-strands to analyse.'

'A moment, please,' said Orlandriaz, laying his hand on Corax's arm as the primarch turned away. Corax glanced down in annoyance at the magos's clutching fingers, noticing that the tech-priest's fingernails looked to be made of a dull bronze. Realising his error, Nexin took his hand away and nodded his head in apology.

'Forgive me, Lord Corax,' said the magos. 'Whilst taking a break from our analystical studies, the Chief Apothecary and I engaged in a debate that was without resolution. I seek your opinion on the matter.'

'What debate?' asked Corax, darting a look at Sixx, who was frowning at his companion.

'It is my belief that your plans could be taken a stage further,' said the magos.

'It is out of the question,' said Sixx, making a cutting motion with his hand. 'It is against our every principle.'

'What is?' said Corax.

'It seems that we might actually make our task easier if we were to incept the project from an initial cellular generation, rather than hybridisation of an existing organism.'

'Cloning,' snapped Sixx. 'The magos thinks we should clone new warriors from scratch rather than modify the gene-seed for implantation. I reminded him that there are many more complications associated with such a process, not to mention the problems it will create in the future.'

'Your arguments were irrational,' said Orlandriaz, scowling back at the Chief Apothecary. 'Emotive.'

'Every possibility must be explored,' said Corax. He raised a hand to silence a protest from Sixx. A passing thought of the Emperor had surfaced in his mind, a

philosophical point his creator had concluded when the
primarchs had been taken from him.

'With that said, direct cloning must be considered only
as a final option if there is no other solution. Magos,
there is good reason why the Emperor did not directly
clone his new Legions from a single template cell. The
resultant legionaries would be identical. Without the
random mutation present in the wider human genetic
structure, there is no possibility for variation. The
Legiones Astartes are successful because we are similar,
but not identical. Qualities such as leadership, intellect
and aptitude for different disciplines allow us to be flexible and to fulfil many roles.

'Even the primarchs were not created equal in all
measures. The Emperor understood the importance of
variation. Beyond that, there is another consideration.
The Legiones Astartes are humanity's warriors, separated
and superior in many ways, but always raised up from
amongst those they lead and protect. A legionary may
be a neo-human, but he *was* once human. A legionary is
the incarnation of the Emperor's plan, a perfect symbol
and example for mankind to aspire to, not simply a tool
of war. It is humanity that the Emperor will lead in the
conquest of the galaxy, not some new species made to
order in a laboratory.'

'Thank you, lord,' said Sixx, with a sidelong look at
Orlandriaz. 'More eloquent than I could ever phrase it.'

'I understand your position and reasoning,' said the
magos. 'I will comply with your direction.'

'Make it work,' said Corax. 'That perfect symbol has
been tarnished by Horus. I would see it shine brightly
again.'

THE ATMOSPHERE IN the docking bay changed as the primarch entered, Commander Branne following a few
steps behind. Navar Hef felt the increase in tension and

reacted, standing just a little straighter, puffing out his chest just a little further. It was only the second time he had seen the primarch in person. The first had been on his acceptance into the recruits for the Raven Guard. Now Corax was here, only eight days after his return to Deliverance, ready to inspect the next generation of recruits. Navar's eyes followed the primarch as he strode along the gallery at the end of the hall, as did two hundred and ninety-nine other pairs. It was testament to the primarch's thoroughness that he was taking the time for this, when there would be so many other demands made upon him.

The three hundred novitiates stood to attention, a block of black-robed young men with lean bodies, close-cropped hair and eager eyes. Navar felt the wave of pride that flowed through the group as Corax nodded his head in acknowledgement of the massed recruits. A simple, easy gesture for the primarch, but one that spoke of a respect that could not be matched by any other individual, save if the Emperor himself had come to see them.

The orders for the recruit company to pack their few possessions and gather at Ravenspire's Centrus Terminal had started a wave of speculation throughout the novitiate blocks adjoining the great tower. Navar was of the opinion that they were going to be shipped out direct to the fighting, as many were. He had heard, second-hand unfortunately, of the losses the Legion had suffered on Isstvan V, and knew that Corax would not take such a defeat lightly. Some had said they were being evacuated to Terra, that Deliverance was under immediate threat and the whole Legion was retreating. Navar had argued against such nay-saying. The Raven Guard would defend their home to the last man, he was sure of it.

There were some who claimed that the stories circulating about Horus's treachery were simply a test of their determination, rumours circulated by the primarch to

see who had the fortitude to be a true legionary. Some,
a boring few in Navar's opinion, reckoned that after
the hiatus following Branne's departure, the normal
procedure was being implemented and they were simply being moved on to the next stage of their training.
Navar was equally dismissive of these claims; he knew
he was an able fighter and physically superior to most of
Deliverance's youth, but at ten Terran years old he and
many of the others were simply too young to begin the
enhancement process yet.

That Corax had deigned to address them personally
added to Navar's conviction that something out of the
ordinary was occurring. His idle thoughts melted away as
the primarch spoke. Corax's voice was quiet but assured,
full of conviction and authority. It was impossible not to
listen, and Navar quickly forgot all of the rumours and
gossip, drawn in by the primarch's irresistible tone.

'You have proven yourselves to be exemplars, the fittest
and brightest humanity has to offer,' said Corax. 'Every
new generation of Raven Guard are to be lauded and celebrated as bearers of the Legion's traditions and future
warriors of the Emperor. Those of you gathered here will
be more than that. You will embody the Raven Guard
and the ideals of Deliverance like no others before you.
You are shortly to become legionaries, and you should
take pride in that. Yet you must also reconcile yourselves
to a burden the likes of which no previous generation
has borne.'

Corax leaned on the metal rail of the balcony and
bowed his head for a moment, eyes closed. When he
opened them, Navar felt swallowed by their blackness.
His awe evaporated, replaced by dread as Corax continued.

'Much of what you have heard in recent days is true.
The Warmaster, Horus Lupercal, is a traitor to the
Emperor. The Raven Guard have suffered badly from his

treachery and our strength is much diminished. You will be the first legionaries that start us back on the road to recovery, the first generation to fight for a return to glory. Your elevation takes place at a time more troubled than any in the Legion's proud history. You will be tested, physically and in your hearts, like no other legionaries before you.'

The primarch's mood brightened, and it seemed as if the hall itself lightened in reflection of this.

'Take heart that you will not be found wanting. Your dedication and courage will not fail. As novitiates you have proven yourselves worthy of bearing the colours of the Raven Guard. The ignorant may look at you and see fresh faces and young hearts, but they do not see what I see. I see the same valour and pride in you that I saw in the eyes of the young men and women who fought beside me to free Deliverance. It is their example you must follow, and their example that you will surpass. If you don't believe me, ask old Branne here. I remember when he was just a babe, mewling for his mother's teat!'

Navar laughed along with the others, amused and not a little disturbed by the thought of the hoary commander having once been an infant. The laughter subsided as Corax's expression grew grim again.

'The trials begin now. Your patience, endurance and trust will be sorely tested by what you are about to undergo, but they are nothing more than practice for the tribulations that await us further down the road. You will act as Raven Guard. You will endure and grow stronger.' Corax lifted a fist above his head. 'I salute you, recruits of the Raven Guard. Your transports await. You leave Ravenspire as novitiates, but will return as warriors of the Legiones Astartes!'

'For the Emperor and the Legion!' bellowed Branne, duplicating his lord's salute.

'For the Emperor and the Legion!' Navar shouted

along with the others, raising his fist as high as he could reach, straining to make his voice a manly roar.

THERE WAS A time for stealth and a time for violence. Since he had arrived on Kiavahr, Omegon had exclusively practised the former, but he felt a sense of release, almost joy, as the sentry's head imploded within his closing fingers. Flicking skull fragments and slick brain matter from his gauntlets, Omegon stepped over the twitching body while Rufan and Alias stooped to pick up the corpse. The two Alpha Legionnaires casually tossed the remains into a nearby chem-pool. Noxious fluids bubbled as the body sank, releasing methane-tainted puffs of air.

With gore-stained fingers, Omegon wrenched aside the bars across the sewer inlet, the corroded steel turning to flakes in his hands. Turning sideways, the primarch lowered his bulk into the channel beyond, the culvert barely large enough for his armoured frame. A thin sludge of slimy effluent trickled along the bottom of the rockcrete tunnel, stinking but harmless to his enhanced physiology.

As they entered, the ruddy light from outside grew dimmer. Omegon activated his suit lamps, two cones of yellow springing from powerful emitters fixed around his eye lenses. Treading carefully, footfalls muffled by rubber-like overshoes, the three warriors of the Alpha Legion advanced forty metres up the gently sloping pipe, stopping by another barred opening. The barrier was no more obstacle than the first, and within a few seconds, Omegon was stepping through the breach into the room beyond.

The chamber was hexagonal, the ceiling a little higher than the primarch could reach with his fingertips, the floor coated with a thin layer of chemical effluent fed by inlets on each wall. Looking up, Omegon was pleased to see that Armand Eloqi's information had been correct: a circular access hatch punctured the centre of the ceiling. The building had once belonged to Eloqi's guild, now turned into communications relay for the Mechanicum.

Alias and Rufan lifted Omegon up so that he could reach the rusted turn wheel. After a little initial resistance, it spun easily in the primarch's hands. A clank signalled the disengagement of the lock. Omegon pushed open the hatch, took hold of the lip and pulled himself up, shoulder pads scraping the side of the hole. At a crouch, Omegon turned around and headed in the direction Eloqi had told him, while the other two dragged themselves up behind.

'Cutter,' said Omegon, holding out his hand behind him.

Rufan took the device from his belt and placed it in Omegon's grip. It looked like a snub-nosed pistol, two gas canisters where the magazine would have been. Thumbing the valve open, Omegon pressed the trigger and a white-hot flame erupted from the muzzle. Reaching above him, the primarch turned on the spot, slicing an almost complete circle in the metal decking above him. When he was done, he turned off the cutter and passed it back to Rufan.

Shuffling back a few steps to give himself space, Omegon lay on his back and kicked upwards. The rough circle of metal broke free and landed with a clatter on the floor above. With room to stand now, Omegon examined the small alcove he had broken into. A nest of wires crisscrossed each other from dozens of circuits and switches. In a few seconds, he had analysed the layout, creating a schematic in his head. There was not a communications system he could not access and this one was crude by Mechanicum standards.

Opening up a plate on his right vambrace, Omegon pulled free several wires and plugged them into the required sockets in the switching boards around him. He activated his communications suite, quickly scanning the frequencies around him until he could home in on the signal he was looking for. An insistent beeping became louder in his ear and he turned left and right, rearranging and rewiring a few of the relays to fine-tune the signal. On the roof above, the dishes would be turning on their gimbals, aligning themselves towards Deliverance.

'Effrit code, hydra-seven-omega,' grated an artificial voice. The primarch smiled as he locked down the receiver, the words he had heard confirmation of what he had hoped for. At least one of his legionnaires had succeeded in infiltrating the Raven Guard.

'Access cryptoduct, *theru gaili ta nurun*,' said Omegon. The words were meaningless syllables known only to the twin primarchs. '*Gaion sackrit kess.*'

There followed a few seconds of static as the connection was established with the tiny stealth-fielded satellite that Omegon had left in orbit over Deliverance. It was no larger than a fist, just a piece of debris, but the cryptoduct device was capable of detecting, decoding and recording any signal within a narrow range of frequencies, frequencies known only to the Alpha Legion. He was also able to implant messages onto the cryptoduct for access by others. It was the perfect go-between, ensuring that both sender and receiver were anonymous and since it could be accessed from anywhere within several hundred thousand miles, their locations would remain unknown.

'Lord Effrit, this is Alpharius,' said the message. Omegon smiled again. It was a conceit, perhaps, but never failed to amuse him. 'Infiltration successful. Objective identified as primarch genetic data. Location is Raven-delve. Awaiting instruction.'

The transmission ended. Omegon had been expecting

many things, but not this. Corax had access to the primarch project? The implications were immediately obvious, both the risks and benefits of the current plan. For a moment Omegon considered changing his objective. If the Raven Guard were able to rebuild their Legion with this knowledge, the swift victory of Horus, and the ultimate destruction of the Primordial Annihilator, could be put in jeopardy. The prudent approach would be to destroy the technology before its secrets could be gleaned by Corax.

Despite that, Omegon could not quite convince himself to follow this course of action. The danger presented was but the weight on one side of the balance. On the other side had to be set the advantages of claiming this technology for the Alpha Legion. Omegon did not doubt that Corax had a good chance of cracking the primarch gene-seed open, certainly a better chance than the Alpha Legion, even with the assistance of the Order of the Dragon.

For the moment it would be best to allow the Raven Guard to continue their investigations. When they had discovered something of value, the secret could be stolen and the Raven Guard destroyed. If the discovery was of the magnitude Omegon imagined it to be, it would herald a new beginning for the Alpha Legion. To possess the secrets of the primarchs was a prize worth a few risks.

With everything the Alpha Legion did, there was always some extra agenda that could be forwarded, some additional objective that could be achieved. In the case of the Raven Guard, Omegon and Alpharius had decided that they would first relieve the Legion of the Terran technology that would be imparted to them, and then the Raven Guard would be destroyed, with all news of the event carefully contained from both the Emperor and Horus. Kiavahr would become loyal to Horus and, finally, the Raven Guard would live again, with Alpha

Legionnaires masquerading in place of the dead Legion. The scope to cause confusion and mayhem would be vast once Omegon had achieved these three goals and he paused in his work and grinned at the thought of it.

He adjusted his connection to the relay, switching to a transmission format.

'Effrit code, omega-seven-hydra,' he said. 'You are Contact One. Assigned sub-channel alpha-three. Orders will be forthcoming.'

As he cut the link, Omegon noticed something else he had not expected. He checked his findings, and found his initial instinct had been correct. The signal to the cryptoduct had been made from a triple-secure Raven Guard source.

That it came from Ravenspire was not a surprise. That it was on the highest-level command channel was.

'I WISH THERE was some soundproofing down here,' said Sixx, walking between the cages that had been built in the western vestibule. A cacophony of howls, growls, whines and screeches heralded his progress along the corridor. 'I am worried the recruits can hear all of this racket.'

'I am sure I will be able to obtain some form of sonic dampening field from one of my fellow magi,' replied Orlandriaz, walking beside the Apothecary.

'Out of the question,' said Sixx. 'The primarch was clear in his instruction: no contact with the Kiavah-ran Mechanicum. Even your presence here suggests something of what we are working on. It must remain undisclosed.'

'A grave mistake, I am sure,' said the tech-priest. 'Aside from that technology which we recovered from Terra, the facility here is exceptionally sparse.'

'You think that the resources of the Raven Guard are limited?' Sixx was incredulous, almost stopping in his stride. 'You realise that we have been implanting gene-seed into recruits for decades?'

'Yes, and the systems you use have not progressed at all in that time,' replied Orlandriaz. 'Even without the primarch data, I am positive I could have increased your productivity by ten, perhaps even fifteen per cent.'

'We are not a manufactorum, Nexin. The creation of legionaries is not a production line process.'

'It will be, when we have completed our task.'

The Chief Apothecary's reply was silenced as the door at the far end of the corridor opened, revealing Commander Agapito. His expression was all Sixx needed to know that their latest report to Corax had not been received well.

The Commander of the Talons stalked along the passageway, boots ringing loudly. Snarls and spitting erupted from the nearby cages.

'You don't have to say anything, commander,' said Sixx, as he came up to Agapito. 'Lord Corax wishes for more encouraging results, yes?'

'I hope you have at least a small success story I can take back to him,' said Agapito. He glanced into the cage to his left and shook his head with disgust at what he saw within. 'He is keen… No, that doesn't really convey his mood. He is *adamant* that you proceed beyond these pointless trials and begin work on perfecting the formula for the recruits.'

'Pointless?' Orlandriaz bunched his fists and his lip twitched in irritation. 'I am sure the primarch would be even more angered if we had turned his first batch of legionaries into these…'

He waved his hand to encompass the long line of cages. Beyond the bars, mammalian and reptilian things hunkered and paced. Some were unidentifiable, little more than mewling, distorted conglomerations of flesh. Most were warped by over-sized muscles, others had bony growths splitting their scales or fur. Several had extra limbs, additional eyes, overgrown fangs or distended spines.

A green-furred mouse the size of a dog lunged against the bars of one cage, its claws sheathing and unsheathing spasmodically, tusks protruding from its lower jaw. In another enclosure, a two-headed snake, several metres long, coiled menacingly, its tail tipped with a jagged barb. From every cage, deformed monstrosities glared and snapped, regarding the legionaries and tech-priest with predatory intent.

'Corax thinks it is a mistake to use animal subjects,' said Agapito. 'He does not suggest that you introduce the new gene-seed directly to the recruits, and Branne certainly won't allow it. By the other hand, introducing primarch genetic material to non-human hosts will never be successful.'

'Then we are caught in a bind,' said Sixx. 'How are we to ensure the new gene-seed works if we cannot trial it in organic hosts? Our data modelling can only prove so much.'

'That is not my problem, it is yours.'

'We will have to return to base cell analysis,' said Orlandriaz, eyes fixed on a massively-shouldered lizard with horny growths protruding from its spine. 'We can certainly eradicate more of the anomalous reactions.'

'But nothing of cerebral impact or behavioural side-effects,' said Sixx.

'Aggression is not necessarily a bad thing in a legionary,' said Orlandriaz.

'We'll leave the mindless ferocity to the World Eaters,' replied the Apothecary. 'We need disciplined, efficient warriors.'

'What shall I tell Lord Corax?' asked Agapito. 'He will expect me to return with some news of progress and a firm plan for resolving any problems.'

Sixx and Orlandriaz looked at each other. The Apothecary sighed and nodded.

'I'll euthanise these abominations and study the cellular breakdown,' said Sixx. 'That should give us some new data to incorporate into the models.'

'I will restart the base cell experiments with a modified gene-seed,' said Orlandriaz.

'How long?' asked Agapito. 'I understand that you need to get this right, and I will support you in every way I can, but the primarch is understandably impatient. Every day we spend now is a day closer to Horus being ready to launch an attack on Terra.'

'When we are successful, time will not be an issue,' said Orlandriaz. He pointed to the creatures in the cages towards the far end of the corridor. 'Those are the results of our implantation since we compiled the latest report. We introduced the genetic template into infants to record the time required for full maturation of the gene-seed.'

The animals in the cages were full grown, some of them showing the mutation of the others, but a few seemed to be ordinary specimens, large for their species but otherwise normal. Agapito shook his head in confusion and amazement.

'You only submitted your report forty hours ago,' said the commander.

'Thirty-seven point three hours, to be exact,' said Orlandriaz, smiling thinly. 'Given the longer maturation period of the average human male, I estimate the entire process, once perfected, will take between seventy and eighty Terran hours.'

Agapito shook his head again, this time with a grin.

'That is remarkable. Eighty hours to turn a boy into a legionary? Well, in body at least.'

'Not just physiologically, commander,' said Sixx, now becoming more enthusiastic. 'Our recruits will emerge from the process with mental and physical aptitudes beyond anything we've seen before. They'll be quick learners too. A little bonus of the primarch material. Our new legionaries will be primed and ready from the outset.'

'That is fascinating news,' said Agapito. 'To pass on to Corax, of course. Take as much time as you need to complete the gene-seed. There is no reason to proceed with anything less than a perfect sample. I look forward to hearing of your success as soon as possible. If what the primarch says about broadening out the recruitment base is true, there could be a near-limitless supply of legionaries. I'll inform Lord Corax of your findings.'

'Yes, commander,' said Orlandriaz. Agapito and Sixx exchanged nods of respect before the commander strode away. Neither Apothecary nor tech-priest said anything until the door at the end of the passage closed behind Agapito.

'I am pleased the commander seems so eager,' said Orlandriaz. 'His brother has been much more reticent in his approval of our project.'

'He used to be one of the staunchest Legion tradition-alists,' Sixx said distractedly, still looking at the closed door. 'He and Branne were hard-headed about their Deliverance heritage, hammered it into me and the rest of the recruits from the first day we were made noviti-ates. I suppose losing so many warriors on Isstvan has changed his mind about being so selective.'

'I fear he may over-represent our progress to your primarch,' said Orlandriaz. 'We should continue our studies with a degree of alacrity.'

'Agreed,' said Sixx. 'If we cannot produce something tangible soon, Lord Corax may become even more impatient. I've never considered him rash, but he is very determined to begin the rebuilding.'

'Adversity often creates desperation,' said Orlandriaz.

'Not ever!' snapped Sixx, rounding on the tech-priest, remembering words spoken by his primarch during the long retreat from the dropsite massacre. 'We are Raven Guard. Deliverance was born out of determination and perseverance. Strife is our sustenance, adversity is our ally. Attack, withdraw and attack again. That is our creed, the lifeblood of the Legion. The Raven Guard do not become desperate when circumstance does not favour us. We become more dangerous.'

The slap of bare feet on black-painted ferrocrete brought back memories to Alpharius as he stood watching the recruits running circuits of the main hall. He knew the memories were not his own – they had been removed by the Alpha Legion's Librarians – but the recollections were exceptionally vivid, coming to him as brief snatches: scenes and tableaux that lasted a few seconds each. His training had taken place in Ravenspire rather than down here on Kiavahr, but he had performed the same drills as the youths around him.

'Ready weapons!' barked Branne from the stage area at one end of the vaulted chamber. 'Form up for firing practice.'

The recruits dashed to the crates at the centre of the hall and took up simple automatic rifles from within. These were training weapons duplicating the weight and bulk of a bolter to a full-fledged legionary; without gene-seed enhancement even a full-grown man could not train with a proper Legiones Astartes bolter. The snap of magazines being slipped into place joined the patter of running feet.

In groups of five, the recruits lined up in front of Branne's position. He waved each squad forwards. Panting, red-faced young men lifted their weapons to their shoulders, took aim at the ceramite target tiles on the far wall and opened fire. The rattle of shots and tinkle of expended cases filled the room.

After firing for a few seconds, the first group peeled away and the second squad took up position. One of the recruits was struggling with the magazine on his weapon and approached Alpharius.

'I can't get it to eject, sergeant,' said the boy, face screwed up with frustration. He looked up at Alpharius – the novitiate's eyes were just about level with the bottom of the legionary's breastplate. 'It's stuck solid!'

'Calm down and try again,' said Alpharius. 'What is your name, novitiate?'

'Hef, sergeant,' said the recruit. He struggled again with the release catch, sweaty hands slipping on the smooth metal of the rifle. 'Navar Hef.'

'Let me see,' said Alpharius, holding out his hand. He took the rifle, examined it quickly and handed it back to Hef. 'The last round did not properly clear the chamber. Look.'

The novitiate examined the rifle, shamefaced. He manually expelled the spent casing and then ejected the magazine.

'Punishment, ten laps,' said Alpharius. 'Battle pace. Move!'

Hef took hold of his rifle properly and set off towards the edge of the hall, perspiration glistening from his shaved scalp. Alpharius could hear him counting out the rhythm of his strides between gasping breaths. There was innocence and dedication there. Hef was a fine recruit.

It was a shame he would be killed along with the rest of the Raven Guard.

Alpharius felt uncomfortable at the thought. More than uncomfortable, in fact. He was not sure how he would define the emotion that made his chest a little tight as he watched the novitiates continue their weapon practice. Guilt, perhaps? It certainly was not a sensation he had felt before, and the Alpha Legionnaire did not like it at all. He cleared his throat in agitation and snapped out a reprimand to a pair of recruits who had sagged down to a crouch at the back of the line. They stood up sharp at his words.

It seemed such a waste. Corax and the senior commanders would never be moved to join the Alpha Legion, but these novitiates were fine young men, who would be ideal recruits for the Legion. Their deaths seemed a little unnecessary.

Alpharius was not sure where these doubts were coming from. He blamed the false memories. They had been increasing in recent days. He could clearly recall the first time he had set out from Ravendelve into the atomic wasteland, though nothing of what had happened after leaving the armoured compound. Names of fellow legionaries haunted him, Raven Guard that had fallen on Isstvan. His fellow legionaries referred to them sometimes and he would have a flash of a face, or instinctively smile at some half-remembered joke, or briefly relive a moment in battle alongside the fallen warrior.

He had to focus. He was not a legionary of the Raven Guard, he was an Alpha Legionnaire. His primarch was not Corax, his oaths had been made to Alpharius and Omegon. In their wisdom, the twin primarchs had chosen to back Horus's rebellion, and he had to trust that it was for good reason. The fall of the Raven Guard, the taking of the gene-tech, would serve a greater purpose.

Holding on to that thought, Alpharius suppressed the memories bubbling up from the depths of his altered mind. I am Alpharius, he told himself. I am Alpharius.

DESCENDING THE RAMP of his Stormbird, Branne was surprised to find Controller Ephrenia waiting for him in the docking bay. She held a data-slate, which she wordlessly passed to the commander as he walked towards the bay doors. With so many lost at Isstvan – legionaries and ordinary humans alike – the controller had been promoted from strategium officer on the *Avenger* to the command centre at the tip of Ravenspire.

'What am I looking at?' asked Branne. 'I have come back to answer a summons from the primarch.'

'Transmission data, commander,' said Ephrenia. She took the tablet back for a moment, tapped the screen twice and returned it to Branne's grip. 'As per your orders, we conducted a survey of all communications logs that the Word Bearers Chaplain had access to, both from Deliverance and via Kiavahr's network. We detected several anomalous transmissions.'

'Anomalous?' said Branne. Pistons wheezed as the great doors to the dock opened up in front of him. He stopped to look down at the controller. 'Be more specific.'

'Non-Mechanicum and non-Legion frequencies and channels, commander.'

'Not that surprising, really,' said Branne, resuming his stride. 'There are many commercial vessels, Imperial Army ships and other non-affiliated ships in the system.'

'These transmissions have a Legiones Astartes signature, commander,' Ephrenia said patiently.

Branne stopped again and studied the tablet with more deliberate intent. The controller was correct, there was a Legiones Astartes cipher and modulation pattern to the recorded transmissions.'

'All are flash-traffic, commander,' continued Ephrenia. 'Compressed, in my opinion.'

'Wait, I recognise this transponder code,' said Branne, highlighting one of the entries with a jabbed finger.

'Yes, commander, it is a Ravenspire access cipher,' the controller said. Her voice lowered as she continued. 'I came to you directly because of that. It is Commander Agapito's broadcast channel.'

'I see,' said Branne. This information perturbed him, but he assured himself his brother would be able to offer a sensible explanation for its purpose. That did not explain the mystery of the remaining transmissions. 'What of the others?'

'Some are old Lycaen security frequencies, and two are on the defunct guild networks, commander. Impossible to pin down a source, but they originate on Kiavahr.'

'Dissidents, no doubt,' said Branne.

'A significant peak in traffic, commander. Previous communications detected on those frequencies were sporadic and clustered. The pattern here is more sustained. I believe it might signify some attempt to reestablish the old guild structures.'

'Good work,' said Branne. 'I will take care of this matter from here. Nothing to get too worried about yet. I shall perform further investigations before I distract Lord Corax with this information.'

'As you wish, commander,' said Ephrenia, with a bow.

'Wait a moment,' said Branne as the controller made to step away. 'Contact Commander Agapito and request him to meet me in my chambers in an hour.'

'Yes, commander.'

'And set up a monitor on Commander Agapito's channel. Let me know if there are any further irregularities.'

'Yes, commander. Is that all?'

'Return to your duties.'

Ephrenia strode down the corridor, leaving Branne with uneasy thoughts. The pro-guild sympathisers on Kiavahr were stirring up trouble, he was sure. It was inconvenient but not a significant threat. It would be simple enough to inform the Mechanicum of the matter.

He took a step and then stopped with a hissed curse. If he warned the Mechanicum of any surge in dissident activity, they would be required to perform a scouring of the rad-wastes, or at the very least intensify their

observation and security of the area. That would lead
to greater scrutiny around Ravendelve, a turn of events
Lord Corax would be keen to avoid.

Branne rubbed in his chin, caught between courses
of action. He was sure that the dissidents could pose
no military threat to the facility, but their timing was
inconvenient. With so much out-system traffic coming
through the star system at the moment, it was quite possible that agitators sent by Horus were stirring up trouble
to keep the Raven Guard occupied.

It was just a theory, and he would need more solid
evidence before it was worth notifying the primarch.
Lord Corax was intent on the gene-tech project, spending most of his time bunkered up in Ravendelve with
Sixx and the tech-priest. Even when he was back on
Deliverance, the primarch spent most of his time poring
over the reports and studies, incommunicado except for
urgent matters.

Unsure how to proceed, Branne realised he was going
to be late for his meeting with Corax. He folded up the
data tablet and hurried along the corridor, hoping the
primarch would not remark on his tardiness.

TWELVE

Brothers in Conflict
Mark VI
Creation of the Raptors

SITTING ON A shallow chair in his rooms, Branne stared at the data tablet laid on the table in front of him. A perfunctory knock on the metal bulkhead preceded Agapito's entry. Branne glanced up at his brother and waved him to the couch opposite.

'What is it, brother?' asked Agapito, choosing to stand. 'Lord Corax tells me there has been a significant development in the gene-project. We are to accompany him to Ravendelve.'

'Yes, I heard,' said Branne. He glanced at the digital chronometer on the table next to the data-slate. 'We have a little time.'

'You seem preoccupied,' said Agapito. He lightened the comment with a smile. 'Is Commander of Recruits proving more of a challenge than you thought?

'I keep having to put myself between Sixx and that magos, with the primarch constantly demanding updates. But that's not what I want to talk about.' Branne handed the slate to his brother, the transmission data highlighted. 'Can you explain that?'

Agapito looked at the tablet and frowned. He glanced

at Branne and then looked back at the data-slate.

'That is my command channel,' said Agapito.

'I know,' replied Branne.

'I don't recognise the transmission code, though. Some kind of glitch in the system?'

'You tell me, brother.'

Looking sharply at Branne, Agapito dropped the tablet back on the metal table with a clang.

'Those are ominous words, Branne,' said the commander. 'I detect accusation behind them.'

'Just interest,' replied Branne. 'Call it my curiosity. Tell me, why is there an irregular transmission from your channel, broadcast on a non-Legion frequency?'

'I do not know, brother,' said Agapito. 'If you have some charge to make, then speak it plainly; your crude hinting is testing my patience.'

Branne stood up and met his brother's gaze directly. He folded his arms across his chest and regarded Agapito for a few seconds, gauging his expression. The commander of the Talons looked genuinely confused and upset.

'You offer no explanation for this?' said Branne.

'None,' replied Agapito, his tone belligerent. 'Do you offer any explanation for your suspicion?'

Breathing in deeply, Branne considered his next move. It was likely that Agapito was genuinely ignorant of the transmission, which gave him a bigger problem: someone had accessed the command communications without authorisation. Branne was not sure which was the worst scenario.

'All right,' he said. 'I will have Ephrenia look into it more closely. Maybe it is a glitch.'

'Are you sure?' said Agapito. 'Don't you want to take me down to the Red Level and subject me to a more rigorous interrogation?'

Branne snarled, offended by the implication. The Red

Level was where the punishment cells had been located during the years of Kiavahran suppression. They had had a bloody reputation back then, and the thought of the tortures that prisoners had undergone in that dark place set Branne's teeth on edge even now.

'Sorry, brother, that was uncalled-for,' said Agapito, offering out his hand in apology. Branne took it after a moment's hesitation.

'I don't understand you, brother, not since Isstvan,' Branne confessed. 'It worries me.'

'No need for it,' said Agapito, with a grin that Branne could clearly see was forced. 'You have plenty of concerns already without adding me to the list.'

'Yes, I do,' said Branne, with another glance at the chronometer. 'We had best get armoured, the primarch will expect us at the dock soon.'

'You can talk to me, brother,' said Agapito. 'About the recruitment project, if you need to. I have not been able to pay half as much attention to it as I would like, not with all of my time taken up with the Legion reorganisation.'

'How are the Talons shaping up?'

'Good. Better than expected, given the circumstances. A few discipline problems now and then, but nothing I can't straighten out. They've had a hard time of late.'

'Don't go easy on them, brother,' said Branne, indicating for Agapito to head for the door. 'It's going to get a lot harder.'

As he watched Agapito leave, Branne could not shake off a question that he wanted to ask but could not bring himself to voice: why are you lying to me, brother?

IN AN ANTECHAMBER of the infirmary in Ravendelve, Corax waited with a mixture of anticipation and foreboding. Cabinets lined one wall, shelves laden with a mass of medical devices on the opposite side. Metal benches had been cleared of other equipment to serve as seats. It had been four days since he had authorised the first implantation sequence. Vincente Sixx had been cautious in his advice, but Orlandriaz had been adamant they were ready to proceed to the next logical stage.

Agapito and Branne waited with their primarch. Sensing his mood, they had said little, but Corax detected an undercurrent of tension between the two commanders. Corax was sure it was due to disagreements about the gene-project.

A scrape at the door caught the attention of all in the room. Corax took a sharp breath, but let it out when he saw that it was Solaro and Aloni. They offered terse greetings and sat themselves next to their fellow commanders.

'Let's hope this has worked, eh?' said Aloni.

'Nothing to lose,' said Solaro. 'If it does not work, we are where we started out.'

'It will work,' said Corax. He had spent every moment he had to spare on the gene-seed manipulation, combining his own knowledge and fragments of the Emperor's memories with the research of Sixx and Orlandriaz. The primarch had scrutinised every gene-sequence and permutation and was convinced the Chief Apothecary and tech-priest had found the solution.

With that assurance, the commanders waited in silence. Agapito fidgeted, tapping his fingers on his kneepads, stopping when he earned himself a scowl from Branne. Corax wished he could have overseen the final implantation himself, as the Emperor had personally attended to the primarchs' creation, but his sheer size had made it impractical for him to stay in the sterile chamber where the process was taking place.

The door opened again, revealing Vincente Sixx. The Apothecary was dressed in surgical robes, a smear of blood across the front. He peeled off a pair of thin gloves and stuffed them into a pocket across his stomach.

'How are they?' asked Corax, standing up.

'Come and see for yourself,' said Sixx.

Corax followed the Apothecary out of the door, the commanders behind him. Stepping into the main infirmary, the primarch was struck by how cold it was. He remembered that the recruits had been placed in a brief cryobiotic state as a precaution against rampant cell reproduction – a stage in the process Corax hoped to eliminate with the next group of recruits if this proved successful. The chill was emanating from the nine men standing bare-chested, close to their beds alongside one wall. They wore loose trousers and soft boots, the air around them filled with faint vapour from their warming bodies.

All nine were the same physically, as tall and broad as a legionary. Some of their facial structure remained distinct, allowing the primarch to identify each with the recruits he had wished well before their transformation. Their bodies were free of hair still and their skin was pale – almost albino like their primarch. He also noticed that every subject had dark eyes. Not quite the black orbs he possessed, but certainly far greyer than even those of previous Raven Guard.

There were identical surgical marks on the bodies of all nine, though the scars were already becoming indistinct. The pattern was instantly recognisable to any member of the Legiones Astartes, as was the discolouration beneath the skin of their torso and shoulders.

'They have their black carapaces already?' said Solaro.

'They have every enhanced organ you possess, commander,' said Orlandriaz, emerging from behind the group of giant post-humans. 'The black carapace must still be implanted as before, it being a mostly artificial construct.'

'And the rest are grown naturally?' said Branne. He

took a step closer to the new legionaries, examining them carefully. The recruits stood to attention with eyes firmly fixed ahead, not reacting to the scrutiny of their superiors.

'Yes,' said Sixx, gesturing for one of the men – Corax remembered his name as Halvar Diaro – to step forwards. 'Several of the gene-seed implantations will not be necessary when the process is perfected. They serve only to prepare the body for later implants and have no direct effect after maturation.'

'What about the progenoids?' asked Solaro. 'Do they mature quickly too?'

'They do,' said Orlandriaz, with something of a smirk. 'However, they will also become unnecessary once we have completed our work. Once the modified gene-seed is finished, we will be able to reproduce from source. There will be no need of the antiquated in-host maturation you currently rely upon.'

'We can make as many gene-seed sets as we like,' explained Sixx. 'Numbers will only be limited by the availability of recruits.'

Corax only half-heard the exchange as the commanders continued to ask questions about the recruits' capabilities and physical enhancements. He was captivated by the nine men, marvelling in their existence. He knew every cell in their bodies better than he knew the Ravenspire, yet to see them in the flesh was breathtaking. They were perfect examples of the Legiones Astartes.

'Where is the tenth man?' asked Agapito, breaking through Corax's admiration. The primarch turned a raised brow to the two men who were architects of the project.

Sixx and Orlandriaz shared a look. The Chief Apothecary sighed.

'A minute defect in the heart, microscopic, was ruptured by the accelerated cell generation,' said Sixx. 'It would have happened even with regular gene-seed.'

'Avoidable,' added the tech-priest. 'More thorough screening will eliminate the problem.'

'I thought the plan was that we would be able to relax the recruitment criteria,' said Agapito.

'In time, we will,' said Corax. He walked up to the man who had stepped forwards and laid a hand on his shoulder. He glanced back at the commanders. 'The next stage of development will be to introduce sequences in the gene-seed that will be retroactive. Genetic weaknesses and minor physical discrepancies will be eliminated by the introduction of the superior gene-seed.'

There were looks exchanged between the others in the room as they absorbed the full portent of Corax's words: an almost limitless supply of legionaries.

'If that can be achieved, if the gene-tech can be passed on to the other loyal Legions, those loyal to the Emperor would outnumber the traitors within months,' the primarch continued, meeting the gaze of Diaro. 'These nine are the first of thousands – tens of thousands when we have finished. It is for that reason we must do everything we can to force Horus to hold back his attack on Terra. Not only will we gain time for Dorn to build ever greater defences, we buy ourselves the space to rebuild after the losses of Isstvan.'

The group of commanders circled around the recruits, examining them from every angle. Corax felt a moment of concern, realising the attitude he had towards these newest Raven Guard. They were not just experimental subjects, not just benchmarks on a path to recovery. They were warriors of the Legiones Astartes.

'I have an important question to ask you,' he said to Diaro, crouching so that he was level with the man's eyes. 'Answer it truthfully.'

'Yes, Lord Corax,' the recruit replied, his voice now deep, edged with a husky timbre.

'How do you feel?'

Diaro looked at the other newly-created legionaries and they all broke into smiles. Another of them answered the question first.

'I feel good, Lord Corax. Strong, healthy.'

'Ready to fight?' asked Branne.

'Yes, commander,' said Diaro. He banged a fist against his heavily-muscled chest. 'Ready to kill traitors.'

THE INTERNAL COMMUNICATIONS chime disturbed Corax's study of the latest test reports on the new legionaries. He paused the flow of information across the three screens in front of him and activated the receiver.

'Lord Corax, your presence at the command chamber is required,' said Ephrenia. The primarch thought he could detect barely-suppressed laughter in her voice. 'We have a situation that may need your intervention.'

'Please be more specific,' said Corax, reaching out to a mug of water balanced on the edge of his metal desk. He realised he had been cloistered in the study room for more than twelve hours.

'We have detected two Imperial Fists vessels approaching Deliverance, lord,' Ephrenia explained.

'Report to me when you find out what they want,' said the primarch. He took a gulp of water, savouring it as if it were fine wine. 'The watch commander can surely handle this?'

'Branne is on watch command, lord,' said Ephrenia. Her smirk was almost audible. 'The Imperial Fists vessels are under the command of Captain Noriz. The exchange is getting quite heated.'

Corax sighed, switched off the data screens and stood up.

'Very well, I'll be there soon,' he said. 'Make sure Branne doesn't do something hot-headed, like opening fire.'

'Yes, lord, I'll do my best,' said Ephrenia, trying not to laugh.

Running fingers through his thick hair, Corax stretched his shoulders and cracked his knuckles. It had been six days since gene-seed implantation had been completed on the first recruits and there was a stream of genetic data and physiological examination reports for him to digest if he wanted to take the project to its next stage. Whatever the reason for Noriz's arrival, it was inopportune at best, and suspicious at worst. Was Dorn sending his man to keep an eye on the Raven Guard?

The primarch made his way to the conveyor and rose up through Ravenspire to the command chamber close to the pinnacle. As he entered, he could hear Captain Noriz's voice over the vox. Branne was hunched over the communications console, a vox-link clasped in his gauntleted fist.

'Your security protocol makes no sense, commander,' Noriz was protesting. 'I can see no benefit to such a delay.'

On the other side of the chamber, standing pointedly in front of the weapons armament panel, Ephrenia caught Corax's eye. He walked over to her as Branne stabbed a finger into the reply switch.

'You cannot enter Deliverance orbital space without prior authorisation, captain,' said the commander. 'Observe proper protocol and we will proceed.'

'Commander Branne is demanding that the Imperial Fists leave orbit and request permission to approach,' said the controller.

'I have already explained the reason for not doing so,' said Noriz. 'You are compromising our mission here.'

'Branne!' snapped Corax. The commander spun around, obviously having not noticed the primarch's arrival. 'Explain.'

'The Imperial Fists sent no hail after entering the

system, lord,' said Branne. 'Our protocols dictate that they stand out from the vicinity of Kiavahr and request permission to approach. At the moment, Ravenspire is within range of their weapons.'

Corax crossed the room, forcing Branne to stand aside at the console. The primarch took up the transmitter.

'Captain Noriz, this is Lord Corax,' he said. 'Why did you not declare your approach to Deliverance?'

'As I told Commander Branne, Lord Corax, I wish knowledge of our presence here to be minimised,' said Noriz after a slight delay. 'A long-range hail would have announced our presence as surely as chorus of blaring trumpets. It is imperative that I speak with you. I have messages from Lord Dorn and the Sigillite.'

'Commander Branne is correct,' said Corax. 'Please withdraw by one hundred thousand kilometres and prepare your ships to receive boarding parties. Commander Branne will meet you in person aboard your vessel to hear what you have to say. If he deems it necessary, he will then grant you authority to approach Deliverance and send a delegation to Ravenspire.'

There was a longer pause before Noriz replied.

'As you wish, Lord Corax,' said the Imperial Fists captain. 'I take it that I should treat Commander Branne as your absolute authority?'

'For certain,' said Corax. 'If you wish to keep a low profile, I suggest you retire out-orbit, to place Deliverance between your ships and Kiavahr. There will be no further long-range communication until Commander Branne has assessed the situation.'

'Understood, Lord Corax.'

Corax turned to Branne and saw an expression of self-satisfaction, an expression that changed to one of contrition when the commander saw the anger in Corax's eyes.

'I might expect such behaviour from a lower officer,

but you are a commander and you must set an example,' Corax rasped. 'You will be cordial and cooperative with Captain Noriz and extend him every assistance he requires.'

'Aye, lord,' said Branne, looking down at the decking. He raised his eyes for a brief moment before turning his gaze away again. 'I admit that perhaps I was over-zealous in my application of procedure. In my defence, the Imperial Fists did breach our security and I was only telling them to do the same as you did.'

'You forced me to support your stance, Branne,' said Corax, voice edged with irritation. 'I am not about to countermand the orders of one of my commanders in front of another Legion, but I do not agree with your response. Do not allow personal feelings to impede your duty again. I am returning to my chambers to continue my work. The next interruption I expect will be your full report on why the Imperial Fists have come here.'

'Understood, lord,' said Branne. He turned away and called to Controller Ephrenia. 'Signal Alpha Dock to ready me a Thunderhawk.'

Corax watched the commander stride from the control room and felt a moment of worry. Something was eating at Branne, something between him and Agapito. The two of them had shown moments of ill-discipline since the return from Isstvan and their behaviour at Ravendelve had bordered on antipathy towards each other. Corax was determined to root out the cause, and if necessary he would find new commanders.

Despite his concern, Corax decided that, for the moment, it would wait. The gene-project was more pressing. When the next generation of Raven Guard was secure, the primarch would turn his full attention to the existing one. He was eager to move on to wider implantation, and chafed at the thought of waiting for the results of more tests. Within moments, his mind was full of thoughts on how to refine the new gene-tech, the problems with his commanders forgotten.

As the primarch made his way back to his chambers, he told himself to have patience. A moment of rashness now might ruin all of the hard work and achievements that had come before. Feeling calmer, he sat down at his desk and started the dataflow again.

THE INTERIOR OF the *Wrathful Vanguard* was very different to the inside of a Raven Guard vessel. It resembled more closely a fortress than a starship, the walls layered with plates of bare metal etched with Legion mottoes and ferrocrete slabs carved with the sigils and devices of the Imperial Fists. Buttresses reinforced every corridor, doors were arch-shaped and made of heavily bolted wood and bulkheads were cross-barred with gilded girders.

Branne did not think it ostentatious – not like some of the vessels of the Emperor's Children he had travelled on – but there was an aesthetic that he found artificial and pompous. Raised in whitewashed cell blocks, the Raven Guard preferred the functional over the ornamental, and even since liberation Deliverance was only sparsely furnished and decorated.

The commander followed Noriz along a central passageway to a heavy elevator. A squad of Raven Guard followed a little way behind and they in turn were tailed by ten warriors of the Imperial Fists. Branne had not remarked on this welcome, still smarting from Corax's admonishment, and had allowed Noriz his prideful show of authority.

The conveyor descended with only a whine of electric motors, unlike the clanking, rattling elevators of Ravenspire. There was room enough for all of the legionaries, allowing the Raven Guard and Imperial Fists to stand a few metres separated from each other.

They could not have been more dissimilar: the sons of Corax in their black, patched-up armour and the warriors of Dorn resplendent in yellow and gleaming gold. The Imperial Fists stood to attention in a uniform line, bolters held at their waists; the Raven Guard had gathered in a clump, bolters slung on their belts, arms crossed or hands on hips.

'How are things on Terra?' Branne asked, feeling that he should break the stony silence.

'The fortification continues,' replied Noriz.

Branne waited, but there was no further comment forthcoming. He looked at the Imperial Fists.

'Your legionaries are turned out well,' he said, thinking of something complimentary to say. 'They are a credit to the Legion.'

'We were fortunate not to be involved in the debacle at Isstvan,' said Noriz. He glanced at the Raven Guard. 'It is understandable that after such a disaster certain standards must be compromised.'

Taking in a deep breath, Branne resisted the bait.

'We're ready to fight, despite our appearance,' he said.

'I know you are, commander,' said Noriz. 'It was not a condemnation of your preparedness or your ability. Your armourium has shown remarkable ingenuity in affecting such modifications.'

'We adapt, as ever. Hide some salt for the gruel, as we say.'

'An interesting motto,' said Noriz. It was hard to tell his mood from the modulation of his armour's external emitters, but Branne detected amusement. 'I am not sure what it means, though.'

'You weren't born in a prison, obviously,' said Branne.

'No, I was not, commander.' The conveyor shuddered to a stop and the doors slid open. Branne's armour detected vacuum as air blew out of the elevator in a gust that tousled the lanyards hanging from Noriz's shoulder pads. 'I hope you now understand why I insisted on full armour.'

They stepped out into darkness, footfalls silent in the void, the light from the conveyor casting long shadows over a floor of unpainted metal.

'The vacuum is a precaution only,' Noriz continued as he led the way. Suit lamps automatically sprang into life from the group as they moved further into the chamber. Turning, Branne saw that the walls were some considerable distance away, thirty metres or more. 'We wished the cargo to arrive in pristine condition.'

'Cargo?' said Branne. His question was answered as his suit lamp played over a figure a few metres ahead. He stopped suddenly, taken aback.

As the legionaries converged, several rows of armoured suits reflected back their lamps. The metal and ceramite were bare, the suits silver and dull grey. Lifeless masks gazed back at the commander as he turned left and right. There were several dozen sets of armour, each locked in place against a strut welded to the floor.

'Mark VI,' said Noriz. 'The latest design from Mars.'

Branne said nothing as he approached the closest rank of empty armour. It looked instantly familiar, at first glance little different from the Mark IV armour he wore. On closer inspection, the Raven Guard commander could see the subtle differences in panel shape and bonding, the thicker material of the flexible joints, the solid greaves covering the knees. Most obvious was the bolt-reinforced left shoulder plate and the helmet design.

'They still require a little further work, I'm afraid,' said Noriz. 'Lord Dorn wished them shipped out to you as soon as we were able. They're artificer-made, pre-production. You'll be the first Legion in the Imperium to be issued with Mark VI.'

'A nice gesture,' said Branne. He ran his hand over the

studded shoulder pad. 'We performed combat tests on the prototypes for two years, during the campaign through Scalland sector. I see they've solved the problem of the abdominal plating we reported.'

'Most of the improvements your Legion suggested were implemented,' said Noriz, almost wistfully. 'Protection is no better than the Mark IV, but the internal systems are far more efficient. The external cabling you see is supplemented by back-ups within the armour plate itself without compromising defence or adding excessive weight. Auto-senses have also been improved. In particular, auditory and olfactory pick-ups are much more sensitive. You will, no doubt, be pleased to hear that the stealth capabilities of this suit exceed that of any other variant.'

Branne nodded. 'You called it Mark VI. What happened to Mark V?'

Noriz pointed at the Raven Guard legionaries.

'With full production not yet begun on Mars, these are the only suits available. Our companion transport has another fifteen hundred of them, on top of the five hundred we are carrying. In the absence of reliable Legion supply lines, the Mechanicum have designated all non-standard or stop-gap designs as Mark V. Many of the improvisations made by your armourium after the drop-site massacre are being passed on to other Legions in the absence of replacement parts for Mark IV. Your legionaries already have Mark V, commander.'

'Why us?' said Branne. 'I'm thankful for the help, but this is a long way to come to pay us a favour.'

'In recognition of your part in testing the suits, and because you need them most. You have been honoured. The Mark VI is to be known as the Corvus suit.'

Branne laughed and jabbed a finger towards the conical faceplate in front of him.

'Because we're the Raven Guard and the armour has a beak?' he said. 'Some honour!'

'It is named after your lord, as thanks for the part you
have played and the losses you suffered when testing the
prototypes,' said Noriz, addressing his words to all of
the Raven Guard. 'Lord Corax is insistent that the Raven
Guard will take the fight to Horus's forces. Lord Dorn
sends these gifts to your Legion as a mark of support and
to assist in that endeavour.'

'You think we don't deserve them?' said Branne, picking up on the captain's tone. 'They would be better used
by the Imperial Fists on Terra?'

'On the contrary,' said Noriz. 'If I were to put desire
before duty, I would like just as much as you to strike
back at the rebels. As it is, I must deliver this cargo and
return to the Legion.'

Silence followed the captain's remarks. He gestured for
the group to return to the conveyor. Branne considered
the Imperial Fist's words, surprised by them. The doors
to the elevator shut behind them and air hissed into the
compartment. With a jolt, the conveyor began to ascend.

'It must have taken quite a bit of effort to get to Deliverance,' said Branne. 'What with the warp storms and
everything else.'

'Navigation continues to be very difficult, yes,' said
Noriz. 'In fact, the Seventh Legion fleet which Lord Dorn
originally dispatched to–'

'So it's going to be a long journey back for you.'

'It is, commander. I sense you are trying to imply
something, but I do not know what it is.'

'How many legionaries do you have with you?' asked
Branne, looking at the Imperial Fists squad.

'One hundred and fifty,' said Noriz. 'I do not see how
that would be relevant to our journey time.'

'In your assessment, how many of your Legion are
defending Terra?'

'When I left, there were more than forty thousand
Imperial Fists stationed at the palace,' said Noriz. He

grunted. 'I think I understand your meaning, commander. One hundred and fifty legionaries would be a far more significant addition, relatively, to your force of a few thousand.'

'I would have said that we need you more than Lord Dorn at the moment, but it comes to the same place,' said Branne. 'Communication is difficult though. We haven't had more than a few scraps from Terra since the storms started. The astropaths are trying hard, but they can't break through the disturbance. You won't be able to confirm a change of orders from your Legion command.'

'I know that you think we Imperial Fists are intractable, commander, but we do not abhor initiative as you suggest.' Noriz extended his hand. 'If Lord Corax agrees, I would be honoured to suborn my command to the Raven Guard for the moment.'

Branne looked down at the proffered hand and then took it in a firm grip.

'Glad you agree, captain,' said Branne. 'Happily for you, you'll be under the direction of Commander Agapito, not me.'

'Despite our early issues and personal differences, Commander Branne, I would have no problem serving under you. Against overwhelming opposition, you rescued Lord Corax and the remains of your Legion from Isstvan. That is a feat worthy of respect and praise. You are a Hero of the Imperium, commander.'

'I am?' laughed Branne. There were chuckles from the other legionaries, both Raven Guard and Imperial Fists. Since Isstvan, the commander had felt as if he had failed. The most important battle in the Legion's history and he missed it. He and his warriors had been apart from the others, isolated from the bond that had brought the rest of the Legion together, Terrans and those of Deliverance. To hear Noriz speak of his actions in such terms allowed him for the first time to think differently about the matter. 'If that makes me a Hero of the Imperium, we'll have to come up with a new title for whoever kills Horus.'

'It'll be Russ,' said one of Branne's honour guard. 'Just you wait. Once the Space Wolves get involved, this'll be over quick.'

'Maybe we'll get to him first,' said another.

'Sanguinius,' said Noriz, silencing the debate. 'The Sons of Fenris are far away, still likely dealing with the aftermath of Prospero. As much as I admire your enthusiasm, the Raven Guard cannot match the might of the Luna Wolves. No, when the Blood Angels hear of this treachery, there'll be no stopping Sanguinius. Lord Dorn calls him the Angel of Death, and I can't imagine Fulgrim, Perturabo, Lorgar or any of the others wanting to step between Horus and the Angel's vengeance. It'll be Sanguinius, mark my words.'

Branne reached into his belt and pulled out a ring with two large keys on it. They were dull, much scratched and slightly bent, the wear of decades plain to see.

'I took these from the first man I killed during the liberation war,' said Branne. 'If Sanguinius kills Horus, they're yours.'

'A wager?' said Noriz.

'If you like,' said Branne. 'What do you offer up?'

Noriz glanced at his legionaries and received nods of encouragement.

'All right,' said Noriz. He unhooked a golden shield from the lanyard on his right shoulder plate and held it up to Branne. It was inscribed with a single word: 'Narandia'. 'My first battle honour, awarded for slaying an ork commander. If Russ gets to Horus first, you can have it.'

This was greeted with claps and a cheer from the Raven Guard.

'I'll be watching your back, to make sure that you

survive long enough to hand over that shiny medal,' said
Branne.

'And I will be watching yours, commander,' replied
Noriz, slapping his hand against Branne's breastplate. 'I
have always desired to own a rusty set of keys.'

Returning the keys to their pouch, Branne hoped that
one of them would prove right. If Horus reached Terra,
nothing would be certain.

THE SLOW DRUMMING of Agapito's fingers sounded from
the metal desk. He stared at the communications log,
angered by the single highlighted line of data.

Someone had broken his personal cipher and endangered everything. He wondered who it might be, and
narrowed his suspicions to a few individuals, legionaries
that had caught his eye by their idiosyncratic behaviour.
There was nothing solid on which to base his accusations though, just an uncertainty that nagged at him.

With Branne scrutinising everything he was doing,
Agapito felt trapped. His questions had been off the
mark, but they were unwelcome attention. Branne
was stumbling around, searching for something but
not knowing what it was. His careless investigation
threatened to uncover everything by accident, and that
couldn't be allowed. Not before Agapito had a chance to
make his move.

A vox-chime interrupted his thoughts. He switched off
the display and activated the speaker.

'Commander Agapito, I have a matter to discuss with
you.' He recognised the voice of Custodian Arcatus. The
Custodian Guard had kept to themselves for most of the
time since arriving on Deliverance, quartered in the mid-
levels of Ravenspire that had once been home to the lost
companies. Every now and then they would emerge,
conducting inspections of the armourium, the docks
and other secure areas. That was another inconvenience,

but Corax had been adamant that the Custodians were given free range of Deliverance and Agapito's protests had been ignored. The one concession the commander had managed to extract meant that the Custodians were not entitled to travel to Ravendelve. That would have been too much for the primarch, who guarded the gene-project and its secrecy the same way he had guarded his followers during the uprising.

'I am in my chambers now, Custodian,' said Agapito. 'We can talk here.'

'Very well, commander, I am on my way.'

Agapito wondered what subject would be up for discussion. It was unusual for the Custodian Guard to interact with the Legion in this way. He wondered if Branne had got involved somehow, and his thoughts soured again. At least the gene-tech and new recruits seemed to be a complete success. Branne would soon have no time to ponder other matters. As Commander of Recruits he would be kept occupied at Ravendelve.

IT SEEMED A pointless exercise, but Alpharius was not going to attract attention by mentioning it. He lowered into a half-crouch, arms a little apart, and circled around the recruit. As he sidestepped to the left, he could see Corax and Branne out of the corner of his eye, watching him and Kaddian gauging each other.

The newly-enhanced Kaddian looked the part: taller than, but not quite as broad as, Alpharius, with rangy limbs and a determined glare. He might possess the physical qualities of a legionary, but he had none of the training and experience. Alpharius had noticed the Raven Guard were prone to wagers, and had bet Sergeant Dor that he would best Kaddian within two minutes. The stake was ten days of armour maintenance. Alpharius flexed his fingers as he pictured the sergeant polishing his suit.

The two warriors wore only loose black trousers for the bout, leaving little for Alpharius to grip for a throw. He lunged, attempting to grab Kaddian's left wrist, but the recruit was two steps away within a heartbeat, Alpharius's grapple missing badly. The recruit's face was a mask of concentration, eyes flicking between Alpharius's hands, feet and face, looking for any warning of his next move.

Circling again, Alpharius could feel the expectation from the rest of the squad, urging him on to victory. There was no cheering though, just studied silence from everyone in the hall, the only sound coming from the slap of the combatants' feet on the hard floor.

Kaddian sidestepped and swept a leg out, trying to trip Alpharius. The Alpha Legionnaire jumped just in time, already moving his weight forwards to shoulder-charge his opponent. He landed and leapt, only to find himself not connecting with Kaddian but running through empty air. A kick to his back sent Alpharius onwards a few more steps before he could halt his impetus and turn.

Immediately he was forced to throw up his arms to block a combination of punches aimed at his head, catching the blows on his forearms. Alpharius aimed a kick at Kaddian's abdomen, catching a glancing blow on the recruit's hip as he dodged back. Pressing forwards, seeking to exploit Kaddian's imbalance, Alpharius again tried for a grapple. He seized hold of the recruit's left arm and twisted, trying to force him down to the ground.

With a suppleness and strength that Alpharius had never encountered, Kaddian arched his back and heaved up with his trapped arm, lifting the legionnaire from his feet. Dropping to the floor, Kaddian turned to toss Alpharius over his back, forcing the legionary to release his grip to turn a hard landing into a forward roll.

A punch to the spine sent Alpharius sprawling, the

attack coming so quickly from behind he had no idea
how Kaddian had regained his feet in the half-second
that had passed. He half-rolled to his right, coming up
to face his opponent.

Just in time for his chin to meet the heel of Kaddian's
right foot.

Slamming back into the rockcrete, Alpharius smashed
his head against the floor as he fell. He rolled away as
the recruit's foot slammed down onto the floor where
Alpharius's throat had been a moment before. Kaddian's
other foot lashed into his ribs almost instantly, forcing
the air from the legionnaire's lungs.

He anticipated the next kick, managing to twist far
enough to grab Kaddian's ankle in both hands before
his foot connected with Alpharius's gut. Surging to his
feet, the Alpha Legionnaire heaved up, seeking to force
Kaddian to his back.

With precise timing, Kaddian used Alpharius's hold
on his ankle for support, surging up to crash a knee into
his chest. Alpharius toppled backwards and the two of
them fell in a heap. Alpharius let go with one hand and
hammered a fist into Kaddian's side, even as the recruit
slammed the tip of his elbow into the legionnaire's
cheek. Snatching his foot free from Alpharius's grasp,
Kaddian turned and knelt across his throat, pinning him
down. Gasping, Alpharius locked eyes with Kaddian and
saw ferocious intent. The recruit drew back his fist, aiming for Alpharius's face.

'Stop!' Branne's shout cut through the pounding of
blood in Alpharius's ears.

Kaddian jumped up and stepped away immediately,
retreating with light steps. Alpharius's head was ringing.
The ceiling swam in and out of focus for a few moments
before his vision cleared.

Sergeant Dor approached, hand outstretched to help
him to his feet. Irritated, Alpharius ignored the assistance

and pushed himself up. He glanced angrily at Kaddian, who was looking at him with a polite smile. Behind Kaddian, the other eight recruits were grinning at their companion's victory.

Still smarting from his defeat, Alpharius returned to his squad, ignoring the smug look on Dor's face. Another recruit and another legionary were called forwards, and the next bout began.

Recovering his senses, Alpharius could hear the conversation between Branne and Corax, standing not far to his left.

'Reactions and strength are better than a matured legionary,' said Branne. 'I've never seen anything like it.'

'Which is fine for unarmoured, unarmed combat,' replied Corax. 'Those advantages will be much reduced when they have their power armour.'

'I've been thinking about that, lord,' said Branne, eyes fixed on the two warriors sparring. 'The new Mark VI suits... They're far superior to anything else we have, except for a few artificer suits for officers, and even they're pretty bashed up. We can't implant the experience and guile of a veteran into these men, but the new armour and their advanced systems would go some way to helping with that.'

'I was thinking the same,' said the primarch. 'These are not just recruits, they are the start of something new for the Legion. I have told Sixx to progress with another one hundred implantations. If we can successfully scale up, you'll have a fighting force within fifty days. Commander of Recruits doesn't seem to reflect your role properly.'

Branne glanced at his leader.

'You said this would be a combat force when you gave me the title, lord.'

'They need a name, Branne,' said Corax. 'We can't keep calling them recruits, but it isn't right that they simply get absorbed by Agapito's Talons.'

'I have a suggestion,' said Branne.

'Then share it, commander.'

'We have the Talons, Falcons and Hawks, lord. I think we should be the Raptors.'

'The Raptors?' Corax smiled and placed a massive hand on Branne's shoulder. 'Yes, that will suit perfectly. Swift hunters. You are the Commander of the Raptors now. I'll inform Agapito, Solaro and Aloni.'

With a grunt and a thud, the legionary duelling with the Raptor ended up face-first on the floor, one arm twisted hard against his back. The Raptor snaked an arm around his neck and pulled, eliciting a pained snarl from the legionary.

'Stop!' Branne called.

The Raptors, thought Alpharius, looking at the line of warriors nodding encouragement to their companion as he returned to the rank. If Corax was right, and the Raptors would be battle-ready within fifty days, Omegon had to hear about this. Alpharius had held off making any report so far, but this was news worthy of the risk. Whatever the Alpha Legion primarch was planning, he would have to move swiftly if he was to counter the resurgence in the Raven Guard's fortunes.

Corax seemed to be content with what he saw. Alpharius watched him leave. Just before the primarch passed through the large doors from the hall, he stopped and looked back, deep in thought. A frown creased the pale skin of his brow, not of anger but of concern. It lasted only for a few seconds, and Alpharius was left to ponder what had passed through the primarch's thoughts as he had gazed back at the young Raptors.

The guard's visor shattered inwards, sending shards of reinforced transpex into the man's eyes. He fell back, howling. Corvus drove his fist into the screaming man's chest, silencing him in an explosion of bone fragments and pulped organs.

The rattle of automatic weapons fire sounded behind him and he felt a stinging sensation across his back. Looking over his shoulder, Corvus saw three men at the outpost rampart, a jutting defence position that overlooked the approach from Wing Two to the vehicle compound. More gunfire chattered and another hail of bullets pattered from his pale flesh, flattened rounds tinkling to the floor around him.

The rebel leader reached down and took the rifle from the dead guard's hands. The finger guard was too small for his huge digits, so he wrenched it off. Though in reality a large calibre weapon, the rifle felt like a child's toy in his hands. Lifting his arm, he turned and sighted on the men in the guard post. They were about two hundred metres away and he adjusted his aim a fraction to account for the poor charge in the rifle's bullets. The muzzle of the rampart gun flared again, ripping chunks from the pockmarked wall behind Corvus, rattling against his left arm.

He pulled the trigger.

The man firing the rampart gun sagged across his weapon, a hole punched through his left cheek just beneath the visor. His finger tightened as he died, sending a burst of bullets into the ground as the gun swung on its mounting.

Firing again, Corvus put his next shot through the throat of the loader, exposed by the swinging of the weapon. The third man turned to run. He was pitched from his feet as Corvus placed his third shot between the man's shoulder blades, shattering his spine.

'Here,' said Corvus, seeing Delpha running past without a weapon. He handed the youth the rifle. The rebel leader jerked his head towards the body. 'There are spare magazines in the guard's belt.'

The first wave had nearly reached the gate. The guards had sealed it from inside, believing themselves to be safe behind three interlocking layers of steels and ferrocrete. They were wrong.

Corvus lifted the radio transmitter from his belt.

'Constantin, enact the override.'

'Yes, Corax,' came the tinny reply. The word meant 'saviour'. Corvus had asked his followers to call him by the name he had already been given, but more and more of them insisted on the honorific. If that was their attitude, he was determined to prove them right and live up to their expectations.

Seeing a discarded shotgun, Corvus strode forwards and snatched it up. The fighting was about to get close and brutal. He pulled his knife – in fact, it was a security colonel's parade sword – from his belt and quickly caught up with the front of the mob streaming down the wide corridor towards the gate. If they could secure the garage facility, they would have enclosed vehicles to cross the airless wasteland outside. The strategic advantage of being freed from the confines of the prison buildings had made the compound one of Corvus's priorities.

'Override in five seconds, Corax,' reported Constantin.

'Press on!' the guerrilla leader roared, waving his shotgun towards the gates.

He was only a dozen strides from the blank surface of the portal. If the charges he had placed within the mechanism during his last unseen infiltration had been discovered, he was about to look very stupid.

A ripple of tiny pops rang through the metal. Corvus reached the lockdown lever a few seconds later – the corpse of the man who had pulled it lay crumpled at the rebel's feet. If all had gone as Corvus planned, the lockdown was anything but secure. He pushed the lever up, feeling no resistance. In that moment he knew he had been right.

Sirens blared and warning lights spun along the top of the gate as the massive portal ground open.

'Ready weapons!' Corvus bellowed over the deafening rumble of immense gears.

The door had lifted no more than half a metre from the ground when a hail of bullets erupted from beyond it, ripping through knees and shins. More than twenty men and women fell screaming, clutching at their ruined legs. A swathe of the inmates turned and ran to avoid the same fate.

Corvus's eye was drawn immediately to Lensa. She lay on her right side, left leg pulled up, her foot hanging off by a few scraps of sinew. Her young eyes met Corvus's and she relaxed. Her shrieking stopped and she smiled.

A second later, another hail of bullets thudded into her body, tearing off half her face and punching great holes through the rest of her body.

With a snarl, Corvus dropped to the floor and rolled under the ascending door. He came to his feet in front of two men standing behind a heavy stubber, its tripod lowered as far as possible. The shotgun roared in Corvus's hand, ripping through the protective vest of the closest guard. The second fumbled for a pistol, pulling it free from its holster at his hip just as Corvus pumped another round into the chamber.

The guard frantically pulled the trigger, sending bullets bouncing off Corvus's chest. The gun clicked empty several times and the man's face fell in horror. A hail of shot tore through his arm and shoulder, sending him spinning to the ground in a fountain of ruddy droplets.

The other gun crew was trying to turn their weapon towards the rebel leader. Tossing aside the shotgun, Corvus heaved the stubber from its mounting, kicking the tripod aside. He slung the belt of ammunition over his arm and brought the weapon to bear on the remaining men. Three short bursts were enough to kill them, the shots carefully placed not to damage the other heavy stubber.

The gate was now about a metre and a half off the ground and more rebels were pouring through. Corvus directed Branne, Agapito and Starken to take possession of the heavy weapon.

'Keep moving!' Corvus shouted. 'Keep moving!'

THIRTEEN

Corax's Hope
Hydra Contact Two
The Path to Victory

THE LINE TOOK one pace forwards, winding along one side of the corridor and back down the other. Navar Hef glanced to his left through the open doorway to see what was going on. The recruits – they weren't allowed to call themselves Raptors yet – were filing past Commander Branne. Next to him was Sergeant Nestil with a box covered with black cloth. Each recruit dipped his hand into the box and pulled out a hexagonal nut. Some were black and some were white.

Those who pulled out white nuts sighed and slipped away. Those lucky enough to produce a black nut – about one in three of the recruits – stepped into the room. They were the ones who would be next in line for the transformation.

Navar had seen the new Raptors training in the hall. They were an inspiration, more so even than the legionaries that Navar had looked up to for his whole life. He could remember each and every one of the First Nine when they had been like him, just a few weeks ago. Now they were sparring with the legionaries and practising fire drill with bolters and heavy weapons.

GAV THORPE

It was so close. If Navar could pick out a black nut, he would be one of the next cadre of recruits to become Raptors. The wait was agonising, taking one step at a time away from the door and then back towards it. When he had turned at the end of the corridor, by the double doors that led to the mess, Navar had realised how close he was to the back of the line. There were fewer than twenty other recruits behind him.

His hands were shaking with the excitement and his mouth was dry.

There were only five more recruits between Navar and Commander Branne. The next drew out a white nut: failure. Four more to go. The recruit who stepped forwards was Navar's squad leader, a fair-haired youth a couple of years older than him called Molo. Navar could barely breathe as Molo reached into the box, one eye closed as if fearful of seeing what he brought out.

It was a black nut.

'Good for you, Molo,' whispered Navar, and received a nod of thanks and wink in return.

'That's it,' said Branne, stepping out into the corridor.

'Commander?' said Navar, his gut tightening with disappointment.

'That's the next hundred,' Branne explained. 'Go back to your dorms and be ready for training at Falling Hour.'

Branne stepped back into the room and the door clanged shut, leaving the remaining recruits with sagging shoulders and scuffing feet. Navar felt like he had been kicked firmly between the legs, the knot of ache in his stomach much the same. He hadn't been one of the First Nine. He wouldn't be one of the Second Hundred.

'Never mind,' said Caol, slapping Navar on the shoulder from behind. 'We might not be the first, but we'll be Raptors soon enough. We can wait a week.'

A week seemed like an eternity to Navar.

* * *

ADJOINING THE COMMAND hall, Corax's control chamber was a square room a dozen metres across, every wall filled with screens and analytical engines. Robed technicians and wheezing servitors busied themselves at the consoles, collating the data flow into revolving star maps and ever-changing tables of information.

Branne, Agapito, Solaro and Aloni sat around the glass-topped table at the room's heart, while Corax stood to one side, a portable terminal in one hand. Apart from the others, silent in a corner of the chamber, stood Arcatus, invited out of courtesy by the primarch. Branne had just finished his report on the transformation of the second intake of Raptors. Two had died during the process; the rest were as impressive as the first wave.

'Sixx says he has created enough gene-seed for two thousand more, though the facilities at Ravendelve only allow us to proceed with implantation on two hundred and fifty recruits at a time. He has requested that we shift the whole operation back to Ravenspire.'

'Not yet,' replied Corax. 'What about the new armour?'

'Tests are nearly complete,' said Branne. 'The Raptors are learning to use the enhanced systems quickly. I've had the first thousand suits painted up in Legion livery. We'll need to finalise the squad organisation before I can pass on the insignia requirements to the armourium.'

'I have drawn up a list of potential sergeant candidates,' said Agapito, activating the touchpad on the table in front of him. 'The Raptors may be well-prepared, but we'll need to draft in Talons for some command experience.'

'Agreed,' said Corax. He glanced at the list. 'All fine warriors, I'll leave the final decision up to the two of you. Solaro, what is the vehicle situation?'

'Poor, relatively speaking,' said the commander. 'The armourium has received three shipments from Kiavahr since we returned, mostly Rhinos, but we're woefully light on heavier armour. Whatever you plan to do to get back at Horus, I hope you don't have a tank battle in mind.'

'It'll be an infantry assault,' said Corax. At a stroke of his hand, an image appeared on the surface of the table, of a star map showing the sector around Deliverance. A red circle highlighted a star towards the edge of the display and the image zoomed in.

'Narsis?' said Aloni. 'That's the objective?'

'We've compiled reports from several Navigators who have been travelling in the vicinity,' explained Corax. 'While the warp storms are still raging, turbulence around the Narsis system is much reduced. Given the world's proximity to several forge-worlds, as well as the resources of Agrapha, Chopix and Spartus, I believe that Narsis will be used by the rebels as a staging post to attack the sector.

'The Perfect Fortress,' said Branne. 'The Emperor's Children brought Narsis to compliance and built the Perfect Fortress there.'

'Typical arrogance of Fulgrim,' said Aloni. 'No fortress is perfect. Still, we don't have the heavy materiel for a siege.'

'Nor the time,' said Corax. 'I have a plan for the Perfect Fortress, but that is not an issue yet. I need to know whether the Raptors will be ready for the fight.'

'In theory, yes,' said Branne. 'But they're untested in real battle. Drills and firing ranges are one matter. The fire of war is another. I wouldn't want to pitch them up against the Perfect Fortress in the first engagement.'

'What about Cruciax?' said Solaro. He adjusted the table's display so that it veered towards another star system, much closer to Deliverance. 'Small moon base in a dead system. It was set up by the Word Bearers, probably a monitoring station. We can test the Raptors and close off one of the traitors' intelligence channels in the sector.'

Branne rubbed his chin and studied the schematic, while Corax nodded.

'How soon?' asked the primarch.

'How many do you want to test?' replied Branne.

'The first five hundred,' said the primarch. 'A proper battle, not some training skirmish. I expect the Raptors to fight independently of the Talons, Falcons and Hawks. They are our first strike formation.'

'Ten days to complete implantation, another ten preparing and arming,' muttered Branne. 'Who can say how long it will take us to get there. Fifteen days at least given the warp conditions.'

'Very well,' said Corax. 'You will lead the Raptors on a raid against the facility at Cruciax. I will accompany you for first-hand observation of their performance. What else do you need to be prepared in time?'

'Just some sergeants,' said Branne, looking at Agapito. 'Other than that, we've got everything in hand.'

'I'll have the new squad leaders reassigned and sent down to Ravendelve in the next two days,' replied Agapito.

'You'll still need some recon,' said Solaro. 'I can have my squads ready whenever you need them.'

'We'll rely on orbital data,' said Corax. 'This is just a small engagement. The force will deploy on the *Avenger* only, no need to risk getting a flotilla scattered in the storms. We hit the Word Bearers, destroy the station and withdraw. That is all.'

'Understood, lord,' said Branne.

'Are you sure?' said Corax. He looked at each of the commanders in turn. 'Narsis is our main objective. I want to be ready to launch a full-scale attack on the Emperor's Children garrison within fifty days. We *must* strike back at the traitors soon.'

'Have your plans been approved by the Emperor?' asked Arcatus, rising from his seat. 'What support can you expect?'

'There has been no meaningful contact with Terra,' said Corax. 'The Emperor granted us autonomy when he allowed us to take the gene-tech from the vault. We can

expect no other forces for the moment. It's just the Raven
Guard, nobody else. I don't know the situation with the
other Legions, so we can only rely on ourselves.'

'My Custodians will accompany you to Narsis,' said
Arcatus. 'If possible, we will secure prisoners from the
Emperor's Children for transportation back to Terra.'

'That is a secondary concern,' said Corax. 'Our primary
goal must be the elimination of the Perfect Fortress and
its garrison. It will hamper our enemies considerably if
Narsis falls into the hands of those loyal to the Emperor.'

'It is your command privilege, primarch,' said Arcatus. 'Remember that though you may fight alone at the
moment, there are others who will be waging this war
too.'

'I have not forgotten them,' said Corax. 'It is for them
that the Raven Guard will place themselves into the jaws
of the beast and draw its bite.'

THE ACID-CLOUD HAD reduced visibility to less than a
hundred metres, and was already etching strange sworls
in the paint of Alpharius's armour. He stepped forwards
carefully, avoiding the forming pools of corrosive liquid. Everything in the rad-zone was tinged with a ruddy
hue, the shadows of the ruined buildings ahead a darker
blot against the crimson skyline.

The bleeping of the rad-detector was insistent but
steady, low enough that his suit had not yet started
pumping counteractive agents into his bloodstream. The
recycled air he breathed was growing a little stale, but
was far from intolerable despite the antiseptic tinge.

Stepping over the corroded remnants of a rail track,
Alpharius looked to his right, where the rest of the squad
was advancing with weapons ready. The in-vision schematic in the corner of his eye showed that they were
seven hundred and fifty metres from the Ravendelve
beacon, five hundred short of the patrol limit.

Skirting around a molten heap of slag that had once been a line of rail carts, the squad crossed the cargo yard at a steady pace. Nemron walked a little ahead of the others, bolter in one hand, auspex in the other. Periodically he would declare no contacts.

The patrol was a standard procedure to ensure that the perimeter of the facility was secure, but with the Raptors recruitment stepping up, Alpharius had detected a greater sense of importance in the orders of Commander Branne. It was not a good sign, an indicator perhaps that the Raven Guard upper echelons might have heard something about the rebellion Omegon was inciting. The patrol range had been pushed out by five hundred metres, covering the outskirts of the desolate transport hub.

Another hundred metres further on, the cloud was thickening even further as the squad moved into a depression caused by the subsidence of underground tunnels and hallways. Descending over broken ferrocrete, Alpharius felt something new. There was a small but insistent pressure at the base of his skull, nestled next to the vertebrae in the gap where one of his progenoid glands had been removed.

He recognised the cause immediately and took a sharp breath. The microscopic Alpha Legion implant set into his spine had detected an alert broadcast. Somewhere within a hundred metres was a Legion transmitter.

'Sweep right, strafe fifty metres,' he said, pushing the rest of the squad away from his line of advance. 'Nemron, active scan of that building seventy metres to the right.'

Alpharius stayed on his course, opening up a gap between himself and the rest of the legionaries. The ticking sensation in his neck was becoming more distinct. Glancing at the others, he saw them only as half-seen shadows in the corrosive mist, and was sure they could see little of him.

He stopped and concentrated on the signal the implant was detecting. He sensed a minor increase in the device's alert tempo as he stepped to his left. Looking around, he saw the remnants of a power pylon, collapsed and folded as if it had been made of wet paper. With one more glance to ensure he was unobserved, he headed towards the pylon, the ticking in his skull becoming quicker and quicker.

He made a quick survey of the rubble around the base of the crumpled tower but could not see any obvious sign of disturbance. He was glad there was nothing to see. He didn't have to have access to the node station to interact with it. Kneeling down, he opened up the access panel in his right forearm and disabled his squad monitor.

'Sergeant, losing your signal,' came the immediate call from Gallid, the vox-link heavy with interference.

'Rad-pocket, nothing to worry about,' Alpharius replied in a measured tone. 'Continue sweep, I will rejoin you shortly.'

The Alpha Legionnaire activated the short-range receiver/transmitter, a small coil of aerial extruding from the back of his gauntlet.

'Effrit code, omega-nine-hydra,' came the electronically muffled voice of the transponder. 'Contact Two. Make report. Action imminent. Ready yourself for commands.'

'Effrit code, hydra-nine-omega,' said Alpharius. 'Contact Two understood. New formation designated "the Raptors". Gene-tech highly stable. Twenty-three days until first operations of Raptors. Target secure but ingress route has been established. Ready for orders.'

A loud crackle surprised Alpharius, indicating a live link was being established.

'Contact Two, this is Effrit. Confirm status of Raptor development.'

'Effrit, Hydra Contact Two. Implantation sequence scaled up. Full processing imminent. Estimate return of enemy to military threat within seventy days. Orders?'

There was a lengthy delay until the reply crackled through. Alpharius guessed that his news had required some deliberation for his master to resolve.

'Report understood, Contact Two. Orders to stand by remain.'

The link closed with a hiss and Alpharius retracted the transmitter. He was a little worried by the response. Though it was hard to tell through the layers of tampering, the Alpha Legionnaire thought he had detected hesitancy in Omegon's message, as if he had been taken back by the swiftly moving current of events.

There was little Alpharius could do at the moment, and the standby order implicitly instructed him not to make any attempt on the gene-tech yet, nor to interfere in or obstruct the ongoing recruitment process. He hoped his primarch had a plan and was ready to act soon. If not, the Raven Guard would be well on their way to recreating their Legion.

'TOUCHDOWN IN FIVE... four... three... two... one. Mark.'

The Thunderhawk rocked heavily and a plume of grit and sand billowed up past the port. Branne was already out of his harness and heading towards the assault ramp. The rest of the thirty Raptors aboard quickly lined up behind him, their newly painted armour gleaming in the combat lighting, their bolters shining with fresh oil.

'Second strike has crippled eastern defence turret, you are clear for disembarkation,' announced the pilot.

The ramp lowered quickly, filling the interior of the gunship with harsh blue light. Branne's auto-senses filtered out the worst of the glare as he thudded down the ramp and onto a wind-swept dune.

'Standard dispersal, Corron take left flank, Nal on the right,' snapped Branne.

The Raptors fanned out quickly, their armour dark against the light grey desert. One squad split to either side and the third followed Branne straight ahead. In front of them, the monitoring station squatted beneath a rocky cliff, its flat roof a tangle of communications dishes and sensor arrays.

Three missiles streaked down from overhead, detonating towards the western end of the station, to Branne's left. Rockcrete exploded outwards from the bunker-busters, showering debris over a sand-choked yard.

'Breach achieved, third unit moving forwards, second unit provide fire support,' said Branne.

The sand was shifting constantly, making the ground underfoot unstable. The heavy legionaries surged through the drifts in clouds of grey, weapons aimed at the low building ahead. The scream of plasma jets erupted overhead as another Thunderhawk made a pass, its lascannons punching through heavily shuttered windows on the southern face of the station. Downblast from Branne's gunship momentarily swathed the advancing Raptors in a storm of grit as it lifted off to take up a covering position above.

'Targets, point fifteen, third window,' snarled Branne, seeing armoured figures moving at one of the destroyed windows. A moment later, bolter rounds spat from the inside of the building, streaking towards Sergeant Nal's squad.

Return fire blazed from Corron's warriors, a hail of bolter shells and plasma blasts. Branne signalled for the squad accompanying him to lay down their own covering fire as Nal and his legionaries pressed on into the defenders' fire.

'Keep them busy,' said Branne, drawing up his combi-bolter. He fired both barrels simultaneously, sending a hail of bolts through the window and into the twisted metal frame around it. The bark of bolters intensified, joined by the thunderous beat of the squad's rotary autocannon, wielded by Kavin. The heavier shells of the autocannon ripped out chunks of plascrete from the wall.

Branne realised this was the first time he had fired at other warriors of the Legiones Astartes. Like the Raptors he led, he had not fought on Isstvan, and it was a moment he was proud to share with the new recruits. He wondered if Corax had been even smarter than the commander had realised when he had put Branne in charge of the Raptors. Not having shared the experience of the dropsite massacre and escape, he had found it hard to relate to the legionaries that had. There was no such divide between him and his new command.

This attack was not just to prove the capability of the Raptors, it was a chance for him to demonstrate to his brother, and the rest of the Legion, that he was as determined to press this war against the traitors as any warrior who had seen his battle-brothers cut down on Isstvan V.

'Thermal scans show the enemy are responding in force towards the southern attack.' Corax spoke slowly and calmly. The primarch had not joined the attack in person, preferring to observe proceedings from the *Avenger* in orbit over Cruciax's largest moon. The gas giant itself could just about be seen as a large arc of dark red beyond the jagged line of mountains behind the monitoring post.

'Hold position, draw fire,' Branne ordered his companions. They had made great display of their landing and first attack, but theirs was a diversionary assault designed to bring the Word Bearers to one side of the compound. Meanwhile, another force was approaching on the opposite side, from atop the cliff, unseen by the defenders.

A bolt cracked into Branne's right arm. Splinters of ceramite pattered against his chest and faceplate. He saw that an access door had been opened about fifty metres to his right, from which a squad of red-clad Word Bearers was pouring fire into his three squads from the flank. One of Nal's legionaries went down, pitching face first into the sand. Another spun to the ground a second later, arcs of energy crackling from a punctured backpack.

Switching his grip to his left hand, the commander fired back with a salvo of ten rounds. Kavin swung his autocannon onto this new threat before Branne had spoken the order. Autocannon rounds punched into the squad sheltering in the doorway, felling a Word Bearer and forcing the others out of sight.

Branne glanced at the secondary chronometer display in his visor: 22.03 seconds until the main attack was in place.

'Keep it up! Keep them busy!' he yelled. The Raptors would not be allowed to fall short of the standards demanded by the Raven Guard. He would not be found wanting either.

THE TOP OF the escarpment was littered with loose rocks, but it did not hamper the legionaries as they bounded across along the slope with long strides. As part of the Ravendelve garrison, Sergeant Dor's squad had been temporarily attached to the Raptors, honorary members it seemed, and so Alpharius found himself descending on the Word Bearers outpost alongside the warriors of the Raven Guard.

It was a strange feeling, almost as odd as the sensation he had felt when the primarch had given the order to open fire at the dropsite ambush. They had been warned then of the plan to back Horus's defiance of the Emperor, but the reality of firing on another Legion had quite surprised Alpharius. Far from being shocked by it, he had

found it liberating. Decades of being overshadowed by
the extravagant exploits of the other Legions had built
up in him a resentment that he had not acknowledged
until the moment he first pulled the trigger.

There had been a sense of vindication then, but now
Alpharius was feeling more pragmatic. The Word Bearers had proclaimed their loyalty so loudly, had spouted
their liturgies and oaths so proudly, it was perhaps their
rebellion that was the most unseemly and least like true
legionaries. Alpharius had always thought they had protested their dedication to the Imperial cause too much,
and when he had found out they would be siding with
Horus it had come as no surprise.

They were allies, as much as any of the Legions that
had collaborated to destroy the Emperor's task force, but
that didn't mean Alpharius had to like the bombastic,
preaching turncoats. He could well imagine them extol-
ling the praises and virtues of Horus as loudly as they
had once proclaimed the righteousness of the Emperor.
Of all those who had taken part in the massacre, it was
the Word Bearers he considered the most hypocritical.

'Ready for drop,' announced Sergeant Dor.

They were almost at the lip of the cliff overlooking the
facility. Two hundred Raptors, and twenty of the former
Talons, surged through the sandstorm.

The Raptors were a strange sight with their beaked
facemasks and new armour, looking the part of hunting
birds of prey. Alpharius had already accessed the technical schematics of the new Mark VI armour, and was
waiting for the opportunity to upload them to Omegon.
It was probably not much of a revelation, considering
the tendrils Horus had infiltrated into the Mechanicum,
but how much of that information the Warmaster was
willing to share with the Alpha Legion was questionable.

A squad to Alpharius's right reached the edge of the
cliff first. They carried on, leaping into the swirling sand.

Alpharius took a breath and followed, hurling himself into thin air. The roof of the compound was twenty-three metres below, a distance that posed little problem to a fully armoured legionary even in normal gravity, and that of Cruciax's moon was two-thirds Terran standard.

Clouds of dust billowed up as Alpharius thudded onto the pitted rockcrete roof. The fibre bundles in his armour bunched as he landed, a sudden flicker of systems reports scrolling past his right eye.

'Meltas!' said Dor, pulling one of the charges from his belt. Alpharius did the same, slapping the melta bomb onto the roof in front of him and setting the timer for three seconds.

He stepped back half a dozen paces and readied his bolter in one hand while arming a frag grenade in the other. With a white-hot detonation, the melta charge blasted through the rockcrete, creating a hole just over a metre across. Dor's bomb went off half a second later, widening the gap. All around him, the Raptors were doing likewise, opening up cracks across the compound. Alpharius tossed the grenade into the opening. He grabbed his bolter in both hands and jumped down through the breach as he heard the crack of the fragmentation charge detonating.

Tiles split underfoot from the impact of his landing. There was dust everywhere, the floor littered with shards of rockcrete that crunched as he took a step. The only light came from the breach above, the harsh glare creating a column of blue around him. With a glance in front and behind, he found himself in a short corridor, open archways at each end. He stepped forwards again, aiming ahead as Sergeant Dor dropped into the station. Alpharius swung his bolter to the right as a door opened a little way ahead of him, but he relaxed his finger on the trigger as he recognised the distinctive profile of a Raptor in the gloom.

The bark of a bolter ahead spurred Alpharius into action. With the rest of the squad thudding down behind them, he and Dor advanced on the archway, five Raptors emerging from a side room to join them.

A figure appeared at the archway. In the swirl of dust it was impossible to tell friend from foe and Alpharius checked his fire. The warrior ahead took a couple of steps closer, revealing a legionary clad in crimson armour. There was something strange about him, a hunched look that unsettled Alpharius.

Dor opened fire first, the Raptors adding their own salvoes an instant later. The Word Bearer stumbled backwards out of sight, pieces of armour flying in all directions.

'Come on!' shouted Dor, breaking into a run. 'Clear out this room.'

Alpharius followed on his heels, bursting through the archway with his finger already tightening on the trigger of his bolter. He swung the weapon left at a pair of legionaries crouching by the shattered sill of a window. His first blast ripped into the backpack of the closest. The second was aimed higher and crashed into the Word Bearer's sculpted helmet.

Or at least that was what Alpharius had first thought.

The Word Bearer toppled sideways, blood pouring from his shattered skull. What Alpharius had taken as an ornate helm was no such thing – the Word Bearer's head was misshapen, a small horn protruding from his brow, canine teeth jutting down to his chin. His skin was bronze-coloured and the blood that pumped from the hole in his skull was black and thick.

Alpharius fired again with a shout of disgust, pulverising the Word Bearer's misshapen head. The other legionary spun around and fired, his burst catching Alpharius in the gut. A cable ruptured, artificial muscle bundles fraying in a welter of white sustaining fluid.

A Raptor surged past Alpharius, bolter blazing, opening up a line of bloody craters across the Word Bearer's chest. The traitor swung his bolter like a club, but the Raptor was too quick, deftly deflecting the blow with his own weapon, before repeatedly smashing his elbow into the side of the Word Bearer's helm. The Raptor hooked a foot behind the traitor's leg and tripped him with another blow to the head.

One foot on the Word Bearer's chest, the Raven Guard warrior fired, bolt after bolt punching through the traitor's armour, coating the Raptor's greaves with gore.

'Move on,' said Dor, pointing towards a sealed archway on the opposite side of the chamber.

Looking around, there were no Raven Guard casualties. Alpharius counted five dead Word Bearers, another of them showing bestial, twisted features similar to the one he had slain.

'Let's not think about that too much,' said Dor, guessing Alpharius's thoughts from his posture. 'According to the pulse survey, there's a reactor two levels down, almost directly below us. Look for a stairwell.'

It was impossible for Alpharius not to think about what he had seen. There had always been rumours. Less than rumours, more fanciful soldiers' tales. Ships had been lost and found with their complements ravaged by some horrific power. Every legionnaire who had spent time in the warp had a story about a strange dream or discomforting occurrence. Alpharius had half-glimpsed bizarre things on the cusp of wakefulness while in warp transit and Legion command had never directly denied that the warp was inhabited. Seeing the contorted faces of the two dead Word Bearers reminded Alpharius of those vague dreams and he wondered just what was happening to the Legiones Astartes who had sided with Horus.

Another corridor led them into a mess hall that ran the

width of the facility, nearly seventy metres long. A fire-fight was already raging when they arrived. The air was filled with criss-crossing salvoes, bright sparks of bolt propellant and fiery detonations reflecting from steel-topped tables and laminated shelves. The roar of bolters and ring of impacts was deafening. The Word Bearers had taken up positions behind overturned tables and in the galley at the far end, and were exchanging fire with two squads of Raptors pinned down at a set of double doors opposite Alpharius.

A burst of shots greeted Sergeant Dor as he ran into the room, bolter on full automatic fire. He heaved over one of the long bench tables and hunkered behind it, splinters of metal spraying around him, bolt detonations sparking across his armour.

Without hesitation, the Raptors piled into the hall from behind Alpharius. The first was taken off his feet by a plasma bolt that melted through his chest plate and incinerated his innards. The Raptors exacted instant vengeance, blazing away at the plasma gunner, the Word Bearer's armour and a glass-fronted cabinet behind him exploding with hits.

'Flank move, squad three!' The order was snapped out by one of the Raptors as he bounded up on to a table with a grenade in hand. He lobbed the grenade over the serving counter separating the hall from the galley. A blossom of fire erupted in the heart of the galley, setting off a chain of secondary detonations from ruptured power lines.

The black-clad Raptors surged down each side of the hall, racing forwards without firing. Two more were sent tumbling by the volleys of the Word Bearers but the dark-armoured legionaries pounded on, ignoring their casualties.

'Keep up, old fella,' one of the Raptors laughed at Dor as he sprinted past the sergeant.

'Cheeky bastard,' snarled Dor, powering himself over the fallen table, bolt-rounds blasting down the hall from his weapon. 'Support fire!'

Alpharius sidestepped into the hall and squeezed off a salvo of five rounds, targeting a Word Bearer bringing a plasma gun to bear from behind a trolley stacked with water jugs. The ewers disintegrated into shards and silver slivers, the Word Bearer forced to dive out of sight, the fresh red paint of his armour pockmarked by several direct hits. The rest of the squad dashed into the hall and took up firing positions, bolt-rounds hammering into the metal counter and tables shielding the Word Bearers.

The Raptors reached the far end of the hall, pulling free combat knives to hurl themselves at the waiting Word Bearers. Alpharius saw one of them shredded by the combined fire of three traitors, moments before his squad-brother vaulted over the counter, his bolter firing point-blank into the face plate of a Word Bearer. The Raptor slashed his knife backhanded through the throat seal of another even as his left pauldron shattered in a hail of ceramite fragments from a bolt impact.

The Word Bearers had not expected the sheer swiftness and ferocity of the Raptors' attack. Black-armoured legionaries were pouring between the shelves and cupboards of the galley, overwhelming the traitors with bolter and knife.

At a word from Dor, the squad started forwards, ready to cover the Raptors if they were forced back. There was no need for such caution. Alpharius saw a Word Bearer go down, bludgeoned by the bolters of three Raptors. Another traitor was lifted off his feet and hurled bodily into the power cables exposed by the grenade, sparks and arcs of lightning scorching across his twitching body.

The last time Alpharius had seen anything like it had

been the World Eaters' charge into the Salamanders at
the dropsite. That had been raw carnage on a scale he
had never imagined possible. The fight in the mess hall
was far less of a spectacle, but the lethal efficiency of the
Raptors was no less impressive.

He pictured the superhumans ahead of him in the
colours of the Alpha Legion, tearing through Ultramarines or Dark Angels. There was an irrepressibility
about the way they fought, a disciplined fury coupled
with extraordinary speed and precision. And they were
just fresh recruits. Alpharius imagined the Alpha Legion
descending on Terra with fifty thousand such warriors,
hardened by previous battles, with the canniness and
guile they would learn from the primarch.

That was a force Horus would respect. Suddenly,
Alpharius realised just how important his mission
could become and why he had not yet received orders
to destroy the gene-tech. This was not about stopping
the Raven Guard. This was about strengthening the
Alpha Legion.

The hall fell quiet, the death cry of the last Word
Bearer quietly ringing from the steel walls. Alpharius
moved into position to secure another doorway ahead,
while the Raptors moved amongst the traitors, wordlessly ensuring they were all dead with knives to the
back of their necks.

'New orders!' barked Dor. 'The reactor has been set
with charges. We're leaving now. Thunderhawks for
extraction at grids seven-sixty and seven-ninety. We
have sixty seconds. Move!'

'That's it?' said Alpharius, before he could stop himself. 'We're done?'

'Strike and withdraw, you know the procedure,' the
sergeant replied. 'Mission was to destroy the station. In
fifty seconds, we will have been successful.'

The Raptors needed no repeat of the orders. Squad by

squad they fell back from the galley and across the mess hall. Alpharius retreated, still keeping a wary eye for any counter-attack.

'Are the enemy eliminated?' he asked.

'They will be when that reactor explodes,' Dor said with a laugh. 'No time to hang around.'

They withdrew to the corridor along which they had advanced and clambered out of the shattered windows. A stream of black-armoured legionaries was pouring back into the sandstorm, disappearing from sight. Alpharius felt grudging respect for the Raven Guard as they melted away as quickly as they had appeared. Forging through the sand drifts, he glanced back but the facility was now enveloped in the dust storm and obscured from sight. Ahead, his locator locked on to the signal of a descending Thunderhawk. Ramp open, the drop-ship plunged down into a dune, adding to the swirl of sand.

The ground shook underfoot just as Alpharius reached the ramp. Stepping aboard the drop-ship, he turned to see a dark red ball of flame expanding in the hazy distance. Moments later, a violent wind swept the dunes, sending a wall of sand hurtling into the open compartment of the Thunderhawk.

'We're full,' the pilot announced over the internal announce system. 'Clear the ramp.'

Dor dashed out of the cloud and leapt onto the ramp as it started to close, grabbing Alpharius's arm to haul himself into the main chamber.

'Mission complete,' Corax announced over the main vox channel. 'We are victorious. The Raven Guard have shown that they cannot yet be ignored in the battle-plans of our foes. The Raptors have proven their worth and earned their first battle honour. The fight against Horus has begun.'

Alpharius lowered himself into his seat and pulled on the harness as the Thunderhawk banked sharply. The entire engagement had lasted less than ten minutes: ten minutes that might have changed the course of the whole war.

THERE WAS A jubilant mood at Ravendelve as the last of the shuttles from the *Avenger* disgorged its cargo of warriors. Even the loss of fourteen of their number had not dampened the spirits of the latest Raven Guard recruits, though it was cause for some sombre reflection for Branne. The casualty ratio was a little high for his liking, considering the Word Bearers could not have numbered more than fifty legionaries against four hundred in the main assault, but his concern came from another source. Corax had said little about the operation except for his short victory speech, and had cloistered himself in Branne's command chamber for the trip through the warp, giving the commander no opportunity to voice his doubts.

While the Raptors were being returned to their dormitories, Branne and Corax travelled back to Ravenspire, to report on the mission to the other members of Legion command. They were waiting in the briefing room when the primarch and Branne arrived. There was still a large amount of activity going on, as Legion attendants gathered as much intelligence as they could regarding Narsis and the Perfect Fortress. Solaro, Agapito and Aloni sat at the table like giant statues amidst the bustle of the command functionaries.

'The outpost at Cruciax is destroyed,' Corax announced as he entered the chamber. 'The Raptors, whilst a little tactically naive, performed beyond expectation and the victory signals to me a new beginning for the Raven Guard.'

'A one hundred per cent success?' asked Solaro.

Corax did not answer, but instead looked at Branne.

'I wouldn't say that,' replied the commander of the

Raptors, staring right back at his primarch. 'We sustained avoidable casualties.'

'They will improve, given experience,' said Corax. 'Their exuberance will be tempered.'

'They were foolhardy, lord, not exuberant,' Branne said, sitting at the table. 'While all combat is a risk, there were many that took unnecessary gambles and that not only cost valuable lives, it potentially threatened the success of the mission.'

'If we take them to the Perfect Fortress in that state of mind, they will be slaughtered,' said Agapito. 'We've been studying what information we have in the archives, and it is a formidable obstacle. I expect the Emperor's Children have been further fortifying Narsis since their alliance with Horus. It is no place for rash action.'

'The Raptors will only be part of the force,' said Corax, frowning with irritation. 'You judge them harshly for a little poor discipline during their first engagement. They knew they were being tested, and overcompensated in their enthusiasm. I remember you and Branne trying to impress me with your heroics when you were young.'

'A good point, lord,' said Agapito. He looked contrite for a moment, then shook his head. 'But there is a difference between two adolescent prison boys and several companies of transhumans armed and armoured with the best weapons we currently have available. As legionaries, they should impress you with dedication and discipline, not raw zeal. Attention to dut–'

'You do not think they are ready?' snapped Corax. 'You sound like one of those Word Bearers Chaplains, speaking of empty duty and discipline. We are involved in a war that will decide the fate of the Imperium! I expect every warrior to carry himself with pride and to do his utmost to ensure victory.'

There followed an uncomfortable silence for a few seconds as Corax turned away, jaw churning with anger.

When he looked at his commanders again, he had calmed himself.

'The Raptors will learn discipline,' he said. 'In time, when there are more of them, we will be able to spread them through the Legion as we would any other recruits and the presence of the veterans will mollify their young spirits. Remember that most of them were little more than children only a hundred days ago. Your transformations took years, during which you learned patience and discipline. Branne, if you are so concerned, you must take extra effort to instil such qualities into your warriors, because we don't have the luxury of several years to test their mettle and forge their battle-spirit.'

'Aye, as you wish, lord,' said Branne. 'A few more turns through the rad-wastes will calm their humours.'

'How soon will we move on Narsis, lord?' asked Solaro. 'Even with the Raptors, we cannot muster more than five thousand legionaries and other ranks.'

'I aim to tackle the Perfect Fortress with twice that number,' said Corax. 'Sixx and Orlandriaz have received instruction to move to the next scale of implantation.'

'Five thousand more Raptors?' said Agapito, almost horrified by the suggestion. 'We have no more than five hundred novitiates left to implant. Where will you get new recruits?'

'From Deliverance and Kiavahr,' said Corax. 'As I told you before, the new gene-seed allows us to take younger and less fitting candidates with equal results.'

'Forgive any disrespect, lord, but that does not make sense,' said Agapito. 'Just a moment ago, we were discussing the immaturity of the Raptors, who have each been subjected to Legion tradition and teaching for several years already. To take untested boys and turn them into super-soldiers seems rash.'

'There is no alternative,' said Corax, showing no signs of anger at Agapito's criticism. 'I understand your

concerns, and considered them on the way back from
Cruciax, but Horus's treachery has backed us into a corridor with only one way out. Either we turn over Raptor
production to its full potential, including casting our
recruitment wider, or we must give up any desire to
strike at Horus's forces. As we are at the moment, it is
a simple case of numbers: we don't have them in our
favour.'

'I would like to register my disapproval,' said Agapito.
He looked at Corax, and then pointedly turned his gaze
to Branne, with an expression of frustration bordering
on desperation.

Branne sympathised with his brother's position, but
he had seen first-hand what the Raptors could do, even
in their inexperience. To have five thousand such warriors would be an incredible weapon. There was also the
question of loyalty to the primarch. Agapito's strange
behaviour since Isstvan gave Branne cause to doubt his
motives for opposing Corax's plan. Perhaps he feared
that the Talons would lose honour and prestige. It was
certainly the case that the seemingly preferential treatment – the armour and weapons – given to the Raptors
rankled at Agapito.

There was another reason to agree with the primarch,
a far more personal one. The action at Cruciax had not
erased the doubts Branne felt about himself for his fail-
ings at Isstvan. It had proved to him more than ever that
he needed to redeem himself in the eyes of the Raven
Guard who had fought there. A large force of Raptors
would make him the pivotal commander at Narsis,
granting him an opportunity to prove his worth on a
stage far more fitting than a raid on an isolated outpost.

'It is fitting,' said Branne, 'that we extend the chance to
become Raven Guard to as many as possible. We fought
a war to liberate the people of this star system, so that
they might enjoy the benefits of freedom. The Raven

Guard prosecuted the Great Crusade across hundreds of worlds to bring that same freedom to others. Now it is time for them to answer our call and repay those efforts with their own.'

'You're not suggesting conscription?' said Solaro.

'No,' said Corax. 'I'll not have that. I do not think we will be troubled by a shortage of volunteers.'

'Word will get out, lord,' said Agapito, gripping the edge of the table tightly. 'So far we have kept secret our plans and our renewed strength. If you recruit on a scale like this, the news will travel back to the traitors and they will send a force to exterminate us entirely, a force we will not be able to resist. Surprise is our greatest asset, and we will surrender it with this sort of declaration.'

'It will be too late,' said Corax. 'We will strike quickly enough that there will be no time for our enemies to prepare. We will begin with the implantation of the remaining recruits at Ravendelve as soon as possible. Branne will organise the mass induction of candidates and we will make our final preparations for the assault on Narsis.'

'What about weapons and armour?' said Solaro. 'At the moment, we can make Raptors faster than we can manufacture Mark VI suits.'

'I already have a manufactorum on Kiavahr stepping up production based on the designs brought to us by Captain Noriz,' answered the primarch. 'As for weapons, we have stockpiles worthy of a Legion that was once eighty thousand strong. A few thousand bolters are not an issue, despite the losses on Isstvan.'

'Transportation?' said Agapito, with the sigh of a man who knew he had lost a battle. 'The *Avenger* and surviving ships cannot carry that many into battle.'

'We will requisition transports from wherever we can,' said Corax. 'We don't need dedicated assault ships, as long as they can launch Thunderhawks and Stormbirds.

Whatever problems you foresee, we will overcome them. The Raven Guard will be prepared to attack Narsis within twenty-five days. I have waited long enough, and I can wait no longer. The fight back against the traitors has already begun, it is time to accept that and strike a blow that will make them nervous.'

'Aye, lord,' said Agapito, his reply echoed by the other commanders. 'It will be as you command.'

FROM A VANTAGE point in the irradiated ruins surrounding Ravendelve, Omegon looked at the fortified facility through the magnification of his auto-senses. Contact Three had been able to transmit from Deliverance, warning of a step-up in activity at the Raptor base. Corax was showing no nerves and was plunging headlong into the implementation of his plan, judging by the number of vehicles and shuttles that had been coming and going over the last few days. Mechanicum and Raven Guard attendants in rad-suits had been extending the complex with prefabricated buildings, almost doubling its size.

He considered his options, none of them with any particular favour. The most obvious course of action would be to signal his operatives to destroy the gene-works now, before the Raptors could be increased in size. That almost felt like a failure to the primarch, when his prize was so close at hand.

The insurgents were nearly ready to attack Ravendelve, an army of several thousand. Fifty Alpha Legionnaires were also only three days away, aboard the *Beta* hiding out in the dust clouds beyond Kiavahr. They would be the spearhead of any assault. It was a balancing act. If he committed too early, without the full involvement of the rebels, his warriors would be cut down to no effect. If he waited too long, the Raptors' ever-increasing numbers would prove insurmountable.

His only hope lay in a swift, decisive strike to secure

the gene-tech and then destroy what remained. He needed time, just ten more days, and everything would be in place to see that plan come to fruition.

The scuff of boots on rubble caused the primarch to turn, his bolter ready. A lean, robed figure picked his way through the debris below: Magos Unithrax. It disturbed Omegon that the tech-priest needed no protection against the radiation and pollutants in the air. Looking closer, he saw Unithrax's sallow face had a half-decayed appearance, only the metal implants holding together the flesh beneath his hood.

'I have a solution for you,' said the magos. He dipped a withered hand into his robe and pulled out a canister the size of a grenade. 'A genetic virus, tailored with the information provided by your operatives. If one of your agents can introduce this to the gene-template being used by the Raven Guard, it will halt their expansion.'

Omegon dropped down to the ground, rubble grinding to powder beneath his weight. He took the canister from Unithrax and looked at it. It hummed softly with a small stasis field, but otherwise looked like a rations canteen used by the Raven Guard.

'What will it do, exactly?' asked the primarch. 'A polluted gene-seed is of no use to us.'

'Exactly?' said the magos. He coughed uncomfortably and looked away. 'I cannot say exactly what the effects will be, though it will be severe. It will be a simple matter to extricate the virus from the gene-strands again once we have them in our possession.'

'It is a blatant move and will raise the suspicions of Corax,' said Omegon, tossing the canister from hand to hand. 'They have already increased security at Ravendelve considerably. I cannot afford for them to lock down the whole facility.'

'They will suspect themselves first,' said Unithrax. 'The virus will mutate the gene-seed from within and it will appear to be an unforeseen side-effect of the implantation process. Unless they specifically look for the viral contagion they will find nothing that cannot be explained by a random but explainable mutation of the genetic material.'

'I will consider it,' said Omegon. 'What will my agent have to do?'

Unithrax produced a small crystal sliver, no larger than a fingernail.

'This data-chip contains the necessary instructions,' he said. 'Pass it along to your operative with the virus container and he will be able to access the data through any terminal in Ravendelve. You should also tell him to destroy both the crystal and the canister on completion of the task.'

'Of course he'll destroy it, we are not amateurs,' said Omegon. He looked at the container again and held out his hand for the data-chip. He slipped both into a pouch at his belt and fastened it tight. 'How proceeds the work of the Order of the Dragon? Are they in position to act when I give the word?'

'We are ready,' said Unithrax. 'Our supporters have made contact with sympathisers amongst the Kiavahr hierarchy. When your guild rabble is in a position to reveal themselves, we will put in motion our part of the agreement.'

'The guilds need only a little more encouragement and then they will do as I please,' said Omegon. He turned and looked out of a mangled window at the silhouette of Ravendelve and rested a hand on the pouch containing the gene-virus.

He would have it retrieved by his contact. It would not be long now.

FOURTEEN

Diversion
A Legionary is Born
The Poison Seed

THE CORRIDORS OF Ravendelve were filled with the din of blaring sirens. Alpharius was in the makeshift armourium, running through maintenance drills with several squads of Raptors.

'Attack warning, form up in the main hall!' he snapped, lifting his own helm from a bench behind him.

'Is this part of the training, sergeant?' asked one of the Raptors as they filed out of the room.

'No, this is real,' Alpharius replied, knowing that no exercise had been planned for that day. The attack warning could only signal a genuine threat to Ravendelve, and he knew exactly what it meant.

While the other warriors in the facility converged on the mustering area, Alpharius took a detour, passing by his squad's dormitory. It was empty, his legionaries having already answered the call to arms. He crouched beside his bed and pulled out a box of battered metal from underneath it. With a glance towards the door, he opened the lid and sorted through the items within: bolter magazines, oils, paints, small replacement parts for his armour, a few fangs and other trophies belonging to the warrior he was imitating and a collection of ration packs and canisters. He rummaged through the last of these until his suit detected the minute vibrations of the stasis field holding the gene-virus. Placing this in his belt, he closed the box and pushed it back under the bunk with his foot.

He had already memorised the instructions for its introduction to the gene-template, and destroyed the data-crystal in Ravendelve's incinerator. He brought to mind this information as he broke into a run, unslinging his bolter from his waist as he entered the main hall. Branne was on the stage and directed a scowl towards Alpharius, noticing his tardiness. Alpharius raised a hand in apology as he fell in with the rest of his squad.

'As I was saying,' Branne said. 'Perimeter sensors have detected a large, unidentified movement out in sectors three and five. A patrol has been despatched. Armourium crews to man the defence turrets. Squads one through four are to embark on the Rhinos in the armourium and provide rapid response. Squads five through twelve will provide sweeps to the remaining perimeter. All other squads, get yourselves at Delta and Gamma gates and make ready for an extended counter-offensive.'

Branne stopped and cocked his head to one side as the buzz of a communication could be heard from his receiver. He nodded to himself.

'Understood, Patrol One,' he said, looking at the assembled Raptors. 'We have confirmed the presence of at least one hundred anti-Imperial insurgents at the perimeter. They appear to be massing for an attack around the rail depot and ruins of the counting house. Squad orders will be forthcoming. You are warriors of the Raven Guard. Fight for the Emperor and Corax!'

'The Emperor and Corax!' Alpharius shouted the refrain with the others, banging a fist against his chest-plate in salute to his commander.

Omegon's timing of the diversionary attack had been

perfect. Alpharius and his squad were on the armourium rotation, responsible for manning the defence turrets and securing Ravendelve. Alpharius ordered his squad to their assigned duties as the rest of the Raptors thundered from the main hall, heading to their respective positions.

'Dieta, I want you to do a check of the new buildings,' he told one of his legionaries. 'There may have been dissidents amongst the work crews. Who can say what they've left behind.'

'We conducted a thorough security sweep of all buildings after they left, sergeant,' protested Dieta, obviously dismayed by the appointment of such a laborious and seemingly pointless duty.

'Take Calden with you,' said Alpharius, pointing to another legionary.

'I'm supposed to secure the infirmary,' said Dieta.

'I'll handle that, just get moving,' snapped Alpharius. The two Raven Guard responded with smart salutes and set off at a run.

Alpharius headed directly for the gene-bank located in the infirmary wing. When he arrived he found several novitiates lying on the bunks, none of them older than ten years Terran standard, Vincente Sixx and Magos Orlandriaz tending to them. A number of robed orderlies stood close at hand with trays of phials and various surgical apparatus.

'We have to clear this area,' said Alpharius.

'Impossible,' replied Sixx. 'These boys have just been given the priming agent for implantation. We cannot move them now, and we have to proceed with the gene-seed introduction before they go into cellular shock.'

'If it must be so,' said Alpharius, realising that the Apothecary and tech-priest would be too busy with the implantation to pay him much attention. 'Do you have the gene-seed?'

'Yes,' said Sixx. 'We have everything to start the procedure.'

'Good, then I'll lock down central storage,' said Alpharius.

'You don't have access,' said Sixx. 'I will come with you. Orlandriaz can begin without me.'

Alpharius was taken aback by the offer and had to think quickly.

'The codes will be changed the moment lockdown is over,' he said, affecting a nonchalant disposition. 'No risk to security protocol, and there's no point in me dragging you away from this important stage of the process.'

'He is correct,' said Orlandriaz. 'I suspect the threat to the facility is minimal. Let us not waste time with this distraction.'

Sixx nodded and pulled a chain from around his neck, on which hung a two-tined digital spike. He tossed the necklace to Alpharius, who caught it easily.

'Check none of my attendants are in there before you lock down,' said the Apothecary, turning back to the closest bunk. 'Command override is peta-orpheus-epsilon.'

'My thanks,' said Alpharius, heading through the ward at a brisk pace. The airtight door cycled opened at his approach, allowing him to pass from the main infirmary into the inner chambers.

He quickly got his bearings from the description he had been passed, locating the sealed stasis cell in which the gene-template would be located. He pushed the digi-key into the lock of the main door and spoke the override code. Bolts hammered into place with a loud clang, securing him against discovery.

Working quickly, he pulled out a cipher-breaker from his belt; an ingenious piece of Alpha Legion-devised kit that he had kept hidden since his infiltration had begun. Plugging Sixx's digi-key into one of the ports on the reader, he activated the code sequence, unlocking all of the cipher signals held within the sliver of metal.

A tiny readout on the side of the cipher-breaker showed him what he needed to know and he took the digi-key to the stasis vault. Inserting the key brought up a hololithic display. Counting off the code from the reader, he entered the required sequence. A hiss of escaping air announced his success and the door to the sealed chamber opened out on two wheezing pistons.

Inside, a cylinder about half his height stood at the centre of a mass of coiled cables, wisps of hyper-chilled air drifting around it. Again, the lock on the storage cylinder gave way to the digi-key. A light flickered into life within, revealing a glassite tube no bigger than a bolter round, hanging in the air between two suspensor units. Inside, in a suspension of pale blue fluid, floated a single thread of genetic material, almost invisible to Alpharius's eyes.

He looked at it for a few seconds, amazed that such power could be contained within something so miniscule. Life, superior transhuman life, was held in that molecule-thin sliver of material. The ability to create legions of unstoppable warriors floated just in front of him. All he had to do was dash that glassite tube on the floor, and the doom of the Raven Guard would be sealed. Yet the primarch had a far grander purpose. The same secret formula would make the Alpha Legion an unstoppable force. Captivated by the thought, Alpharius realised that he had a choice. What he did next might well decide the outcome of Horus's war against the Emperor, could decide the fate of the entire galaxy.

Did Horus deserve such a gift? What grievance against the Emperor could be so vast that such a war was needed to settle it? Alpharius knew that there were greater forces than him at play in this rebellion, but at that moment none of them held the power he did.

He laughed quietly at himself, embarrassed by his

grandiose thoughts. The primarch had made it clear that
the destiny of the Alpha Legion lay alongside Horus's,
for the good of the Legion and all of mankind. Alpharius knew his primarch would not make such a statement
unless he knew for certain that it was true.

Dismissing his doubts, Alpharius plucked the capsule
from the grip of the suspensors and turned, looking for
the gene-coder as he had been instructed. He located it
on one of the work benches, a large machine with several receptacles the same size as the gene-tube, hooked
up to a bank of analysing engines.

He switched on the gene-coder and placed the template material into one of the apertures. Punching in
the command sequence he had learned, he activated the
coding mechanism. As the machine purred into life, he
took the virus container from his belt and opened it up.
Inside was a near-identical glassite phial. He made the
mistake of looking at the contents. The gaseous mixture
inside writhed with a life of its own, changing colour
and contorting madly, sliding against the phial as if trying to escape. For some reason it reminded him of the
descriptions of the warp he had heard from Navigators:
ever-shifting and restless.

Swallowing his revulsion, he placed the virus into
another receiving pod and closed the lid.

His fingers tapped away at the keypad, allowing the
gene-template and viral solution to mix inside the coding
machine. He stopped as he felt a tremor shaking Ravendelve: the defence turrets were opening fire. Alpharius
had to move swiftly. The time he had taken would either
be noticed by Sixx or one of the turret crews, or the attack
put in motion by the primarch would soon be hurled
back and the lockdown would be ended.

He finished the input sequence and waited a few
seconds while machinery whirred in the depths of the
gene-coder. An alert pinged the completion of the task

and the phial casket opened with a hiss.

He retraced his steps, returning the gene-template to its stasis chamber and sealing the door. Using the cipher-breaker, Alpharius entered the data logs and deleted the entries reporting his interference. It was not as secure as a complete wipe, but he did not have time for such a precaution. With implantation reaching the level it had, it would take a deep auditing scan to pick up on the anomaly, during which the system would have to be shut down. Such an event was unlikely, given Corax's determination to build up the strength of the Raptors as fast as possible.

With everything back where it should be, Alpharius exited the central chamber. Sixx and the tech-priest were engrossed in their labours, stooping over one of the implant recipients. Not drawing any attention to himself, Alpharius left the digi-key on a shelf and slipped out.

Once in the corridor he broke into a run, heading for Turret Three where he was supposed to be guiding the defence gunnery.

THE WHEEZE OF the autolung and staccato rattle of the monitor needles was oddly soothing. Navar Hef felt disassociated from his body, a state induced by a cocktail of preparation agents and hypnotic suggestion. He flitted between wakefulness and shallow sleep, barely aware of what was happening, the fleeting moments of lucidity serving to reassure him that Vincente Sixx and his attendants were never far away, constantly observing his progress.

There was pain, but his trance-like state allowed him to siphon the sensation to a part of his mind where it did not impact his thoughts. Navar's body felt as if it was burning, within and without, yet he remained icy cold in his mind.

Organs were moving and growing, bones were thickening and lengthening, cells were duplicating and mutating. He dreamed he was a shadowmoth, hanging in its chrysalis from a gantry in one of the prison wings. Navar's body was in flux, a semi-solid construct transforming from the physique of a human youth to the transhuman physiology of a legionary.

Time passed without meaning. Occasionally Navar felt a surge of energy or agony, flares of feeling from limbs or innards undergoing implantation. Such sensations were confined to his mind, his body fixed in a paralysis that prevented screams and laughter. The lights hanging from cables above dimmed to darkness or became blindingly bright, sensed through his closed eyelids. He wondered if this marked the passing of the day and night or simply reactions to the changes in his body.

More than anything, when he experienced any emotion, Navar felt joy, a constant ecstatic feeling of becoming his true self.

Locked in his thoughts, the Raptor-to-be formed a picture of himself as he was and as he would be. He could vaguely sense the huge increase in his mass, his chest and arms and legs becoming heavily muscled. At some point he realised there was a different rhythm to his heartbeat, the familiar pulsing in his throat accompanied by a secondary beat, more rapid but weaker. He breathed and tasted the air in a way he had never tasted it before. Sweat and antiseptic, ozone and brushed metal lingered on his enhanced tongue and in his improved olfactory sensors.

Even his brain was changing. As if from a distance, he observed new structures and pathways forming in the grey matter of his thoughts. He came to realise that there were no drugs in his system any longer. His fugue state was being maintained from within by an interaction of his newly grown catalapsean node and sus-an membrane.

It was then that he knew the process was complete. With an effort of will, Navar forced himself from his semi-sleep, gaining clarity of thought and sense. The ward surrounded him in sharp focus: the scuff of the attendants' feet, the whine of Magos Orlandriaz's servitors, the smell of blood and adrenaline, the flickering of the light fittings.

He sat up, suddenly aware that he was ravenously hungry. Despite being intravenously fed proteins and nutrients throughout the implantation, his body had devoured its store of fat to fuel his massive growth.

Navar chuckled as he realised his feet were at the end of the bed. When he had lain down just a few days ago, they had barely reached two-thirds the length of the sheet. He lifted his right hand and formed an immense fist, knuckles flexing underneath hardened skin. Bunching the muscles in his arm, he marvelled at their power and felt the urge to crush something in his grip.

'You must move to the rehabilitation room,' said an orderly, all but her eyes hidden under hood and behind face mask. Navar could see the flecks of grey in the blue of her irises, and every tiny blood vessel in the whites. He saw his reflection in her pupils, a naked giant lying on bloodstained sheets. Her breath carried wisps of *caroumal*, a sugar-rich supplement used by the Raven Guard and their serfs to fuel short bursts of energetic activity. The bags under her eyes and lines around her brow offered testament to her fatigue.

'Please, follow me to the rehabilitation room,' she said, taking Navar's wrist. He could detect the minute inflections in her voice, the weariness that caused looseness in her larynx. It seemed to Navar that she almost slurred her words, whereas a normal man would have just heard the same familiar tones.

He swung his legs from the bunk, and stood up. There was another moment of delight as he towered over the

attendant. He saw his shadow engulfing her and was
filled with a sense of mastery. She was not impressed,
having dealt with dozens of Raptors in recent days.
Without further word, the attendant turned and walked
towards a set of double doors with glass windows. Navar
heard the pad of her slippered feet and swish of her
medical robe as loud as heavy boots and piston-driven
armour.

Something caught in Navar's throat and he coughed.
The attendant pointed to a metal bucket on a hook
beside the door. An awful stench rose from it.

'You'll need to expel some dead tissue from your
lungs,' said the attendant.

Navar hawked and spat a thick clot into the bucket.
He took a deep breath and found no other obstruction.
The attendant pushed open one of the doors, revealing
rows of benches and loose robes. There were several
dozen Raptors cleansing their bodies from long troughs,
sloughing away blood clots and thick sweaty residue.

Several turned and grinned at Navar, and he smiled
in return. If he understood correctly, these would be his
battle-brothers within a matter of days, fully grown and
combat-ready.

'Thank you,' he said to the attendant, and stepped
through the door to join the rest of the Raptors.

THE EMPTY FUEL tank ruptured from the impact of Omegon's fist, a hollow clang resounding around the deserted
freight terminal on the outskirts of Nairhub, hidden in
the rad-wastes of Kiavahr. With a snarl, Omegon looked
to the heavens through the gaps in the metal sheets of
the roof; skeletal craneworks jutted up into the cloudy
red sky, around them chains hanging from scaffolding
and walkways like creepers of an industrial jungle. Pulling his gauntleted hand from the ragged hole he had
made in the steel drum, the Alpha Legion's primarch

directed his murderous glare to Magos Unithrax.

'Do you have an explanation?' Omegon demanded. He rested one hand on the hilt of his chainsword, and curled the fingers of the other around the grip of the bolter slung at his hip. 'Another batch of Raptors has undergone transformation without a hitch, and no hint of your virus.'

'Your operative must have made an error when he attempted to introduce it to the gene-template,' said Unithrax, meeting the primarch's anger with a calm, cold stare. 'Perhaps he compromised the integrity of the viral code.'

'He followed your instructions *precisely*,' Omegon replied. 'My operative is not at fault.'

'The viral agent will have mutated the gene-seed if the procedure has been correctly implemented,' the magos insisted, assured of the truth of what he said.

'This is not satisfactory,' said Omegon, calming himself so that he could think clearly. Whoever was to blame could be dealt with later. He had to devise a secondary plan, and quickly. 'Is it possible the virus is somehow still dormant? What sort of safeguards did you engineer into it to ensure it would not spread out of control and become infectious?'

'The virus is a common variety, harmless on its own,' said Unithrax. He shrugged, and a third arm, mechanical in nature, momentarily appeared from under his robes in imitation of the gesture. 'It is merely a vehicle to introduce the corruptive element.'

'And what corruptive element have you used?' said Omegon. 'Does it need time to activate?'

'It is warp-based in origin, the stuff of the immaterial rendered into solid form,' the magos said quietly.

'Warp tech? It's notoriously fickle,' snapped Omegon. 'Why would you use such a thing?'

'Not so much warp technology as something more

primordial, primarch,' said Unithrax. 'The viral agent uses modified daemon blood.'

'What?' Omegon snarled the question as he snatched hold of the tech-priest's robe. 'You exposed my operative to the taint of Chaos?'

'A near-synthetic compound utilising trace amounts,' said Unithrax, unperturbed by the primarch's outburst. 'Daemons do not have blood, as such, it is merely a useful euphemism. It contains minimal daemonic power in itself, but its presence is a powerful mutagen. If it was correctly mixed with the gene-template, there will be corruption.'

'Well, it has not worked,' said Omegon. He released his hold and began to pace, and then stopped himself, annoyed by the display of agitation. Reaching a decision, he fixed Unithrax with a hard stare.

'The Order of the Dragon is ready to move?' said the primarch.

'Give us the word and we will act,' replied Unithrax.

'Good,' said Omegon. 'We have delayed long enough; it is time to begin the final phase of the project. I will organise a little testing skirmish for our Raven Guard friends while you begin the coup. Corax will have his eye fixed on Ravendelve and he will not see your preparations until it is too late.'

'Very well, primarch,' said the magos. 'Unless I receive a signal from you, we will make our move at the temple council in three days' time.

'Be sure that you do,' said Omegon. 'The Seventh and Nineteenth Legion vessels are still at high anchor close to the Lycaeus moon. I will bring the *Beta* stealthing into closer orbit and have my warriors shuttled down, if you can guarantee the protection and secrecy of the agreed landing site.'

'The Starfall docks belong to the Order of the Dragon. Your troops will arrive without remark or record.'

Omegon dismissed the magos with a wave of the hand, and equally dismissed him from his thoughts. The guilds would not move until they had seen some solid sign of the support of Horus, which would be given to them when the Order of the Dragon turned their weapons on the Mechanicum. Until then, Omegon would have to find some smaller force to attract Corax's attention and increase the security measures at Ravendelve; measures that he would need to cover the involvement of his legionnaires.

He had the ideal candidate, someone whose loyalty had been assured from the earliest days of the revolution, a man who would not hesitate to lay down the lives of his followers to protect his own. Omegon set up his cipher-net communications equipment and established a signal. A few minutes passed before a connection was made.

'Greetings, Councillor Effrit. This is Armand Eloqi.'

THE CHEM-CLOUDS WERE thicker than anything Alpharius had seen before, causing him to wonder if the insurgents had some control over their formation. It seemed too convenient that a thick swathe of noxious vapours had swept over Ravendelve only hours before their attack.

Along with the rest of his squad, he stood at the western rampart, looking for targets. Residual fallout was playing havoc with his auto-senses, no matter which spectrum filter he used. Now and then, he or one of the other squad members unleashed a bolt-round or two into the cloud mass, spying a swirl that might betray enemy movement, or aiming at darker patches in the fog.

To his right, Turret Four pounded out a steady stream of macro-cannon shells, the buildings in the distance blazing with detonations that set alight gas pockets and carved fifty metre-wide craters in the heaped rubble.

Secondary emplacements roared with heavy bolters and
chaingun fire, churning through the thick mist but hitting little.

'No aerial support available,' came Commander
Branne's voice over the vox-net. Alpharius was not surprised in the least. Without Thunderhawks or Stormbirds
to fly recon, the Raven Guard would be forced to patrol
on foot or in Rhinos, exposing themselves to ambush.
For a Legion that prided itself on strategic flexibility and
the mobility of force, they had been neatly trapped in
Ravendelve by the initial attack.

Leaning over the rampart, Alpharius could see the piles
of bodies from the first wave: dozens of mangled corpses
left by the Raven Guard fusillade. If this was Omegon's
attack to secure Ravendelve, it was very poor. Alpharius
could not believe that the long preparations of his primarch would lead to something so desultory, but he had
received no instructions. All he could do was stand on
the wall and continue to play his part as a loyal Raven
Guard legionary. To do anything else would expose his
secret without reason.

'South gate opening, direct fire to cover column,' said
Branne.

Under the sergeant's orders, Alpharius and the squad
moved closer to Turret Four, to set up a fire position covering the blind spot beneath the high tower. There was
nothing to see, no targets to fire at. There was sporadic
las-fire in the distance though, bursts of energy bolts
leaving fiery trails through the contaminated fog. The
insurgents had certainly not abandoned their attack.

'Stay keen,' said Sergeant Dor. 'They're planning something. Be ready.'

IN THE HULL of the second Rhino in the column, Navar
Hef sat on the narrow seat with his bolter across his lap.
The transport rocked wildly from side to side as it sped

over the uneven ground of the rad-fields, but his suit
compensated for most of the movement so that he just
swayed back and forth a little.

'Rapid deployment, thirty seconds!' snapped Sergeant
Cald. 'Weapons check.'

Navar went through a quick inspection of his bolter
and grenades. He unhooked the fastener on the sheath
of his combat knife and tested the magnetic grips on the
spare magazines clamped to his belt and thighs. All was
in order, as it had been when he had boarded the Rhino.

'Stand ready!'

Cald and his nine Raptors stood up and turned
towards the rear hatchway. The bumping of the Rhino
was more pronounced, but the gyrostabilisers of the
Mark VI armour kept Navar balanced. He took a step
backwards as the Rhino trundled to a halt.

Drop-bolts exploded along the sides of the hatch,
dropping down the access ramp. Navar was the fourth
out, fanning to the right with three other squad members. He saw movement through the doorway of a
collapsed building ahead and fired without hesitation.
His bolt-round found its mark, an arm swathed in band-
age-like cloth sent spinning into view.

'Enemy, twenty-five metres, secondary arc,' Navar
reported breathlessly.

The squad reformed without any need for command,
laying down a curtain of fire into the rubble of the ruined
building, leaving contrails in the ruddy miasma and fist-
sized holes in the rockcrete walls.

'Cease,' ordered Cald. 'Section one, move up. Section
two, flank protection.'

Navar was in section two, so he held his ground and
kept watch to the right. The sergeant led his team of five
men towards the ruins, their black armour almost disappearing in the haze.

They were nearly out of sight, no more than twenty

metres from the closest broken wall, when light flared
through the gloom. An arc of lightning erupted from a
stairwell leading down to a basement level, earthing into
the lead Raptor. His armour and body exploded, sending bloody fragments of bone and ceramite thudding
into the legionaries around him. Navar had never heard
mention of anything like it during the training exercises.

'Emperor's oath, that's a stormcannon!' yelled Cald.
'Saturation fire! Level that building!'

Switching his bolter to full automatic, Navar emptied
the remaining bolts from his magazine into the enemy
position, the crackle of the detonations just a few flickers
amongst the storm that engulfed the stairwell. Behind
Navar, the remote cupola of the Rhino opened up, hammering away with combi-bolter fire. As he slapped home
another magazine, the Raptor's hearts kicked into high
combat pulse, flooding his body with adrenal compounds, seeming to slow time as his nervous system
surged in response.

His auto-senses blacked momentarily. When they
returned, Navar saw the fiery trail of a plasma jet streaking through the mist. The Rhino's point-defence missile
had passed within a metre of him, causing the black-
out. It detonated in an airburst just above the insurgents'
den, showering white-hot promethium across the stairs
and wall.

'Pull back to the Rhino,' said Sergeant Cald, calm and
authoritative. The lead team started to withdraw as the
promethium melted through the rockcrete, turning it to
a dwindling pile of burning slag. 'Commander Branne,
encountering guild-tech weapons. We might have a
problem.'

As they returned, one of the surviving Raptors from the
forward section stumbled. At first Navar thought he had
just lost his footing, but as the Raptor pushed himself to
his knees, he spasmed violently, his bolter flying from

his grasp. Navar had not seen any weapons fire and his first thought was of some other unknown guild-tech the sergeant had not warned them about. Just as he thought this, Navar heard grunting over the squad vox-link and turned to see the Raptor to his right falling to one knee, his head rocking madly forwards and back.

Tightness gripped Navar's chest. It reminded him of the sensation of fear he had used to feel before his transformation, though he felt no dread attached to the cramping. A sudden burning shot up his spine, causing Navar to gasp with pain. He tried to fight the urge to crouch, his legs and pelvis felt as if they had been shattered.

'Hef? Lastar? Devor?' He didn't recognise the voice, but the panic it conveyed was something he had never expected to hear from a Raven Guard.

The Raptor realised he had fallen to his knees and looked up to see Sergeant Cald standing over him, looking rapidly to the left and right. Another surge of flaming agony roared across Navar's chest, his muscles contorting, throwing him to his back. He couldn't help the scream that erupted from him. He smelled and tasted blood inside his helm.

'In the Rhino! Get in the Rhino!' Cald was bellowing. The sergeant grabbed one of Navar's arms and started dragging him to the transport.

'I can... make it...' Navar snarled, pushing himself to his feet. He stumbled a few steps and hurled himself onto the Rhino's ramp. The impact sent another shuddering burst of pain through his body.

'Command, command!' Cald's voice over the vox was almost lost under the pounding in Navar's ears. 'Urgent evacuation needed. All Raptors are down. I repeat, all of the Raptors non-combatant.'

'I know,' came Branne's terse reply 'It's happening across most of the squads. No assistance available. Get them back to Ravendelve as best you can.'

Navar felt himself lifted bodily into the Rhino, seeing the helm insignia of his sergeant through a crazy patterning of hyper-inflated blood vessels in his eyes. He was dumped onto the floor, landing on top of another Raptor; the marking on his shoulder pad rim marked him out as Devallia. Navar saw Devallia tearing at his helmet, trying to rip it free. After a few seconds, the seals snapped and the helm came off, tossed away by the frenzied Raptor.

He found himself looking into a pair of inhuman eyes, almost completely red with blood, save for pupils that had shrunk to dark pinpricks. Navar was gripped with horror as he saw veins and muscles pulsing beneath blackening skin. Devallia cried out, and in opening his mouth revealed another row of sharpened teeth erupting from his gums. Corrosive saliva dribbled onto his chestplate, hissing and spitting where it fell.

The Rhino jerked into motion, rolling Navar to his back. He stared up at Sergeant Cald, who was crouched at the open ramp, one hand held to the brow of his helm as he shook his head in disbelief.

'Sergeant…' The words were difficult to form, Navar's tongue feeling swollen in his throat. He held a hand out towards Cald and noticed long claws had broken through the fingertips of his gauntlets. 'Sergeant? What's happening to me?'

Cald looked at him for several seconds, as if he had no answer to give. Then he stepped closer and stooped over Navar, clasping his deformed hand in his own.

'Stay strong, legionary,' said Cald. 'Remember who you are. You are Raven Guard.'

PART THREE

MONSTERS AND MARTYRS

FIFTEEN

The Fortunate Ones
Divided Loyalties
The Legionnaires Revealed

HE HAD ONLY wanted to buy a little more time, but as he crouched next to the receiver beneath the bent girders of a toppled viaduct Omegon was delighted with the static-broken message passed on by the cryptoduct. The poor quality of the signal was due to a communications block being broadcast from the Ravenspire. It was the response Omegon had been depending on, though it meant his own transmissions would be severely hampered. The message was from Contact Three, who knew nothing of his fellow Alpha Legionnaire's action.

Omegon played the recording again, his fingers adjusting the dials of the receiver to get the best possible signal. The report was still quiet and fragmentary, and only his experience and superhuman hearing allowed him to pick out words and phrases from amongst the white noise that was blanketing every frequency.

'...*widescale degradation throughout the latest batch... degenerate, bestial... more recent recruits are worst affected... Corax has ordered... nearly a thousand of the poor... suspects mutation due to some mistake in the gene replication for large scale implantation. Apothecary Sixx housing the   howls and roars like caged animals. Security has been tightened around*

the gene-tech, but access still possible. There seems… overall
mission integrity intact. Awaiting…'

The sacrifice of Eloqi's guild had been worthwhile,
after all. In the grand scheme, their survival or success
was irrelevant. The guild insurrection, and the Order
of the Dragon who had instigated it, were simply the
means to pry open Ravendelve.

The *Beta* would be moving into position, while the
Order of the Dragon was ready to strike their final blow.
It was time that his operatives knew their full part in the
endgame. He shut down the receiver and packed it away,
going over the final parts of the plan in his mind.

Tomorrow, twenty-nine Terran hours from now, the
Alpha Legion would make their move.

THE PAIN HAD subsided for the last few hours, leaving
Navar with a deep ache in his flesh and bones. He
sat in the corner of the cell, not able to look at Marls,
Kharvo, Dortaran, Benna and the other twenty Raptors
who shared the room. They were amongst the fortunate
ones, apparently, though Navar did not feel fortunate
as he looked down at the jet-black talons jutting from
his fingers.

He had seen a few of the worst-affected, as Sixx and his
attendants had hurried them into the quarantine area
that had been quickly established in the depths of Ravendelve. It was only temporary, the Apothecary had said,
reversible if they could isolate the mutated strands in the
gene-seed. Navar knew he had not experienced much of
life, but he recognised a comforting lie when he heard
one, even if Sixx had been lying to himself as much as
the Raptors.

He could hear the muffled yells and screams of the
most degenerate and could not push away the visions he
had seen. Some of them had been bent almost double
by elongated spines, others had been twisted by insane

muscle growth, their limbs warped and engorged. Bony growths split their skin, fangs punctured their lips, and all had the same bloody eyes as Navar.

As a child, Navar had never suffered nightmares. Growing up in the shadow of the Ravenspire was more assurance than any mother's words that there were no monsters that could harm him. Yet the sight of the degenerated Raptors was something from the darkest recesses of his imagination, causing a primal revulsion and fear that no amount of Legiones Astartes discipline and training could eradicate. That he was counted amongst the monstrosities only increased his unease.

His brain, his body, no longer produced the fear response of a normal human, but on that primitive level, in the core of his mind, Navar was distressed and unable to articulate his worry. It was if he could not form the thoughts, could not grasp the concepts required to voice his dread.

Navar stood up to ease the pressure on his lower back, where one of Sixx's attendants had surgically removed a vestigial tail. The Raptor's knees and hips ached, wound about with tight, overgrown ligaments and sinew. He started to walk, completing a circuit of the room, which was bare save for the thin training pads on the floor that had been provided as rudimentary bedding, the best the Legion could offer for the moment.

He neared the door, and heard voices. The door was not locked, not for them. Elsewhere, the most bestial sufferers had been taken to the cages that had once housed Sixx and Orlandriaz's animal subjects. They could not be trusted to stay where they would be safe, though none had been violent towards their fellow Raven Guard.

The voices grew louder and Navar recognised the deep timbre of the primarch. He gestured to the others and they rose from their positions to crowd as close as they could get. The conversation seemed to be taking place a little further down the corridor beyond, near to the infirmary entrance.

'…is an intrinsic problem with the gene template, I am sure of it,' they heard Orlandriaz replying to something said by Corax. 'There is no error in the replication process.'

'Then why are the first five hundred Raptors unaffected?' said Corax. 'At some stage, we have made a mistake. The reduplication to this scale must be responsible.'

'Unless there has been degeneration in the source material,' replied Sixx.

'It is kept in stasis, how could it change?' countered Orlandriaz.

'Incrementally,' replied Corax. 'It is removed from stasis for reprocessing new batches of gene-seed. Perhaps it has degraded a little during each removal, so slightly that we have not noticed it.'

'That would suggest there is an inherent flaw,' said Sixx. He cleared his throat before continuing, apparently uncomfortable with what he had to say. 'The flaw is not in the Raven Guard gene-seed, it has been verified many times over since its creation.'

'What are you suggesting?' said Corax.

'That there is something wrong with the primarch data,' said Orlandriaz, as coolly as if he were discussing inclement weather.

'Or our analysis of it,' Sixx added quickly. 'The traits we are seeing, the deformations, are consistent in their own way. Not entirely random.'

'I fail to see that,' said Orlandriaz.

'I do not,' said Corax. 'We know that there are elements of non-human structures within the primarch data. Similar strands are encoded into every gene-seed. The Legiones Astartes make-up owes a small part to characteristics found in other species, introduced by the Emperor into the gene-seed. The scales, horns and other growths may be indicative of these traits being accelerated, out of step with the rest of the adaptation. Whatever was holding them in check, maintaining the balance, has deteriorated. Judging by the timing of the change, I would start by looking at those physical functions under greatest stimulation during combat. It seems that the something in their enhanced metabolism triggered this.'

'An uncomfortable thought,' said Sixx. 'To think that all of us contain the potential for such transformation.'

'Not all of us,' said Corax.

'Apologies, lord, I did no–'

'I don't mean my primarch heritage,' Corax continued. 'The standard Raven Guard gene-seed is stable, as you said before. We have done something to destabilise it. Isolate that cause, and perhaps we might find a means to reverse the errant genetic material.'

'It is a possibility,' said Orlandriaz. 'I shall conduct more tests to compare the initial Raptors created with the most recent, to see if I can identify a consistent differential.'

'I'll concentrate on making them as comfortable as possible,' said Sixx. 'If we can't…'

'We will!' said Corax. 'They are Raven Guard and deserve our greatest effort. Keep me informed. I must return to Ravenspire to discuss the attack on Ravendelve with the command council.'

'You fear it is the start of something more threatening, lord?' asked Sixx.

'We all but wiped out the insurgents, so the threat is debatable. That proscribed guild-tech weapons have surfaced cannot be ignored, though. We could do without further distraction while we resolve the issues with the gene-template.'

The noise of the conversation receded, followed by the

clank of the infirmary door closing. Navar turned back to
the others.

'You heard Lord Corax?' he said. 'They'll find a way to
change us back.'

Some of the other Raptors smiled, a few sadly shook
their heads. Navar headed back to his corner and sat
down, ignoring the pain in his rump. The primarch
believed that there was a way, and he had the most bril-
liant mind imaginable. Feeling a little happier, Navar
leant back against the wall, closed his eyes and tried to
sleep.

THE DISCUSSION BETWEEN the commanders and Corax had
lasted for several hours. Branne was happy to leave the
command chamber, the last of the council to do so,
having been intensely questioned by Corax regarding
the insurgent attack, and he was anxious to return to
Ravendelve and oversee its defence. The primarch had
been adamant that the timetable for the attack on Narsis
was not changed. If the Raptors could not be included in
the force, the Raven Guard would adjust their strategy.
Branne definitely wanted as many legionaries as possible to take on the Perfect Fortress, and so his place was
at Ravendelve to provide an encouraging presence for
Sixx and Orlandriaz.

As he stalked towards the conveyor down to Alpha
Dock, he was met by Controller Ephrenia. She held a
data tablet in her hand, a sight that Branne did not find
encouraging.

'A moment of your time, please, commander,' said
Ephrenia.

'Walk with me,' Branne replied, continuing past.

'We have found several odd signals, commander,' she
said. Branne stopped.

'Commander Agapito's channel?' he asked quietly.

'No, commander, not this time,' said Ephrenia. She

handed Branne the data-slate. 'There have been several encrypted messages concealed within normal Legion traffic. Hidden amongst the data-pulse between Raven-spire and Ravendelve, riding the pulses to bypass the communications block. They appear to originate from several places on Kiavahr.'

'So we've found out how the guilders are communicating? Good work. Can we stop it?'

'I already have, commander,' said Ephrenia, looking a little hurt by the implication. 'One such transmission that was hijacked was a routine upload from the infir-mary core in Ravendelve. In picking apart the entwined codes, it became apparent that the core log had been tampered with. The log was accessed and then the access was crudely wiped.'

'There are only a handful of us with access to that log,' said Branne. 'Why would any of us try to hide such action?'

'Digital markers indicate that it was Commander Agap-ito,' Ephrenia said, her voice hushed. She stepped closer to Branne, though he could hear her lowered voice with ease. 'I was about to tell Lord Corax, but as you are here I think that perhaps you should deal with the matter.'

'Thank you, controller,' said Branne. 'I'll handle this.'

Branne turned around and headed back towards the central transporter that ran the full height of Ravenspire. Whatever reason Agapito had for accessing the gene-tech datalogs, it could not excuse an attempt to conceal the act. The commander quietly fumed as he made his way up to the personal chambers of his brother. He did not knock, but threw open the door, ready to demand an explanation from Agapito.

The chambers were empty, and showed no sign that Agapito had returned here after the command council. Branne activated his vox.

'Spire command, can you locate Commander Agapito?'

'One moment, commander.'

Branne waited impatiently, pacing around Agapito's main room. He spied a tablet on the arm of a couch and picked it up. Activating the slate, he brought up the last screen display. It seemed to be a duplicate of the files Branne had been given by Ephrenia no more than ten minutes before.

His communicator chimed.

'Commander Agapito authorised a pilot and Storm-bird for launch, commander,' the Legion functionary in the command chamber told him. 'Course logged was for Ravendelve.'

'When?' demanded Branne.

'Two and a half hours ago, Terran standard, com-mander.'

Branne cut the link and threw both data-slates to the floor.

'What are you doing, brother?' he asked the empty room. Two hours was enough time for Agapito to already be at Ravendelve. Branne ran from the room, heading for the Thunderhawk waiting for him at Alpha Dock.

THE SCANNER TICKED monotonously, every pulse accompanied by an image on the screen in front of Alpharius. He turned his chair and checked the audio pick-ups, seeing nothing detected except for the wind. The gun towers had been constantly manned since the last attack, and Alpharius and the rest of the squad had been on watch since dawn. Nothing was happening, there had been no sign of any insurgent activity in the last twenty hours.

The chair creaked as he leaned back, laying his hands in his lap. Behind him in the control room, Sergeant Dor was cleaning his bolter, cloth and tools laid out on an instrumentation panel. Marko was also there, monitoring the communications station.

'Time for another visual sweep,' said Dor, not looking up from his work.

Alpharius said nothing as he stood up and moved to the reinforced door. He keyed in the security code and the door extended out and slid to one side. Stepping into the airlock, he sealed the door behind him. He took his helmet from his belt and fitted it before opening the outer seal. Wind rushed in, bringing the acrid taint of pollution.

Stepping out onto the rampart, Alpharius glanced down at Ravendelve. Searchlights from the towers and walls scoured the surrounding ground, their beams lost in the hazy air no more than a hundred metres out. He could see armoured figures patrolling the walls beneath him, their eye lenses bright yellow dots in the gloom. Unslinging his bolter, he walked around the rampart, passing under the shadow of the huge twin-barrelled cannon in the emplacement atop the tower.

He performed a point check, using the magnification of his auto-senses to inspect the gatehouse, armourium doors and other points of entry. All he saw were Raven Guard, patrolling tirelessly or standing sentry. One thousand Talons had been sent down from Ravenspire to reinforce the garrison, taking the place of the Raptors who had succumbed to the genetic corruption.

It had pained Alpharius to see the tainted legionaries, some of them wracked with agony, all of them a perversion of the Legiones Astartes. It would be a mercy to kill them, and when the time came, the Alpha Legion would surely grant them swift release from their torment. The Raven Guard were enemies, but Alpharius had a great deal of respect for the warriors of Deliverance, having shared in their tribulations.

He continued on his circuit, moving to the outside of the tower to look out over the rad-wastes. He already knew from the sensor reports that there was nothing out there, but the Raven Guard were highly suspicious of guild-tech and left nothing to chance. It was possible that the insurgents possessed something that might mask them from the scanner sweeps.

There was nothing to see, only a tortured landscape of flattened buildings and cratered rock.

He started towards the door to complete one loop around the tower, but stopped at the corner to look into the far distance. To the north-east, five kilometres away, the outskirts of Nabrik jutted from the bank of red fog like the fingers of a drowning man breaking the surface of the water. Lights blinked from their rooftops and the lamps of armoured airships passed sedately between them.

Alpharius was about to turn away when he noticed a flickering in the gloom, close to the base of one of the towers. A series of flashes illuminated the fog. Moments later, a dirigible erupted into flames, the mangled remains of its gondola sent plummeting into the city. A second or two later, the Alpha Legionnaire heard the muffled but distinct rap of heavy cannons drifting over Ravendelve, followed by the *crack* of the airship's detonation.

Astounded, he watched tracer fire erupting from several of the cloudscrapers at the heart of the city, and more explosions billowed into life further into Nabrik. He thought it to be just another insurgent attack at first, targeting the Mechanicum following recent defeats against the Raven Guard, but then several things happened at once.

Two huge detonations rocked one of the soaring towers, almost cutting it in half. The upper storeys crumbled and toppled, crashing into the streets below in a huge cloud of flame and smoke. Alpharius's first thought was that it was a bomb, but his amazement grew as a

gigantic figure appeared silhouetted against the growing
column of fire. It was at least ninety metres tall, its right
arm a massive multi-barrelled cannon, the left another
immense weapon that gleamed with the blue sheen of
plasma generators. Its armoured carapace was packed
with turrets that streaked laser and shell fire into the city:
an Imperator-class Titan!

As he watched the Imperator unleash a ball of raven-
ing blue energy from its plasma annihilator, Alpharius
heard Marko shouting over the vox.

'Full alert, man stations! Threat imminent.'

'Powering up defence cannons,' announced Dor.

The words had barely sunk in when the macro-
cannon above Alpharius opened fire. The shockwave
from its twin muzzles hit the Alpha Legionnaire, his suit
warning icons flashing amber and red as the concussive
blast enveloped him. Two shells the size of battle tanks
screamed into the distance, exploding kilometres away.

Just as the noise of the shell detonations reached
Alpharius, a ticking started in his skull, a double pulse
different from the one he had felt before. He knew immediately what it meant: Omegon had remotely activated
the tracking function. The implant was now homing in
on the devices of the other Alpha Legionnaires.

It's started, Alpharius thought, his hearts racing. The
Alpha Legion were making their move. He had to get
into position and meet with the others.

Increasing the magnification of his sight, Alpharius saw
four columns of vehicles and infantry snaking through
the ruins where the cannon had fired, passing between
flames and rising smoke from the double impact. There
were transports and tanks, flanked by three armoured
walkers, each twenty metres tall. One of the Warhounds
– the walkers were clearly scout-class Titans – was enveloped by a shimmering dome of purple and black as its
void shields collapsed from the initial macro-cannon

bombardment. The other two Warhounds raised their
weapons and returned fire as shots from Turret Two
shrieked across Ravendelve to pound into the metal
body of the compromised Titan.

Alpharius hurled himself to the rockcrete a moment
before the cannonade erupted around him, showering
him with stone-like shards and fragments of the plasteel reinforcing rods within the tower wall. Two white
beams lanced out of the shifting fog, punching through
the armoured casement of the macro-cannon.

Propelling himself towards the door, Alpharius was
engulfed by a storm of sparks and fiery debris from
above, spitting and clattering on his armour. He hauled
open the outer door and threw himself inside, slamming
the armoured portal as another volley of shells hammered into the rampart where he had been only two
seconds before.

'Nord and Falko are down,' Sergeant Dor reported.
'Cannon is non-operational. Withdrawing to central
structure, there's nothing we can do from here.'

The tower shuddered again from more impacts as the
airlock cycled through the filtering process. Alpharius
paced back and forth for a few seconds, waiting for the
inner door to open. The interior of the tower had been
plunged into darkness, lit only by sparks bursting from
fractured consoles. Dor and Marko were waiting by the
stairwell that linked the tower levels.

'What about the others?' asked Alpharius, glancing up
to the landing above. Automatic fire suppression systems had flooded the gun casement, filling it with white,
dusty smoke.

'Done for. Let's get moving,' said Dor, setting off down
the steps. 'Muster at station four.'

Alpharius could not afford to be drawn into the general muster. His instructions from his primarch were to
get to the main gate.

'Go on,' said Alpharius, waving Marko to follow Dor.

The Raven Guard turned his back on Alpharius as the Alpha Legionnaire unsheathed his combat knife. Alpharius drove his boot into the back of Marko's knee, forcing him down even as he plunged the blade towards the side of the legionary's neck. He sawed the serrated edge through Marko's flesh, almost decapitating him.

'What's the delay?' Dor shouted back up from the landing below.

Alpharius dropped Marko's corpse to the floor, readied a grenade from his belt, and moved to the rail above the steps.

'Take this!' he called out, dropping the primed grenade.

Dor caught it out of instinct. A slow second passed as he realised what he had done, the grenade falling from his fingers, but too late. The grenade exploded, hurling the sergeant from his feet, razor-edged shrapnel cracking against his armour. Alpharius knew that a single grenade would not be enough to take down a legionary and vaulted over the rail, bolter in one hand.

He thudded onto the landing as Dor was pushing himself to one knee, chainsword already drawn. Gas hissed from split piping and oily fibre-bundle lubricant mixed with the blood leaking from the sergeant's midsection. Alpharius's first bolt hit Dor in the left side of his helm, where the communication pick-up was located, silencing any warning he might broadcast.

Dor roared and leapt at Alpharius, who dodged back a moment before the spinning teeth of the chainsword would have taken off his arm. He fired blind, hammering bolts into the sergeant's chest, the cascade of detonations sending Dor sprawling again. Alpharius followed up quickly, placing his next shot through the eye lens of Dor's crumpled helmet. The already damaged helm split apart as the bolt detonated inside, spraying blood and brain matter across the metal floor.

Stopping only to prise the chainsword from Dor's dead grip, Alpharius headed down the tower.

LOOKING UP AT the colossal form of the *Magnus Casei* as the Imperator Titan unleashed another miniature star into the heart of the city, Omegon felt a little trepidation. He had known that the Order of the Dragon had extensive resources, but had not appreciated just how much influence they had extended into the Mechanicum of Kiavahr. He had expected a distraction, infighting amongst the different temples. What the Order of the Dragon had delivered was all-out civil war.

The streets were packed with tech-priests and Mechanicum functionaries fleeing the carnage. Slack-faced servitors wandered around, unable to process what was happening, staring vacantly at the explosions and flames. Here and there, soldiers in reflective bodysuits herded the crowd away from the fighting, urging them out of their lines of fire with their rifles. Praetorian servitors – half-human war machines even larger than Omegon – watched over the exodus with chainguns, lascannons and sonic disruptors.

Guild forces were pouring into the city, thousands of warriors clad in armoured environment suits. The distant crackle of las-fire and thunder of heavier weapons cut through the sound of flames and the panicked shouts of the surging throng. Here and there, the fabric of the streets themselves exploded from below as indiscriminate mole mortar fire raked the city from the outskirts.

Screaming and shouting erupted with renewed fervour as the *Magnus Casei* lifted its foot and stepped along the broad boulevard between two smoking hab-blocks. Defence turrets atop its buttressed and crenellated carapace barked into life as the vapour trails of aircraft cut through the sky above the city.

Amongst the surge of fleeing civilians, Omegon had perfect cover. He stepped from the doorway of a forgehouse and into the crowd, head wrapped in a thick scarf, heavy robes concealing his immense frame. He had discarded his armour, sinking it into a chem-pool in the wastes; it was stealth and not physical defences that would protect him now.

Allowing himself to be pulled along by the stream of people, he flowed with them to where the boulevard broke into a large plaza. There the crowd began to fill the square and their panic grew. Squads of the Mechanicum's soldiers – the skitarii – were blocking off the exits, forcing back the refugees with electro-staves and warning shots from their autoguns. Tracked weapons platforms were positioned at the intersections, their cyber-augmented crews alert for danger.

It was simple enough for Omegon to use his bulk to force a path through the throng, heading for one of the other roads leading into the plaza. Shouldering aside a tech-priest, he strode to the skitarii cordon. He was met by a company leader, the plates of his carapace armour engraved with Mechanicum runes. The officer looked up at Omegon with mechanical eyes, lenses reflecting the flames consuming the cloudscraper behind the primarch.

'Captain Vertz of the Talons, let me through,' snapped Omegon, not allowing the officer a chance to speak. 'I must report to Ravendelve.'

'Yes, sir,' said the officer, waving for his men to drag aside part of the barricade they had erected across the street. 'There is a column from the sixth district assembling at Foundry Arc, responding to a request from your primarch. You might want to join with them.'

'Thank you for the information,' said Omegon, stepping past the skitarii leader. He was genuinely grateful for the knowledge, as it would mean the next phase of his plan would be made a lot easier.

He broke into a run, heading out of the city towards the edges of the rad-wastes.

THE CRASH OF falling masonry announced the destruction of another turret. Ravendelve's main building shook with the impact as the lights flickered and warning sirens screeched. Agapito had no time to wonder about the significance of this development as he pounded down a flight of stairs towards the armourium.

He was met at the next landing by a squad of Raptors, who were assembling a multi-laser on its tripod. For the last few days, he had spent much of his time with Captain Noriz, taking his advice on the basic defensive strategies his Legion employed. Agapito's mind was brim-full of attrition ratios, specific killzones and interlocking deployment patterns.

'That's no good there!' he snapped. 'If the enemy get this far in, it'll make no difference. Move it to the south transept for a decent field of fire.'

'Yes, commander!' replied the squad's sergeant, even as Agapito continued on his hurried course.

Besides, he thought, I still need an escape route open to me if things get out of hand.

As AGAPITO ENTERED the armourium level he found the area almost deserted. A few servitors trundled back and forth, hauling ammunition onto the bed of a bulk carrier. They paid him no heed as he ran past. Hearing voices ahead, the commander sidestepped into one of the practice ranges. Footsteps rang on the floor outside and then passed away.

When the sound of the legionaries had faded, Agapito emerged into the main corridor, checking that he was not seen. If his presence was remarked upon he would surely be called upon to take charge in Branne's absence, a delay he could not afford. He did not know how long he would have, but every second wasted might see his opportunity lost.

ALPHARIUS ENTERED THE gatehouse with a confident stride to find an assortment of Raven Guard already there. Most were Talons, but a squad of Raptors manned the controls of the lascannon batteries overlooking the approach. There were certainly too many legionaries for him to overcome in the same way he had disposed of Dor and Marko.

There was a commotion at the other door as Sergeant Nestil entered, flanked by two warriors from his squad.

'Activate landing beacons,' the sergeant ordered. 'Reinforcements are arriving. Be ready to open the sub-gate to let them in.'

Checking a snarl of frustration, Alpharius moved away from the massive doors of the main gate. His task had been to secure the gates and open them for the arrival of more Alpha Legion troops, but with even more Raven Guard arriving it seemed like a foolhardy move. The implant in his skull was ticking madly, telling him that another Alpha Legionnaire was close at hand, probably within the bastion of the gatehouse. He could not risk arousing suspicion by revealing himself just yet.

Under Nestil's instruction, the lock bars on a smaller gateway set inside the huge slabs of adamantium-sheathed ferrocrete were disengaged. The postern opened on hydraulic rams, revealing a view of the landing apron between the gatehouse and outer wall. The gatehouse was soon going to be very full, so Alpharius headed up the stairwell leading to the observation gallery that ran above the gates themselves. He found himself in the company of five other Raven Guard, sitting in the cradles of the quad-heavy bolters mounted along the gallery's outer wall.

Ignoring them, Alpharius looked out of the metre-thick

glasteel window. The flare of ramjets descended through
the ruddy murk and he recognised the shape of an
approaching Thunderhawk, another a hundred metres
behind. Touching down on the apron, the black-
armoured drop-ship lowered its ramps to disgorge
several squads of legionaries moving at the double. As
soon as the last Raven Guard disembarked, the Thunderhawk pilot gunned the engines and took off. The second
touched down as the first wave of reinforcements filed
towards the open postern gate.

At a loss, Alpharius glared down at the two lines of
black-armoured figures jogging towards the gatehouse.
He watched the second Thunderhawk lift off again as
the first wheeled around a few hundred metres from the
wall. Something struck him as odd about the Thunderhawk's manoeuvre and he paid closer attention to the
gunship's approach.

Increasing the magnification of his auto-senses, he
zoomed in on the gunship and saw that the locking
arms on its missiles had been disengaged. It was about
to make an attack run.

He sprinted back towards the stairwell. Four near-
simultaneous blasts filled the gallery with flying shrapnel
and fire, the shockwave hurling Alpharius through the
doorway to send him clattering down the first flight of
stairs.

Head ringing, he pushed himself to his feet as he
heard the report of bolters from below. The vox was
suddenly alive with shouted warnings, before being cut
off by deafening static. Two Raven Guard backed into
the stairwell beneath, one blazing with his bolter, the
other sending a stream of burning promethium from his
flamer at some unseen enemy in the main gatehouse.

Alpharius levelled his bolter and opened fire, cutting
down the legionary with the flamer. His companion
turned in surprise, weapon lifting towards Alpharius.

Before he could fire, a ball of plasma screamed through the doorway, exploding against his left side, incinerating half of his body in an instant.

Holding his bolter in one hand to pull free his looted chainsword, Alpharius advanced slowly down the steps, eyes fixed on the doorway. He stopped as he reached ground level, hearing the sounds of fighting lessening. Bolter held out, he stepped around the edge of the arch. The ticking in his head was near-constant now.

He saw Sergeant Nestil striding through a pool of burning promethium, almost on top of Alpharius, flames licking from his breastplate and left arm.

Alpharius readied the chainsword and sprang at the sergeant, sweeping the weapon towards his throat.

Nestil saw the attack and pivoted, catching the side of the chainsword with his forearm to deflect the blow onto his shoulder plate. Monomolecular teeth screeched, churning through paint and ceramite.

'Hydra!' Nestil yelled, bringing up his combi-bolter.

'Effrit,' Alpharius replied instantly, the counter-signal. He stopped mid-swing, letting the chainsword drop to his side. Nestil also lowered his weapon.

'Nestil?' said Alpharius, not quite able to believe that the veteran sergeant was really an Alpha Legionnaire.

'I am Alpharius,' the sergeant replied. 'Ort?'

'I am Alpharius.'

'So am I,' said a voice behind the pair. 'What a coincidence.'

Both Alpha Legionnaires turned.

'You?' said Nestil, shaking his head. 'One of us is a commander?'

SIXTEEN

The Bombardment of Kiavahr
Ransacked
Sixx's Revenge

THUNDERHAWKS AND STORMBIRDS were already soaring away from High Dock as Corax entered the landing area. Controller Ephrenia ran to keep up with his long stride, relaying the flow of information being sent to her by the command chamber.

'Fighting is localised to two cities, lord,' she said breathlessly, the vox-unit held to her ear. 'Supreme Magos Deltiari says that he has mobilised the Legio Vindictus to respond. A corps-strength column of skitarii has been despatched to assist in the defence of Ravendelve. The Mark VI manufactorum is under heavy attack but holding out. Guild-loyal forces have besieged Prime Forge and are moving to occupy the old guildhouse at Santrix Tertia. Captain Noriz is already aboard the *Wrathful Vanguard* with his Imperial Fists, and is requesting permission to join the counter-attack on Kiavahr... One moment, lord, receiving direct transmission from Ravendelve. Routing it through.'

She handed the receiver to Corax and he stopped at the ramp to his Stormbird.

'Commander Branne?' he said. 'Report.'

'Not Branne, lord, it's Vincente Sixx,' came the reply.

'Commander Branne has not arrived yet. Commanders Agapito and Solaro are here, though I cannot contact either at present.'

'Understood,' said Corax, pushing aside for the moment the question of where Branne was and what was occupying the other two commanders. 'What is the situation?'

'Lord, we are under fire from Warhound Titans, as well as several mobile artillery platforms. There's a guilder column only half a kilometre from the compound, with battle tank and heavy weapons support. I think our defences have been breached, but I cannot confirm that. What should we do?'

'What do you mean?' snapped Corax. 'Defend Ravendelve!'

'The gene-template, lord,' said Sixx. 'We cannot allow it to be taken by guilders. Who could say whose hands it might end up in?'

Corax stopped himself from replying immediately, forcing himself to evaluate the situation objectively.

'If we destroy the gene-template and research, we condemn nearly a thousand legionaries to a miserable existence,' said the primarch. 'We need that template to reverse the effect of the gene contamination.'

'I understand, lord, but can we risk it?'

'You will have to use your own judgement, Chief Apothecary,' said Corax. 'Lock down the implantation facility and round up some legionaries as a final guard. Have charges set, ready to destroy the gene-template and all associated material. It's up to you to decide when the risk is too great. I will be at Ravendelve in ninety minutes.'

'Understood, lord,' said Sixx. 'We'll do everything we can to protect it.'

Shutting off the connection, Corax gave the receiver back to Ephrenia. Her words were lost in the roar of a

DELIVERANCE LOST   413

Thunderhawk taking off a short distance away.

'What did you say?' said Corax.

'Commander Agapito, lord,' the controller repeated. 'There have been several potential security breaches connected to Commander Agapito. I brought them to the attention of Commander Branne. That may account for their current incommunicado status.'

'I don't have time for a full explanation,' said Corax, stepping onto the ramp. 'Send an order to Ravendelve for Solaro to find and detain both of them.'

'Understood, lord,' said Ephrenia. 'I will ensure that any important developments are relayed to your Stormbird channel.'

'I know you will,' said Corax, turning back to carefully lay a hand on her shoulder. A smile creased her elderly face. 'My commanders might be absent with their own agendas, but I can always rely on you, Nasturi.'

He ran up the ramp, calling to the pilot to take off. Seating himself in the custom-made harness in the main compartment, the primarch stared out of the window. The Stormbird shuddered as its engines growled into life, the black of the landing apron dropping away.

The Stormbird turned and accelerated away from the Ravenspire, bringing Kiavahr into view. Corax eyed the planet suspiciously. Like a thorn he had left to fester in his flesh, the guilds had returned to plague him. He had been so keen to leave, to take up the mantle of primarch and join the Great Crusade, he had underestimated their persistence. He chastised himself for the oversight, and added another reprimand for not expecting them to make a move. They had to have heard of Horus's treachery and now was an ideal opportunity for them to make their play for power.

He remembered a time long past when he could have ended it once and for all.

'We can't let them attack again,' argued Reqaui. 'They got thousands more troops to send and don't care none about their losses. It don't matter that we have an army of men willing to lay down their lives, we just can't match them. They'll come again and again and again until we're dead or back in the cells.'

'I wish I had never considered it,' said Corvus, staring at the orb of Kiavahr through the wide window of the guard officers' mess. The couches were ripped and bloodstained, the ornately carved and lacquered tables and cabinets riddled with bullet holes and scarred by las-fire. 'It is too extreme. There are millions on that world who labour under the yoke of the guilds as much as we did, and who have committed no offence against us.'

'Reqaui is right, Corax,' said Nathian. The sub-commander of Wing Two lay on one of the couches, a decanter of distilled spirits balanced on his chest. He sat up, took a swig from the crystal bottle and pointed past Corvus, jabbing his finger at Kiavahr. 'The bastards deserve it.'

'I never said that!' said Reqaui. 'Didn't say they deserved it, said it would be the quickest way to bring peace.'

'You're drunk,' said Corvus, crossing the room in three strides to snatch the decanter away from his lieutenant. He placed it on the ripped velvet surface of a snareball table, noticing that there was a detached finger in one of the net pockets.

'But I ain't stupid,' Nathian replied. 'Kill all the bastards and there won't be nobody left to fight. That's peace, right there.'

'What do you think?' Corvus asked, turning his gaze towards Branne and Agapito. The two brothers were seated at a table with a collection of maps of the Kiavahran cities laid out between them.

'I don't even know if it's possible,' said Branne. 'How do we get them to the surface?'

'We'll drop the first charges down the gravity corridor onto

Nairhub,' said Corvus, but then stopped himself, offering no further explanation. 'It doesn't matter. I've decided we can't do it.'

'Then we better get the defence lasers charged up again,' said Agapito. 'The last bombardment severed the mainline cables to the bunkers protecting Wings Four and Five.'

'We'll go down fighting, glorious deaths all around!' said Nathian, using the opportunity to retrieve the decanter and take another mouthful.

'If that's what it comes to,' said the rebels' leader. 'Every one of us is prepared to make that sacrifice.'

'We have to do it, Corvus.' Attention turned to Ephrenia, who had not yet uttered a word during the entire debate. She sat on the floor with a bandaged and splinted leg raised up on the remnants of a side table. 'If we do not win, Lycaeus will never be free, and neither will Kiavahr. You have to survive, Corvus. If you die, any hope of liberty dies as well. Thousands, tens of thousands, even hundreds of thousands will be killed, but millions will be freed.'

Corvus couldn't make that choice. There was no guarantee it would work, and what sense was there in crippling Kiavahr, condemning the population to a slow death of thirst and starvation, if it did not bring victory?

'Break the power of the guilds,' urged Reqaui.

Corvus nodded reluctantly. There was no other way.

'Great,' said Nathian. 'Let's get a move on, no time to waste.'

'It has already been arranged,' admitted Corvus. He sank down into the couch vacated by Nathian, long legs stretching out across the burnt carpet. 'Turman and Wing One have loaded five atomic charges into drop-shuttles. Their guidance systems have been locked on to Nairhub, Toldrian Magna and Chaes. All I have to do is send them the order.'

Ephrenia pulled herself up with a grunt of pain and hobbled across the room. She lowered herself to the floor beside Corvus and rested her arm on his knee.

'Time won't make it any easier to give that command,' she said, looking up at him with soft eyes.

With a sigh, Corvus gestured to Agapito, who pulled the radio from his jacket pocket and tossed it across the room. Catching it easily, Corvus flicked the switch to transmit.

'Turman, this is Corvus,' he said slowly. 'Launch the shuttles.'

The guerrilla commander switched off the device and let it drop to the floor. He turned his head to look through the window. After a few minutes, the engines of the drop-shuttles could be seen moving away into the darkness that separated Lycaeus and Kiavahr.

'Shit,' said Nathian, flopping into a chair. He raised the decanter in Corvus's direction. 'We're actually going to win, aren't we?'

'Branne, I want you on the main transmitter,' Corvus said, staring at the ruddy orb of Kiavahr. The light of the system's star was just starting to spread across the continent called Garrus. He pictured the thousands of people who were just waking to report for the first work shifts, thousands who would not finish those shifts. There was no point trying to hide from what he had done, though he knew the innocent would be incinerated along with the guilty. 'I want you to make a general broadcast on every guild channel when the charges go off.'

'No problem,' said Branne. 'What message should I send?'

'Tell the guilders that over centuries of subjugation, they stockpiled one thousand three hundred and twenty atomic charges on Lycaeus. I have only used five.'

THE CLOUDS OF Kiavahr filled the view from the Stormbird, streaming past in vermillion tatters. Corax would be at Ravendelve in less than thirty minutes, but to the primarch it felt like it might as well be a century. He flexed his fingers in agitation, frustrated by the course of events that had overtaken the Raven Guard. Superstition was anathema to the Imperial Truth, and he had never been an irrational person, but it seemed as if his Legion had been cursed since they first made planetfall on Isstvan.

He corrected himself. They had survived Isstvan, when other Legions had not. Through determination and courage, the Raven Guard had endured, and would endure their current tribulations.

The chime of the communicator set into the head rest of his seat broke his thoughts, signalling a transmission on the command channel.

'Establish contact,' he said, leaning back from the port. 'This is Corax.'

'Lord Corax, this is Branne.'

'Where in the Emperor's name are you?' snarled the primarch. 'Ravendelve is in danger of being overrun.'

'Lord Corax, you mustn't land at Ra–'

Another chime interrupted Branne's reply, and it was Ephrenia that Corax heard next.

'Lord, we have registered a target signal directed at Ravendelve from orbit,' the controller said hurriedly.

'Source?'

'It's from the *Avenger*, lord!'

'I can confirm that, lord,' said Branne as the two channels merged.

'How?' said Corax.

'Because I am aboard the *Avenger* and have four cyclotronic torpedoes loaded and aimed at Ravendelve, lord.'

Corax could scarcely believe what he was hearing. It took him several seconds to digest the information.

'Why would you be doing that, commander?' the primarch asked, his tone as cold as ice.

'If there is any possibility of the guilders obtaining the gene-tech, I will vaporise the entire site,' Branne said, his voice quiet. 'Lord, we have made hard decisions before now to protect the Legion.'

'There are Raven Guard on the surface, commander,'
Corax said, choosing his words carefully. 'Why would
you fire on your own Legion?'

'Only out of necessity, lord,' Branne replied evenly.
'Please do not land at Ravendelve, that would compli-
cate things.'

'Are you trying to force my hand, commander?'
snapped Corax. 'Is that a threat?'

'No, lord, it is a plea,' Branne replied. 'If you land at
Ravendelve, I will not open fire, but we may lose the
gene-seed.'

Corax lashed out, his fist buckling the bulkhead
beneath the port.

'Why did you not wait for instruction from me?' he
demanded.

'I feared you would overrule my decision, lord,' Branne
said. 'Your desire to rebuild the Raven Guard has consumed you of late, and weighs on your ability to make
clear judgement.'

Corax threw off his harness and stood up, seething.

'Corvus, you have known me for many years and
I have never been anything other than loyal to you,'
Branne's voice continued through the speaker. 'We will
find another way to survive if we have to. Please do not
land at Ravendelve. The Legion, the Emperor and the
Imperium, need you to stay alive. I await your orders.'

The words cut through the primarch's anger. It was the
same voice that had been with him when Lycaeus was
freed and Deliverance born. It was the voice that had
calmly relayed his orders over a hundred battlefields.
It was the voice that had welcomed him back after the
nightmare of Isstvan.

It was a voice he trusted.

Corax was breathing heavily, blood surging through
his body, his thoughts a whirlwind. A face appeared in
his thoughts, contorted with hatred, black eyes filled

with venom, the face of a creature prey to dark passion.
The face of Konrad Curze, the Night Haunter, whom he
should have slain.

He could not let love of his Legion destroy him, the
way hatred had destroyed Curze.

'Very well, commander,' he said. 'Remain on station
and await my order. If Ravendelve is to be destroyed, it
will be by my command.'

CAUGHT BETWEEN SEVERAL courses of action, Sixx had
begun the lockdown process but not finalised the
protocols. He needed to secure some thermal charges
from the armourium, but every squad seemed to be
occupied in defending the curtain wall. Neither Solaro
nor Agapito could be raised, leaving the Apothecary in
a quandary: should he leave the infirmary to fetch the
explosives himself?

He decided that the infirmary was not under immediate threat, so he would have to risk making the trip in
person. Sealing the outer door with his command key,
Sixx hurried along the corridor to the conveyor. It was
not there and he urgently pulled the call lever.

He stepped back in surprise as the elevator doors
slammed open just a few seconds later, leaving him
standing face-to-face with Commander Solaro. He was
flanked by a handful of legionaries, their black armour
glinting in the blue glow of the commander's drawn
power sword.

'A great mercy!' said Sixx. 'Commander, I need you t–'

Solaro lanced his blade through Sixx's chest without a
word. Blood bubbled up the throat of the Chief Apothecary, turning his exclamation of shock into a gargling
flurry of crimson bubbles.

Solaro pulled the power sword free, leaving Sixx to
drop face-first to the ground.

'Get the digi-key,' said Solaro, heading up the corridor.

Sixx could do nothing as one of the legionaries crouched down and tore the chain from around his neck. As blackness swept over him, Sixx's last thought was of the terrible mistake he had made.

'WHAT'S THE DELAY?' demanded Nexin Orlandriaz as he threw open the top hatch of his crawler. He swivelled in the cupola to glare back down the column of tanks and transports snaking back into the mist. His lungs stung in the acrid air, but the pollution was nothing his modified body could not process.

The skitarii corps consisted of two thousand cybernetically enhanced warriors travelling in eight slab-sided Dominator mobile fortresses, another five hundred marching alongside. Around the armoured behemoths were several more of the small recon crawlers, hidden behind a rag-tag assortment of tanks that had been gathered together to provide further protection: Imperial Army Leman Russ battle tanks and Falchions, Predators that had been destined for the Raven Guard and three Iron Angel-class heavy walkers that stomped along on four legs, their hulls bristling with anti-personnel weapons.

'Some of the praetorians got bogged down,' a ballistae sergeant shouted back from the back of his four-man self-propelled assault gun. He jabbed a thumb over his shoulder to where large figures were emerging from the fog.

Each was as large as a legionary or bigger, vat-grown for the purpose, and each of the dozen combat servitors was armed with an assortment of chainguns, rocket pods and multi-lasers. Some weapons were carried on armoured harnesses, others replaced limbs or were riveted and welded into the artificial flesh of the praetorians.

Alongside them strode the herakli, more vat-grown

giants clad in thick robes and cowls covered in Mechanicum sigils, chests and shoulders protected by plates of ceramite. They hefted multi-barrelled cannons and heavy lasers as easily as a skitarii carried his lasgun. One of the herakli stopped beside Orlandriaz's crawler, staring up at him with his face hidden by the shadow of his hood. This caused the others to pause and gaze at the magos.

'Taskmaster! Keep them going forwards,' Orlandriaz bellowed.

A functionary in heavy coveralls and visored helmet barked orders at the servitors and they lumbered on again.

They were only half a kilometre from Ravendelve; Orlandriaz had met them at the two-kilometre cordon to escort them in safely. Two Warhound Titans were blasting away at the curtain wall to the west, scourging the rockcrete with Vulcan bolters and turbo-lasers. The booming of artillery fire was near-constant, as was the ripple of detonations slowly cracking apart the thick outer shell of the main compound. Orlandriaz could see nothing of the new buildings, but the thick columns of smoke billowing up from where they had been erected did not bode well.

Sinking back into his command chair, Orlandriaz barked an order into the metal ear of the pilot servitor. The crawler lurched forwards and then settled, tracks churning through the slick dirt. The magos pulled back his hood and slipped on the communicator headset.

'Colonel Kuerstandt, have half the Dominators redirect against the rebels,' the magos said.

'I'll send the tanks too, they'll be no use inside the wall,' the skitarii commander replied. 'What about the rest?'

'We go in through the main gate and into the central courtyard. I am trying to raise a contact with a

Raven Guard commander, but there is no response at the moment. However, our alliance broadcast is being received and secure approach signal has been sent back, so we are safe to enter.'

'Affirmative, magos,' said Kuerstandt. 'I will personally command the counter-attack against these Omnissiah-damned traitors.'

'Of course,' said Orlandriaz. 'With all speed, colonel. We must ensure the guilders do not breach Ravendelve.'

TWO OTHER DISGUISED Alpha Legionnaires guarded the door while Solaro, Nestil and Ort gathered up everything they could that was related to the gene-tech project. Ort and Solaro scoured the archive databases, copying thousands of files onto crystal chips while Ort used Sixx's key to access the gene-template sanctum.

Nestil knew exactly what to do, and opened the stasis chamber. He still had the stasis container that had held the gene-virus, and into this he slipped the glassite tube containing the primarch material. It looked different now, darker and thicker.

'Delete everything,' said Solaro, slipping a data crystal from its slot in the main archive bank. 'Let's not leave anything to be found.'

Ort moved from console to console, activating the scour programme as Nestil started picking out test slides from a micro-analyser, gathering them into a belt pouch. Solaro powered up a vacant terminal and punched in the command access codes.

'The Thunderhawks are still on the landing pad,' he said. 'That will be our extraction point. The others have formed a cordon to stop the skitarii reaching us. When we arrive, we'll fall back by squads and then get out of here. I will signal *Beta* to begin her run into orbit for the rendezvous.'

'Just because you're pretending to be a commander,

doesn't put you in charge,' Nestil said with a laugh.

'Have you got a better plan?' snapped Solaro. 'We don't have time for games.'

'Calm down,' said Nestil. 'The Raven Guard don't have a clue we are here. Let's just move to the main gate and not draw attention to ourselves.'

The bead in Nestil's ear crackled into life.

'Effrit-hydra-omega. All contacts, report progress.' The primarch's voice was distorted and muffled.

'Contact Three reporting,' said Ort. 'All three contacts have met with assistance forces. Mission accomplished. Establishing our exit route.'

'You are a credit to the Legion, all of you,' said the primarch. 'You are ahead of schedule, so I have one final task.'

'Yes, we're ready,' said Ort.

'The Raven Guard moved their gene-seed store to Ravendelve to aid in the implantation process,' said Omegon. 'It is located in a vault adjacent to the infirmary.'

'That is correct,' said Nestil. He twirled the chain with Sixx's digi-key around his finger. 'We have the key-codes. What do you want us to do?'

'Destroy all of it. Deactivate the stasis field and destroy every last scrap of gene-seed. I want there to be no chance of the Raven Guard recovering from this attack.'

'Understood,' said Solaro.

'Before you do this, secure the gene-tech data. Give it to one of the assistance force and have him place it in the weapons locker at the east end of the north corridor. I will despatch another operative to retrieve it.'

'Another operative?' said Ort. 'All three of us are here.'

'That is not your concern, legionnaire. Do as I command.'

'As you will it, lord,' said Solaro.

He took a storage box from a nearby work bench and

upended it, spilling long syringes to the floor.

'Put everything in here,' he said. 'You heard the primarch.'

DUST FELL FROM the cell's ceiling as another blast rocked
Ravendelve. Navar and the others sat or crouched in a
circle in the middle of the chamber, glancing up with
every shell impact. They were under orders to stay where
they were, but it was unnerving to do nothing while they
knew Ravendelve was under attack.

A thud against the door caught their attention. Navar
got up and waved for the others to be ready.

'Careful,' Kharvo said, exposing pointed teeth.

Navar nodded and raised a clawed hand to strike. He
fumbled at the handle with the other, his talons making
it hard to grip. Pulling open the door, he was forced to
step back as a bloodied body fell into the room.

'It's Vincente Sixx!' said Navar, kneeling over the
wounded Chief Apothecary. Blood pumped from a
poorly cauterised gash in his chest, soaking his white
robe. Sixx's wild eyes roamed across the ceiling for a
moment as the other Raptors gathered around.

'Traitors,' whispered Sixx. 'Infirmary. Protect... Protect
the gene-seed.'

With a blood-caked hand, he pulled open the front
of his robe, revealing the black bodysuit beneath. There
was a bolt pistol in a holster at his hip. Navar nodded in
understanding and pulled the weapon free.

'No...' said Sixx. He coughed up more blood and
waved his hand weakly towards the inside of his robe.

'There's a pocket,' said Kharvo, reaching inside. He
pulled out a triangular piece of metal with a Raven
Guard symbol embossed on one side. 'It's a command
key.'

Sixx's face contorted with pain, but he forced himself
up on one elbow.

'Weapons lockers, bay seven,' said the Apothecary. 'Was getting charges.'

'We'll fetch someone to tend you,' said Navar, standing up.

'Gene-seed!' hissed Sixx. 'Your future.'

'We will protect it,' said Benna, gripping Sixx's shoulder with a scaled hand. 'Keep strong.'

The Raptors moved out into the corridor, Navar leading the way with the bolt pistol. They came to the next door and opened it. Fifteen deformed Raptors looked up from their makeshift bunks.

'Hef, take five others and bring back weapons, we'll gather the rest of our brethren,' said Benna, who had been a squad leader before implantation. He pointed towards the doors leading to the infirmary chambers. 'Kharvo, keep watch down there.'

The Raptors divided without debate, Navar taking the digi-key from Kharvo. It was good to stretch his legs as he sprinted down the passageway towards the weapons lockers with Marls, Ghoro, Tandrad, Myka and Hal close on his heels. As they reached the doors, a huge explosion rumbled above them, followed by the thunderous crash of falling masonry.

'Sounds like Turret Two is down,' said Myka. 'We'd better hurry up.'

Slamming open the doors, Navar looked left and right down the passageway beyond, Sixx's pistol gripped tightly in both hands. He saw a Raven Guard legionary standing guard by the archway to the loading bays above the armourium. The legionary turned in surprise and lifted his bolter.

'It's all right,' said Ghoro, lifting up his hands. 'Raptors! The infirmary is under attack.'

'Watch out!' yelled Marls, barrelling into Ghoro as the legionary opened fire. The bolt caught Marls in the arm, ripping through flesh and bone just beneath the shoulder.

Navar fired without thinking, acting out of instinct, his first shot catching the legionary in the side of the chest, sending the traitor's next shot into the wall beside Ghoro and Marls. The next two shattered the legionary's shoulder plate as he stumbled back to his feet.

The legionary turned his bolter towards Navar and time seemed to slow. The Raptor felt a ripple of cold racing through his body as he aimed the bolt pistol at the legionary's face and pulled the trigger again. As he felt the recoil of the launch charge kicking the pistol, muzzle flare erupted from the legionary's bolter. Two flickering trails of propellant passed each other.

Navar's shot hit a moment earlier, punching through the grille of the legionary's mask before detonating inside his helm. An instant later, pain screamed through Navar's side as the counter-shot tore a chunk from his chest, sending fragments of white-hot metal into his fused ribs.

Navar stumbled back and was caught by Myka and Tandrad. He looked down at the wound, a fist-sized hole just beneath his pectoral on the left side.

'Check him!' snapped Ghoro, jabbing a finger at the downed legionary.

'Why did he shoot?' asked Marls. 'What's going on? If it's our own legionaries, how can we tell who is on our side?'

'Let's just get to the infirmary,' said Ghoro. 'Sixx said they were there. Anyone else we meet, we'll just have to take our chances. Get to the arms locker, I'll help Navar.'

Navar was passed into the arms of Ghoro, who lowered him to the floor, back against the wall.

'It's not too bad,' Ghoro said with a grin.

Navar looked down. The wound was already sealing over with a thick scab, the Larraman cells in his blood clotting almost instantly. The pain had already subsided to a dull ache as other compounds flooded his system.

'Guess there are advantages to being a monster,' said Navar. He gestured for Ghoro to help him up, feeling his strength returning.

The other Raptors returned a couple of minutes later, carrying plasteel weapon and ammunition crates between them, bags stuffed with grenades and other supplies slung over their shoulders. Opening up one of the crates, the Raptors armed themselves with the bolters inside and took several magazines each, tying the bandoliers around their thighs and arms.

Feeling a lot more confident, his injury almost forgotten, Navar opened the next crate. Inside was a melta-gun, and several spare casks of pressurised gas.

'I'll take that,' said Ghoro, lifting the weapon from its padded cradle. He looked at the others, perhaps expecting protests, but there was no time for arguments. Shutting the lids on the boxes, the Raptors headed back to the cells where the others were waiting.

SEVENTEEN

Attack, Withdraw, and Attack Again
Cut Off the Head
The Truth of It

THERE DID NOT seem to be anyone in command, but the Raven Guard prided themselves on their autonomy and initiative. Lacking orders from their superiors, the sergeants mustered their squads to the defence of Rav endelve. Balsar Kurthuri found himself with Sergeant Caban and an ad-hoc squad of seven other legionaries, heading through the murk of the rad-wastes towards the enemy attack. Macro-cannon rounds screamed overhead from the remaining defence towers, answered by shells, las-fire and plasma bolts from the renegade Titans escorting the column.

The residual atomic fallout was interfering with Balsar's auto-senses, leaving him half-blind in the thick fog, unable to use thermal or wide-spectrum scanning. He deactivated his armour's sensors, relying on his own augmented vision to pierce the gloom. The black-clad warriors to either side of him were barely visible, but their armour transponders relayed their locations to a schematic in his visor. Sergeant Caban was at the front, and it was from him that there came a crackled warning over the vox.

'We have movement, fifty metres ahead and right. Infantry. Disperse right, thirty metres. No friendly forces in the area, engage on sight.'

Balsar picked his way over a pile of slag, casting his gaze to the left and right. It would be so easy to open up his othersight, allowing the potential of his mind to flow outwards to detect the enemy. It would also be simple enough to incinerate them with a psychic blast once they were found, and the temptation to use his powers was almost overwhelming.

There were no Chaplains left within the Legion to enforce the Edict of Nikaea, and Balsar recalled Lord Corax's words from outside the vault room. The situation had changed, and it was surely sensible to use every weapon available against the traitors. Balsar was still not sure what had happened next. He had definitely felt a connection with the psychic locks placed upon the door, intricately beautiful and impenetrable. It had been an urge from within to engage his psychic powers, and had Balsar ever wanted to discuss the event with another, he would have claimed he had been guided by the Emperor. It certainly had felt as if an outside agent had been controlling his thoughts for those few moments, and remembering the complexity of the seals placed on the door, Balsar was sure he would not have been able to dismantle them on his own.

If the Emperor had acted then, as seemed to be the case, then surely that was license for Balsar to use his powers again?

A deeper shadow emerged from the fog just to Balsar's left. The Raven Guard fought back the urge to reach out with his thoughts. Instead, he brought up his bolter and opened fire, hitting the figure low in the torso with two rounds.

'Enemy!' he announced over the vox. 'One down.'

He opened fire again at more silhouetted targets,

telling himself it was not his place to second-guess the judgement of the Emperor.

THE AIR IN the antechamber was well below freezing point, the walls crusted with ice. Five more Alpha Legionnaires stood watch in the corridor outside, masquerading as Raven Guard, while Ort and Nestil went through the process of shutting down the stasis field generators in the main vault. Solaro stood ready with the digital key, idly snapping small icicles from the cover of the keypad with the tip of his finger.

'Why the delay?' Solaro asked, looking over his shoulder at Ort. The other legionary stood at an open power relay panel shaking his head.

'Is this really necessary?' asked Ort.

'The primarch was specific,' said Solaro. 'Just shut it down.'

'I don't know,' said Ort, stepping back from the relay. 'It's one thing to take the Raven Guard out of the war. It's another to wipe them out entirely. When Horus defeats the Emperor, we'll need allies to rebuild the Imperium.'

'You're an idiot,' said Nestil, pulling out a transformer switch. 'The Raven Guard will never serve Horus now, not after Isstvan. Corax is too stubborn. When we win, they will just disappear like they always do, and continue fighting us at every chance. Do you want to spend years watching your back, wondering when the Raven Guard will come for us?'

'We've all seen what that mutagen did to the Raptors,' said Ort. 'It's tainted, unnatural. And the Word Bearers? We all saw them at Isstvan, and I saw them up close at Cruciax. I don't think it's Horus that's behind this war, it's something a lot worse. You know what I'm talking about.'

Nestil turned, a cluster of wires in his fist.

'More fool them,' he said. 'I know what you're talking

about and we all heard Corax's speech. This war was coming, like it or not, and we had to choose a side. Better that we are with the victors than the losers. The Emperor's forces were crippled at Isstvan. That could have been us between the guns of the Word Bearers and Iron Warriors. Be thankful the twin primarchs made the right choice.'

'It's too late to have second thoughts,' said Solaro. 'What the Word Bearers choose to do is up to them, we don't have to pay attention to them any more. Let them dabble in their sorcery. It'll burn them in the end and we'll be the ones left laughing.'

'Besides,' said Nestil, returning to his work, 'with this gene-tech, the Alpha Legion will be the ones who will hold the balance of power. Us, not Lorgar, Angron or even Horus.'

Ort said nothing as he stepped back up to the relay panel and began to disconnect the cables.

'What was that?' said Nestil, glancing towards the door.

Solaro had heard it too, a shot ringing out against the background of the bombardment.

'Maybe those stupid guilders have actually managed to get through the curtain wall,' said Ort.

'No, that was inside, close by,' said Solaro.

Suddenly the bark of bolter fire filled the corridor outside.

'Keep working!' he snapped, moving towards the door.

The Alpha Legionnaires on watch were firing down the corridor to the right, blazing away freely. Bolt-rounds were screaming past them from the direction of fire. Drawing up his bolt pistol and power sword, Solaro stepped out and turned just as one of the legionnaires crashed to the ground, armour riddled with jagged holes.

From the direction of the infirmary, a group of mis-shapen warriors were attacking, taking cover behind the roof supports that jutted from the bulkheads every few metres. Solaro looked into dozens of fury-filled red eyes, in faces contorted with horns, fangs and tusks. Some of the attackers were covered in scales of red or green. Some were muscle-contorted monstrosities whose biceps and shoulders bulged under the fabric of their robes.

All of them were armed, the hail of bolter fire intensifying as more poured through the doors at the end of the passageway and emerged from the chambers connected to the infirmary. A round glanced from Solaro's shoulder pad, sending splinters of ceramite flying.

'Forget that!' he snapped, ducking back into the vault's entry chamber. 'We're too late. It's time to leave.'

Ort and Nestil stopped what they were doing and snatched up the bolters they had set aside to work on the energy relays. They closed in behind Solaro, who stepped to the corner of the door and snapped off a few shots at the incoming Raptors.

'We'll cover you,' said one of the Alpha Legionnaires, slamming home a fresh magazine into his weapon as bolt detonations erupted on the stanchion he was sheltering behind.

'Run!' Solaro barked, waving his power sword. 'Before they cut us off.'

Pounding out into the passage, the three operatives turned and fled from the Raptors, not even pausing to fire a shot. Solaro glanced back as they reached the far doors, and saw that all but two of the Alpha Legionnaires had been taken down, selflessly putting themselves between the withdrawing operatives and the Raptors. They were making good account of themselves though – at least a dozen robed bodies sprawled across the floor of the corridor.

'Make for the landing apron,' said Nestil as the security door hissed open in front of them.

When they had passed through, Ort turned and fired

into the lock control pad, bringing the door slamming down.

'Let's see them come after us now,' he said.

'You abandoned our legionnaires back there,' said Nestil.

'They'll go down fighting,' said Solaro, taking a turning to the right. 'We have to get out of here.'

They sprinted through across the upper level of Raven-delve and made for the stairwell close to the main gate, which Solaro hoped was still in the hands of their comrades. Taking the steps three at a time, they launched themselves down the stairs, heading for the gatehouse.

Reaching the bottom, they paused and looked around. In the courtyard behind the gatehouse were several legionaries in the livery of the Raven Guard, but it was impossible to tell if they were sons of Corax or simply masquerading as such. Two gigantic praetorian servitors flanked the gate itself, along with a handful of the Mechanicum's herakli warriors.

'Through here,' said Ort, gesturing with his bolter towards the east tower guard room.

'Calmly now,' whispered Solaro. 'No need to rush.'

The defenders by the gate paid little attention to three Raven Guard striding into the gatehouse, though Solaro felt a small amount of relief once they were out of sight again.

'How do we get out?' said Nestil.

'The gallery is in ruins,' replied Ort. 'Our Thunder-hawks saw to that. We'll be able to jump down easily enough.'

'I'm not sure about leaving the gene-tech here,' said Solaro. 'What if the other operative can't retrieve it?'

'It's too late to go back,' said Nestil. 'We have done as we were ordered. It's time to extract.'

Solaro conceded the point with a nod and they made their way to the inner stairwell. The floor above was a rubble-choked ruin, the shards of the shattered gallery window scattered amongst the debris. The fog had thickened again, but standing on a pile of pulverised ferrocrete, Solaro could make out two bulky shapes out by the landing field.

'The Thunderhawks are still here, as I thought,' he said, sheathing his power sword and holstering his pistol. He grabbed hold of a twisted plasteel reinforcing rod jutting from the remains of the outer wall and swung out of the gallery. 'Come on.'

They had to drop the last few metres to the ground, but there was no sign of any Raven Guard in the vicinity. The steady thunderous report of the surviving macrocannon punctuated the whine and boom of falling artillery shells, but the guilders seemed to be targeting the other end of Ravendelve. Overhead, Stormbirds and Thunderhawks were diving through the clouds, their cannons and missiles raining fire down onto the guilder column. Solaro could see a plume of bluish fire dancing above the curtain wall, the leaking plasma reactor of a Warhound Titan.

As they approached the closest Thunderhawk, Solaro felt a creeping unease. He activated his vox-link, trying to hail the pilot, but received no reply. Approaching through the mist, he discovered that the cockpit canopy was shattered, and there were several smoking holes in the fuselage.

'Let's hope the other one is undamaged,' said Nestil, cutting to the right under the Thunderhawk's wing.

'Hope is a weakness,' a voice called out from behind them. 'It is the first step on the road to disappointment. If you were Raven Guard, you would know that.'

Solaro turned, drawing his weapons. A black-armoured figure stood at the edge of the landing pad. He had a lascannon held up to his shoulder, aimed at the Alpha Legionnaires, its cable snaking down to a power

pack on the ground beside him. He stood with one foot
on an octagonal box that had a thick metal grip-handle
running around its circumference. Lights winked in
sequence on a small display beside the Raven Guard's
foot.

'It's over,' the figure called out. 'You have no way of
escaping. The *Wrathful Vanguard* and the *Triumph* are
moving in to blockade the planet even as I speak.'

His surprise fading, Solaro recognised the voice.

'Agapito? It's me, Solaro! What are you doing?' he
called back.

'You might have his face, but you are not the Solaro
that I knew,' said Agapito, the lascannon directed at the
faux-commander. 'The company you keep tells me that
for sure.'

'You're making a mistake, Agapito,' said Solaro,
putting his pistol in its holster. 'See? Don't do anything
rash.'

'What do you mean about the company he keeps?'
said Ort, glancing at the other two Alpha Legionnaires.

'I didn't know about you, Ort, or whatever your name
is. Unfortunately for you, your companions were not
as thorough in hiding as they thought. Nestil, how did
you recognise the *Phalanx*? The Raven Guard have never
served in the same warzone as the Imperial Fists fortress.
And Solaro, who else would have clearance to break my
command codes and use my personal channel? It certainly wasn't Branne or Aloni.'

'You're just one legionary,' said Solaro. 'What do you
hope to achieve?'

'You never fought for Deliverance, Solaro,' said Agapito, tapping his foot on the box beneath his boot. He
pointed the lascannon at the device. 'But I'm surprised
you don't recognise an atomic charge when you see it.
Five hundred kilotons: more than enough to wipe out
Ravendelve and every traitor in it. You can't escape with

the gene-tech. I'll level this whole place if you try.'

'You won't do that,' said Nestil, taking a few steps back, bolter in both hands.

Solaro heard a distinct thrum and glanced over his shoulder. Twenty golden-armoured warriors were standing in the fog, power fields flickering along the blades of their halberds. The Custodian Guard were between the Alpha Legionnaires and the main gate.

'How many more of you have turned? What did the traitors offer you?' Agapito snarled. 'What was the price the Warmaster placed on our primarch's head?'

'Our primarch?' said Ort, with a laugh. 'You know nothing of our p–'

Solaro lashed out with the power sword, slashing through the fool's throat before he could say any more. The Alpha Legionnaire collapsed face-first to the ground, gasping his last bloody breath into the acid-tinged puddles.

'Tell me!' roared Agapito. 'Tell me what you know and you will be granted quick deaths. If not, I am sure Lord Corax will make an exception to the ban on the Red Level. Even a legionary cannot endure the torments on offer there.'

Solaro looked at Nestil, and though they could not see each other's faces, their subtle nods indicated they were in agreement.

'What makes you think you can take us alive?' Solaro snarled.

He lunged, thrusting his power sword through the heart of Nestil as the sergeant pulled the trigger and sent a bolt-round smashing through Solaro's helm. The two of them fell into each other and twisted to the ground, locked together in death.

CAUGHT BETWEEN THE wall of Ravendelve and the advancing forces of the Mechanicum, the outnumbered guilder force was pushed back into the rad-wastes. Reinforcements from Deliverance harried the retreating foe, exacting revenge for those who had fallen, and the Imperial Fists under Captain Noriz lent their strength to that of the Raven Guard. The battle continued well into the night, the sky awash with explosions and las-fire. In the city, the arrival of the Titans of the Legio Vindictus halted the Order of the Dragon, though great swathes of the city were left as blasted wasteland, the rubble choked with the dead of both sides. The sky above Kiavahr was filled with the smoke of thousands of fires, blotting out the stars and moons. Mechanicum aircraft dropped incendiary bombs and plasma charges onto the guild houses where the Order of the Dragon held out, while the guns of the Legio pounded away with shell and las-blast.

Under the orders of Corax, Ravendelve was sealed, the warriors of the Raptors and the Custodians slaying several Raven Guard that tried to leave under the cover of the confusion. With the immediate threat to the gene-tech quashed, the primarch ordered Commander Branne to stand down the *Avenger's* torpedoes and arrived to oversee the aftermath.

He was met at the ruins of the main gate by Agapito and Arcatus, with a bodyguard of loyal warriors standing ready to escort the primarch.

'I want an explanation, commander, and I want it now,' demanded Corax as he strode through the remnants of the gatehouse.

'The situation is very confused, lord,' said Agapito. 'Ravendelve is secure from attack, but the threat within is uncertain. We tallied the dead from the fighting and have found more than thirty legionaries who do not appear on our records.'

'Infiltrators,' growled Corax. 'Traitors wearing the colours of the Raven Guard.'

'What of Solaro and the others?' said Agapito. 'Why would they turn against us?'

'I am not so sure they did,' said Arcatus. Agapito and Corax looked at the Custodian for explanation. 'You have been the victims of a devious masquerade. My order understands intimately the means by which an intruder can enter an organisation unnoticed. It is our sole task to thwart such attempts. I believe there is only one Legion capable of such deception.'

'The Alpha Legion,' said Corax, growling again. 'This treachery bears their hallmark.'

'We shared air with Solaro for a long time. If he and the others were Alpha Legion in disguise, how can we say for certain that any of the others are loyal?' said Agapito.

It was a tricky problem, but Corax knew the answer almost immediately.

'My true sons will bear my mark,' said the primarch. They had reached the main hall, where the remaining Raven Guard had handed over their weapons and were being watched over by Custodians and first generation Raptors. 'My genetic data is wrapped up inside every cell of your bodies, while any infiltrators will bear the code of another primarch. Have Vincente Sixx screen every legionary for genetic markers that do not match the Raven Guard gene-seed.'

'Sixx is dead, lord,' said Agapito. 'He died defending the gene-project.'

'What of Orlandriaz?' said Corax. 'Has he survived?'

'He is in the infirmary, working out what damage has been done by the traitors,' replied Agapito.

'You cannot expect to continue with this project?' said Arcatus. 'Not after what we have witnessed here? We barely stopped the traitors escaping with the genetic material. It is too much of a risk, I cannot allow it.'

Corax stopped, stung by the Custodian's words. He looked at the ring of Raptors in their combat-scarred armour, standing guard over their battle-brothers without hesitation or complaint.

'What about those Raptors who have suffered from our mistakes?' said Corax. 'Do we condemn them to their sorry existence?'

'Spare them the pain,' said Arcatus. 'Each of them contains the seed of what you have done here, and perhaps locked within their twisted bodies is the means to achieve what you hoped. They are just as much a threat as the data contained in the gene-vault.'

'No,' said Agapito. 'We cannot kill them out of hand! What reward is that for the service they have done for the Legion today?'

'Agapito is right,' said Corax. 'I cannot murder them in cold blood. They have the bodies of beasts, but they have proven that their hearts are Raven Guard.'

The primarch rubbed a hand across his brow, conflicted in his thoughts. Was it folly to believe that he could right the wrong he had done to the Raptors? He had left Terra convinced he could rebuild the Raven Guard and despite all that had happened, the need to confront Horus's forces still existed.

Corax left the hall with Agapito and Arcatus beside him and made his way to the infirmary. At each conveyor and stairwell, armed Raptors stood guard, their distinctive armour marking them out in the dim emergency lighting. The trio headed along the north corridor, passing by shuttered weapons lockers emblazoned with the icon of the Raven Guard. Two hulking herakli stood guard in front of one such row of metal boxes, their multi-barrelled cannons tracking the primarch and his companions as they passed. A Mechanicum acolyte loitered in the shadow of one of the brutes, fussing over the belt of his robe. With the Raven Guard garrison held under guard and the reinforcements engaging the guilders in the atomic marshes, Orlandriaz and a contingent of his allies had provided much-needed security within and without Ravendelve.

'If the Alpha Legion is involved, we must assume that they will not be content with simply destroying what they found,' said Arcatus as they reached the conveyor that led to the infirmary. 'If you continue with this experimentation, you will attract the attention of Horus sooner or later.'

Corax lifted a portable vox from his belt and opened up a command channel.

'Let us see what the Commander of the Raptors thinks,' said the primarch. 'Branne, have you heard what was said?'

'Aye, lord,' Branne replied over the communicator. 'Every word. Agapito and the Custodian make good points, but I have a different view. If we continue, there is the possibility that we might find a means to reverse the predicament of the tainted Raptors. On the other hand, how many more recruits do we risk before its discovery? Lord, I think it is time that we closed this door and locked it forever. If we are to rebuild the Raven Guard it has to be through the means we know and can trust.'

'Wise words, commander,' said Corax. The group stepped into the conveyor, Corax bowing his head to avoid the ceiling. As the elevator shunted into life, the primarch made a decision. 'There are no swift answers to our situation. We have done all we can, but our efforts have fallen short. The gene-project will be terminated immediately and any research that was missed by the Alpha Legion will be destroyed.'

'What of the Raptors?' said Agapito. 'They are not to blame.'

'And I do not hold them at fault,' the primarch replied. 'I cannot – I will not – kill them out of hand. They were accepted into our brotherhood of warriors and as members of the Legiones Astartes they will be granted the same fate as all of us: to die with honour in battle against the Emperor's foes.'

'It is still your intent to launch an attack against the traitors?' asked Arcatus. 'Your Legion is in disarray, primarch.'

'The assault on Narsis will commence as planned,' said Corax. 'If this episode proves anything, it is that the Raven Guard do not sit well when idle. In battle we thrive, not in contemplation. More than ever, we need a victory, to restore spirits and forge a new brotherhood within the Legion. We have been divided for too long, between those of Terra and the men who liberated Deliverance, between those who survived Isstvan and those who saved us, between the veterans and the Raptors. No more. We are Raven Guard and we shall show the Imperium that we are united.'

They found Magos Orlandriaz in the infirmary. The wards were full of casualties from the fighting, most of them the Raptors who had taken on the infiltrators without armour. Several dozen of the beds contained still forms, the bloodstained sheets drawn up over their faces. Corax stopped beside the bed of one of the Raptors, who had heavy bandaging around his chest.

'The Legion owes you a great debt, legionary,' the primarch said. He knew the face and name of every man under his command, and the Raptor was no different. 'It's Hef, isn't it? Navar Hef?'

'Aye, Lord Corax,' said Navar, grimacing as he struggled to sit up.

Corax waved him to lie still. 'I'm just happy that we could serve you.'

'You still can,' said Corax. He raised his voice to address the wounded across the ward. 'Who among you thinks they are still battle-ready?'

There was a chorus of shouts and enthusiastic calls.

'For the Emperor and the Raven Guard!' said Agapito, raising his first.

'For the Emperor and the Raven Guard!' the Raptors replied as one.

Corax nodded and walked back into the inner sanctum, where he was met by Orlandriaz, who had been talking with Arcatus.

'The Custodian tells me you wish to gene-test the whole Legion, lord,' said the magos. 'I can begin testing within a few hours.'

'And it will root out any Raven Guard who is not what he seems?' said Agapito.

'I can assure you that no legionary will be able to hide his true nature, commander.'

RECALIBRATING HIS THERMAL regulator, Catho Juliaxis settled to his haunches with his back against the wall. He closed the metal shutters that served as eyelids in his altered face and wondered when he would be relieved of the tiresome duty of monitoring the herakli. The mute monstrosities were no company for a man of intellect.

His aural detector picked up the sound of one of his charges moving. Opening his eyes, he looked up to see one of the herakli standing over him. Gazing into the shadow beneath the construct's hood, he was surprised to see intelligent eyes staring back at him.

'Wh–'

The immense herakli rammed his cannon under Juliaxis's chin, crushing his windpipe and snapping his neck with a single blow. The other beast looked on, confused by the behaviour of its companion.

Pulling down the shutter of the locker, the dead acolyte's body concealed within, Omegon slipped the box of gene-data inside his robe. Affecting the lumbering gait of the herakli, he calmly walked out of the north corridor and headed for the gatehouse.

It had been so tempting to gun down Corax when he had walked past, but the triumph would have been fleeting. The Alpha Legion understood better than all others that the greatest victories were often those that were unheralded and unnoticed. Better to slip away with the mission accomplished than attract attention for a temporary thrill.

There were Mechanicum forces all about Ravendelve and it took Omegon only a few minutes to mingle with the other herakli. Soon he found himself being led out of the compound to join the hunt for the guilders. As the mists closed around the group of skitarii, a ticking started in the base of his skull, indicating that a gunship from the *Beta* was within five hundred metres. It was time to leave Kiavahr for good; he had what he came for.

There were shouts of panic as he opened fire, mowing down the other herakli and their skitarii minders in a few long bursts. Leaving their bodies to be swallowed by the fog, Omegon headed into the murk to make rendez-vous with his transport.

EIGHTEEN

The Raven's Wings
Horus Claims His Prize
Narsis

THE MOOD IN the Carnivalis was sombre, the assembled legionaries standing silently in ranks as Corax walked the length of the hall to the stage. Agapito, Branne, Aloni and the new commander of the Hawks, Nuran Tesk, flanked the raven-carved lectern. All of the Raven Guard were present, including the disfigured Raptors capable of fighting. The armourium had modified their prized suits of Mark VI, providing reinforcement where it was needed, cutting holes for horns and spinal growths, adjusting joints and seals for contorted limbs.

The ranks had been cleansed; as Orlandriaz had begun his gene-testing, those warriors pretending to be Raven Guard had attempted to flee or had ended their own lives. Drawing on what he knew of the meta-seed of the primarchs, Corax had been able to confirm that the infiltrators were from the Alpha Legion. The mark of Alpharius was in their blood and bones and flesh, and condemned them as certainly as their actions.

Mounting the stage, the primarch received nods of respect from his commanders. Corax turned to face the Legion. He was clad in full battle gear, one hand sheathed in the lightning claw that had survived the fight with Lorgar and Curze, the other holding the power whip he had wielded to such devastating effect in the retreat on Isstvan. He held up both hands, showing the armaments to the Raven Guard.

'The Legiones Astartes conquered the galaxy for the Emperor,' he began, but his voice faltered as he looked out at rank after rank of his warriors. Were these the last days of the Raven Guard? Was he about to lead them into their final campaign? He swallowed hard, remembering the adversities he had faced as guerrilla leader of the Lycaen rebels. The task then had seemed as insurmountable, but he had triumphed. He would not give in to fear, not of his enemies and not of what he might become.

He started again.

'The Legiones Astartes conquered the galaxy for the Emperor. We were created by his hand, moulded in flesh by his will and given the best weapons and armour conceived by mankind. Yet it was not our guns or our bodies that made the Great Crusade possible. It was belief. Belief in our cause, in the spreading of the Imperial Truth, gave us conviction beyond the superstitions and raw courage of our foes. Trust in our commanders and in ourselves gave us the strength to overcome any obstacle set before us.

'Belief and trust are just as much casualties of this war as the dead who fell on Isstvan and at Ravendelve. It is hard to comprehend that Horus, the Warmaster chosen by the Emperor, has turned renegade. It is difficult to accept that our brothers-in-arms, warriors of the Legiones Astartes, have defied the Imperial Truth and broken their oaths. Yet it is belief and trust that will remain our greatest weapons.

'I have always taught you that hope is needless. There is only action and consequence. I still adhere to that creed. There is no hope for the Raven Guard. We will do as we see fit and the consequences will follow. We have suffered not one but two grave attacks. The first was cowardly, but open. The second daring, but hidden. Neither ambush on Isstvan nor corruption from within has destroyed us and so we learn and grow stronger. It is not in our nature to bow our heads to defeat. We will not be meek while traitors seek to overthrow the Emperor.

'Today is the day that Horus and his treacherous allies learn that the Raven Guard cannot be dismissed. Today we set aboard our ships and take the war to our enemies, as we have done so many times before. Some of you were there at the beginning, when this hall was the site of bloody battles between men and women who yearned for freedom and the oppressors who would deny them. Some of you set out beside the Emperor, leaving Terra to forge a new empire across the stars. Some of you cannot claim such heritage, for you were fortunate to be raised into the Legion in later times. And some of you had your first taste of battle at Ravendelve.

'It does not matter. We are all Raven Guard. We are all warriors. The Emperor will not judge you by your medals and diplomas but by your scars. That is not a platitude; it is the reality of what we are. We live to fight the Emperor's battles, and we die to bring the Emperor victory.'

Corax paused and looked towards a group of yellow-armoured warriors who stood alongside the Raven Guard: Captain Noriz's Imperial Fists. His gaze moved to the golden warriors of Custodian Arcatus.

'Horus sets his eye on Terra and the palace of the Emperor. Many are those who will lay down their lives in its defence, and we salute them now for their sacrifice. Yet it is not for us to stand behind the walls, for we are the shadow that kills, the hidden death that none suspect.

'Horus and his craven companions think themselves beyond retribution. The Raven Guard will prove them wrong. The accursed Warmaster and his confederates believe victory is inevitable and that the Imperium will bow to his will. The Raven Guard will prove them wrong. In our defiance we shall light the fires of battle that will burn across the length and breadth of the galaxy. The citizens of the Imperium will know that they have not been abandoned. We will show them that the torch of Enlightenment shines brightly. The Legiones Astartes will never be destroyed whilst one of us draws breath.

'We do this because mankind needs to believe that Horus can be defeated. We do this because humanity must be shown that the Legiones Astartes can be trusted. We are few and our enemies are many, but every traitor we kill sends a message to our foes and allies alike: the Raven Guard will never surrender!'

A wordless shout erupted from more than four thousand throats, ringing around the vaulted ceiling of the Carnivalis. Energy fields crackled as the Custodians lifted their halberds in salute to the primarch.

An expectant hush settled as a small detachment of Raven Guard broke from the ranks. They were led by the Techmarine, Stradon Binalt, and carried with them a large object draped in one of the Legion's black banners.

'What's this?' asked Corax, turning to his commanders. They shook their heads and shrugged, as surprised as their primarch.

Binalt and his entourage mounted the steps to the stage and approached Corax. The primarch stepped away from the lectern to face them, and as one they each fell to one knee, except for Binalt who met his lord's inquiring stare.

'On Isstvan, the Raven Guard suffered a heavy blow,' said the Techmarine, the precision of his words betraying a speech practised many times. 'The raven had his wings clipped and our fortunes have suffered. It is fitting then that at a time when we must learn to soar once more, the raven should have his wings restored.'

Binalt tugged the banner away, revealing Corax's ornate flight pack, long thought lost. Its newly enamelled finish now gleamed in the lights of the Carnivalis, the two graceful, newly-fashioned wings sweeping to either side of the apparatus.

'I couldn't quite match the original artificer in craft, but I hope it will suffice, lord,' said Binalt, bowing his head.

Corax took the flight pack in both hands and lifted it up, marvelling at its construction. He looked down at Binalt and smiled his thanks, but before he could say anything, the hall was filled again with a thunderous shouting, springing from the ranks of the Raven Guard.

'*Corax! Corax! Corax!*'

THE WARMASTER'S CHAMBER was as gloomy as it had been during Alpharius's last visit. As before, he was met by Horus, flanked by Abaddon and Erebus. There was another as well, lurking within the shadows behind the Warmaster's throne. He was dressed in the armour of the Emperor's Children, with a thin face and darting eyes.

'You have something for the Warmaster?' said Erebus, as the door slid shut behind Alpharius.

'Why do you say that?' Alpharius replied. 'Am I to make tribute now to our glorious leader?'

'Watch your tongue,' snapped Abaddon. 'We know that one of your vessels has just joined the fleet, though you attempted to hide its presence from us.'

'I have done no such thing,' said Alpharius, stretching out his hands in a gesture of mock innocence. 'All of my vessels employ a certain amount of stealth. It is a central pillar of our security. No deception is intended.'

'Then you admit that your mission regarding the Raven Guard is a success,' said Erebus. 'You have obtained that which you sought?'

Smiling, Alpharius produced a data crystal from his

belt and held it out in the palm of his hand.

'Not an unqualified success,' said the primarch. 'Some of the Raven Guard, Corax included, survived our attack. It is of little consequence. We have, as you assert, acquired our prize.'

Erebus took a few steps forwards and reached for the crystal, but Alpharius snatched away his hand.

'It is for the Warmaster only,' said Alpharius, his smile fading.

'Watch your step, Alpharius,' said Abaddon. 'Your attitude will earn you the Warmaster's displeasure.'

'No words for your brother, Horus?' said Alpharius, looking at the Warmaster, who had been fixing Alpharius with a neutral gaze throughout the exchange. 'Do your minions do all of your talking for you now?'

Horus stood up and Alpharius thought for a moment that he had pushed things too far. His doubts were dispelled by Horus's smile, as he beckoned the stranger to come out from behind the throne.

'This is Apothecary Fabius,' said the Warmaster. 'You will entrust your prize to his care. On my behalf, of course.'

Alpharius tossed the data crystal to Fabius, who caught the glittering shard and looked down at it with a covetous smile.

'We shall see what secrets Corax unearthed, for certain,' said Fabius. He bowed to Horus and withdrew into the shadows.

'Is there anything else, Warmaster?' said Alpharius.

Horus's eyes narrowed with suspicion as he regarded the Alpha Legion's primarch.

'You hand it over so easily, I suspect you are hiding something,' said the Warmaster, stepping closer.

'I do have another confession to make,' said Alpharius. 'I have retained the original gene-material for myself. I thought it wiser to share our fortune. You will find the research of Corax quite extensive. I do not understand much of it, but I am sure Apothecary Fabius is as talented as rumour would have us believe.'

'Oh, he is,' said Erebus. 'He will unlock the primarch secrets, and with that information we will destroy the Emperor.'

'A worthy use of such a thing, so hard-fought for,' said Alpharius. He met his brother's penetrating gaze with a stare of his own. 'I believe we have concluded our business here. Unless there is anything else you wish to discuss, brother?'

Horus jerked his head towards the door to dismiss Alpharius, and returned to his throne.

'Good,' said the Alpha Legion primarch. 'Now that this matter is settled, perhaps we could actually begin to prosecute this war. Even now, I am sure the Emperor is getting impatient for our visit.'

'He will wait,' said Horus. 'The war is well under way already, Alpharius. Just because you have not been fighting it does not mean that others have been idle. The Ultramarines will be destroyed and the Blood Angels will join our cause. We will be ready to make our move soon.'

That seemed unlikely to Alpharius, but he said nothing and left without further comment.

THE COMMAND DECK of the *Avenger* was filled with people. As well as the officers and functionaries of the Raven Guard, the battle-barge was hosting the command corps of the newly-arrived Therion Cohort. Sub-Caesari Valerius had shuttled across to the capital ship with a small army of notaries, praefectors, tribunes and vice-tribunes to compile the orders for his force.

It had been a tortuous journey from Therion, negotiating the storms that still raged across the warp. Several ships had been lost entirely and more than a dozen

more had been waylaid or forced to translate, scattering
the fleet over light years of space. Despite the problems,
Valerius had managed to hold the vanguard intact, and
as per Corax's instructions had redirected while en route
to Deliverance to rendezvous with the Raven Guard in
Taurion, a system neighbouring Narsis.

His previous encounters with Corax had left Valerius
awestruck, but as sub-Caesari he felt his station better
suited his position within the command council. His
promotion had not, however, done anything to quash
his amazement at the primarch's strategic abilities.
While Valerius needed his contingent of advisors and
adjutants to keep everything in order, Corax was able to
control the whole council with nothing more than a few
notes on a data-slab. The dispositions of dozens of ships
and thousands of warriors, their armaments and their
commanders were all locked inside the primarch's mind
and even the smallest detail was retrieved effortlessly.

The order of battle and general approach had already
been agreed, with the Therions forming the first wave,
the reflex-shielded Raven Guard vessels following
behind. So far it had been as Valerius expected, having
fought alongside the Raven Guard for several years during the latter stages of the Great Crusade.

The final approach and landing was giving him a lot
of trouble.

'If I understand you correctly, Lord Corax, there is to
be no preparatory bombardment?' said Valerius. Pelon
appeared at his shoulder with a glass of water, which
Valerius took without comment. He took a sip to calm
his agitation. 'Our drop-ships will be shot out of the air.'

'Orbital defences will be eliminated as normal,' replied
the primarch. As was his habit, he stood to one side
while the commanders were crowded around the central
table. 'Once orbital supremacy has been established you
will have to conduct a landing under fire.'

'I have three battleship-class vessels, lord, each quite capable of eliminating any ground defences. There will be no need for your Legion to reveal its presence at the onset, I guarantee that. Isn't that right, Captain Willhelms?'

The commander of the battleship *Resolute* nodded.

'Torpedoes and lances will do the job,' said Willhelms,

'Can you guarantee the lives of the ten million people living in that city?' asked Branne.

'We will endeavour to avoid any civilian casualties, of course.' Valerius glanced at Praefector Antonius, who made some quick calculations on his data-slate and handed it to the sub-Caesari. 'Perhaps no more than five thousand?'

'This is not an ordinary city,' said Corax. 'Fulgrim was not idly boasting when he named it the Perfect Fortress. My brother declared that it was not enough for a fortification to house a garrison, it had to protect the population. The Perfect Fortress is not an area within the city, it *is* the city. Fulgrim reasoned, quite rightly, that the populace was best protected if they were integral to the fortress's design.

'He decided to use the civilians as shields?' said Valerius, horrified by the thought.

'That was not his argument at the time,' replied Corax. 'In the case of an invasion, they would spontaneously form a militia to help with the defence. That is of no matter. There is no separation of defence and civilian construction. Habitat towers house defence lasers. Factories are protected by bunkers and concealed trench lines. The layout of the roads was the work of Perturabo, to allow swift response from the defenders whilst hindering attack.'

'To destroy the fortress we have to destroy the city,' said Branne.

'Which we will not do,' said Corax. 'The people of

Narsis are innocent in this. We are here to act as messengers for the Emperor's cause, not to kill his followers. We cannot spread our message by obliterating the populace.'

'A thorny problem,' admitted Valerius. He finished his water and absent-mindedly handed the glass back to Pelon while he pondered. He gave up with a shrug. 'I cannot see a landing without orbital support being anything but a disaster. We will be dropping right onto their guns.'

'There is a potential landing site,' said Aloni, bringing up a schematic of the area surrounding the Perfect Fortress. He pressed a key and a crosshair appeared on the map. 'Here, in the hills to the north-east.'

'That is at least twenty kilometres away!' said Valerius, standing up to examine the diagram. 'We do not have that many tanks and transports.'

'Twenty-eight, actually,' said Agapito. Valerius did not like the hint of amusement in the commander's tone.

'You will attack on foot,' said Corax. 'You will land under cover of night, though do not expect that to be much of an advantage because the enemy will have scanners and thermal imaging.'

'March nearly thirty kilometres overnight to attack a city-fortress?' Valerius had a sinking feeling about this whole endeavour and felt it was his place to be honest. 'That is a strategy doomed to failure.'

'Exactly,' said Corax. The primarch's smile was unsettling. 'I don't expect you to take the Perfect Fortress by yourselves. That's why we're here.'

THE HOLOLITHIC DISPLAY showed just how hopeless the situation was for the fools. Captain Hasten Luthris Armanitan of the Emperor's Children prowled the command chamber of his tower, watching every data report and scan relay like a hawk. The natural topography to

the north-east would funnel the attackers towards the
Eighth Avenue gate, beyond which lay a broad thor-
oughfare dominated by three cannon batteries located
at one–hundred-metre intervals along the road's length.
To either side, the city became a maze of interlocking
corridors of fire overlooked by bunker positions and
sally ports.

'Their foolishness shall be the cause of their defeat,' he
said, speaking more to himself than the Legion serfs at
the consoles. 'So typically weak, to assault without prior
bombardment. What do they hope to achieve?'

'Cordon Two has been overrun, captain,' reported one
of the serfs. 'Last report was of a massed infantry assault.
Enemy casualties heavy.'

'I suppose there is a little wisdom in leaving behind
their armour,' said Luthris. 'All of those anti-tank rocket
batteries are going to waste. Have their crews stand down
at Cordon One and get them to man the line.'

'Affirmative, captain,' said the attendant.

Luthris checked the time display. There was a little
over three hours, Terran-standard, until dawn. The first
wave of attackers would have barely reached the wall
before his troops had full visibility. Then the carnage
would really begin.

THE OUTSKIRTS OF the Perfect Fortress had an appearance
utterly at odds with their purpose. Elaborate hanging
gardens sprawled from the roofs and walls of the white
buildings, the scent of their flowers filling the air. Colonnaded frontages and overhanging galleries provided
cover for the Therions as they advanced towards the gate
tower looming over the buildings ahead. The Emperor's
Children had sacrificed nothing of their aesthetic sense
in the city's design, so that colonnaded, alabaster buildings might equally serve as administration offices or
tank depots, it was impossible to tell from the outside.

Valerius marched with his men, determined that they would push home the attack with every last iota of strength, even if they were doomed to failure. He had been forced to swallow the ignominy of sacrificing his last command at Isstvan for a diversion, and was determined that his next would not end so ingloriously. The Therions would give a good account of themselves, whatever Corax expected.

A few Sentinel walkers had survived the hours of missile and shell bombardment on the approach to the city. They were several hundred metres ahead, scouting for the three-hundred-strong advance guard. Valerius only knew of this from the constant commentary being fed to him by Tribune Calorium, who followed the sub-Caesari a few steps behind.

'Sir, lead squadron encountering another defence line,' Calorium reported, the cup-like vox-receiver clamped to one ear. 'Taking fire from overhead balconies.'

Valerius glanced up at this news, seeing anew the lines of galleries over overhangs above him. It had been the same ever since entering the city: seemingly innocuous architectural features revealing their true purpose as killing sites, weapons platforms and minefields.

Sensing their commander's nervousness, Valerius's bodyguard closed ranks around him, their golden carapace armour and white fatigues stained and muddied by the advance from the landing zone.

'Perhaps we should move into cover, sub-Caesari,' suggested vice-Tribune Callista.

'And where is that, exactly?' Valerius snapped in return. He had already lost four men from his command section when they sheltered in a flower bed that turned out to have been laced with trip-mines.

Callista looked around uncertainly.

'Never mind,' said Valerius, continuing to stride along the middle of the road. It had been frustrating, fighting against unseen enemies, coming face-to-face with his foes only when he saw them retreating to the next defence line.

Not that he was in a mood for such a confrontation. The purple-and-gold-armoured warriors would no doubt take an even heavier toll once they decided to stand and fight. There was small comfort in reaching the city proper; the shelling from towers deep in the fortress's heart had stopped, no doubt to avoid fire falling on their own warriors.

'Advance teams are suffering badly,' announced Calorium. 'Requesting reinforcement.'

Glancing at the tribune, Valerius's heart sank.

'Have Third and Fourth Companies move up in support. See if they can outflank the enemy position. Order Fifth and Sixth to move up from the rearguard. How is Praefector Magellius proceeding?'

The tribune spoke for a short while and then sorrowfully shook his head.

'Second Phalanx is being pushed back, they've lost a third of their men,' said Calorium. 'Sir, Third Phalanx is also reporting a stalled advance. They are being cut down by the gate defences.'

An explosion less than two hundred metres ahead sent a plume of ash and smoke into the sky. A few seconds later, debris showered down on Valerius and his men.

'What was that?' he demanded, though Calorium was already talking quickly on the vox.

'Macro-cannon, sir,' the tribune said. 'Sited at the junction ahead, concealed on the third floor of a tenement.'

There was shakiness to the tribune's voice, and looking at the other soldiers around him Valerius could sense their fear. If he continued to push them forwards, they would break and rout. That would not be at all to his liking.

'All right, send to all command sections,' he snarled.

'Company-by-company withdrawal. Establish a perimeter at the edge of the city. This is to be an orderly retreat. We will have no running away and no panic.'

'Yes, sir.' Calorium's manner and tone betrayed his gratitude for the sub-Caesari's decision.

Valerius stopped where he was and stood with hands on hips, glaring at the distant towers. He had reached the city, an achievement it itself, but even his reconnaissance forces were more than two kilometres from the inner defence line.

It did not matter what Corax intended, it still tasted bitterly of defeat.

'THE ENEMY ARE withdrawing en masse, captain.'

'Ridiculous,' Luthris replied. 'They have not even begun to test our defences.'

'Visual confirmation of scanner data, captain. The enemy are pulling back into the outer reaches.'

The Emperor's Children officer made a slow lap of the command centre, examining every data stream and display. The evidence was incontrovertible: the attackers were giving up ground on all fronts. It seemed a disappointing end to a lacklustre attack.

'Any sign of low orbit vessels?' he asked, settling in his chair.

'None, captain,' came the reply. 'All enemy ships are keeping out of ground defence range. No sign of dropcraft.'

It made little sense to Luthris as he returned to his command throne, but it was foolish to consider the motivations of lesser warriors. No doubt they had been ordered to attack and had complied without knowing the full extent of the opponent they faced. He was not about to be forgiving of the error.

'Assemble counter-attack companies at gates three and four,' he ordered, his finger on the comm-switch set into the arm of his chair. 'Prepare the armourium for mobile columns to make a swift encircling move via the under-city ramps. These fools do not attack our city without retort. Mission objective is the total destruction of all enemy forces. Counter-attack to commence in fifteen minutes.'

He released the comm-switch and leaned back, the chair adjusting to the movement. He looked over his shoulder to Sergeant Turan, who stood by the doorway, plumed helm under one arm.

'Prepare the assault force, sergeant, I shall personally lead them into battle.'

'As you will it, captain,' Turan replied with a bow of his head. He fixed on his helm and banged a fist against his chestplate in salute. 'We will murder these dogs wherever they try to hide.'

A LASCANNON BLAST burst through the edge of the balcony, obliterating the man to Valerius's right. Showered with dust and blood, the sub-Caesari crawled back from the parapet to hunker down in the ruins of the window behind. Calorium was still by his side, one arm in a sling, the communications pack on the floor next to him. He looked at Valerius with bloodshot eyes and shook his head.

'No reply from Praefector Tigurian, sir. I think our left flank has broken.'

'Two thousand men, tribune, two thousand men!' said Valerius, slumping against the frame of the window. 'None of them are left?'

Calorium shrugged in reply.

For an hour the Therions had retreated, and for another they had held against the counter-attack of the Emperor's Children. Marcus had done all he could, cajoling and encouraging his commanders to stay and fight, to hold the line at all costs, but there was little time left. He risked standing up, snatching his magnoculars from his belt. Training them to the south-west he could see several dozen armoured figures advancing along the road, no more than half a kilometre away.

'Please leave!'

Valerius turned and glared at the old man whose chambers he had commandeered as a temporary command post.

'And go where?' the sub-Caesari snarled.

'My wife, she wants you to leave…'

'Really? Perhaps she thinks that Horus would be better suited as leader of the Imperium?'

'I wouldn't know anything about that, sir. I just know that when the legionaries get here, they'll not leave any of us alive if we're sheltering you.'

Valerius said nothing more. He could not blame the elderly couple for their fear. He had been fearful before, then desperate, and now had emerged into a state of strange calm about the situation. Nearly ten thousand Therions had lost their lives in the last eight hours, but he felt sanguine about the losses. A sense of numbness had filled him since losing contact with Second Phalanx, an acceptance of the inevitable.

He looked again at the Emperor's Children. They were taking their time, checking every building along the road. Overhead, Thunderhawks prowled, seeking targets for their cannons and heavy bolters. The streets had become a bloodbath from their initial strafing runs, forcing every Therion to take shelter inside. To their credit, what little it counted for, the Emperor's Children had not fired on the buildings; perhaps they still believed they were protecting these people.

He drew his pistol. It seemed important that he had a weapon in his hand.

'Forget that,' he told his tribune, looking at the vox-unit. 'Get your lasrifle.'

Calorium pushed the heavy pack aside and dropped the receiver. He flinched as another las-blast tore into the sculpted architrave above them, melting through the relief of a war chariot charging against a horde of barbarians. On his knees, he crawled over the dead Therions and retrieved his weapon before returning to Valerius's side.

'You said to trust you,' Valerius muttered to himself. 'Weather the storm and trust you. Well, Corax, the storm is upon us.'

THERE WAS LITTLE honour in slaughtering the poorly-armed soldiers. Their lasguns were pitiful against Legiones Astartes armour, their gold-coloured flak vests no defence against boltguns. Luthris could not even enjoy the slaughter: it was too one-sided and little test for his tactical acumen or his physical prowess.

At the head of his squad, he strode up a sweeping staircase leading to the upper floors of a guesthouse. He fired his bolt pistol at the men hunkering down behind the balustrade above, his shots finding their marks between the wooden pillars.

'Squad Andilor, proceed to the third floor,' he said, shooting another soldier in the leg. The bolt tore the man's hip apart, sending him sprawling. Luthris casually drove his sword into the man's chest as he stalked past. 'Squad Collonius, fourth floor.'

'Heavy weapon on the roof opposite, captain,' reported one of the sergeants. 'Multi-laser.'

'Call in a Thunderhawk strike, sergeant,' Luthris replied. 'Must I make every decision?'

'Affirmative, captain. Calling in airstrike.'

With an armoured boot, the Emperor's Children captain kicked open the door at the end of the landing. He quickly scanned the rooms beyond but they were empty. With a sigh of disappointment he turned back to the stairwell.

'Captain!'

The shout came from below, not over the vox. Striding to the edge of the landing, Luthris saw Squad Argentius backing into the foyer, bolters aimed towards the outer doors. One of them yelled a warning and they opened fire, but Luthris could not see their target.

'What's happening?' the captain demanded. 'Speak to me!'

Before he heard the reply his comm-bead crackled into life.

'Captain, we have detected sub-orbital craft, approaching at speed.'

'From where? How did they launch?'

'We do not know, captain. Orbital scan is clear.'

Even as he tried to absorb this information, Luthris watched the squad below. Two of the legionaries were heaved into the air, blood spilling from gaping rents in their armour. The others fired at nothing, though their bolts seemed to deflect from thin air, exploding against emptiness. Sergeant Argentius stepped forwards with his chainsword roaring. A moment later his arm and head flew away, cut clean through by some invisible force.

Luthris could not believe what he was seeing. Within a few seconds, the whole squad were dead: dismembered and decapitated.

'Sorcery,' he muttered. There was no Librarian close at hand to help him.

Bringing up his power sword, he took up a guard position at the top of the stairs. He thought he saw something for a moment and fired his pistol. The shot detonated a few steps up from the bottom of the stairs.

A moment later he was looking into two jet-black eyes, centimetres from his face. Stepping back, he realised what it was that confronted him. The warrior was half again as tall as Luthris, armoured in pure black splashed with gore, a winged pack upon his back. His face was bone white, his hair shorn at shoulder length. In one hand the warrior held a crackling whip; the other was sheathed in glowing claws. The apparition bared its teeth in a wordless snarl and raised its talons.

'For the Emperor!' it whispered as the claws slashed down.

CORAX MOVED FROM room to room, slaying any Emperor's Children he came across. His claws cut them to ribbons and his glowing whip sliced through polished armour. Reaching the highest storey of the building, he walked out onto the balcony overlooking the main street. Looking up he saw the dark blur of drop-pods falling from the heavens. Beyond them came the contrails of Thunderhawks and Stormbirds.

It was time to head for the gate.

THE DROP-POD OPENED up like the petals of an iron flower, metal ramps crashing into the wall rampart. Navar was the first out of his harness, bounding down to the wall with easy strides. Unarmoured soldiers were manning a gun post ahead of him. Slipping a taloned finger into the guard of his bolter, he gunned them down with three shots.

Behind him, Carval growled and hissed. With a glance back at his fellow Raptor, Navar nodded. He had no idea what Carval had tried to say, but he understood his brother legionary's intent.

'For the Raven Guard!' Navar cried as he dashed along the wall, opening fire when a squad of Emperor's Children burst out of the tower ahead.

Bolt-rounds flickered back and forth between the two squads, ripping chunks of ceramite from armour. A shadow fell over Navar and he glanced up to see Lord Corax soaring over the edge of the wall. The primarch's whip lashed out, shredding two of the Emperor's

Children from the waist up. Behind Corax came more Raven Guard, dropping down from the top of the tower ahead, their jump packs flaring to slow their descent. Plasma pistols and chainswords ready, the assault squad fell upon the rear of the Emperor's Children.

There was shooting from inside the wall. Navar glanced down to his left and saw three yellow-armoured squads fighting their way across a narrow courtyard, pushing back the Emperor's Children. Captain Noriz's Imperial Fists would not miss out on the victory. On a rooftop further from the wall, two more drop-pods were opening up. Custodian Guard in their gleaming gold armour stormed out, unleashing bursts of energy from their guardian spears, cracking open the power armour of their foes.

Beyond the wall the Therions were advancing again, taking revenge on the Emperor's Children who had slaughtered their fellows. Though their lasguns were not as powerful as their foes' bolters, their weight of fire and tenacity was driving the traitors back towards the gates.

Lord Corax circled once, no doubt taking stock of the battle's progress, before he landed a little ahead of Navar. The primarch pointed towards the centre of the city, to where the central tower of the Perfect Fortress soared more than three hundred metres above the buildings surrounding it. Navar looked to where Corax gestured and saw thousands of Raven Guard pouring out of drop-pods around the tower. He recognised the beak-faced Mark VI armour of the first Raptors as they led a charge against the central citadel, alongside loping and shuffling warriors of the last generation. Bolters, plasma and laser scoured the gardens and porticos of the enemy installation. Other legionaries, from the Hawks and Talons, jumped down from hovering Thunderhawks to set up crossfires on rooftops and inner walls, cutting down the retreating Emperor's Children. Stormbirds looped slowly, their guns blazing at pockets of resistance, reserves of more Raven

Guard inside ready to commit to the fight.

It was a joyous sight, the whole Legion acting in concert, and Navar understood why his primarch was grinning.

'NOT SO PERFECT,' said Agapito.

Corax had gathered his command council in the chambers of the garrison commander. It reminded him of the officers' mess hall on Lycaeus where he had decided to use the atomic charges on Kiavahr. The carpet underfoot was thick, the walls panelled with red lacquered wood. Finely sculpted statues stood on marble plinths around the edge of the room.

'We certainly can't hold it,' said Branne.

An exquisite alabaster bust of Fulgrim toppled to the floor with a dull crash as the commander leaned deliberately against its pedestal. Glancing down at the fragments, Branne dropped a heavy foot onto the remnants, crushing them into the carpet. 'You know that Horus will respond.'

'I am counting on it,' said Corax. 'We will not be here.'

'So what was the point?' demanded Valerius. He looked like a child, sitting in a deep armchair made for one of the Legiones Astartes, his feet off the ground. Behind him, his aide had salvaged a decanter of wine from a cabinet and was hunting for an intact glass amongst the ruin of shattered cupboards and shelves. 'A lot of Therions died just to hand this world back to the traitors.'

'We're leaving, you're not,' said Corax. 'The rest of your Cohort will be arriving, nearly five hundred thousand men. The Legio Vindictus has already departed from Kiavahr with a dozen Titans. Other Imperial Army elements are also on their way, nearly a million more soldiers. Horus will be getting a hot welcome if he does come here.'

'So we stay here and keep fighting?' said Valerius. 'You have levelled half of the defences.'

'It won't come to that, sub-Caesari,' said the primarch. He stared out of the window, watching smoke drift over the ornate towers and gardens. 'The Raven Guard are leaving, but not for Deliverance. Khalghorst is our next target. There is a Word Bearers garrison there. We'll have hit them before Horus even has word of what has happened here.'

Corax turned and looked at his commanders.

'This is not the Great Crusade. There is no compliance, no garrisons. We fight as the Raven Guard always have. We fight and we withdraw. We hit hard and elude the counter-blow. There are others that will stand and take the brunt of the traitors' fury, and they have my sympathy, but this war will not be won with kind regards. And we will rebuild our numbers, slowly as before, but growing stronger as our enemies are weakened. The traitors allowed the Raven Guard to survive, and that will prove a costly mistake.

'We will take this war to Horus wherever and whenever we can and we will bleed his forces dry. We cannot win this war alone, but we will ensure he wins no quick victory.'

EPILOGUE

Aboard the *Alpha*, Omegon walked to his shared chamber without thought, his feet guiding him through the corridors and levels without conscious effort. He knew that Horus had accepted the gene-data, which left him with just one more loose end to tie up.

Entering the quarters, Omegon was immediately confronted by Athithirtir, the alien's enviro-globe bobbing around in agitation.

+I sense that you are being duplicitous.+

'Your sense is annoyingly correct,' said Omegon, sitting on the bunk so that his face was level with the gas-filled sphere.

+It is unwise to pass on the primarch genetic material to Horus. It will alter the balance of power in his favour. You risk giving victory to the Primordial Annihilator.+

'Then it is fortunate that the data we handed over is flawed,' said Omegon. 'Fabius will never perfect the technology. The servants of the Primordial Annihilator will expend countless lives and endless hours in the pursuit of the impossible.'

+I sense that you are feeling proud of this conclusion. You are hiding something from me.+

'Your empathic ability is becoming tiresome,' said Omegon. 'We no longer need an envoy from the Cabal. We are capable of determining our own fate from now on.'

+That is not an option. The Cabal must steer this war to the correct conclusion. To do otherwise risks victory for the Primordial Annihilator. You are being disobedient.+

'We do that a lot,' said Omegon. He stood up and grabbed the globe in one gauntleted hand. Anti-grav motors gave out a high-pitched whine as the sphere struggled against the primarch's grip.

+This vessel is impervious to you and your weapons. Your attempt to harm or threaten me is pointless.+

'I am not going to hurt you at all, my gas-filled friend,' said Omegon.

He walked to the doorway and keyed open the lock. Leaving his quarters, the primarch headed for the closest conveyor. Athithirtir screeched all the way as they rode the elevator down to the docking levels, but Omegon had already issued orders to ensure there was no other soul along their route. The area around dock four was empty. Passing through the armoured door, Omegon walked between the secured Thunderhawks lined up on each side of the flight deck.

+I do not understand your intent. Your behaviour is unacceptable.+

'I am simply taking you to your ship,' said Omegon, letting go of the globe. Athithirtir floated up out of reach, ranting unintelligible curses at the primarch.

+I do not detect my ship.+

'I am sure it will be here,' said Omegon. He walked back towards the doors. 'Maybe in a century or two.'

Sealing the doorway behind him, Omegon opened a communications frequency.

'Dock four control, this is your primarch. Open inner and outer doors immediately, full atmospheric cleanse.'

'Affirmative, lord,' came the reply.

Warning sirens blared while Omegon imagined the huge armoured portal shielding the flight deck opening, revealing the field of stars outside. The air would blow out like a hurricane, taking the intrusive little alien with it. Content that his task was complete, he headed back to his quarters. There was still a lot more to be done. With the gene-tech secured in the *Alpha's* vaults, in time his warriors would truly be *legion*.

ABOUT THE AUTHOR

Gav Thorpe has been rampaging across the worlds of Warhammer and Warhammer 40,000 for many years as both an author and games developer. He hails from the den of scurvy outlaws called Nottingham and makes regular sorties to unleash bloodshed and mayhem. He shares his hideout with Dennis, a mechanical hamster sworn to enslave mankind. Dennis is currently trying to develop an iPhone app that will hypnotise his victims. Gav's previous novels include fan-favourite *Angels of Darkness*, the Time of Legends trilogy, The Sundering, and the Eldar Path series amongst many others.

You can find his website at
mechanicalhamster.wordpress.com.

**An extract from *Legion of the Damned*
by Rob Sanders**

WARHAMMER
40,000
A SPACE MARINE BATTLES NOVEL

LEGION OF
THE DAMNED

ROB SANDERS

April
2012

UK ISBN: 978-1-84970-142-6   US ISBN: 978-1-84970-143-3

**Available from
*www.blacklibrary.com***

'How GOES THE Feast, brother?' asked Ezrachi.

'Badly,' Corpus-Captain Shiloh Gideon lamented. 'For the Excoriators, at least.'

'How many?' enquired the Apothecary as he approached. His right leg was a full bionic replacement and almost as old as the Apothecary himself. While robust and powerful, it sighed with hydraulic insistence and lagged a millisecond behind its flesh and bone equivalent, giving the impression of a slight limp.

'Too many,' Gideon snapped, running a palm across the top of his tonsured scalp. He grasped the hair that grew like a silver crown around his skull in obvious frustration. 'We lost three more this morning. Occam, Basrael and Jabez. Occam fought well, but not well enough. I thought Jabez was dead. I don't think anything is going to stop that Crimson Fist. The Feast may already be theirs.'

'Brother Jabez will live,' Ezrachi assured him. 'Just.'

Gideon didn't seem to hear the aged Apothecary.

'Shame begets shame,' the captain said. 'Our failure at the Feast is tied to the loss of our Chapter's sacred standard. I can feel it.'

'Your head is full of Santiarch Balshazar's sermons. I honour the primarch, but Dorn lives on through our flesh and blood, not dusty artefacts,' Ezrachi insisted. 'The loss of our standard is a mighty blow, but in truth it was but a blood-speckled banner.'

'Rogal Dorn himself entrusted his sons – our Excoriator brothers – with that item over ten thousand years ago,' the corpus-captain said. 'It displays the Second Founding's decree and is threaded with the honours of every battle fought in our long, bloody history. It carries the distinctia of the Praeses Chapters and our service in garrisoning the Eye. It bears the stigmartyr – the emblem that the Chapter adopted as its own.' Gideon turned to present his own ivory shoulder plate, adorned with the scarlet symbol to which he made reference: a gauntleted fist clenching the length of a thunderbolt-shaped scar. 'It is much more than the blood-soaked rag to which you allude, and I'll have you mind your irreverence, Apothecary.'

'I meant no offence, corpus-captain,' Ezrachi replied plainly. 'As you well know, there is more than a little of my own blood splashed across that standard.'

'Our brothers fight for a broken honour,' the captain continued, oblivious to Ezrachi. 'We are accursed. The Emperor's eternal fortitude, once absent in the brother that surrendered the banner, is now absent in us all. It is our collective punishment.'

'Is it not our way?' Ezrachi put to him. 'Do not the Excoriators, of all Dorn's sons, feel the loss of the Emperor deepest? Do not the Excoriators alone know our primarch's true grief, the agony of his redemption and the cold wrath of his renascence? Do we not purge his weakness and our own from this shared flesh through the Rites of Castigation and the wearing of Dorn's Mantle?'

'This is beyond our inherited sin,' Gideon said miserably. 'The loss of the honoured First Company, the near assassination of our Chapter Master, the failure and decimation of the Fifth and now this – one hundred years of humiliation in the making, right underneath the disapproving noses of our kindred. All as spiritual censure for the loss of Dorn's gift – the very embodiment of our Adeptus Astartes honour.'

'We have lost a great symbol,' Ezrachi admitted, 'but not what the standard symbolised. That is alive and well in the hearts of every Excoriator who bears his blade in the Emperor's name. As they do here brother, at the Feast of Blades.'

'Blades drawn in disbelief and sheathed in failure,' the corpus-captain said grimly.

'Is our standing in the Feast really so dire?'

'I'm pinning our hope on Usachar and Brother Dathan. Usachar is a squad whip and a veteran. Dathan is young, but fast, and has a way with a blade.'

'Some hope, then,' Ezrachi said.

'Usachar is chosen against Knud Hægstad of the Iron Knights and young Dathan has drawn Pugh's champion,' Gideon reported. 'It's never easy crossing blades with those chosen to wear the primarch's plate, but with the Imperial Fists defending their title and the Feast fought on a world they conquered, I don't rate our chances. Even if they win, they'll have to face that damned Crimson Fist in the next round. It's fairly hopeless.'

'So,' the Ezrachi put to the corpus-captain, 'it is time.'

'I would enter the arena myself, but for the desperation it speaks to our brethren.'

'Making your decision all the easier and more forgivable,' the Apothecary persisted. 'You have no choice. Give the order.'

'I would not do this for a hundred worlds,' Gideon snarled, 'but for the dishonour we would endure in exiting the Feast so early and the disgrace to carry back to Eschara. I promised Master Ichabod a victory to lift the Chapter and carry our brothers through these dark times. I cannot return with both empty hearts and hands. News of our failure would likely finish what the filth of the Alpha Legion started. I fear the disappointment alone might end him, Ezrachi.'

The Apothecary shook his battered head. 'Quesiah Ichabod is the greatest Excoriator to have ever lived. Those armoured serpents were lucky – and perhaps born so – but even they, with their lies and infernal ways, could not take him from us. Besides, he is now on Eschara with one of our best – the Chief Apothecary.'

'I can't look my Chapter Master in the eye and tell him I did everything in my power to secure victory when I did not.' Gideon seemed to come to a dismal decision. 'I'd privately hoped that it would not come to this. Nine Excoriators have fought for their Chapter in the Feast, yet ten were sent for such a hallowed duty. Only Dorn knows why Master Ichabod insisted upon his inclusion, but that is now the choice laid before me. Can he be made fit for anything, let alone battle?'

'I believe so. We are pure of heart, but not of blood. As part of a former Legion and now as a Chapter, we are not alone in our experience of genetic deficiency. The Wolves and the Angels carry the flaws of their blood heritage on to new generations.' The Excoriators Apothecary paused before continuing. 'When the Darkness takes one of our number, it might appear to us a wretched palsy: the slackness of the jaw, the tremor of the limb, the blankness of the eye. Surviving Excoriators report the experience as a living nightmare, a sleeping wakefulness in which they relive the bottomless woe of Dorn's most trying time – the grievous loss of our Father-Emperor, at least as we knew him. This is both our father's genetic blessing and his curse to his sons. To know the possibility – for even a second – of an Imperium without the Emperor. To feel what Dorn felt. The profound misery of a primarch. The paralysing fear that even one as great as he experienced, for himself and for humanity, over the Emperor's shattered body. To live the Darkness.'

'Such details have little meaning for me, Apothecary,' Gideon told him. 'The Adeptus Astartes are bred for battle. We exist only to avenge the Emperor and put the enemies of humanity to the blade. I need warriors, not dreamers. Whatever the actual nature of this affliction, it does not befit one of our calling. If it were me, I'd rather my brothers ended such a vegetative existence than watch me live on in such a senseless state.'

'Since the Darkness can strike any of us at any time, corpus-captain, I'll bear that in mind,' Ezrachi promised with a subversive curl of the lip. 'While we dwell on such matters, you should know that the procedure I intend is untried and that the brother in question might not survive it.'

'For the calamity he has brought down on all of us, I would lose little sleep over that.'

'I suspected as much,' the Apothecary said. 'I inform you only that it in turn might inform your strategy for our brothers in the contest. You do know it is possible that his suffering caused the loss of the Chapter standard rather than his failure being the cause of the Darkness.'

'What do I care for that?' Gideon snorted. 'He failed his primarch. He failed his Chapter Master. He failed us all. The only care I have in this is to find use for such traitorous hands. What will you do and how long do you need?'

'Santiarch Balshazar has his way of managing the afflicted,' Ezrachi replied. 'A spiritual treatment that those suffering the Darkness survive or they do not. While I respect the symbolic significance of the Santiarch's practice and the rituals specific to our Chapter cult, my method might seem comparatively direct.' The Apothecary indicated a point at the back of his skull, where in the fashion of the Chapter, his thinning hairline met a scarred and shaven scalp. 'The catalepsean node is located here on the brain stem. As the implant responsible for modifying the circadian rhythms – our patterns of sleep and elongated periods of consciousness – it seems possible that a malfunctioning node could be responsible for a loss of motor control and the experience of a 'living nightmare'. I plan to drill through the bone and insert a hypodermic lightning rod into the brain. There I shall issue a localised shock to the catalepsean node, hopefully interrupting the affliction of the Darkness and reinstating the natural function of the implant.'

'It sounds painful.'

'Undoubtedly.'

'Good,' the corpus-captain said before taking his leave. 'I must travel down to the surface with Usachar and Dathan. The Rites of Battle begin for the next round shortly. The Feast waits for no one. Send word if your experiment meets with success. I'll also need informing if our fallen brother fails us once again.'

'How do you define failure?'

'A living death. Or an actual one,' Gideon told the Apothecary as he left. 'It makes very little difference to me when it comes to Zachariah Kersh.'

I AM IN a place… of darkness. I have never been here, yet I know it well. My mind – like my body – is in sensory overdrive. Something far beyond my genetic inheritance, beyond the rigors of Chapter indoctrination and the suprahormones roaring through my veins. This moment feels more acute, vivid and keener than any I have formerly experienced. Every molecule of my being is devoted to it, like the seconds have been honed to a razored-edge.

Despite the intensity of this experience, the world about me is dark and indistinct. Everything, from the walls to the floor beneath my feet, is cloaked in a peripheral haze. I try to focus, but anything upon which I settle my eyes assumes the quality of screaming shadow. The howling gloom spreads like a stain, running into everything else and framing me in a vision of smeared charcoal.

I wander the labyrinthine nightmare of this place, weapon in hand, searching, splattered with blood that is not my own, knowing that brothers both lost and true clash about me. There is gunfire. There is death. I can hear calls of distant anguish. I cannot make out the words but know that they are laced with venom and cold reason. The hot ring of blades fills the air, before power beyond my comprehension is unleashed in the bleakness beyond. I feel its unnaturalness wash over me. My heart hammers. I am running, fearful, but not for myself.

I erupt from the maze and come to a halt in an open space. A giant archport blazes with the light of a nearby globe, set against a pin-prick darkness. I know not this world, yet its reflected radiance draws me in. I am where I cannot have been: above Holy Terra. The vista rolls and I feel the movement deep inside of me. I am aboard a vessel. A bastion of Angels, a cathedral amongst the stars. The bridge expanse beckons.

As I step between the armoured bodies that litter the deck in anonymity, I come to realise that this is not a colossal command deck. It is a throne room. Before me are three titans: fallen and terrible in the murderous ruin they have committed, one upon the other. Two mighty brothers lie twisted and broken on the steps. Their god-flesh is still, their fratricide over. The chime of battle hangs about their corpses. Their weapons decorate the deck. My own falls to the floor.

Then, the centrepiece of the slaughter. The father of all lies amongst his fallen family. The Emperor of Mankind. A beacon in the darkness. Withering to look upon, impossible not to.

I approach as one might his doom, hesitant and uncomprehending. Child-like. The moment overwhelms me and tears cascade down my blood-flecked cheeks. I fall to my knees. I weep over my Emperor, for there is nothing left to do. No higher power to whom I can appeal. With His body held to mine I roar my defiance, like an infant freshly ripped from the womb. A new coldness clings to me. It saturates me with its despair. I sink deep within myself and find a greater darkness there. An Imperium without an Emperor. A fatherless humanity. An eternity without direction.

I quake. I know only fear and fury at an empty cosmos, devoid of answers. His head, in my arms, rolls to one side. His eyelids fall open and his divine gaze fixes upon the blazing archport. Dead eyes set on the dead space beyond. But there is a figure. Something I had not seen before. There and yet not. An armoured figure that steps from the darkness into silhouette, glorious against the Terran glare. Unlike my stygian surroundings, or the Emperor, eclipsed by His own brilliance, the figure falls into harrowing focus. Its movements are slow and deliberate and as it walks towards me it grows in stature and menace.

An ally? An enemy? There are no shortage of either, dead on the deck about me. I think of my Emperor and tighten my grip on His malevolence-mauled body. I clutch only the crisp air of the bridge to my chest, for the Emperor's hallowed form has gone. I remain kneeling, as though my legs are now part of the deck. My face is that of a simpleton and my mind is overwhelmed with a grief beyond grief. I sit. I watch. I dread.

The revenant approaches. Its searing plate is of the blackest night. Each ceramite boot is wreathed in spectral flame. I look on as its incandescent steps fracture and frost-shatter the metal of the deck beneath them. The ghost-fire curls and crooks its way about the figure as one burned at the stake. It slows to an appalling stop and looks down on my kneeling form. Before me is an Angel of Death. A brother of the beyond. Devoid of Chapter markings, the armour speaks only of the grave: a rachial nightmare of rib and bone, a skeleton set within the surface of the sacred plate. Beneath, the ghastliness goes on. The faceplate of its helmet is smashed and a ceramite shard missing. The bleach-white of a fleshless skull leers at me. The glint of a service stud. The darkness of an eye socket that burns with unnatural life. Perfect teeth that chatter horribly.

'What are you?' I manage, although it takes everything I have left to brave the utterance.

It says nothing, but reaches out with a raven gauntlet. A bone digit protrudes from the splintered ceramite fingertip. I watch it drift towards my face with horror. The thing touches me. And I scream.

Legion of the Damned – released April 2012